To Mary

With aff... ...on a

best wishes Always.

Arabella

23. 7. 1990.

THE END OF THE FAMILY

After a disastrous fire at his Isle of Man stud farm in which four men are killed, David Ismay disappears off the face of the earth. For his spirited sister Emmeline and his gentle wife Christabel, the suggestion that he is guilty of arson and manslaughter is unthinkable; for the police the connection is obvious.

In the weeks that follow, the lives of the two women are plunged into unimaginable horror as their family name is dragged through the mud and they realize they will have to sell their beloved home to clear their debts. Only the arrival of Karl Ryan, son of old family friends from South Africa, offers any solace at all. While Christabel daily retreats further into a fantasy world on the brink of madness, Emmeline and Ryan struggle against the odds to find out just what has happened to David – and who is behind the mysterious forces plotting *The End of the Family*.

Writing with all the verve and passion which so marked *The Sins of Rebeccah Russell*, Arabella Seymour has created a Gothic drama of suspense which will long live on in the reader's mind.

THE END
OF THE FAMILY

Arabella Seymour

COLLINS
8 Grafton Street, London W1
1990

William Collins Sons & Co. Ltd
London · Glasgow · Sydney · Auckland
Toronto · Johannesburg

First published 1990
© Arabella Seymour 1990

BRITISH LIBRARY CATALOGUING IN PUBLICATION DATA

Seymour, Arabella, 1948
The end of the family.
I. Title
823'.914 [F]

ISBN 0–00–223476–9

Photoset in Linotron Sabon by Wyvern Typesetting Ltd
Printed and bound in Great Britain by
William Collins Sons & Co. Ltd, Glasgow

She heard his footsteps echoing on the flagstone floor, the sound of a door opening and closing shut. Then there was silence ... she was to remember that sound of footsteps and the closing door for the next sixty years.

For Lewis – here's to friendship!

PROLOGUE

THE BOY LAY CURLED UP, foetus-like, in the cocoon of under-growth, his chin resting in his hand. The playthings he had brought with him to his secret hideout lay scattered near his feet: a battered cricket ball, a home-made catapult, assorted marbles and fivestones in a grubby linen bag.

He hadn't meant to fall asleep. He hadn't meant to stay for so long in the small, secret place that he had made his own, near the entrance to the badger sett. But the only way to watch the shy, secretive creatures was to lie in wait after darkness fell, hoping that they'd emerge. Knowing his mother would never allow him to come out here alone after dark, he'd waited until everyone in the cottage was asleep before dressing himself and creeping downstairs, his excitement at the forbidden adventure jostling with his fear.

But the badgers hadn't come and his eyes had grown heavy; only meaning to lie down and close them just for a minute, that was the last thing he'd remembered, staring through the tangled undergrowth towards the mouth of the sett.

It was the strange light, playing across his closed eyelids that stirred him, then jarred him from sleep. He was aware of a sudden, painful stiffness – pins and needles in his hands and legs. Rubbing his eyes, he hauled himself up into a sitting position and stared upwards through the thick but leafless branches of the trees. The sky above him, far away in the distance to where the edge of the woods stopped and the gentle slope that stretched down to the Ismay stud below, was streaked with red.

Dazedly, his heart racing, he stumbled up and out of the thick tangle of undergrowth, and along the muddy track that led to the edge of the woods. He tried to run faster, tripping and sliding in the darkness and on the uneven ground, strewn with fallen twigs

11

and half-rotted tree trunks, knocking out of the way the branches that cut at his skin and tore at the sleeves of his jacket.

Panting, trying to get his breath, he at last reached the edge of the woods and stared down, disbelievingly, to what he saw far below.

Sheets of flame tore up through the roof of the main stud building, enveloping everything in their path. Like red and orange torpedoes, they whipped around the adjacent barns and stables, and showers of sparks, burning hay and straw, spilled out into the blazing night sky, lighting it like a fantastic firework display. The terrified cries of the horses trapped inside the buildings reached his ears, even from this distance, mingling with the frantic shouting of the men and the awful, sickening sound of the buildings caving inwards as the wood was incinerated by the merciless intensity of the fire's heat.

The boy could see the black dots that were people hauling some of the plunging, rearing horses out of the buildings; futilely, rushing towards the blazing inferno with buckets of water. Then, catching sight of something else so unexpectedly that he caught his breath, he stumbled backwards towards the cover of the trees.

Half-way up the slope that led from the burning stud buildings to the wood, three shadowy figures began to move. He had not noticed them at first. They had materialized, suddenly, from the darkened cluster of boulders that stood closely packed together near the summit of the ridge. Then, with more speed, they seemed to be moving directly towards him. Terrified, the boy turned and ran.

Back along the overgrown footpath, wildly pushing the tentacles of bushes and trees from his face, he clawed his way back to the safety of his hiding place where he lay, face down, heart beating fast, one hand over his mouth to smother the laboured, frantic breathing. Minutes later he heard running feet; then the rough, strange, breathless voices of men speaking in a language that he had never heard before. Gruff, guttural, alien. They were the Kaiser's men, German soldiers invading the island to extract revenge because they had lost the war with England; and German soldiers, his mother had said, ate babies and bayoneted naughty children. He shook, his limbs shivered in remembering those words; through the sweat that was running into his eyes he could see the booted feet of one of them so closely that he could have reached out and touched him. Then the same man flung something down on the ground, inches away from him, before he heard the three of them move off in the opposite direction.

He lay there for so long that when he tried to get up it took him several minutes before the circulation came back to his arms and legs. He was stiff with cold, paralysed with fear. What if the Kaiser's men had gone to his mother's cottage and set fire to it like they'd set fire to Mr Ismay's stud? What if they were out there somewhere, hiding in the woods, waiting to waylay him as he crept home along the path? He would have to take another, longer route back, just in case.

The sky above him to the west was still brightly lit up, streaked with the red and orange of the blazing fire. Somehow he must get back. Somehow he must reach home without being seen, without being caught.

Suddenly, an owl above him in the branches of a tree hooted and screamed, drowning his own shout of fear as he ran.

Drenched with sweat and dashing the soot and grime from his streaming eyes, the head stud groom tugged the stallion's halter forward with all his might. The terrified animal plunged and reared alarmingly, his eyes rolling with fear at the sight and smell of the awesome ferocity of the fire. All around them beneath the inexorable mercilessness of the flames, the stud buildings shrivelled and caved in one by one, the crashing timbers drowning the last panic-stricken death cries of the horses who were trapped inside.

There was no hope of saving any more. There was nothing he could do. Tying the stallion's leading rein tightly to the nearest object well out of reach of the rapidly spreading fire, the stud groom collapsed against the wall, exhausted, burned and bleeding, tears of anguish and hopelessness mingling with the salty perspiration that stung his eyes. Somewhere behind the billowing wall of acrid smoke he could hear somebody shouting orders, men rushing to and fro in a fruitless attempt to salvage whatever was left from the clutches of the fire.

The most valuable, the most important animal at the stud had been saved; that was all the groom could think of. How the blaze had started, which horses, which men had died, were questions he

13

would only be capable of asking later. For now he was too weary even to move from the spot where his body was slumped, all the fight, all the breath knocked out of him.

From the noise and pandemonium he heard somebody call his name. As he glanced up through the protective cage of his grimy fingers, the massive roof of the main stud building crumpled like a deck of cards, and the night air was filled with the final heart-rending cries of men and animals who he would never again see alive.

ONE

LIKE A SOLITARY GHOST she moved silently along the deserted Boat Deck, looking this way and that. She put up a hand to shield her eyes from the strong glare of the sun. All around her the deck was empty; the whole ship for as far as she could hear or see was devoid of any sound, any sign of life.

The space beside the deck rail where her brother had been standing just a moment ago, was curiously empty now. Even the noise of the belching steam from the ship's great funnels had abruptly ceased.

She walked on and on, past the empty officers' quarters and the deserted Marconi room towards the first class vestibule, then she opened the double doors and stood at the top of the grand staircase and looked down to the floors below.

The light from the chandeliers shone and glinted on the exquisite carvings of the wooden balustrade, on the rich gilded ironwork and fittings, on the bronze cherubs that decorated the banister ends, the gilt clock set into the ornate woodwork of the A Deck foyer. But there was still no sign of life.

Slowly, her heart beating faster, she began to descend the stairs one by one. At the bottom, to her left, lay the leaded glass double doors to the first class dining saloon. She pushed them open and went inside.

To her astonishment, the huge room was empty. Her eyes travelled quickly, disbelievingly, across the deserted tables, only moments ago aloud with the noise of chatter, laughter, the chink of glass and cutlery. On the starched, snow-white linen tablecloths, nothing had been touched: the gold-rimmed crystal glasses, the silver place settings, the matching table napkins folded into pyramids and set beside each place.

She stepped backwards towards the double doors and pushed

15

her way through them; then she began to run in panic. Back into the deserted A Deck foyer, past the entrance to the first class staterooms. Along the empty corridors shrouded in eerie, inexplicable silence, on and on until she found the right door. She opened it and stumbled inside.

Everything was exactly as she remembered it a short while before; nothing had changed; nothing had been touched. Her mother's lace dressing-gown lay across the back of an upholstered chair; her father's leather brush case was still on the little polished table beside the bed. The lights still burned brightly from their fittings on the cabin walls, casting a soft, golden glow across the satin eiderdown. A string of pearls lay on the dressing-table top. A diamond hair comb. A pair of gloves. On the padded stool, half open, a black ostrich feather fan. But both her mother and father had disappeared.

Slowly, she walked back along the corridor the way she'd come. She pushed open the leaded glass doors that led back into the A Deck foyer. Then, she began to climb the grand staircase to the Boat Deck above.

It was then that she heard it: a strange, terrifying rumbling sound from somewhere overhead. Instinctively, she stopped in her tracks; instinctively, she gripped the wooden balustrade with both hands. Suddenly, the stairs beneath her feet began to sway and rock dangerously, and she lost her balance, as down the huge staircase rushed an enormous wave that crashed over her and drowned her frantic screams.

Her body was tossed like flotsam in the swirling water, all around her floated pieces from the ship; a woman's silver hair brush and comb, a child's china-headed doll; deck chairs, blankets, cutlery, clothing, a violin. Then, the bodies. Nameless faces, their flesh bloated and green; a bloody limb, a hand; a man in evening dress, a woman floating face downwards, her white nightgown billowing out beside her, seaweed matted in her hair.

She could feel herself going under. She struggled to breathe, to keep her face above the waves. Then, suddenly, mercifully, she caught sight of him, her brother, standing in a life jacket at the top of the stairs. He strode towards her through the swirling, foaming sea water, holding out his arms.

'*David* . . . !'

*

16

Emmeline Ismay woke, seconds later, still screaming out his name.

She was wet with perspiration, even though the fire in the grate had long since gone out and the room was bitterly cold. She was shaking all over. Her heart was beating too fast. She started up from the chair, pulling the blanket tighter around her, willing herself back from the old nightmare into reality. Slowly, she eased back into the depths of the chair. She rubbed her tired eyes. Then her glance fell on the disorderly pile of newspapers that lay on the carpet beside her chair. *21st September, 1919.*

After a while her hands grew steadier. She lay back and closed her eyes. Weariness pulled her back into a fitful half-sleep, until a noise woke her again.

She looked up through the gloom and glanced at the clock. Fifteen minutes past midnight. It must have been the lights from his car that had woken her, the crunch of the wheels on the gravel in the drive. He was late. More than an hour late. She guessed that either there had been a hold up on the line or he'd had trouble starting the car when he reached Epsom station.

She got up and yawned. She was glad that she'd waited up for him. The old blanket trailing behind her, she went out of the room and through the big hall towards his study, knowing where everything was, even in the pitch darkness.

A light shone from beneath his door. She smiled and went in.

'Emmeline! You shouldn't have waited up. It's gone midnight!' He was sitting behind his desk with papers strewn in front of him. 'I told you if I wasn't back by eleven, to go to bed.'

'What happened?'

He rubbed his eyes. 'I was late leaving Delauney's office and I missed my train at Victoria. Then when I finally reached Epsom, I had trouble getting the car to start. The cylinders were damp.'

'I didn't mean that.'

For a moment they looked at each other. Then he held his head in his hands and sighed noisily. His dark brown eyes had a haunted, hopeless look in them.

'Delauney received a preliminary report from the island police. It isn't conclusive, not yet; but there's evidence to suggest that the fire at the stud wasn't an accident.' She stared at him in disbelief. 'The insurance company have refused to pay out; every owner

17

who lost stock that was in our care is demanding immediate refund of fees, plus the full market price for the animals that perished in the fire. I can't blame any of them; in their places I'd probably do exactly the same. Most of those mares are irreplaceable; and they're not in the horse breeding business for a game. But if the insurance company refuse to support us and the owners sue ... Emmeline, you know as well as I do what that means.'

All her tiredness left her.

'But they must support us! Could anyone in their right mind even think that you'd start a fire at the stud deliberately? It's madness. We were brought up with horses, we've lived and breathed them all our lives ... horses have been the family livelihood for more than seventy years – longer, if you count the days of Edward Brodie at Newmarket! Don't they understand, for God's sake, just how much you stand to lose from that fire?'

'Unfortunately, they don't see it the way you do. The implication is that I would have everything to gain.'

Her blue eyes flashed.

'David, I don't believe I'm hearing this!'

'If the fire was started on purpose, I'm the chief suspect. My motive? The insurance money. Isn't more than a quarter of a million pounds more than sufficient motive for anybody? See it with their eyes. I did it because the stud's a millstone round my neck, because it's too far away for me to be able to keep my finger on its pulse, too costly for all but the wealthiest owners to send their mares there. The Isle of Man and back is more than a whole week's trip ... all that time wasted when I could be here, in Epsom, doing much more important things, like taking full advantage of the post-war racing boom; make a quick fortune and get out before the whole industry sinks in the inevitable slump that's coming in the next two years!'

'David – '

'I know exactly what you're going to say – that when the fire happened I was here, half the country and the whole of the Irish sea away, with Christ knows how many witnesses. But that doesn't count with them. I could just have easily arranged it, couldn't I? How the hell do I prove to them, to the police, the insurance company, the owners, that I didn't? It's only my word against the evidence.'

'Evidence? What evidence?'

18

'A box of matches, found a quarter of a mile away from the stud grounds in Ballakeighan Forest.'

'Anyone could have dropped it there, for God's sake!'

'A box of matches, a stone's throw away from a stud that's just gone up in flames? Isn't that a little too much of a coincidence?'

'If the stud was a millstone around your neck you'd sell it, wouldn't you? Haven't they got brains?'

'And where would I find a buyer, in a country that's on its knees, gut-shot and impoverished by four years of war, who'd be prepared to give me anything like the figure I'd stand to get from the insurance claim?'

'Anyone who knows anything about you would know that you'd have rather died in the fire than caused anything to happen to those horses.'

He got up from behind the desk, went over to the window and stared out into the night.

'It's my fault it happened, Emmeline. I should have brought the stallion back here and stood him at Epsom.'

'And closed down the stud so that everyone working there lost their living? Come on, David, you know as well as I do that you'd never have done that!'

'Yes, you're right . . . I would never have done that.'

'Because you *cared* about the people who worked for us at Ballakeighan. Is someone who does that capable of burning down the very place those same people are dependent on for their daily bread? Let anyone accuse you, and we'll sue them for every penny they've got!'

He turned away from the window. He managed a half-smile.

'I'll have to go there. To Ballakeighan. As soon as possible. It can't wait.' He ran a hand through his already untidy hair. 'I should have gone as soon as we heard the news. I would have, but there was so much to do, so many things here that needed my attention. Maybe I should have dropped everything straight away, maybe it would have looked better for me if I had. Once this gets out, about the so-called "evidence", the rumours will start flying. Every enemy I've ever made will crawl out of the woodwork and try to cut my throat.'

'Not while I'm around, they won't.'

He came across to where she stood and reached out to stroke her hair. He bent and kissed her forehead.

19

'You know, you should never have cut your hair.'

'That's what Christabel said. But have you tried running a stableyard and helping the Red Cross tend wounded soldiers at the same time, with a mane of hair trailing down your back?' She gave a hoarse little laugh. 'Anyhow, it's the latest fashion, didn't you know that? Shoulder-length bobs for women.'

'Like hobble skirts and showing your ankles? Wouldn't our grandmother have been shocked?'

'That's what I thought, when Janet and I went rummaging through the old trunks up in the attic and found some of her things. Those gowns! The material in one walking dress would make outfits for at least six women in the WRVS. I was going to cut them up and make something . . . but in the end I couldn't bring myself to do it.'

He pulled the blanket tighter around her and tapped her on the nose playfully, like he'd done ever since they were children.

'Under that steel-plated armour of yours you're just a pure, old-fashioned sentimentalist, aren't you, little sister?'

'If you say so.'

Both knew already what the other was thinking; it had always been that way; they'd always been able to communicate their thoughts without words, so close were they to each other. A half-raised eyebrow, a single look, the almost imperceptible movement of the head; a kind of uncanny telepathy had always existed between them that had astonished their parents, other people, but never each other. Even before he'd come back from London she'd known instinctively that something was wrong; as soon as he'd looked at her face a few moments ago when she'd come into the room, he knew that she'd known. It happened so often that neither of them ever thought of it as being uncanny any more.

'David, it's so cold in here, and damp. Let's go down to the kitchen and sit by the stove awhile; we can talk there. It's the only place in the whole house that's warm.'

'But you're tired; you should go up to bed. We can always talk about this tomorrow.'

'It is tomorrow.'

'Ah, so it is. Later then. When we've both got some sleep and I can think more clearly. But you shouldn't have waited up for me when you've been working all day.'

'Do you think I could go to sleep now knowing that someone's accused you of planning arson? Or that we could be facing total financial ruin?'

'I'll go to Ballakeighan and find out the truth.'

'Not alone you won't. I'm coming with you.'

He sighed. He opened his lips to protest; to give her at least half a dozen cast-iron reasons why it would be better for both of them if she stayed; but the words remained unsaid: he knew by the look in her eyes that she meant to come with him whether he agreed to it or not.

He nodded slowly. Then he picked up the oil lamp on the desk and led the way through the house to the kitchen downstairs. They paused, side by side, in the cold, draughty old hall. Patches of mildew stained the once-fine wood panelling; the elaborate cornices of the plasterwork on the ceiling were dirt-encrusted and crumbling; everywhere was permeated by the smell of damp.

Neither of them spoke, neither of them looked at the other, for both of them were thinking the same thoughts: remembering the house as it used to be, as it had been a long time ago when they were children; before the war, before the *Titanic* foundered, before the *Lusitania* had been sunk. It had been polished and shining then, loved, lived in; full of happiness, warmth, laughter. Enormous fires had blazed in the massive grates, every room, summer and winter, had been decorated with giant vases of garden or hothouse flowers, even the attics and the servants' hall. An army of them had tended every room with loving care, at Christmas the hall had been hung with boughs of ivy, mistletoe and holly, and a huge fir tree grown on the estate had stood at the bottom of the grand staircase, festooned with little baubles and wooden ornaments, all around it knee-deep in gifts for family, servants and friends. Carriages would arrive in the courtyard outside, bearing friends and relations and their mountains of luggage; every guest room would be full.

How sad and silent and bare it all seemed now. So eerily noiseless, so dark, so neglected, so lonely. So still that they could almost hear it weeping. Without a word, they both walked away and went down into the kitchens.

She sat there, on a wooden bench, while David lit all the lamps.

Shadows leapt up across the bare walls, and she gazed around her. Cobwebs lay dark and thick in the corners of the ceiling; everything seemed coated with dust. The top of the giant cooking range that had once gleamed like jet was dull and stained with burned-on fat. Drawing her knees up to her chin, Emmeline sighed.

'David, what are we going to do? There must be a way we can fight all this!'

'There is . . . if you believe in the old family motto. There's always something you can do about everything.'

'But what did Delauney say? Surely he doesn't think that anyone who knows the first thing about you would lend credence to the idea that you could be responsible for what happened? For Christ's sake, David! The most valuable horse we've ever had could have been burned to death in that fire, with more than half of our gross annual profit along with him!'

'But he wasn't. Although most of the visiting mares and their foals all died. Delauney's a lawyer and lawyers only care about facts that can be proved in court. I didn't do it. I know it. So do you. So does anyone who knows me for what I am. But at this moment in time I can't prove that I didn't, and proof is what counts. It isn't enough to know the truth.

'In the report that the island police sent it says that they have strong reason to believe that the fire was started deliberately. The only suspect they have is me because I'm the only one who stood to gain. That Ballacragan was one of the few horses that survived only makes my motives – to them – seem more suspicious. Think like them, Emmeline. If I did plan it, and if I did get away with murder – and remember four stud hands died in that fire – then I stood to gain not only a massive insurance payout but I still had our most valuable piece of bloodstock: Craganour's full brother.'

'You just said that you can't do anything without proof. That cuts both ways. What proof do they have other than that box of matches?'

'It's more than enough to start them off on a longer and darker trail.'

'A trail that'll lead them to nowhere because there's nowhere to lead them to.'

'Maybe. But if that report is right and the fire really was arson, it means only one thing. Because if I didn't start it then someone else did. And I mean to find out who if it's the last thing on this earth that I ever do.'

There were several moments of silence between them, while he

22

wrestled uncomfortably with the other thoughts that were foremost in his mind, causing him almost as much disquiet as the question of arson at his stud. There had never been any secrets between them, him and Emmeline; by keeping this other thing from her he felt guilty, troubled, uneasy. He wanted to tell her everything, but now was not the right time. It would take too long, and time was something that he was desperately short of.

'Is there something else?' Her voice, sharp and quick, from across the room. How well she knew him!

He turned, and smiled reassuringly.

'We'll have a long talk later . . . tomorrow, when I get back.'

'Who, David? Who could ever hate you that much to want to destroy you?'

'All the way up to London, all the way back again sitting on that train, I asked myself that. But the only thing I was certain about is that whoever it is could never be a racing man, not someone who'd spent his life around horses. Only a man with no soul could be responsible for having more than forty mares and foals burned to death in their stables, and four men along with them.' He looked across at her. 'I don't know anyone who could do something like that.'

'Maybe the only way we can ever find the answer is to go to Ballakeighan.'

'Yes.' He lay back in the old rocking chair and stared into space. 'Sometimes I fancy I can almost hear the old house weep, can you? The way it was, once, in the old days when Mumma and Father were alive, and before that, when Mumma was a little girl. The grand balls, the banquets, the house parties, every spare bedroom used for guests. This kitchen, all bright and whitewashed, with the best dinner service gleaming in the plate racks and hams and pheasants hanging in the larder. The smell of those hams.'

She half smiled too.

'Yes, I remember it.'

'I never remember ever seeing a single speck of dust. Not anywhere. Do you know that? Even when everyone had gone home and the guest rooms weren't used, everything was so shining and clean, as if it had never been touched. I used to love the smell of the beeswax that the maids used to polish the furniture. Almost as much as I loved the smell of Mumma's favourite perfume . . .'

She got up quietly, and came across to where he sat. She laid a hand on his shoulder.

'David, you look so tired . . . all that travelling. You need to sleep. We can talk again tomorrow.'

'I used to think of that, the smell of the beeswax polish and Mumma's perfume, in the trenches at Mons . . . little things, things that you never expect to remember. Helping father's lads to clean the tack before a big race, being allowed to sit on the winner's back the day after, for a special treat, cook's apple pies and her white, starched apron, her big hands, kneading dough on this very table. You, with your hair in corkscrew curls, playing with your dolls' house in the old nursery . . . Then I'd think of Mumma, and Christabel, coming down the staircase in their best gowns at Christmas, with the lights twinkling on all the sequins . . .'

'David . . .' Her voice was almost a whisper. As she spoke the big hall clock growled in the depths of the house, and he came back to the present. A small, weary smile creased his face.

'I won't have time for breakfast in the morning. Tell Christabel what's happened.'

'Where are you going?'

'To see John Martin. Nine sharp. I rang him from London and arranged to finalize the transport for Ballacragan and what's left of the bloodstock on the island first thing in the morning. I want those animals back here as soon as he can bring them.'

'Does Stranahan know?'

'I sent him a telegram yesterday, thanking him for his help in stabling the animals at his place, and telling him that I'd let him know in the next few days what the shipping arrangements would be. I can see to that when I get back tomorrow.'

'Do you want me to tell Christabel everything?'

'It might sound better coming from you.' For a moment he felt guilty. Christabel was his wife and yet he'd known for some time they had been inadvertently drifting apart. It wasn't that he had ceased to love her. There had never been anyone else. But her lack of understanding of how much a part of his life the family business was, how much it meant to him, had driven a wedge of silence between them so that he rarely confided in her any more. Not because he didn't want to but because even the simplest thing was difficult for her to understand. Ever since their marriage, five

24

years before, all she had cared about was having a child. Ever since her last miscarriage, more than two years ago, she had become more and more distant towards him. But he still loved her.

Side by side, unspeaking, they went back up the kitchen stairs to the old, musty-smelling, darkened hall. At the foot of the staircase, he stopped.

'You go on up. I'm going to walk down to the old gatehouse and look through some of the obsolete stud records. Delauney thinks that we might find a clue there – a name, a reason, a motive. Maybe he's wrong, but I can't think of anywhere else to look except in the lists of names of everyone we've done business with in the past.'

'Do you have to do it now? If you wait till tomorrow I'll come down and help you.'

'I can think better in the early hours. And when I'm alone.' He smiled, and kissed her cheek so that she wouldn't feel slighted. 'Don't expect me for lunch. I might just be back in time for dinner. But if I'm not, don't wait. Tell Janet to keep mine in the oven.'

At the top of the staircase she turned and looked down again. She shivered in the stark chill air, and stifled a yawn. He blew her a single kiss, and then turned and walked off into the darkness. She heard his footsteps echoing on the flagstone floor, then the sound of a door opening and closing shut. Then there was silence.

She was to remember that sound of footsteps and the closing door for the next sixty years.

TWO

A THIN, HARSH RAY of early morning light filtered across the bed through a chink in the curtains. It snaked its way across the untidy, cluttered dressing-table and part of the carvings on the elaborate chimneypiece, picking out the dust and the disarray, making the room seem even more of a shambles than it really was. Christabel Ismay hated the piercing sunlight. Screwing up her eyes against it in protest she turned over, trying to force herself back into sleep. But it was no good. Her mind had already begun to work and now there would be no peace until she slept again that night.

With a deep sigh, she sat up and looked dejectedly around her. Boxes of powder and rouge, hairbrushes, combs, pins, all lay scattered across the top of her dressing-table; piles of clothes lay draped across chairs and across the foot of the bed. The drawer of her tiny writing table in the far corner of the room was half open, stuffed with sheets of paper and envelopes that she had not had time to put away.

She covered her face with her hands and rubbed her eyes vigorously, as if to force herself awake.

She went on sitting there in bed for several minutes; it was so cold in the big bedroom that in autumn and winter she always hated getting out of the warmth of the bed. Then she flung back the covers, grasped her blue velvet dressing-gown and tugged it on, before going across to the window and pulling back the curtains.

The bedroom looked out on to what had once been the old rose garden, and for a moment she stood there, face pressed against the glass, staring out, remembering the garden in all its glory, as it had once been when she'd first known David. At one time, she had known every variety of bloom off by heart. Almost in

26

defiance of her fuddled, aching head, she tried to recite their names. There was *Gloire de Dijon*, her favourite Bourbon, with its large, globe-shaped flowers and heady scent, rose, salmon, and yellow; there was *La France*, with its scrolled silvery pink buds and strong perfume; Old Pink Moss, Goldfinch, Albertine; the exotic *Rosa Mundi*, the shell-pink climber, *Fantin Latour*; *Belle de Crecy, Desprez à Fleur Jeune*; and her best-loved, *Anna Brodie*, whose buds opened purple and changed to pink, violet and lilac as they faded. The rose of her wedding bouquet, named after David Ismay's great-grandmother who had founded the racing stable and planted the rose garden.

So sad the garden looked now, in the drab, cheerless autumn morning, for the sun had disappeared and the sky looked heavy with threatening rain.

Christabel turned away from the window and contemplated the disarray in the room. She went across to her dressing-table and sat down in front of it; half-heartedly she took up one of the brushes from the clutter stewn across the top and lifted it to her thick, tumbling, disordered fair hair. So much hair to brush. So much hair to arrange into some sort of style; perhaps she should have cut most of it off, like Emmeline, at the beginning of the war. But David loved it so, and her own pride in it had always stopped her. She twisted it into a chignon and then rummaged in the untidy mess for pins.

She got up and went to her wardrobe. How stark and frugal the clothes seemed now compared to the wonderful creations that ladies had worn before the war. She thought, nostalgically, of the vanished profusion of frills, ribbons and frothy lace, the exquisite layers of taffeta and silk; the *broderie anglaise*, the swirling yards of brocade and satin, the glorious hats that were works of art; everything was different now. The war had changed and destroyed so much, besides people's lives.

She reached into the depths of the wardrobe dejectedly. Once it had been a wonderful pleasure to dress; now it was little more than a tiresome chore. The subtle pastels of the Edwardian era had vanished into straight, narrow skirts and dresses that often did not leave room even for the simplest of petticoats, in loud colours that matched their wearers' strident demands for emancipation: strong reds, greens, oranges, sulphur yellow. Boned corsets had given way to long, cylindrical 'foundation' garments that

Christabel had learned to struggle into without the help of a maid, a pre-war luxury that she had somehow learned to do without; but at one time the very idea of a lady dressing herself would have been unthinkable.

Her eyes moved along the rows of clothes; pausing once or twice, then moving on, until she finally pulled out a straight, tubular-shaped dress of dark green velvet, relieved of its plainness by bands of gold embroidery around the neck and cuffs. Half an hour later she left the bedroom and made her way downstairs. A few steps along the landing she hesitated. Then she turned back. But not to her room. Suddenly animated, she started to run along the remainder of the landing and up the next flight of stairs. On and on, up and up; out of breath, she finally reached the door of the room she wanted and almost burst inside. Then all the excitement and pleasure drained from her face.

It was still as it had been left all those months ago, the empty nursery; in slow motion she walked across the floor and stopped beside the cradle, then touched the layers of cold white lace with the tips of her fingers. So exquisite, so beautiful, so incomplete; there was no baby inside it, the baby she had prayed and longed for, and then lost. The delicate gossamer blanket, the satin counterpane, felt icy and damp to her touch.

She looked up, looked around her. In one corner of the room stood a rocking horse; in another a box of toys. A nursing chair, a foot rest beneath it, a basket with a white satin valance, stacked neatly with napkins and gauze squares. Her eyes fell back again to the empty cradle, and she moved it, gently, so that it rocked slowly from side to side. A lump rose in her throat and she fought it down at the sound of approaching footsteps behind her. She sensed another presence in the room but for the moment she was so overwhelmed by her terrible sense of loss that she could not even turn to see who it was. She wiped away the single tear that had welled up in the corner of one eye.

'Oh, there you are, Mrs Ismay!' Janet's voice, breathless from climbing the two flights of stairs. 'Breakfast's all ready, ma'am, an' Miss Emmeline's waitin' for you downstairs. Sent me up to fetch you, she did.'

Slowly she turned her head. She wanted Janet to go away. She wanted so desperately to be alone. None of them understood; none of them knew how hurt she still was inside.

She tried to speak in a normal voice.

'I'll come later. In a minute. Tell her I'll come in a minute.'

'But it's so cold up here, ma'am. Catch your death, you will . . .' Janet's voice trailed away, as she realized what she'd said. She twisted the edge of her starched apron in her chilblained hands. 'I meant, what with there bein' no fire up here since – '

'Everywhere's cold in this house. It always has been, since the war. The war changed everything.'

'Yes, ma'am.'

She went on staring down into the windswept garden, at the naked trees, the box hedges, the unpruned honeysuckle, the crumbling stone sundial in the sunken garden. She thought of herself, the girl she'd once been, walking hand in hand with David; laughing, stopping as he'd kissed her, smiling up into his face; a hundred years ago, a lifetime ago. Had that summer ever really existed?

'Shall I tell Miss Emmeline that you'll be down, then, ma'am?'

Christabel moved away from the window; her eyes fell once more onto the empty cradle. The gush of tears rose up again, and she fought them back. She mustn't cry. Not here, not now; not in front of Janet. Even though the world she had been brought up in with its strictly observed moral codes, its accepted standards of behaviour, had been swept away forever with the advent and aftermath of the war, everything in her upbringing baulked against a display of emotion in the presence of a servant. Composing herself, she made herself face Janet.

'I shall be down presently.'

Janet bobbed a ghost of a curtsey and scuttled away.

She went on looking around the walls, at the unused pieces of furniture that she'd chosen with such joy, excitement, expectation. The room seemed almost like a museum without the one thing that was missing which would have given it life. *'There'll be others,'* the doctor had said, and she had waited. But three years had gone by, another miscarriage, and the nursery she had so lovingly furnished, down to the tiniest detail, was still only an empty room.

David, David. She must find David. She rushed out onto the landing and down the stairs so quickly that she almost lost her footing. When she burst into the dining room, out of breath, Emmeline spun round in dismay.

29

'Christabel!'

'Where is he? Where's David?'

'In Epsom. With John Martin.' She poured out two large cups of dark, steaming tea. 'Making the arrangements to bring the rest of the Ballakeighan stock over here from the island. The sooner the better in the light of what's happened.' She pushed one of the cups towards Christabel's place on the table. 'He got in from London very late last night. He didn't want to wake you. He had to go out this morning before anyone was up and about.'

'Where did he sleep? He didn't come to bed last night.'

'Oh, I expect he fell asleep in his chair.' She smiled, a little wearily. Christabel noticed that there were dark shadows beneath her eyes. 'I sat up waiting for him, to see how he got on. We talked. I went up to bed. He walked down to the old gatehouse to ferret out some of the ancient stud records. He hoped there might be a clue.'

'A clue? A clue to what?' She closed the door behind her and leaned against it. 'What are you talking about?'

'Christabel, I think you'd better sit down.'

'It's a lie! David would never be a party to anything like that!'

'I know.'

'It's so absurd that it isn't even worth answering. It's beneath contempt.'

'I'm afraid that it isn't as simple as that.'

'What do you mean?'

Emmeline sat down at one end of the table. 'The island police contend that they've found proof: a box of matches not far from the scene of the fire. They also say that they have another line of enquiry that would seem to substantiate the suspicion of arson.'

'If it *was* arson then David had nothing whatsoever to do with it!'

'We both know that; so does anyone else who knows anything about him. But the police don't.'

'Do you believe it was arson?'

'If they have found proof, what else could it be? The only difference is that somebody else, not David, is responsible for starting it.'

'Who could want to destroy him that much, Emmeline?'

Emmeline lay back in the huge carver chair.

'I don't know, not yet. But someone does. And we intend to go to Ballakeighan ourselves and find out the truth.'

'Ballakeighan? But I thought you just said that David's gone to arrange for the horses who weren't killed in the fire to be brought back here?'

'So I did. But whatever proof's to be found will be found there. Besides which, Delauney indicated that the island police want a statement from him about his bloodstock affairs and anything else that might or might not be relevant to what happened.'

Christabel took up the spoon from her saucer and slowly stirred her tea.

'I'm frightened, Emmeline.'

'What of? David's entirely innocent. We'll prove that even if it kills us.' Somehow, she managed to smile, more to reassure her sister-in-law than herself. Deep down she felt a strange, uncomfortable foreboding. 'Speak the truth and shame the devil.'

Christabel looked across to the great oak sideboard where two silver domed dishes stood, next to a stack of Spode plates. She stared back into her untouched cup of tea.

'I don't think I could eat anything, not now. I'll wait till David gets back.'

'That might not be until much later. He said not to wait dinner.'

'As late as that? It won't take him all day to make the arrangements for the horses with John Martin, will it?'

'He has other things to do besides that.'

'What things?'

'He didn't go into detail ... I'm only repeating what he told me.' She got to her feet with an air of finality. 'I must go, I have to do the stable rounds with Billy. If you need me after that I'll be in David's study for the next few hours, going over last quarter's accounts.' She hesitated at the door. 'If you'd like to, I thought we could go through my wardrobe this afternoon, and sort out what I'll need to take for the Ballakeighan trip. I could do with your advice.'

'Yes, I'd like that.'

Emmeline closed the door behind her. She leaned against it for a moment. She sighed. Poor Christabel. Every day, day after day, wandering around the enormous house. Nothing to do. Nothing

31

to think about but to dwell on the past. If only the miscarriage had never happened. If only the baby could have lived. If only she had been born more like herself. Emmeline had coped with all the crises in her life so much better than she had: the *Lusitania*; her parents' death; four years of war. She'd seen to the running of the estate and the family business while David had been away fighting at the front; driven ambulances for the Red Cross when the house had been turned into a hospital for the wounded; she'd nursed Christabel through two miscarriages and at the same time sat up into the early hours, wrestling with the stud books and complicated accounts. Whatever had happened she'd always been there, a permanent shoulder to cry on. Christabel had always lagged far behind. She was traumatized by tragedy, unable to adapt, incapable of coping single-handed with anything that differed from the ordinary. Beautiful and wraithlike, she'd wandered pathetically through the makeshift wards in her borrowed Red Cross uniform, bridling at the smallest drop of blood, hampering more than helping the trained, professional nurses. Emmeline had always found herself apologizing for her.

But it was not Christabel's fault. The advent of the war and all the way of life it had swept away had robbed Christabel of the one role she would have filled to perfection. The grand Edwardian lady, in dainty high-necked frilled blouses and elegant impractical skirt, presiding over her household with dignity and grace; benevolent to the servants, charming to her guests, the perfect wife, the perfect hostess, the perfect mother. If only she could have fulfilled that; for all the things she'd lost, been cheated of, that might have compensated.

Poor Christabel. Emmeline walked on through the house to her brother's study, where Janet had lit the fire. She went over to it, holding out her hands towards the blaze, letting her thoughts move away from her sister-in-law to the trouble that was fast looming not only for David but also for herself. Her fast-thinking, practical mind turned over the unpalatable possibilities one by one.

David was innocent, but circumstantial evidence – coupled to the prime motives he himself had outlined last night – could be enough to secure his arrest. And, if that unthinkable thing happened, what would she do then? Temporarily, as she'd always done whenever he was away, she would continue running the business and the estate; but for how long could she go on? The scandal would be enormous ... taking away in one fell swoop the Ismays' good name and the income from their profusion of clients that went with it – more than that, their reputation, goodwill, trust. The very roof over their heads. Everything in the house that had been worked for, fought for, cherished and loved for nearly eighty years would have to be sold, very probably the house itself. Forcing herself to think the unthinkable, she recalled her own words from last night and Christabel's from a moment ago. Who could hate David so much that they would want to destroy him?

Slowly, she moved away from the fire. She sat down behind his desk. He'd made enemies, of course – what successful professional man hadn't? And everything David had ever done always had about it that special touch, quite apart from his good looks and charm; of course there were lesser men who begrudged him his achievements, his position, the name he'd made. She understood that. But what was happening now went far beyond the mundane, petty envy and resentment felt by nonentities and far less successful men. Four stud grooms had died in the fire. If David was accused of responsibility for engineering it, then he would also be accused of their deaths. She closed her eyes tightly and clenched her fists.

It took all her iron will and self-control to concentrate on the account books. Only when Janet came to ask her about lunch did she allow herself any respite.

'I'm too busy to stop now. Could you bring me in something cold on a tray?'

'Yes, miss. But what about Mrs Ismay?'

'She won't expect you to lay out a table just for one, Janet. Ask her what she wants and then take her a tray as well. There's a fire in the library; that's as good a place to eat as any.'

'Yes, miss.' She disappeared and closed the door noiselessly behind her.

Emmeline spent another hour working on the pile of ledgers in front of her, then she stacked them back neatly in their places and went outside.

Despite the early promise of a fine clear day, a mist was beginning to rise. There was dampness in the air, a pervading dampness that dripped from the leafless branches of the trees and soaked the ground, permeating everything she touched.

She toured the stables in David's place, spent an hour discussing the new stock with the head stud groom, then, remembering her promise to Christabel she started to make her way back towards the house. As she reached the front door, she could hear the sound of the telephone bell ringing beyond it. Suddenly it stopped.

The nearest extension was in the library. As she opened the door and went in she caught sight of Christabel, holding up the receiver and mouthpiece with as much trepidation as if they were parts of an unexploded bomb. There was alarm on her face.

'What's wrong? Who is it?' She came in, closing the door behind her.

'It's John Martin.' Christabel's voice was shaking. 'He says that David never arrived.'

Emmeline took the telephone from her and sank into the nearest chair.

'This is Emmeline Ismay. Mr Martin, my brother left the house hours ago ... early this morning. He left before any of us were even up. He told me last night that he was meeting you at nine o'clock.'

At the other end of the line, Martin's voice seemed to crackle and buzz.

'That was the time we arranged between us. But he didn't turn up.' There was a pause. 'I have a meeting in Epsom at three with someone at the bank. If I don't leave in the next few minutes, I'll be late. I thought I'd best telephone you and ask you to give your brother a message when he gets back.'

'Yes, I'm listening.'

'Tell him to contact me in the morning. We can arrange something else then.'

Emmeline apologized several more times, then thanked him for calling her and replaced the earpiece on its mount.

'Emmeline? Did he have any idea where David could be?'

'No, but my guess is that he had more trouble with the car. It must have broken down on the road and he went to get help.' She wanted to say something to allay Christabel's panic; her brother was a big boy now. 'There's no need to worry unduly.' She turned away, going to the window and gazing out into the thickening mist. Christabel came and stood beside her, fidgeting uneasily with her long, elegant hands.

'I know that. But it isn't like David at all.'

THREE

THEY CONTINUED SITTING THERE, one at each end of the massive dining table, glancing every few seconds from their untouched food to the clock. Eleven minutes past ten. In the yawning silence Janet, standing at the sideboard, began to stack the soiled tureens and dishes.

'Shall I fetch in the coffee now, Mrs Ismay?'

They both stared at her suddenly; in the silence her voice had startled them.

'Yes, please, Janet.' Christabel got to her feet. 'We'll take it in here.'

'Very well, ma'am.' It was Winifred's evening off; as she reached the door with her heavily laden tray, Emmeline got up and opened it for her. Janet paused in the doorway. 'If Mr Ismay isn't in in the next half hour, miss, I'm afraid 'is dinner'll be fair ruined. I turned the stove down as low as it'd go – '

'That's all right, Janet. He won't mind.'

The moment they were alone again, Christabel's expression changed.

'Where is he? You reckoned he'd be back hours ago! It's nearly half past ten!'

Emmeline was over beside the reading table, thumbing through a back copy of Weatherby's bloodstock returns. 'I didn't say that. It was just a guess; not words written in stone. You know David when it comes to horses. He could have decided, on the spur of the moment, to go off somewhere or other to see to something connected with the stud. He told me last night that he'd be late for dinner. He made a joke about telling Janet to keep it hot.'

'He could have telephoned.'

Emmeline sat down in a chair and lay the Weatherby book open on her lap. 'It won't be the first time he hasn't.'

36

'It's inconsiderate of him.'

'Where the stud's concerned, David has to put business before both of us; you know that. Now more than ever because of the terrible damage the war's wreaked on the business, on the entire racing industry as a whole; ever since David came back from France we've been fighting for our lives, trying to swim and not sink along with so many others who've been well nigh ruined. If all that wasn't bad enough, he's now got the fire at Ballakeighan to contend with. Only a handful of stock saved and God alone knows how many perished.' Impatiently, she laid the book to one side. Could anyone ever make Christabel understand? 'It isn't like David to be inconsiderate, I agree. But this isn't an ordinary situation. We both need to remember that.' She smiled, to soften the admonition. 'Besides, he couldn't telephone, even if he was able to. The Epsom exchange closes at seven o'clock.'

Christabel's eyes looked brighter.

'Yes, of course it does; I'd completely forgotten. I'm sorry, I suppose you think I'm being selfish, wanting David near me all the time. I can't help it, Emmeline. I just can't. When he's away from me I start to panic . . . I've tried not to, but I can't seem to – to control it somehow. If I hadn't lost the baby . . .' her voice trailed away.

'I know. And I do understand. Really I do. But you must try to fight it. Conquer it. It isn't good for you. Or David. If he thinks you're still brooding about what happened . . .' She hesitated, trying to pick her words with care. 'He needs a completely free mind at the moment . . . to try and sort out all the problems we have . . . and there'll be other babies, Christabel. When you're strong again, the doctor said there's no reason at all why you shouldn't have another child.'

'But I'm strong now!'

'I didn't mean that. The memory of what happened is still raw. Your mind needs time to heal. Thinking about what you've lost is still too vivid, and real. You feel just like I felt after Mumma and Daddy died when the *Lusitania* went down. I couldn't even look at a tub of water or a picture of a ship without shuddering, reliving it all; I clung to the only thing I had left . . . David. Just like you're doing now. I never thought I'd get over what happened; I had terrible dreams, horrific nightmares. Sometimes, I still do.'

'You never told me.'

'I had one last night, when I fell asleep in the chair waiting for David to come back from London. Strange, I never dream of the *Lusitania*; it's the *Titanic*, always the *Titanic*. I suppose it's because we were all aboard her on her maiden voyage; Mumma, Daddy, David and me ... but we only sailed on her as far as Queenstown because Daddy was buying some stallions there. Afterwards, when we heard that she'd struck an iceberg and sunk with enormous loss of life we couldn't believe it – or how incredibly lucky we were ...'

She fell silent when Janet came back, carrying the tray of coffee. For a few moments after she'd gone neither of them spoke. Then Christabel broke the silence.

'Does David ever say anything about me to you? I mean, about what happened when I lost the baby?'

Emmeline began to feel distinctly uncomfortable; these were waters that she'd far prefer to stay out of.

'Discuss you behind your back? Surely you know him better than that?'

'I didn't mean in that way. I meant, did you ever get the impression from him that he felt I should have got over the miscarriage by now, that I'd brooded over it for far too long?'

'Christabel – '

'It isn't easy for a man to understand, is it? Not how a woman feels when she's lost something that was a part of herself; something that can never be replaced. I know what the doctor said to me. I know what the doctor told him. That one day there'll be others. I *do* know that. But there are some things that you can never have again. It was a real person to me, a living thing. Can you understand that? It was mine and it died. Even when we have other children in the future, I'll never forget. Is it wrong of me to feel like that?'

'Of course not.' Emmeline laid a hand on her arm. 'Nobody's asking you to.' Slowly, she extricated herself and began to pour the coffee. 'Look, I can see how tired you are. Why don't you drink this with a drop of brandy in it, then go on up to bed? I'll wait for David. And we can talk to him about Ballakeighan in the morning.'

'But you waited up for him last night.'

'Really, I don't mind. It makes no odds. Besides, I'm far more used to losing sleep than you are, especially at the height of the foaling season.' It was one of her dry jokes and Christabel managed to smile.

'He doesn't want me to come with you when you go to the island, does he?'

The unexpectedness of the question caught Emmeline unawares. In the split second that she hesitated, Christabel went on.

'I suppose I'd be in the way, wouldn't I? More of a hindrance than a help. I'd hold you back. I suffer from travel sickness; I don't ride well. I can't be packed and ready at two minutes' notice like you can. I can't blame David for not wanting to take me.'

Emmeline had had a few moments to think.

'It isn't that he doesn't want you to come, nor me either. There's nothing he'd like better. But you'd be far more useful to him stopping here, holding the fort, looking after things. And you're right – you hate travelling, packing and unpacking every other day, living out of a clothes trunk. That wouldn't suit you at all.'

'How long will you be away?'

'As long as it takes to find out the answers to all the unanswered questions. David's reputation – the whole future of the business – depends on his finding out the truth about the fire. He won't be satisfied until he does.'

After a long moment of silence, Christabel stood up.

'Yes, you're right.' Another weary smile. 'I do feel tired. I don't know why, I've done nothing all day. I never used to feel like this. I always felt so strong and full of energy until . . .' Her voice trailed away. 'I will have that brandy. Just a little. Enough to help me sleep . . .'

Emmeline poured her the brandy and she cradled it in her hands.

'I'll take it up with me.' She kissed Emmeline lightly on the cheek and went out.

Silence settled on the room once more, and Emmeline lay back in her chair. She glanced up at the clock. Twenty minutes past eleven. She wondered where David would be now, what he was doing. There'd been something else, last night, she was sure of it, that had been very much on his mind besides the fire, something that he wanted to tell her but had decided against. She recalled his words as she got up and went over to the window. '*We'll have a long talk later . . . tomorrow, when I get back.*' Pushing aside the heavy fringed draperies, she gazed out into the damp, foggy night. Only the outline of the trees along the drive and the stable roof were visible; no movement. No sound.

She turned back into the room, piled the cups back onto the tray and took it down into the kitchen to Janet.

'Miss Emmeline!' Janet jumped to her feet, the noise of footsteps and jingling crockery had woken her from her dozing in the chair. 'You shouldn't 'ave brought that down 'ere, really you shouldn't. That's my job!'

'And you should have been in bed more than an hour ago. I'm sorry. We got talking and I completely forgot the time. It was thoughtless of me.' She put down the tray. 'Mrs Ismay's just gone up.'

'Mr David not back, then?'

'No, Janet. No, he isn't.'

'Reckon he won't come home till mornin', then. Not wi' this bloomin' fog about. Blokes in the yard when I went out to fetch some coal in, told me the traffic'd all but stopped on the Epsom road; that thick, it is. Mr David'll 'ave stopped over at some pub or other, I shouldn't wonder, and'll drive back first thing. Pity about 'is dinner, though, miss. One o' my specials, too.'

Emmeline paused on the landing outside Christabel's bedroom, listening for any sound. The light still streamed from beneath the door. Gently, she reached out and turned the handle, then peeped in.

The bedside lamp with its ornate and fussy silk shade was still on, casting a peachy glow across the satin eiderdown. Christabel, fast asleep, was still half propped up for reading on a pile of lace-edged pillows, the book still open beneath her hands. Quietly, Emmeline tiptoed across to the bed and eased it from her fingers, then lay it down on the bedside table. For a moment she stood looking down at her brother's wife, at the long, pale lashes, the long coil of golden hair that snaked its way across the pillow, the empty place beside her in the big bed. Poor Christabel. She was so dependent on David that she was hopelessly lost without him.

Though he never said so she often wondered if he felt stifled by her dependence and slavish devotion. It was ironical, too, that he had been brought up among a family of strong women, yet had married one that was curiously weak.

Emmeline bent forward, and turned off the light.

FOUR

SHE WAS UP AND DRESSED in her riding clothes before dawn, long before anyone else was awake. She'd gone downstairs, put the big kettle on for tea, made herself a cup and drunk it. Then, saddling up one of the hunters, she'd ridden along the drive and out onto the Epsom road, where she'd pulled him up, eyes searching for the sight of any approaching vehicle, horse-drawn or car. Nothing. She'd cantered back, given the men their orders for the day, then sat herself by the telephone to wait for the Epsom exchange to open. If David wasn't on his way back already, certainly he'd know how anxious they were and telephone the house straight away. But nine o'clock came and went. Half-past nine. Twenty minutes past ten. By eleven o'clock there was still no telephone call and no sign of him. Christabel was almost hysterical.

'The fog's lifted enough for him to get back! Where is he? Oh dear God, where is he?'

'If he hasn't come back then he has a reason.'

'He's lying hurt somewhere, I know it! He must have had an accident!'

For several more minutes Emmeline paced up and down the library floor. Then she grasped up her leather riding gloves and began pulling them on.

'You're right. Something must have happened. I can't think what. Maybe the car broke down miles from anywhere and David hit his head. Maybe he's suffering from concussion and is being looked after by someone who doesn't know who he is. Maybe when he was on his way to John Martin's he made a detour to see somebody else. We could go on speculating all day and all night. But we can't just sit here and wait any longer.' She turned to Christabel. 'Telephone the police station in Epsom, tell them what's happened. I'm going to get some of the men together and go out searching for him on horseback.'

'But it gets dark so early.'

'We'll take flares.' She was gone before Christabel could move.

It was only half-past three but already the light was failing. The fog, that had seemed to thin out earlier in the day, was rising again; the air was damp and cruelly cold. They were on the high ground now, between Woodmanstone and Hare Warren, looking down in the fast failing light into the narrow valleys and spinneys, the empty, bare, undulating fields and tiny lanes; but, like all the other places they had searched, they could still see nothing.

Emmeline reined in her horse and shaded her eyes; the breath from the others' mounts rose up like steam in the growing darkness, the mist swirled around their legs eerily, so that they looked almost unreal – ghost riders rising from the sea. One of the men edged his horse towards hers, holding his flare aloft; she shivered in her too thin garb.

'It's no use, miss; light's fadin' fast. Wherever he is, we'll not sight him now.'

The light from the flares cast a red glow across her eyes.

'There's another half-hour of daylight; we'll go on searching till it's gone.' She raised her voice so that it carried across their heads clearly. 'I know you're tired. I know it's cold and it's getting late; I know you're hungry. And that you've been in the saddle nearly all day. So have I. But my brother is missing and I must find him.' She looked at each one of them in turn. 'I can't do that without your help.'

'I'm with you, miss! Light or no light!'

'And me.'

'Me too. We'll keep looking till we find him!' She smiled at the chorus of assenting voices. She passed a gloved hand across her tired eyes.

'I'm grateful. Now, listen to me! We've covered every likely inch of ground from the edge of Banstead Downs right across to Walton Parish. We've combed every lane, every rough track, every back road from Epsom Heath right down to Galton Park and Beggars Bush, and there's still no sign of him. What I suggest is that we split into two parties. Moran, you lead the first group and search the ground up to old Nonesuch Park, then make your way back to the house; we'll search in the opposite direction and meet you back there. If we don't find anything, then we have an hour's rest before we change horses and then try again, further afield. Agreed?'

'What if none of us finds anythin' after that, Miss Emmeline?'

'Let's hope we do. Maybe there'll be news when we get back to the house. Let's get going while there's still some light!' She wheeled her mount's head around, tapped him with her heels, then set off down the slope with the rest of the men in her group behind her. In the fast growing darkness the flares one behind the other looked like some giant, undulating snake moving along the ground. At the bottom of the hill she turned in the saddle.

'We'll take the long way round, doubling over some of the ground, just in case there was anything we missed. Then we'll make for the lane through Parsons Green and High Shabden, and reach Brew House from the slopes up behind Oaks Field.'

Every yard they covered yielded nothing. Overhead, the sky grew darker. Nearly an hour later, they suddenly caught sight of the lights streaming from the windows of the house in the distance. Half a mile away across Oaks Field she could see the dark, shadowy outlines of the other riders, their presence illuminated by the flares. Emmeline turned to one of the men behind her.

'Looks like they haven't found anything, either.'

'Miss Emmeline! Down there, in the courtyard!' Spurring his tired horse forward beside hers, he pointed in the direction of the house. 'I can see a car!'

For a single moment she felt her heart leap. She shaded her eyes and peered through the darkness in front of them, willing it to be his. But as she cantered forward down the slope her fleeting moment of exultation sank; for she could see as she came closer that it belonged not to her missing brother, but to the police.

A uniformed constable from the village stood by the steps that led up to the front door; another sat behind the wheel. Emmeline slid down from the saddle, threw her reins to one of the men and ran across the courtyard into the house, fighting down the rising feeling of panic and alarm. As she entered the hall Janet rushed forward to meet her, her face sheet-white.

'Miss, the police are here!'

'Have they found him?'

'No, miss. They're talkin' to Mrs Ismay in the drawing room, and they want to see you.'

Emmeline nodded and ran past her across the hall. She almost burst into the room, knocking off balance the constable who was standing behind the door so that he tottered backwards like a flying skittle.

Four pairs of bewildered eyes turned to stare at her.

'Miss Ismay?'

'Yes, I'm Emmeline Ismay.'

She faced two strange men in long checked coats; one held a fawn bowler in his hands, the other a notebook and pencil.

'Have you any news of my brother?'

The elder of the two men stepped forward and produced an identification wallet from inside his coat pocket. He held it open in front of her.

'Miss Ismay, I am Detective Inspector Lock and this is Detective Sergeant Barnes.'

'From Surrey County Police?'

'No, miss, from Scotland Yard.'

'*Scotland Yard!*'

'I regret to inform you, Miss Ismay, that despite preliminary enquiries, your brother's present whereabouts are still unknown. But, as I've already explained to your sister-in-law, at first light tomorrow – that is, if he still hasn't returned – we intend to mount an extensive search.'

He cleared his throat. 'Mrs Ismay telephoned the local police station at ten minutes past eleven this morning to report that her husband was missing, only a few moments before we were due to set off to interview him about certain events that took place at his stud farm on the Isle of Man three weeks ago.'

There was a blazing fire in the room. The sudden combination of its overpowering heat and the insinuation in his words hit her like a slap in the face. All over her skin began to tingle and burn. She stared at him coldly.

'What exactly do you mean by that?'

'That your brother's sudden disappearance just before he was wanted for questioning must be viewed, I'm afraid, as an extremely suspicious coincidence.'

Across the room she heard Christabel gasp.

'How dare you insinuate that my brother had anything to do with that fire! How dare you even suggest that he'd deliberately run away because he didn't have the guts to face an inquiry! He spent more than two and a half years of his life fighting for this country in the trenches, being shelled, bombed, showered with poisonous gas, up to his knees in mud and filth and the dead bodies of his friends. He never ran away from anything in his life! Ever since our parents died when the *Lusitania* was sunk four years ago, he's worked like a slave to drag the family business out of the slump that the war flung it into. Not just for himself, or me; he cares about the people who work for us. No man who's ever worked for the Ismays will ever find himself thrown on the dole – not like the thousands of soldiers who were demobbed last year and had to suffer the misery and humiliation of it, because the land fit for heroes that the Government promised them wasn't forthcoming once they'd outlived their usefulness as political cannon fodder.

'The day before he vanished, my brother spent the entire day in London discussing the fire with his lawyer; his main concern was that the men and their families who worked for us at Balla-keighan didn't suffer because the death of the horses meant they no longer had any work. When he got back he was very tired but he still talked with me into the early hours about everything. Almost his last words were about how soon we could go to Balla-keighan ourselves to find out the truth.'

'Miss Ismay, I admire your loyalty to your brother and I cast no aspersions on his courage. But I'm here because a crime may have been committed and we believe that your brother can assist us in our enquiries.'

'Do you know what he said that night he came back from London, when his lawyer told him the island police thought there were suspicious circumstances surrounding the fire? That he'd be the first one you accused because on the face of it nobody else had a motive! And he was right!'

'At this moment in time we're not accusing anyone – '

'You don't have to say a word; I can see it in your eyes. We're all under the black cloud of suspicion, anyone whose name is Ismay. It happened before, when the *Titanic* sank and everyone blamed J. Bruce Ismay; it was Charles Bowyer Ismay's fault that the 1913 Derby was a scandal and a fiasco. Now you're pointing the finger of accusation at my brother for the fire. You think he did it for the money, don't you? That's all anyone cares about these days, the money. There used to be higher things, like honour and honesty, but the war's swept all that away. We're all mercenaries, we're all cheap, ruthless, cynical. The police deal with so many liars and cheats that they think everyone they meet is a liar and a cheat too. We're all criminals, to be hounded and accused!'

'That isn't true. All I suggested was that your brother's sudden absence from home and the uncertain circumstances surrounding the fire at Ballakeighan seemed to us more than an ordinary coincidence.'

Christabel came angrily into the centre of the room.

'Your exact words were that it was an "extremely suspicious" coincidence. That isn't quite the same thing.'

'I'm sorry to have given inadvertent offence, Mrs Ismay. And I can fully understand how anxious you must be about your husband . . . especially since we know he was having trouble with his motorcar and that the weather conditions may have prevented him from managing to get in touch with you so far. But I'm only doing my job – '

'So were the Hun when they released poisoned gas into the British trenches.'

There was a short, uncomfortable silence. One of the logs fell from the fire and crashed into the grate, scattering sparks in every direction. Emmeline went over and picked up the tongs to put it back.

'Please, let me . . .' She stepped back and stood aside as Barnes took the tongs from her. So chivalry was not completely dead after four long, weary years of war. So much had changed beyond recognition. A great feeling of weariness overwhelmed her. She suddenly felt the need for a strong drink, though she rarely took spirits; a hot bath, a warm bed with crisp, newly starched sheets. She leaned back against the mantelpiece with a sigh.

'I've been out with the men since this morning, searching on horseback. We covered every lane, every spinney, every conceivable place where my brother might have been; I don't know how many miles we rode. But we found nothing. Not a single clue as to where he might be. But I know my brother. He'll guess how worried we are and he'll either come back or contact us as soon as possible.'

'He could have had a terrible accident!' Christabel again now. Her fine-boned face was white, taut. She twisted her wedding ring round and round her finger. 'In this fog, he could have veered off the road, gone into a ditch. He might be lying injured somewhere!'

The Sergeant laid a hand gently on her arm. 'I'm sure you've no need to distress yourself unduly, Mrs Ismay. If an accident had happened on his way home, your sister-in-law and your men would have found him by now. And in this fog he'd hardly be driving very fast.'

Christabel sat down. 'Yes, yes . . . I suppose so . . .'

'There isn't much more that any of us can do, not tonight. Another half an hour and it'll be black as pitch. We shan't trouble you with any further questions just now.'

'I won't sleep at all, not knowing where David is.'

'Going without a good night's rest won't help anyone, Mrs Ismay. I'm sure you'll have news in the morning.'

They moved out into the hall. Lock closed the door behind him.

'Miss Ismay, can we talk somewhere more private?' He made a sign with one hand for Barnes to go on ahead. 'A few moments more of your time, no more.'

Emmeline opened the door of her brother's office.

Everything was exactly as he'd left it on the night he'd come back from London. There were still the same untouched papers stacked in neat order on his desk; his tray of pens. Ledgers of bloodstock in alphabetical and yearly order methodically filed on the rows of shelves. Emmeline looked in front of her towards the window that led onto the courtyard, the window where David had stood pensively that night. There had been something, she knew it now, that he had wanted to tell her. She still had no idea what it could have been but their uncanny affinity of thought and her own gut feelings told her that it was something unconnected with their bloodstock or the fire.

She was aware that Lock was staring at her.

'You really don't know where he is, do you?'

Slowly, her eyes on his face, she sat down on the edge of David's desk.

'So you believe me?'

'I do now.'

'Everyone guilty until proved innocent?' There was mockery in her voice.

'I'm sorry, but a policeman's job is fundamentally one that has to be based on both facts and supposition; if you were in my place and faced with a case of possible arson coupled with a stud proprietor who seems to have conveniently disappeared just as awkward questions are about to be asked, I think you'd come to the same conclusions.'

'If you'd seen my brother's face when the news about the fire first reached us, you'd have no doubt that it was as great a shock to him as everyone else.'

Lock was silent for a moment.

'Miss Ismay, what I want to ask you now you'll understand I couldn't ask in your sister-in-law's presence. Can you tell me if there were ... other women ... in your brother's life besides his wife?'

He had succeeded in both shocking and angering her in one deft blow.

'You can't be serious?'

'It's a question I have to ask.' He came further into the room. 'Putting the matter of the fire aside for a moment, let's take your brother's sudden disappearance alone – '

'He'll be back tomorrow, you'll see.'

'In nine cases out of every ten with disappearing husbands, I can tell you that there's another woman involved. Please, hear me out. Let's assume that what you believe is true, that your brother knew nothing and had nothing to do with the Ballakeighan fire. Let's assume that there is another lady in his life. From what Mrs Ismay told us before you arrived – about certain tragedies in their personal life that both found very difficult to come to terms with – your brother is coming close to the end of his tether. The tragic death of your parents at sea, the horrors of the trenches, the running down of the business during the war ... then comes the news of the fire, the destruction of his last remaining most valuable asset. Lesser things have been enough to tip a strong man over the edge. Each of us has our own breaking point, Miss Ismay. All I suggest is that your brother, over a period of time, has been under colossal strain and mental anguish. I couldn't possibly have asked your sister-in-law such indelicate questions – even in my capacity as a policeman pursuing official enquiries – as to whether their marriage was happy, or whether she had her own private suspicions about her husband's fidelity; but I must ask you. In times of extreme stress many men turn to other women, for a variety of reasons. It's a fact of life. Much as I find the subject wholly distasteful, I have to get at the truth. I want to know if, to your knowledge, there was anyone else in your brother's life.'

Her shock was not so much what he had said about David and Christabel, but that her mind had been thinking along almost identical lines. His words about having something to tell her when he came back still burned in her head. To give herself time to harness her thoughts she slid down from the desk and went over to the window where she pressed her face against the cold pane and stared out into the foggy night. She could see his reflection behind her in the glass.

'If there had been anyone else, David would have told me. I know he would have told me.'

'Before the news came about the fire at his stud, would you say he was behaving in his usual way?'

'Yes.'

'No unexplained absences? Spending nights away from home?'

At last, Emmeline turned to face him.

'Inspector Lock, my brother was a grown man with widespread bloodstock interests. He was often away from home and he often found it necessary to stay away for days; sometimes longer. But he always let us know in advance and he always gave us the address of the place where he'd be staying. If they had a telephone, that information also. We always knew where we could contact him if we needed to.'

'But not this time?'

'We knew he was on his way to see John Martin, the bloodstock transporter. It was only when he didn't arrive and Martin contacted us that we started to worry.'

'Of course.' Lock gazed around the room. His trained, experienced eyes took in the neat pile of papers, the precisely stacked ledgers on the shelves. A clean blotter, the tray of pens lying side by side. The room of a man who liked tidiness and order, or the room of a man who had left it neat and tidy knowing that he would never use it again? Only time would show him which answer was the truth.

'Can you think of anywhere he might be? Someone he might have gone to in time of trouble?'

'Our uncle, Charles Bowyer Ismay. But he lives in Northamptonshire.'

Lock took out his notebook and began to write.

'He would have telephoned! He would have let me know first!'

'He may have decided to go on pure impulse. A spur of the moment decision. He could have broken down miles from anywhere, and have slept last night in his car. It's possible. Only large houses tend to have a telephone. Your uncle has one, I take it?'

'Yes.' She told him the number. 'I'll contact him first thing in the morning, when the Epsom exchange opens.'

'We could use our special powers and have the post office put through a call out of hours if you wish it.'

Emmeline's face brightened for a moment; then the smile faded.

'If David was there he would have telephoned us.'

'He could have arrived when the local exchange had already closed.'

She came towards him, eagerly.

'Then do it! Please, do it! Even if you have to get the post-master out of bed! Tell my uncle that David might be on his way to him ... and that I'll telephone him as soon as I can in the morning.'

'Very well, miss. Not much more any of us can do tonight, like I said. Thank you for your co-operation.' He noticed that she looked at him sharply as he said this. Of course, how could he expect her to trust him? That would be asking too much. He smiled, and held open the door for her. 'One more thing, though, if you could oblige us. We have copies of press articles about your brother, with pictures. But if you had a recent photograph, a good likeness, that we might borrow ... I'll see that you have it back as soon as may be.'

'I'll go upstairs and fetch one.'

'What about the men, miss?' Janet's voice, behind her in the

51

depths of the dim, draughty hall. 'They're still in the courtyard outside.'

Emmeline flung her cloak around her shoulders. 'You go on to bed; I'll speak to them.'

She walked out into the chilly night air, her breath rising in the fog. The men had long dismounted and were standing around in groups talking in low voices. When they caught sight of her they all fell silent and looked up.

'No news.' A groan of disappointment rippled around the courtyard. 'The police are continuing the search tomorrow, where we left off. All we can do is wait.' She managed a weary smile. 'I don't need to tell any of you how grateful I am for your help tonight.'

She watched them as they murmured good-night and slowly began to drift away until only Herbert Haynes, their stud groom, remained. He touched his cap.

'Foul night, Miss Ismay. Whole air smells of a coal cellar. Reminds me o' London.' He came towards her. 'No need for you to be troublin' yourself with doin' the rounds tonight; I'll see to it.'

Emmeline smiled. She drew the cloak closer around her body.

'I'll come with you; yes, I want to. I need something to distract me.' They began walking side by side towards the main stud buildings in the opposite direction to the house. 'You've known my brother for as long as I can remember. Do you think he'd be capable of starting that fire?'

Haynes' face expressed horror.

'Is that what them coppers said?'

'It was suggested.'

'Let 'em suggest it to me!'

'I think I gave as good as I got.' In the darkness he saw her ghost of a smile. Yes, he'd bet she had, an' all! His eyes shone with admiration. That was what the Ismays did to you: they dazzled, they captivated; once you'd worked for them you wanted to stay with them forever. That was how it was. He remembered Cornelius and Rebeccah Ismay, in the years before the war when he'd come here to learn his trade; his father had worked for her father, James Brodie Russell, and his sense of pride and privilege at belonging to the Ismay empire had outweighed the long hours of toil, the sleepless nights in the foaling season, working outdoors in all weathers. There wasn't a day when he'd have changed places with anyone in the world. And the thrill when a foal that he'd watched come into the world turned out a classic winner was a feeling he couldn't even begin to put into words.

'If only I knew that my brother was safe. That everything is all right.' They went on walking.

'Mr David's got his head screwed on the right way round, miss. He'll be all right, you can bet on it.' They turned down into the stud courtyard and beneath the arched clocktower, their booted feet echoing loudly on the cobbles. 'If Mr David's got a reason for not comin' back tonight, you can bet your last sixpence it'll be a good one; he knows what he's doin'.'

'It isn't like him not to let me know where he is.'

'There's a first time for everythin', miss.'

That made her feel curiously better, somehow more at ease. Haynes' blunt, down to earth common sense. She was being foolish, worrying for no reason. When David hadn't come back to the house this morning as she'd expected him to she'd let herself be thrown into an uncharacteristic panic by Christabel, who panicked at the slightest thing. Maybe the business with the fire over at Ballakeighan had set them all on edge far more than she knew. David would come back tomorrow. If he'd gone on an impulse to Charles Bowyer Ismay, he'd telephone her, first thing.

'Any problems with the foals or yearlings?'

'None, miss. As fine a batch as ever you'd wish to see. Post-war depression or not, this year's youngstock'll be the pick of Tattersalls.' He unlocked one of the boxes and stood back to let her pass through. 'Just take a look at this filly foal. Look at those legs and that depth of chest for a six-month-old.' He held his lantern higher, casting a warm, amber glow across the ankle-deep straw. The animal whinnied softly and came towards them while her dam placidly continued to chomp hay from her manger. 'Look at that shape ... faultless.' He stooped forward and ran a hand gently over the filly foal's forelegs, then her flanks. 'What can you expect with a sire like Zinfandel and a dam like Lady Josephine? That's class. What a useful colt that was!'

Emmeline sat down on an upturned bucket.

'By Persimmon out of Medora? A magnificent whopping great chestnut ... I can't remember but I know my father rated him as one of the best colts he'd ever seen.'

'He was prime classic material, that horse; pity his owner, Colonel McCalmont, died and all his nominations for the next year's races were void. After Lord Howard de Walden got him, he won the Coronation Cup at Epsom – trounced Rock Sand and Sceptre . . . that'll show you how good he was!'

'Well, she should show speed and stamina; Persimmon stock and a sprinting mare.' Emmeline got to her feet and began to pet her. 'My brother was going to make a present of her to our uncle for all the help he gave us after Father died . . .'

Haynes fell silent for a moment, out of respect. Damn Germans, to torpedo a passenger liner with innocent people aboard, Mr and Mrs Ismay among them. As a little boy coming to watch his father work he could remember that dazzling smile . . .

'Your uncle doesn't keep as many horses in training as he did. Is that likely to change?'

'I don't know . . . maybe. It was always his great passion, the turf. But I think after 1913 when he lost the Derby on a disqualification that should never have been, he lost heart.'

'That was a wicked piece of trickery an' no mistake!'

'Just a sample of what can happen when one man has too much power. Eustace Loder, he wanted to run the Jockey Club single-handed! Everyone knew about the feud between my uncle and him. It was common knowledge after the race. And their quarrel wasn't just about horses. I was too young to be told at the time but later my mother said that there'd been an attachment between Uncle Charles and Loder's sister-in-law. To a man like Loder that in itself was more than enough to make bad blood between them.'

'To my way of thinkin', it wasn't any of the Colonel's business what his wife's sister did.'

'He didn't look at it quite that way.'

They both looked around the stable to make certain that everything was in order before going outside and relocking the double door. 'After Craganour was disqualified in the Derby my uncle lost heart, I think. After all, he was first and last a sportsman and the whole affair sickened him; Loder had acted out of malice, not fairness. Otherwise nothing on earth would ever have persuaded him to sell the colt to the Argentine.' They walked on to the next box. 'If Ballacragan had died in that fire it would have been an irretrievable loss to the entire English bloodstock industry. It would have meant the complete destruction of a unique bloodline forever.' She opened the top of the next stable door and looked in; Haynes locked it as she moved on. 'After all, there is blood-stock available that has been sired by Desmond, but not blood-stock sired by him out of Veneration II. After all, she was a half-sister to Pretty Polly.'

'Funny, that,' Haynes said as they continued their way down the row of boxes. 'How you'll get a brilliant race mare like Pretty Polly who's well nigh useless at stud and then you get a sister or half-sister – maybe one who's never even seen a racecourse – and the stock they produce turns out to be brilliant. Uncanny.'

'My father used to say the same, and it's true, if you go back in time. Look at all the great race mares: Eleanor, Blink Bonny, Tagalie, Sceptre as well as Pretty Polly herself, none of them went on to produce anything of note. Strange. Almost as if everything they had to give was burned out on the racecourse. Father used to pick out unraced stock of the best lines who had brilliant winning fillies as full or half-sisters, and he rarely went wrong.'

'Mr Ismay was a genius, and that's for sure!'

The mention of her father sent her into silence. Their footsteps went on echoing around the deserted yard. But doing the rounds in David's place, talking about the horses, had somehow com-forted her. She was grateful to Haynes.

'Well, that's just about it, miss. Will there be anything else?'

She smiled.

'No, not now. You'd best be getting home to your family and your fireside.' She shivered in the chilly night air. 'Thank you for talking. I feel better now.'

'If there's anything you want, miss, you or Mrs Ismay, you've only to let me know.' He touched his cap and began to walk in the opposite direction. 'Good-night, then, miss.'

'Good-night, Haynes.'

Slowly, pensively, Emmeline began to walk away in the direc-tion of the house. Out of the foggy darkness it loomed towards her, a giant murky shadow; lights streamed from the upstairs windows across the lawns. The bare branches of the trees that lined the drive cast eerie shadows like the fingers of a skeleton hand. She wondered where David would be now, what he was thinking. She wondered if he was alone. She turned his words to her that last evening over and over in her mind.

What had he meant when he'd said, 'We'll have a long talk

later . . . tomorrow, when I get back'?

Was she reading something into those words that he had never meant? Or had he meant never to come back at all?

The small boy crouched on his haunches in the dusty yard, watching the others playing with their whip and top. He longed to join in with them, but it was useless to ask because he knew that they would only laugh at him and call him cruel names because of his affliction. In his hand he toyed with his grubby drawstring bag of marbles. After a few more moments, as they disappeared along the village street laughing and shouting, he got up and wandered into his mother's scullery.

She was too busy with the week's mountain of washing to notice him. Sleeves rolled up, soap in hand, she pounded the sheets in the big iron tub against the washboard, pausing every few moments to mop the sweat from her brow. Life had never been easy; now, after the war with the menfolk dead and only her fourteen-year-old daughter to be of any use to her, she was old before her time, and bitter. There was a movement in the open doorway and she glanced over her shoulder.

'Oh, it's you, is it? Well, now you're here make yourself useful and tell your sister to hurry up with that hot water! This lot's turnin' cold and I've all this laundry to get rinsed and hung out before dinner time!'

The boy slunk inside, still fingering the bag of marbles.

'It was th-th-the G-G-G-Germans, wasn't it, M-M-M-Mam, st-st-st-st-started that f-f-f-f-fire. . . ?'

'Out o' the way! What are you on about now, then? Germans!' She dunked another pair of sheets into the soapy water and went on pounding them against the washboard savagely. 'Was the Germans killed your pa, that's what they did, God rot 'em, leavin' me with you and your sister to fend for on me own. Go on, get along wi' you an' into the kitchen!' He went, eyeing her cautiously over his shoulder. 'Well, shift yourself! An' don't get near the copper on the stove!'

Lock and his Sergeant were back at half-past eight the next morning. Emmeline was already waiting for them, dressed in her outdoor clothes, ready to repeat the daily ritual of doing the stud rounds in David's place. Their expressions were dour. Even before Lock spoke she guessed that their telephone call to Charles Ismay had produced no further clues. She showed them inside the house.

'Your uncle was on the point of retiring for the night when we reached him. He was astonished to hear that your brother seemed to have disappeared without trace, without making contact. But he feels certain it has something to do with the fire.'

'The fire?'

'He thinks your brother may have learned something, from an unexpected source and decided to follow it up on his own, on impulse.'

'But how could he? He was on his way to John Martin's place.'

'We could theorize all day and night, Miss Ismay. I was deliberately guarded in what I said to your uncle; after all, your brother's movements have only been unaccounted for little more than forty-eight hours; I think we only need start to concern ourselves seriously if he remains missing for, say, a week without making contact. That would be extremely suspicious.'

Emmeline gave him a cold look.

'You said yesterday that you intended to mount an extensive search first thing this morning if he still hadn't come back; and the fact that the fire might be arson coupled with his sudden disappearance was more than a suspicious coincidence.'

'True . . . and a search was mounted this morning at dawn. I've ordered hourly reports. But I intend to give Mr Ismay the benefit of the doubt. After all, everyone who we've so far interviewed as to his integrity and character speak of him in the highest possible terms.'

The look she gave him spoke volumes.

'We've no wish to inconvenience you, or Mrs Ismay. Or to interrupt the routine of the stud. We would, however, like to interview your men and the household servants. Purely a matter of routine. Also, I'd appreciate it if you could spare me a few more moments of your own time . . . in another room, perhaps?' He glanced towards the table, already set for breakfast. 'I don't think we'll need to trouble Mrs Ismay any further, for the time being at least.'

Without speaking, she led them down along the dimly-lit hall towards the staircase, then opened one of the doors leading off from it. A strong musty smell assailed her nostrils.

'It isn't used now. It hasn't been used for years; not since our parents died and we closed up a lot of the rooms. There seemed no point, really, in keeping them open. More work for the staff. And they were never used any more.'

Lock looked around him, sensing the neglect and sadness of the place. Giant cobwebs clung from the ceiling. The single table and two chairs were covered with faded dust sheets that were themselves thick with dust.

She paused, and let her eyes wander around the bare walls, the uncarpeted floor. 'I think it used to be the butler's sitting room. We don't have one now. We haven't had a proper staff in the house since before the war.' She sat down on one of the chairs. 'Well, what is it you want to ask me? I've told you everything I know already.'

'Miss Ismay, I'm faced with two possibilities here and I need to establish as quickly as possible what line my enquiries have to take. We were sent down from Scotland Yard to investigate your brother's business dealings and the circumstances relating to the fire. Having got here we're now faced with a possible disappearance. We have to ask ourselves — is that connected or unconnected with the fire business? Only time will tell.'

'I already told you yesterday; I know my brother better than I know myself. The stud is his life. If you knew anything about him you'd know that for him to have had anything to do with arson is absurd. On the contrary, we were going over to Ballakeighan together to try and find out how it started.'

Lock nodded.

'And that, I take it, was your brother's suggestion? To which you immediately agreed?'

'What are you trying to say?'

'Miss Ismay, I've been in this job for more years than I care to remember, so let me tell you this: there's nothing so strange or mysterious as the way the human mind works. People who are close to us, people we think we know, are capable of behaving in ways we never dreamed possible. You're sceptical, aren't you? But I know it's true because I've seen it happen. Even if your brother knew nothing of the fire, had nothing to do with it, maybe it was the last straw for him. Consider this. From enquiries we know that racing and the bloodstock industry are suffering a severe post-war depression. Many companies and men who were wealthy before the war have suffered heavy losses, some have been pushed into bankruptcy. Until we check your brother's books we won't know what his financial position is. You'll appreciate that we can't simply take your word for it; it has to be thoroughly looked into. Perhaps on top of everything else he felt he couldn't cope any more . . . so he just went.'

'I've never heard anything so bizarre! David, to walk out without a word to Christabel or me? To leave me to face the music on my own?' There was contempt in her voice now. 'Your years mixing with criminals have certainly given you a warped view of other people!'

'I'm sorry, I meant no offence. But the possibility has to be faced.'

'Go ahead then. Go through the books. Go through everything.' She was at the door now. 'But please excuse me, I have work to do.'

'They're back, aren't they? Why don't they go away and leave us alone? They should be out there, looking for David. He could have crashed, he could be lying hurt – '

'They're only doing their job, Christabel, and I'm sure David can take care of himself.'

'Why are they looking through his papers? What do they think they're going to find? Behaving as if he was some criminal. They think he had something to do with that fire, don't they?'

Emmeline went on watching from the window. Barnes had come out of the house and was walking, briskly, towards a group of stud hands in the middle of the yard.

'They say they have to consider the possibility. Well, I suppose they're right; after all, they don't know him like we do. They're working in the dark. David himself said that he'd be the first one they suspected if arson was proved.'

'If they think he did it for the insurance money it doesn't make sense. If he disappears how can he claim it?'

'You forget, I'm an equal partner in the bloodstock company. If the insurance claim was met then the money would be paid to me – all this is theory, of course. Then, they reason, we join

David wherever he's hiding and divide the spoils.'

Christabel was outraged.

'But that's crazy! Surely nobody could possibly believe that?'

'In the Inspector's long and distinguished career no doubt he's come across plenty of men who would do it.'

'Well, they'll be proved wrong, won't they?' Angrily she stormed away. Emmeline heard her footsteps growing fainter, then the slam of a door. Then Janet's voice, behind her, made her jump.

'It's not right, what they're doin', miss. Not right. Turnin' the place upside down, nosin' into Mr David's business, all 'is books an' papers are in a right mess; I saw, when I went by the room! They'd better put 'em back just the way they were, that's all! 'Fore he gets back. Mr David'd have a fit.'

'If I refused to let them search his study, Janet, they would have been more suspicious. And they'd only have gone and got a warrant.'

Janet looked beyond where they were standing to the door of Christabel's room.

'I'll take something hot in for Mrs Ismay. Something with a nice drop o' brandy in it. That'll help her to bear up. If only Mr David'd come back an' sort everything out, if only he would.'

Heavily, Emmeline sighed.

'We can only go on looking, Janet. Until we do find him. Just go on looking.'

When Janet had gone she went on staring from the window at the dull, cheerless winter landscape, into the distance beyond the dark outline of trees. Sleet was falling now. Dead leaves blew across the empty courtyard.

Where are you, David? Where in God's name can you be?

The police car sped along the winding drive, then halted at the big gates that led out onto the main Epsom road. The windows rattled under a sudden onslaught of sleety rain. The road ahead looked dark, windswept, deserted; not many would be out on a night such as this.

'What a spitfire!' Lock said, drily, keeping his eyes trained on the road ahead of them. 'I can just imagine that one marching with the suffragettes. *Emmeline*. It wouldn't surprise me to find out that Mrs Pankhurst is her godmother. Maybe she was named after her.'

'She can spit fire at me anytime, sir,' Barnes answered, with a smile. 'I like a girl with a bit of spirit.'

'Looks aren't everything, Barnes. And you're supposed to remain objective.'

'Did you see that big picture right at the top of the stairs, sir? A beautiful woman with dark hair and blue eyes in old-fashioned clothes. Just like her, it was. I saw the resemblance straight away, when the maid showed us through. Striking.'

'Don't let a pretty face turn your head. If you do you're in the wrong job.'

'Just an observation, sir. And I'd swear on my mother's Bible that she doesn't know anything about the brother vanishing into thin air. Nor the wife, either.'

'Certainly not Mrs Ismay. A blind man could tell that. Hysterical!'

'And Emmeline Ismay, sir?'

'On the face of it I'd say she doesn't know where he is, either. Not unless she's a brilliant actress, which a lot of women are, mark my words. I've come up against a few in my time; doubtless I'll come up against a few more before I retire. But this one – well, at the moment we have to keep an open mind.'

'She was outraged at any suggestion that Ismay could be guilty. Or that she knew anything about it.'

'Her reaction seemed perfectly genuine. My first instinct is that she's telling the truth.'

'She'd hardly spend the whole day riding all over the countryside trying to find him if she wasn't, surely, sir? She was all in. Cold, wet, hungry. You can't fake that.'

'So that leaves us with the same mystery as we started out with this morning. Where is David Ismay? Why has he disappeared? And why now, when the finger of suspicion over how that fire started is pointing his way? His wife told us that he took his personal effects with him – his wallet, keys, loose change – the things any other man would take. The bank confirms that no large amounts of cash have been withdrawn over a long period of time, or recently. So on the face of it, it seems that he set out for John Martin's place but never arrived. What we have to find out is why.'

'If he'd had trouble with his car, or an accident on the way, somebody would have seen and reported it, even if he'd hurt himself and couldn't. But there's nothing.'

'That leaves us with only one reasonable assumption, Barnes, that he left the house but didn't go to John Martin.'

'Martin, Mrs Ismay and his sister all said that he told them he'd be there at nine o'clock sharp. He treated the meeting as a matter of urgency because he was anxious to ship the horses that hadn't been killed in the fire back to England. What could have happened on the way?'

'We have to assume that he didn't drive to Martin's house. That for some reason that we don't know about yet, he went somewhere else.'

'His wife said that he was especially particular about letting people know if he couldn't keep a promise. So why didn't he stop in Epsom and telephone? It's totally out of character, from what we know of him so far.'

'You think there could be another woman?'

'It's possible. Highly possible.' He slipped a hand inside his coat pocket and brought out a single photograph. 'Ismay's a particularly handsome man, the sort of man who'd be highly attractive to almost any woman. We can't rule anything out.'

'From what his sister said, sir, they were very happy. He and his wife, I mean.'

'Few things are really what they seem. Just because they don't throw plates at each other doesn't mean that he wouldn't go off with someone else. Think about it, Barnes. Mrs Ismay, granted, is a beautiful woman, but beauty's only skin deep. Maybe they haven't been happy for years but he's kept quiet and suffered in silence. Then he meets someone else.'

'It's possible.'

'If he arranged for that stud to be put to the torch for his own financial gain and expected to sit tight and get away with it, he must have learnt more than his lawyer told him about what proof was found, so then he took fright and bolted. Otherwise his disappearance makes no sense.

'I'm only speculating, but let's say someone else involved got word to him either before or shortly after he met Delauney in London, that the game was up. He must have done some quick thinking and laid his plans accordingly on the journey back. He tells his sister that he's going to meet Martin, that he'll be out all day. Not to wait for him at dinner. That gives him a whole day to get out of the country.'

'And luck was with him even there! The fog was getting thicker every minute. Nobody worried because when he didn't turn up next morning they assumed he was somewhere, waiting for it to clear. Even the trouble he was supposed to have had getting his car to start could have been more fabrication to gain time. But what about money, sir? The bank confirmed that he'd made no significant withdrawals during the last year. He only took with him whatever he had in his wallet.'

'True. But how do we know what sums of ready cash Ismay might have got hold of through different deals in the last few months? Sums that never went through the banking system. Not all gentlemen are honourable.'

'You think that's the answer?'

'It could be. Not easy to prove. Ismay may be an exceptionally clever man. Perhaps he's been planning this for a long while. If he is guilty, you have to admire the way he's done it – covered his tracks so well that nobody suspects him, not even his wife and his sister.'

The car slowed down as they came into Epsom. Past the Angel and Crown, a fashionable milliner's, a tailor's shop; then left along Folly's Lane to the police station. They got out, shivering in the cold night air and went hurriedly up the steps into the building.

There was a small fire burning in the grate in Lock's office, and he went over to it, rubbing his hands together, while Barnes called to one of the junior constables to brew tea.

'And what's on the agenda for tomorrow, sir?'

'First thing, you go back to the Ismay house. Carry on taking statements from the staff and servants – maybe have a gentle talk with Mrs Ismay. Not that I expect much joy there. We can leave the sister for the time being. If she knows anything else she's not saying. Me, I'm off to London to talk to the Ismay lawyer. After that it's up to Northampton to see Charles Bowyer Ismay – never know what might come of a talk to him – then both of us meet up again here. We compare notes, gather what we've got, then off to Ballakeighan to try and get to the bottom of this fire.'

Barnes sat down on the edge of the cluttered desk.

63

'And if David Ismay's reappeared by then?'

'So much the better. It'll make my job a whole lot easier. But I wouldn't bank on it.'

'You told the Ismay girl that you were giving him the benefit of the doubt.'

'So I was. But at the moment I can't see any benefit, just the doubt.'

The desk junior brought their tea and Barnes drank it gratefully. It was too strong and someone had forgotten to put sugar in it, but it tasted like nectar as he gulped it down. It was so hot it made his eyes water.

'Just one thing still bothers me in all this. Something that doesn't ring true.'

'What?'

'About David Ismay. On the face of it, he has to be guilty, only because he's the only one who has a motive that fits. Why should anyone else do it? So far we've been unable to dig up any real enemies. And yet after talking to his sister I just have this feeling that that's what we're supposed to think – that he couldn't have done it because he isn't that sort of man.'

Lock smiled grimly.

'You mean what she said the first time about him fighting for his country, waist-deep in mud in the fields of Flanders, battling in the face of the enemy against shelling, gunfire and poisoned gas? It's all irrelevant, isn't it? Nobody's accusing him of being a coward.'

'But there are different kinds of cowardice. Would a man like that walk out into thin air and leave his wife and his sister to face the music?'

'He might, because he wouldn't think it was an act of cowardice.'

'I never thought of it that way before.'

Lock came away from the fire now that he had warmed himself.

'Neither did she.'

FIVE

'Miss Emmeline! *Miss Emmeline!* Please, wake up!'

She started up from the chair as Winifred shook her. Her body was stiff, her head throbbed. She couldn't remember falling asleep again, only staring out of the window at the first streaks of light breaking through the darkness of the sky, while she thought of David. Then oblivion.

'What is it? Are the police back so early?' Her mind refused to function, it was still only half light outside the window. She could only have fallen asleep, fitfully, for just a few minutes.

'It's Mrs Ismay, miss. She was gone from her bedroom when I took up her tea. Then I looked out of the window and saw her outside in the garden. She's only got on her lawn cotton nightdress. She'll catch her death . . .'

'All right, I'm coming.' Emmeline flung open her wardrobe, pulled out the first cape she caught sight of and threw it round her shoulders, then hurried after Winifred. On the stone terrace they both paused, breathing hard, looking all around them.

'There she is!'

They both caught sight of Christabel simultaneously, her white nightdress flying out behind her in the strong wind, walking through the tall shrub bushes towards the sunken garden.

When they caught up with her she turned and stared at them almost in surprise.

'I thought I saw something . . . David . . . when I got up and looked out of the window. Do you think he's gone to the old gatehouse?'

Emmeline took her gently but firmly by the arm and propelled her back towards the house.

'Christabel, you shouldn't be out here. It's freezing cold. You should have got dressed first.'

65

'But I thought I saw David . . .'

'It was your imagination. If he'd come back his car would be parked in the courtyard and he'd have come straight into the house. Come on, let's go back.' She took the cloak from her shoulders and draped it around Christabel's. She exchanged a glance with Winifred.

'I want to talk to you, Emmeline.'

'Yes. Yes, when we get back in the house.'

'I had an uncle when I was a little girl – he's dead now – he went missing, too, for a whole month. I can remember it. And I can remember eavesdropping with my sisters when we heard my aunt and my mother talking after he'd come back.'

'Christabel – '

'My aunt had a miscarriage, just like I did. Afterwards, she went into a state of depression. Nobody could talk to her. She'd just sit in the same chair all day long without speaking. That was why he went. He couldn't stand it, it wore him down.' Christabel's blue eyes filled with tears and Emmeline knew what she was going to say before she said it. 'Do you think that's why David's gone? Just to get away from me? Not for good . . . just to be on his own for a while. It isn't ridiculous! Men do that sort of thing – '

'Not David.'

'But he told me more than once that after we lost the baby I should pull myself together. And I couldn't.'

'You're talking nonsense.'

'But he did. I could sense him growing impatient with me, and there was nothing I could do. It irritated him when I kept going into the empty nursery. I tried not to do it but I couldn't seem to help myself . . .'

Emmeline came over to where she was standing and laid her hands gently on Christabel's shoulders.

'David loves you, Christabel. Do you really believe that he'd do anything that caused you one moment of worry or unhappiness? We both know better.'

Christabel's eyes fell to the floor.

'Then where is he? Why hasn't he come back? Why hasn't he made any contact with us? And where is he now?'

'I wish I knew.'

When he had been missing for a week, Emmeline began telephoning her uncle every day in case he had heard any news. A local newspaper reporter turned up at the house and was sent away again. In the town, she could feel people looking at her in a certain way, even those she had known all her life and who knew her and David well. Stories speculating on the cause of the sensational fire that had gutted the stud in Ballakeighan began to appear in large print on the front pages of the national press.

Two days later, the police came back.

She had just finished a long, arduous conversation on the telephone with her uncle during which she had scarcely heard half of what he'd said. She was in a furious temper.

When Janet showed them into the library, she went on leafing through a pile of stud returns while they stood watching her impatiently on the threshold of the room.

She looked up at them with steely eyes.

'I can see by your expressions that you haven't found my brother.'

'Miss Ismay, do you know the registration number of your brother's car?'

She frowned.

'TY 1589. A Morris Cowley.'

'It was discovered about an hour ago in deep undergrowth in Bush Wood.'

She dropped the sheaf of papers in her hand.

'*What?*'

'We'll need you to come with us to formally identify it.'

She felt all the colour drain from her face.

'Was he – ?'

'The vehicle had clearly been abandoned, Miss Ismay. There was nothing inside it. It was discovered by a passing motorist. There was no sign of your brother.'

'But Bush Wood is in the opposite direction to John Martin's house. I don't understand.'

'Neither do we, Miss Ismay. Perhaps we'll learn something more when we've examined the car.' Lock opened the door behind him and stepped back. 'I'd be grateful if you could come to Epsom with us now.'

'All right. Wait until I fetch my coat.'

'And Mrs Ismay? No doubt she'll want to be kept in touch with this development.'

'I won't tell her until I get back. It's best that she doesn't see the car. This has all been too much of an emotional strain for her. Coming face to face with David's empty car – '

'Yes, I understand.'

No, Christabel Ismay wasn't made of the same stuff as this girl; that much he already knew. Twenty-five years' experience in the police force had taught him a lot about human reactions and he'd warrant that this one was a different kettle of fish altogether. He admired her self-possession, the iron control; most women in her place would have reacted with stunned disbelief, followed by hysteria and tears.

He went outside to wait for her in the courtyard.

A dozen paces behind Lock and his Sergeant, she picked her way carefully through the long damp grass and dead leaves, stepping over sprawling tree roots and severed trunks, trying to avoid the potholes filled with rainwater and mud. They came suddenly upon the place where the car had been found, and she abruptly stopped.

All around them the woods were teeming with uniformed policemen, prodding the undergrowth with long sticks; beside the abandoned car she caught sight of a constable with two dogs. He stood up stiffly as he saw them approach.

'We put the dogs in, sir, as soon as we got the word, but the scent's gone cold, I'm afraid. He's been gone from here too long.'

'Pity. But keep casting them around. We might find something else, with a bit of luck.' He turned to Emmeline. 'Miss Ismay, can you confirm that this vehicle is your brother's car?'

She walked up slowly to it, hesitantly, as if she was in a trance. She walked around it, staring at the driver's seat, at the wheel, the gears. She thought, with an almost physical pain, *David was here. He sat there. His hands touched the wheel.* For the first time since he'd vanished, she felt tears burning at the backs of her eyes. But she fought them, defiantly. Surrounded by police, Lock and his Sergeant, this was no place to cry.

She swallowed.

'Why did he come here? Why has he abandoned the car?'

'When he started from home he must have turned left at the gates and come out onto the Banstead side of the main road. Then, instead of making in the direction of John Martin's place, he continued on down Walton Heath towards Dorking. For what purpose we don't yet know. It may be he suddenly changed his mind. Perhaps he'd arranged to meet someone there. But one thing is certain, the car didn't get here by itself. It was driven here and deliberately concealed to delay discovery.' He looked around. 'The entire area will have to be searched; we may find some clue as to which direction he walked in – if he went on by foot at all.' He saw Emmeline stiffen. 'It may be – a possibility that we can't dismiss – that after he abandoned his vehicle here he was met by someone else in a different one.'

'This is all wild speculation.'

'Speculation is all we have at present, Miss Ismay. Facts are few and far between. But having abandoned the car, he must have made for some specific destination, if there was no rendezvous. It hasn't gone unnoticed that once a man left the cover of these woods, he'd be pretty close to the Reading and Reigate railway. The station is only a few minutes' walk from the other side of Bush Wood.'

'But David always used the suburban line, on the other side of Epsom. When he went to London to see Delauney he went and came back from Epsom station. It's much nearer to the house.'

'He may have used the Reading and Reigate, Miss Ismay, because he was not known by the railway staff there as he was at Epsom. That much seems obvious.'

'Why not drive to wherever it was that he wanted to go? Why use the railway at all?'

'More anonymous. Faster. Easy to switch and change routes, unlike a motorcar. Only the more well-to-do people own a motor vehicle. A motorcar would stick out like a sore thumb.'

There was anger in Emmeline's voice now.

'And where do you suggest he went *to*?'

'Miss Ismay, I have something else to tell you. Maybe here isn't exactly the place I'd chose but you may as well hear it here as anywhere. When the story gets out the press will be blazoning it in large print across their front pages anyhow.'

69

'If you mean journalists' speculation about how the fire started and where my brother is, they've done it already.'

He took a deep breath, and to her surprise she realized that he was trying to find an easy way to tell her to soften the inevitable blow. But there was no easy way.

'The report from the island police that we've just received shows beyond any doubt that the fire at the Ismay stud was arson. There's incontrovertible evidence. When we've finished tying up loose ends here, we intend to travel to the island and examine the scene of the fire ourselves.' She couldn't speak. She felt as if she was choking. 'Money and explosives – English money – were found in an abandoned shepherd's hut some distance from the stud land.'

Somehow, she found her voice again.

'They could have been planted there. Because the money was English it doesn't prove that it belonged to my brother. How could it when at the time of the fire he was here in Epsom? I could find a hundred people who knew him to testify to that.'

'Only your brother had a strong enough motive.'

Abruptly, she turned away from him.

'Will you please take me home?'

'We'll need a statement first, I'm afraid. At the police station. Your formal identification of your brother's motor vehicle.'

One of the uniformed police held open the door of the car for her, and she got in beside Lock.

'Anyone could have planted those explosives to implicate David.'

'Who would hate him that much? Exhaustive enquiries have failed to turn up a single name. Not one of his relatives, friends or business acquaintances has any idea who would hate him enough not only to ruin him but to send him to the gallows.'

Icy fingers touched her spine.

'Even if everything you suspect about David was true, manslaughter isn't a capital offence.'

'Whether the death of those four men who worked for your brother was manslaughter or murder would have to be proved or disproved in a court of law. If he arranged to have the stud put to the torch – and most of it was razed to the ground – he would have known that there was little chance for many of those living there to escape; after all, they were all asleep in their beds when it happened. That would be murder.'

She fell into cold, sullen silence until they reached Epsom. Then she got out of the car and went up the flight of steps to the police station before any of them could help her.

A man was blocking her path. She stopped, abruptly, and peered at him through the netting veil on her French velvet toque.

He smiled and stepped back. Even before he spoke she knew instinctively that he was not an Englishman. His strong, sunburned features were in sharp contrast to the pallid policemen's faces; something in his movement, even the assured, casual way he stood, branded him immediately as a foreigner.

Since he wore no hat, he simply inclined his head towards her and said, in a curious accent that she failed to identify, 'Good day.'

Lock was behind her now.

'Miss Ismay, this is the gentleman who found your brother's car.'

For a moment they stared at each other, then his face broke into a smile.

'Miss Ismay? Emmeline Ismay? You're not Cornelius's daughter?'

'Why, yes . . .' She was taken completely by surprise.

He held out his hand to her and she took it; he had a strong grip, even stronger than David's. She looked up into his face and saw that his eyes were not brown like her brother's as she'd first thought, but a dark, slate grey.

'I'm Karl Philip Ryan.' The accent could have been South African, perhaps Australian. 'When I started out from Southampton two days ago I never expected to end up in an English police station.'

'You knew my father?'

'My father knew him well when he worked for the Merritt Bloodstock Company in the States. I haven't seen him since I was a boy.' He smiled. 'He always said that if I ever came to England to look him up. When I boarded the train I bought myself a couple of newspapers and I couldn't believe what they were saying . . . arson at your Isle of Man stud.'

For the moment Emmeline was nonplussed. Inside Lock's office she sank down onto a hard chair.

71

'You were on your way to the house when you found David's car?'

'I'd stopped to have a cigarette and consult my map. Then I noticed these deep tyre marks in the mud near the edge of the wood. Looked as if somebody had skidded badly, so I went inside to investigate. When I found the car in the undergrowth I drove back into Epsom to tell the police, although I still had no idea that the car belonged to your brother. I thought that whoever had been driving might have come off the road and been concussed. They want me to make a statement.'

'And you came here to see my father?'

'I've been away in the Transvaal for the last five years; it seemed a good idea to look him up after all this time en route for Philadelphia.'

There was a sudden silence in the room.

'My father ... both my parents were killed four years ago, when they were aboard the *Lusitania* and it was torpedoed.'

His face registered shock.

'I'd no idea.'

'If you were in South Africa then you probably would never have found out. There were articles in the English newspapers, and in New York because of the family's connection with the White Star Line there. But you wouldn't have known otherwise.'

'I don't know what to say ... Your brother missing, this fire! Is there anything I can do to help?'

'We'll want a statement from you, Mr Ryan,' Lock said, 'about how you discovered the abandoned vehicle; after that you're free to leave. But since you're clearly known to Miss Ismay's family perhaps you could drive her back to the house when you've finished here – if Miss Ismay is agreeable?'

'Yes, of course. I'd be delighted.'

Emmeline got to her feet. In the middle of all the anxiety and turmoil it was a welcome relief to have come across someone who'd known her beloved father, a friend, an ally; but the dark little room in the hostile police station was too much for her to bear any longer. 'Could I make the statement later?' she said to Lock. 'Please, when you've finished here, Mr Ryan, make your own way to the house. Any acquaintance of my father's is more than welcome. I know my sister-in-law would be delighted to meet you, but I'd rather go now. I feel sure you understand.' He

72

glanced almost imperceptibly at Lock and she knew that he did.

'I accept your kind invitation, with pleasure. But if you're certain you want visitors at a time like this – '

'Anyone who knew my father is welcome at the house any time.' She smiled. 'Please . . . I must go now.'

'But you can't walk back!' He stared at her long, dark linen tunic costume, with the tightly fitting jacket and tubular skirt; the veiled toque, ankle-length button up boots with sharp heels.

'It's all right. I'll borrow a horse from the livery stable; I bet I'll be back before you are.'

She left both men staring after her.

She'd always hated riding side-saddle; but now there was no help for it. Her fashionable tight skirt was too narrow to let her ride her favourite way, astride. But the chestnut gelding she'd borrowed from the Epsom livery gave her a good, exhilarating gallop across Walton Heath, then down through Cophill and Banstead Downs, the long way home. She resisted the strong temptation to change direction and ride through Bush Wood. No doubt the army of police who were still searching there would refuse to let her through, and she'd had more than her fill of policemen for one day. She slowed the gelding down to a steady pace as they came in sight of the road, and it was then that she heard the sound of a motorcar engine some way behind her. As it came closer, she eased the animal to a halt.

She recognized him even before he'd drawn up alongside; she looked down at him from her superior height in the saddle, calming the horse with her hands as he began to shy. She waited for him to stop. He smiled up at her.

'Your horse doesn't like the sound of my engine.'

'Most horses don't.'

'I drove all the way along the main road from Epsom when the police had finished with me, looking for you.'

'Then you wasted your petrol, Mr Ryan. I didn't go that way.'

'So I see.' He turned off the engine and came up to her. She could tell at once by the way he stood easily by the gelding, patting it, that he was used to horses. Another point in his favour. 'I asked the livery stable which way you'd be likely to ride back home.' He laughed. 'I should have known better than to take the

73

obvious and the quickest route, but then, I don't reason like a woman.'

'You're colonial, aren't you?'

'Rhodesian.'

'Ryan isn't a Rhodesian name.'

'My father wasn't. He went there as a young man, years before he lived in America. That was where he met your father and where I last saw him. I wish I'd known about the *Lusitania*.' A silence. 'He married one of the daughters from a neighbouring plantation. My mother was a mixture of French, German, and Dutch. I guess that makes me something of a mongrel.'

She decided that she liked him.

'Is the only reason you came to England to look up my father? Or are you trying to ferret out some long-lost relatives?'

'Not a bit of it. I wouldn't know where to start. Besides, the past should stay where it belongs, don't you think? In the past. I've lived in most countries for a time: South Africa, Australia, America – among others. I'd never been to England and my father always wanted me to see it. And I wanted to meet Cornelius Ismay again. I decided to spend a few months here before moving on again. But let's not talk about me. It's you I'm concerned about. All this happening at once would be a terrific strain on anyone.'

She managed to smile up at him.

'Let's go on back to the house.'

'I'm sorry your sister-in-law isn't well enough to come down; I can understand how worried she must be.'

'She hasn't been sleeping well, so I asked the doctor to give her something to help. He must have called while we were in Epsom. Janet says she took the tablets and ten minutes later she was sleeping as sound as a baby.'

They sat down on opposite sides of the fire.

'It's a beautiful house.' Ryan looked around him. His eyes rested on the oil paintings of bygone racehorses, the ornaments, the rows of books. 'Of course, my father knew Cornelius before he married your mother; then Cornelius came to work in England for the Merritt Bloodstock Company and they lost touch.' He took his wallet from inside his jacket pocket and pulled out a faded photograph. 'Here, this was taken in Philadelphia before he

74

sailed.' He held it out to her and she took it, her eyes wide with astonishment and pleasure.

'I can't believe it! He looks so young here! Which one is your father?'

Ryan pointed.

'He looks even younger, no more than fifteen or sixteen.'

'He wasn't. His place in the company wasn't a very distinguished one then; more an errand boy than anything else. But he had a passion for the racehorses and as long as he could be in the thick of what was going on, I think he'd have been almost content to work for next to nothing.'

'And now?'

'I'm the only one left.' He had wandered over to the nearest bookcase and begun to look through the neat rows of leather-bound volumes. His sudden silence when she'd mentioned his family spoke louder than words; obviously, for his own reasons, a closed subject. Emmeline swallowed her curiosity and decided not to pry.

'Do you read a lot?'

'When I have time.'

She came over to where he was.

'What's that you've got? *A History of Capital Punishment*?' She laughed. 'God alone knows who added that to the collection ... certainly before my mother's time. By the look of it, it hasn't been off that shelf for the last fifty years.'

He leafed through the yellow pages.

'Thirty-nine, to be exact. It was printed in 1880.' He replaced it on the shelf. 'For a so-called civilized country, the English judiciary were a bloodthirsty lot.'

'You've studied the subject?'

'No. Just come to the conclusion after twenty-five years that all governments, like the Church, operate the same double standards of justice. It's all a game to them, running countries, making laws, dictating to the people who put them where they are how to live their lives. Think about it: a handful of men in power, ordering tens of millions of their fellow countrymen around like children in school; and they get away with it. They steal the money they earn and call it taxation. They start up wars and get other men to fight them. What they can't make them do by passing legislation they do by getting at their consciences. That's where the Church

75

comes in. Have you ever thought of it like that? I wonder if the day will ever come when half the world comes to its senses and we all rebel. I wonder what the governments and the Church would do then?' The bitterness in his voice made a startling contrast to the easy, unruffled manner of a short time before.

'You sound almost like my brother, David.'

'Oh?'

'Tell me about yourself.'

He took the glass of brandy that she held out to him and settled down in the depths of the nearest comfortable chair.

'I was born in 1893, my family are dead. Like I said a moment ago, I'm the only one left. I've travelled around the world and now I'm here. In England, in your brother's house, drinking his brandy in front of your fire. Tomorrow I'll be somewhere else, and somewhere different the day after that. One day in the distant future, like everyone, I'll die.'

She sat down opposite him. He intrigued her.

'There's something in the past you don't want to talk about?'

'There's nothing in the past I want to talk about.'

For a long moment there was a silence between them.

'I'm sorry,' he said at length, putting down his glass. 'I apologize. After all your hospitality, I didn't mean to seem rude. Or ungrateful.'

'It's all right, I understand.' He'd most likely lost his wife, she speculated, or quarrelled with a sweetheart and she'd left him, maybe to marry someone else. Perhaps he'd had a run of bad luck and lost everything, and had travelled to England hoping to find a new start with his father's old friend, only to discover that he'd been dead for more than four years.

'Let's talk about you, instead.'

She smiled.

'What is it you want to know?'

'Anything you want to tell me.' He leaned back in the chair and crossed his legs. 'After all my father told me about the Ismays, they've always fascinated me. A family apart. Always different from other people – special. They always stood out head and shoulders above the rest. Other families live and die and then that's it . . . all they ever amount to are entries in baptismal and marriage registers, names carved on headstones in some church-yard until the ivy and lichen grow over the stone and the weather obliterates the names; the rest of the family move away or die out and nobody's left. No trace. No memories. That will never happen to the Ismays.'

'Some people would say the family are notorious.'

'Sour grapes. Your great-grandfather founded one of the biggest shipping lines in the world; your uncle built the *Titanic*. His brother's only the second man in history to have won the Derby and then had his winner disqualified – and in the race where a crazed suffragette ran onto the course and brought down the King's horse. And Cornelius ... nobody could ever forget Cornelius ...'

Emmeline looked at him. If he had been anyone else other than who he was – someone who'd been close to her father and for whom she already felt a tremendous sympathy and liking – she would never have spoken about The Past. But he, like the Ismays, was different. For him she could break the rules.

'You mean because he was the key defence witness when my mother stood on trial for her life?'

'My father told me all about that, yes.'

Emmeline hadn't thought, much less spoken about, The Past – as it had always been known in the family – for years, not since the tragedy on the *Lusitania* when in the aftermath of grief everything her parents had explained to her and David when they were both deemed old enough to understand, had come flooding back. Her mother's first, unhappy marriage to another man; an evil man, a man who had wanted her for her grandmother's bloodstock and money, who'd betrayed her with her own half-sister and plotted with her illegitimate half-brother the most gruesome murder. But her father, who had once been his confidant and friend, turned against him, turned queen's evidence and it had all come right. In the end. Slowly, she looked down again at the faded photograph that Ryan had shown her.

'The fourth man ... it's Rufus Waldo, isn't it? My mother's first husband.'

'Yes. I didn't like to say, not at first. I didn't know if you'd ever seen a picture of him.'

She went on staring at it. It was a handsome face, an arrogant face. Looking closer, she could see the conceit and cruelty in his eyes. But to a young, naïve girl such as her mother must have been when they first met, he would no doubt have seemed irresistible. She pointed to the last remaining figure in the photograph.

'Who is this?'

Ryan hesitated, but only momentarily.

'Oh, just another employee of the Merritt Bloodstock Company. Nobody important.'

She held the picture up.

'Would you mind if I had the picture copied? It's the earliest photo I've ever seen of my father. I promise I'll take great care of it. And when it's done I'll cut off the other two and just leave your father and mine.'

Ryan smiled.

'I don't mind at all.' He sipped the remainder of his brandy. 'But you haven't finished telling me about yourself. Or David.'

'Not much else to tell, other than that we were both born here, and then when the war started David was called up. The bloodstock business was left to us both, so I suppose I have to take over the reins until David comes back.'

'I wish there was something else I could do to help.'

'There is. Be our guest for dinner.' She got to her feet and so did he. 'If my father had been here he would have been delighted to welcome the son of an old friend, and I know David would, too. If you'll excuse me for a few moments I'll go upstairs and find Christabel. She must be awake now. And I know she'll be delighted to meet you.'

'David's car, found abandoned in Bush Wood? Why didn't you tell me straight away? I wanted to go there, too . . .'

'I thought it was best that you didn't. You're under enough strain already.'

'But I'm his wife, Emmeline! I had a right to go. And you had none to keep it from me.'

'Look, I'm sorry. I did what I did because I knew how upset you were, and I thought it would make things worse if you saw the car. In any case, there was nothing to see. Nothing was found in it. But Karl Ryan is downstairs and I want you to meet him.' She handed Christabel the old photograph and explained the connection. 'Isn't it incredible, the way things turn out? He's been in Rhodesia and South Africa for the last few years, which is why he didn't even know about Daddy's death. He was shocked, coming

78

here and expecting to look him up after so long.'

'And his father's dead too?'

Emmeline nodded.

'He doesn't seem keen to say much about his family; some tragedy, maybe. But to have the son of an old friend of Daddy's turn up at a time like this . . . I'm so glad he's here.'

Christabel gave her a knowing look.

'He's certainly made an impression on you. Is he stopping long?'

'That's it. He was talking about leaving as early as tomorrow. And now that he's found out about Daddy and the police don't need him any more, I suppose there's nothing here to keep him. But I wish he wouldn't.' She looked down at the picture in her hands. 'Having someone with a link to the family at a time like this is a rare comfort, somehow.'

'And there's no more news of David? The police haven't found any leads?'

'Not yet. But David would never disappear without a good reason. If only we knew what the reason was.'

SIX

EVEN IN THE SUMMERTIME, the tall, narrow, medieval windows
let in only a minimum of light to the room that had once, centuries before, been used by the Abbess as a place for solitude and
meditation. Now half of it was shrouded in the brooding, melan-
choly half-light of oncoming darkness, neither day nor night.
Even the beautifully coloured lampshades and the crystal
chandelier that looked so oddly out of place against the backdrop
of eight-feet-thick stone walls, made little difference now that
daylight was fading; it always reminded Adeline Bausche of the
passage from Genesis that her father would read to them from his
Bible on Sundays in the parlour, the happy family Sundays that
she remembered from her far-off childhood in Cape Town. If she
closed her eyes tightly, willing the ugliness and the emptiness of
the present away, she could still hear his voice; deep, kindly,
gentle. Tears began to seep through her closed eyelids and trickle
down her cheeks.

'In the beginning, God created the Heaven and the Earth. And
the Earth was without form, and void; and darkness was upon
the face of the deep ... And the spirit of God moved upon the
face of the waters. And God said, Let there be light: and there
was light. And God saw the light, that it was good; and God
divided the light from the darkness ...'

Since he had married her, and brought her here to this luxurious prison, her whole life had been covered by shadow.

Dejectedly, she moved away from the window; it was too dark
to see anything now. And maybe she'd been wrong, as she was
about so many things; maybe it was only in her starved imagination that she fancied she'd seen anyone at all.

She shivered, and went nearer to the roaring fire. However
fierce it was, however many giant logs the servants threw upon it,

the room was never warm, even in summer. It was so cold and damp in England, so different from the long, hot, tropical summers of South Africa; even winter in Cape Town was hotter than England on the hottest day. She knelt down and held out her cold, stiff hands towards the blaze, and as she stared into the crackling depths of the fire she remembered that far off afternoon not long after they'd come to Epsom, when she'd first met David Ismay.

She had never loved any man outside her own family before; when she'd married Guy Vogel, so much older than she, it had been because she had to, and not because she had wanted to. For her father's sake, she'd been willing to make any sacrifice. But as soon as she'd caught sight of David Ismay across that noisy, crowded room of people talking about English bloodstock and he'd glanced up and looked at her at the very same moment, her heart had started to thud painfully and her hands shook. Terrified that her husband might notice, she'd somehow managed to turn away, smiling nervously and self-consciously as she'd moved among her husband's guests, longing to turn around again and look at him. It had been late summer then, and she'd been able to wander out into the newly planted gardens where she'd sat down on a stone seat until she'd managed to compose herself.

She remembered the spill of guests following her out onto the lawns, the smell of roses, the sunlight on the water in the pond as she'd sat there staring at the fish that every now and then darted nimbly to the surface. How like them she was in their confined, artificial world, things of beauty to be possessed and looked at; but, unlike them, she knew only too well how much of a prisoner she was. It was then, just as she'd been about to get to her feet and make her way back inside that she'd heard the almost imperceptible sound of footsteps behind her on the grass. And then, across the water of the pond fell the tall shadow of a man.

Instinctively, she knew it was David Ismay and that he had followed her. Slowly, her cheeks burning, she'd turned and looked up into his face. His hair was very dark, almost black, and the breeze blew it back from a broad, strong forehead; his warm brown eyes were the antithesis of the cold, light, cruel ones of her husband.

He'd introduced himself and she'd continued to gaze up at him, mesmerized by his good looks and boyish charm while he'd

81

talked; then she found herself responding and talking back in a gay, animated manner that startled even herself; she was someone else; the happy, laughing, carefree Adeline of long ago, the Adeline she'd thought had ceased to exist. When she'd stood up and stumbled on the grass he'd reached out and steadied her with both hands, and his very touch had sent shivers of indescribable ecstasy running through her. She felt almost reckless, light-headed, painfully young, a raw young animal that, after being confined in a small, dark, silent place, has suddenly been let out into a vast, green, fenceless meadow to run free.

It was like that – she smiling up into his face and he holding her with both hands – that her husband saw them, coming towards them across the grass.

Slowly, she'd turned to look at him and the smile had died on her face. The expression in his eyes had terrified her.

She started up, heart lurching, as she heard the sound of footsteps approaching from outside. Then the great, heavy oak door with its massive iron hinges swung to before she could get to her feet, letting in a blast of icy cold air.

'Livia!'

'Good evening, Mrs Vogel.'

'I thought I saw people coming along the drive earlier. They looked like policemen. I tried to see from the windows, but they'd disappeared.' She finished getting to her feet. 'Did I see someone? Maybe it was my imagination . . .'

'No, they were policemen. From the village. Mr Vogel spoke to them.' The other woman was older than her mistress, dressed in a smart maid's uniform, but without a white starched cap. Her straight black hair was drawn back severely from her narrow face and caught in a gleaming coil at the nape of her neck. 'I'll draw the curtains, madam. Then I'll help you to dress for dinner.' She glanced towards the log basket, half empty, standing in one cor-ner of the room. 'I must send Losch up with more wood for the fire.'

'What did they want, the police from the village?'

'Just making routine enquiries. Someone abandoned a motorcar in Bush Wood, and they wanted to know if anyone here had seen or heard anything.' She smiled; a tight, mean smile that never extended to her eyes. She held the adjoining door open that led into the huge bedroom, where a single lamp bathed the lavender satin coverlet and ornate gold-fringed hangings with a gentle glow. 'Mrs Vogel, it's time to dress for dinner. Mr Vogel is waiting downstairs.'

When they'd first built it, in 986, it had been called Wherwell Abbey; the Abbey of the Holy Cross and Saint Peter, to house the order of Benedictine nuns. It had been founded by Elfrida, widow of King Edgar, in expiation for her sins: being concerned in the murders of her first husband, Ethelwolf, and King Edgar the Martyr so that her son by Edgar could become King. She was buried in the Abbey after spending a lifetime in penitence, but there were some who said that her unhappy ghost still walked, sobbing, in the dour confines of the Abbey she had founded.

There was no trace of tenth-century religious starkness about the converted Abbey now. Guy Vogel had come over from South Africa less than a year before and totally transformed it; renamed it The Hermitage and engaged decorators to modernize every part of its interior. No expense had been spared to transform it from a cheerless, gloomy religious house into a gentleman's luxurious twentieth-century residence; few traces, except the eight-feet-thick stone walls, which in places could never be disguised, remained. Even electric lighting had been installed, much to the envy and dismay of more than a few less advanced neighbours who still used oil lamps and gas. Wealthy racing men around Epsom openly speculated how much the refurbishing of the building had cost; and also how long it would be before its *nouveau riche* colonial owner tried to put his toe in the door of their social world which included membership of the Jockey Club.

But Guy Vogel continued to surprise them. After donating five thousand pounds for repairs to the Epsom grandstand roof, he left the house with his young wife and a handful of servants and went up to Scotland, where gossip filtered back that he had purchased a baronial castle in the lowlands. When he returned, he held a grand dinner-party in the transformed and luxuriously decorated old hall, inviting everyone of any standing within thirty miles' radius of Epsom as his guests. Few declined his invitation; after four dismal, barren years of world war when the entire racing industry had declined – and, from 1916, banned by the Government altogether – the shot in the arm from new, outside wealth was desperately needed; for reinvestment, for breeding programmes, for renovating everything that had been forced to fall into disrepair since the beginning of the war.

Vogel's strong South African accent had sounded oddly at variance among the gathering of English aristocrats and landed gentry; half a century earlier none of their grandparents would ever have even considered sitting with him at the same table. But times had changed. While they were struggling to cope with the vestiges of depleted family fortunes and the aftermath of the war, he was enjoying the continuous fruits of the gold mines in Klerksdorp that had made his father a millionaire two generations back.

There was only one thing that all the guests were sorry for: Vogel's young wife, a little too delicate to come to grips with the harsh English climate, was unable to be present.

'My dear, how lovely you look.' He turned from the huge fireplace that dominated the room, and let his eyes move over her. Instinctively, she felt herself stiffen. 'But then you always do, don't you? Come here. Come closer.'

She came down the remaining steps and stood there in the middle of the room. There were goose pimples on her bare arms. All around them, covering the stone walls, were the massive Flemish tapestries depicting scenes of hunting that she hated. Mounted men, with their spears and knives and arrows, penetrating the flesh of their helpless, dying victims. She always tried not to look at them; the weavers had made the scarlet silks so skilfully look like real blood; to decorate a room where people ate with pictures glorifying scenes of mutilation, suffering and death seemed to her the epitome of callousness and bad taste. She kept her green eyes on his face instead.

'Guy, I saw some policemen from the window today. Livia told me they were here, asking questions about a motorcar found abandoned in Bush Wood. What's happened?'

'Nothing for you to concern yourself with, my dear. Nothing at all.'

The flames from the fire made his thick, unruly, red hair and

84

twirling moustache look redder still; the freckles stood out on his skin. He was holding something in his hands, holding something out to her.

'Guy . . .'

'Do you see what I have here, Adeline? Do you recognize it?'

Her eyes focused. There was a feeling of sickness in the pit of her stomach. In his big, freckled hands he was holding a book. One of her books.

'It's my copy of *Jane Eyre*. I've been searching for it.'

'Take it, if you please, and then tell me what's wrong with it.'

He was nineteen years older than she. Standing there, under that cold, burning gaze was almost too much for her to bear without giving in to the temptation to turn and run. She felt like a naughty little girl caught stealing apples who is about to be soundly thrashed. She had never stopped being afraid of him; but then she knew she had good reason. Her fingers shaking, she took the book and stared at it without comprehension.

'Well?'

She turned it over slowly. She looked carefully through the pages.

'I'm sorry, I don't understand. What is there wrong with it? I don't see anything.'

His tall shadow loomed over her, and she stepped back.

'Open the cover, if you please. Open it and tell me what you see.' There was no pleasantness in his voice now; no trace of warmth. Her hands felt like lead as she did as he ordered her. For a moment she stared at her own handwriting, then up into his cruel face.

'I still don't understand what is wrong with the book.'

'Read the inscription. Read it to me out loud. And then tell me what is wrong.'

'It's only my name. And the date. There's nothing else.'

So suddenly that he made her jump, Vogel tore the book from her hands and ripped out the page. He screwed it up into a tight paper ball and flung it in her face.

'Your name, yes! But Adeline Bausche is no longer your name, is it, my dear? Not since you were married to me. You are Adeline Vogel.' He was trembling with anger. 'Now, pick up the page and throw it on the fire.'

Without speaking, without hesitation, she did as he said. Then

85

she stood there, leaning against the stones of the fireplace, watching it as it burned. Adeline Vogel. No, she would never think of that as her name; she would always be Adeline Bausche, the name she had been born with, whatever he said, whatever he did to her. Nothing could take her real name away. But for her own sake she had to go on pretending. And for her father's.

'I'm sorry.' She spoke the words with difficulty, as if she was trying to force them through a throat that was being strangled with a ligature. She couldn't force herself to turn and look at him in case he saw the truth in her eyes.

'I think I can forgive you, my dear. You look so beautiful tonight. Pale blue silk, with sequins. You look so lovely in pale blue.'

'Thank you.'

He was pouring something into two glasses now, somewhere across the room, thankfully away from her. The silence seemed interminable.

'Guy ... whose car was it ... that they found? Was it anyone we know?'

He stopped what he was doing at once, and she saw that she had made yet another mistake.

'Nothing to concern you, my dear. Nothing to do with us at all. I don't want to talk about it. The subject is closed.'

'But Guy – '

He came across to her and took her by the elbow, pressing his powerful fingers into the flesh of her arms with such force that she cried out. 'Closed, my dear. Closed.' He increased the pressure of his fingers until her eyes watered. 'Do you understand what I say?'

He knew she was afraid of him; he had always known. Her fear had become his substitute for passion because he knew that she would never love him, and for that other reason that only she had knowledge of. And she knew that he would never let her go free.

Karl Ryan got to his feet as the two young women came into the room. He put back the silver-framed wedding photograph that he'd taken from the collection on the small table behind him, recognizing at once the same fair, grey-eyed face in the bridal gown and the girl who was looking intently at him now. He came forward and held out his hand.

'Mrs Ismay?'

'How do you do, Mr Ryan? Emmeline told me that you found my husband's motorcar in Bush Wood.' He could tell by the reddened rims around her large eyes that she'd been crying; the desperation in her voice came across to him clearly. Yes, she was beautiful, but not to his own taste: she was like an ornament, delicate and fragile, something to be admired and looked at but not touched. From all he'd been able to find out about David Ismay, he was not a little surprised by his choice of wife. Against the sister she seemed pale and insignificant.

'I was already on my way here,' he started to explain, 'when I stopped and came across it, quite by chance.'

'Emmeline told me all that. But were there no clues, nothing of David's left inside the car?'

They sat down.

'It was completely empty. But when I left the place the police were going over it again inch by inch with a fine-tooth comb. I went back into the town to make a statement and then they told me I was free to leave.'

Christabel twisted her wedding ring round and round her finger nervously.

'Were there no footprints? There should be soft, muddy ground inside the wood at this time of year.'

'Myself, I didn't see any. The whole area around the car was ankle deep in dead leaves. But from what the police said back at the station they were searching the entire wood. They must find something after that.'

Christabel stopped fiddling with her wedding ring and gripped the sides of her chair.

'It must have been a shock for you to come all the way to England expecting to see David's father, then finding out that he was dead. And David missing.'

'Yes, it was a shock. But now that I'm here if there's anything that I can do, please don't hesitate to tell me.'

Emmeline spoke for the first time.

'Didn't you say that tomorrow you'd be somewhere else – and somewhere else the day after that?'

He smiled.

'A figure of speech. Before I started off on my way here I booked in at a hotel in Epsom. With my father and Cornelius being friends and all, I wouldn't leave with all this going on even if I wanted to. Which I don't.' His eyes rested on Emmeline. 'Before Lock brought you to Epsom after I'd found the car, I overheard him mention to his Sergeant that they were going to the scene of the fire, on the Isle of Man; is there any chance that David decided to drop everything and get there first?'

'We were going there together, when he'd arranged with John Martin for the horses to be shipped back. When David came back from London after that meeting with his lawyer and told me the island police maintained they had proof of arson, he was anxious to get over there and see for himself as soon as the loose ends had been tied up here. He would never have just gone without telling anyone.'

'Can you be sure of that? He might have panicked and acted on the spur of the moment. Felt he had to get there before the English police did. It isn't impossible.'

'I've turned every possibility over in my mind at least ten times, and still I haven't come up with any logical, rational answer. One thing I do know. Until we have news of David I intend to go ahead and carry on just as he'd do; I'll go to the island and see for myself.'

Panic instantly appeared in Christabel's eyes.

'But you can't leave here! There's nobody to run the stud. I don't know the first thing about it, you know that – '

'Christabel, we have the best men in the business. Moran always took over when David had to go away and we couldn't have a better back-up man than Herbert Haynes; what they don't know about the bloodstock breeding industry isn't worth knowing.'

'But suppose something else, outside their scope, comes up? What would I do? I couldn't contact you.'

'Telephone Charles Ismay or David's lawyer in London. The numbers are in his book.'

Christabel wilted in her chair.

'How long are you planning to be away?'

'I can't answer that, not now. As long as it takes to find out the truth.'

'I'd rather come with you. I don't want to be left here on my own. Waiting, wondering what's happening.' Ryan and Emmeline exchanged a discreet glance; politely, he kept silent.

'You know it wouldn't work, Christabel. You hate travelling. Packing and unpacking and moving on at a moment's notice. Strange hotels, strange beds. Besides, we discussed all this before David went missing.'

Christabel fell silent.

'Mr Ryan,' Emmeline was on her feet now, tugging at the bell cord for Janet, 'let's go in to dinner. Christabel will want to hear all about the days when your father knew mine.' She glanced at the table in the corner of the room, its polished surface covered with photographs in silver frames. 'If only he was here now.'

'You can't stop me going to Ballakeighan, Inspector Lock, and I don't recommend that you try.' Emmeline was furious at being disturbed in the middle of dinner, even more furious that he kept insinuating David had run away to duck his legal responsibilities while keeping her and Christabel completely in the dark about what they had been able to uncover. 'My sister-in-law stays here; that's the logical thing for her to do. The sight of all those burned-out stud buildings will only upset her more than she is already; she wasn't well long before my brother disappeared.' Restlessly she paced around the room. 'Myself, I'm going to London in the morning to see our lawyers. As soon as I get back I intend to start packing to leave.'

'I think you should seriously reconsider that, Miss Ismay. In fact I think you're being extremely foolish. There's nothing you can do over there that will be of any help at all to your brother – wherever he is. Gathering evidence is a business for the police.'

'I disagree. Or is it that you're afraid I might find out the truth before you do? That wouldn't do much for your reputation, would it?'

'You're wrong. Nothing would satisfy me more than to find your brother and be able to uncover the necessary evidence to exonerate him. You forget, you and I are on the same side.'

She laughed, harshly.

'If David came back right now the first thing you'd do is arrest him – right or wrong?'

'I'd tell him that I believed he was in a position to assist us with our enquiries.'

'You think like a lawyer, don't you? Or a politician. They never answer with a simple yes or no, either.'

'You don't like me, do you, Miss Ismay?'

She almost smiled.

'I reserve my right to remain silent.'

Yes, he supposed he had deserved that. But he wasn't here to court popularity. For a moment neither of them spoke. Outside, beyond the window, she could hear the men coming to the end of their long day in the yard, the familiar sounds of horses' hooves on gravel, somebody calling out instructions. Everything outside still seemed so normal, so ordinary, yet her whole life had changed.

'So, what now? You wanted to speak to my brother's men and use a room inside the house. Carry on. I shan't be here to get in your way, will I?'

'We'll need to speak also to your uncle, Charles Ismay.'

'And what do you think he can tell you that we can't?'

'It's merely routine to question all available members of the family.'

'I almost admire the way you never give me a straight answer!'

Lock counted to ten. If either of his daughters had ever spoken to him – or anyone else – like that, as old as they were he'd have put them across his knee and tanned their backsides. But at the same time he couldn't help liking her.

'From there, we'll go direct to the Isle of Man and meet forces with the local police there. And, hopefully, find the right answers to all the questions.'

'Is there anything else you wanted to talk to me about, or can I go back to my dinner now? Even though it's probably stone cold and the others have moved on to dessert.'

'Only to reconsider your decision to go to Ballakeighan. For your own sake. I know in these days of women's emancipation it might be considered an acceptable thing to do, but it's a long journey by road and sea, and the island is sparsely populated, the stud in an isolated position. If your theory that someone else perpetrated the crime and sought to incriminate your brother is right, have you stopped to think that you may well be putting yourself in danger by going there?'

'I can take care of myself.'

'You might well think so. But police are few and far between on the island and we'll be there only for a short space of time, to examine the burned out buildings and question your brother's employees. I hope you'll take my advice and think again.'

'I said, I can take care of myself, but I'm more than grateful for your touching concern.'

He looked at her sharply, but her face was expressionless.

'You'd be ill-advised to make such a long journey on your own.' He stopped abruptly, having caught sight of something through the window that attracted his attention. 'That motorcar, parked at the back of the house, it looks like Karl Ryan's – '

'It is mine,' said Ryan from the doorway. He walked inside. 'Miss Ismay invited me to stop for dinner, that's why I'm still here. Nor will she have to travel to the island alone. I would have been prepared to do anything I could to help Cornelius and that extends to the rest of the family, too. I'd be happy to accompany her.'

Emmeline had spun round to face him, not certain whether it was Lock or herself who was the most surprised.

'I don't know what to say, or how to thank you, but it's an offer I certainly won't turn down. Only if you're sure that it won't interfere with your own plans.'

'I don't have any. I came here to look up Cornelius. If he'd still been alive and needed help, I'd have been the first to offer it. I know my father would.'

This was something else Lock hadn't bargained for; interfering outsiders, meddling in things that didn't concern them. And he'd never liked colonials anyhow. Like the younger generation, they had no respect for the old order of things, their elders or the law. Didn't know their place. It was to impress the Ismay girl, of course – what other reason could there be? Amazing, what the power of a pretty face could do. Why else? Who in their right mind would willingly offer to go traipsing off to some God for-saken island miles from the mainland, on what would undoubt-edly be a rough, wearying wild goose chase? Well, as Barnes had already pointed out, the girl was a beauty. Maybe if Lock had been in Ryan's place and thirty years younger, he'd have done exactly the same. But he still didn't like it.

He was unsure how much he could trust the girl. Was she really as innocent as she made out to be ... or did she really know where her brother was? If she was lying to protect him then all he could say was that she was a first-class actress. He'd come across enough of those in his time. In his mind's eye he'd already pencilled in a question mark against her name. Ismay's wife? She was another kettle of fish altogether; no question that she didn't know a thing. He recognized hysteria and panic when he saw it. It was merely routine procedure that dictated that he speak to Charles Ismay as the next step, though he already had a distinct feeling there'd be no joy there. All enquiries into Ismay's character and background pointed to his non-involvement.

After Emmeline Ismay had shown him out of the house and he was on his way back to Epsom, he mulled over in his mind the notes he had already made.

Everything pointed glaringly to David Ismay being guilty, but were his motives too blatantly obvious to be true? Surely only a madman would have his own stud put to the torch for financial gain and even hope to get away with it; and David Ismay was certainly no madman.

If he was innocent, who was guilty? Most businessmen had enemies, but were any of his bitter enough and determined enough to try to ruin him? None of his extensive enquiries had unearthed any candidates so far – but did that mean that he still hadn't dug deep enough?

It was all still a puzzle, a jigsaw with too many pieces that didn't fit, no matter how he tried to match them together. All he could do was go on from the beginning until he got to the end.

'You're very quiet, sir,' Barnes said when Lock was settled by the police station fire with a cup of tea.

Lock went on chewing at the end of his pencil. He glanced up.

'Just thinking how we can go about eliminating possibilities, that's all. From tomorrow, I want a watch put on the Ismay girl.'

'Shall we go back and finish our dinner?'

'After you.' Ryan held open the study door. 'I'm sorry I barged in like that. I didn't mean to interfere. But I saw him come to the door and I thought you might be in need of some moral support.'

'You have a perfect sense of timing!'

He smiled.

'I don't like policemen. Don't know why. I think it's my general hatred of uniforms. They have a strange effect on people who wear them.'

'He's plain clothes division!'

'Well, you know what I mean. I thought he might try and bully you.'

They walked along the passage towards the dining room.

'Well, of course, you don't know me very well, do you?' They both laughed.

'You certainly gave him as good as you got.'

She laughed again.

'How much did you overhear exactly?'

'Enough to show that you were more than holding your own.' He opened the door for her and she walked back into the room. But Christabel had gone.

'Janet, where's Mrs Ismay?'

Janet looked over her shoulder and stopped clearing away the tureens and dishes on the sideboard.

'She didn't wait, miss. Having pudding now?'

'No, thank you. I'm not very hungry.' She sat down and Ryan resumed his place at the long table. 'When I woke up this morning, I thought, this isn't happening to me. It's a dream, a nightmare. Unreal, a crazy figment of my imagination like the dreams I have of being shipwrecked on the *Titanic*.'

'The *Titanic*?'

'We were on her maiden voyage, all of us. More than seven years ago. Somehow it seems like only yesterday. Only as far as Queenstown. Then we and a handful of other passengers disembarked. Daddy had some horses he wanted to see there, and the other people were planning a motor tour of Ireland. Four days later when she went down we couldn't believe how lucky we were. It was fate, wasn't it?'

'Do you dream about it often?'

'I wish I didn't dream about it at all.'

For a moment he was silent; he had enough nightmares in his own life to understand how much it affected her.

'Do you really have no idea at all where he is? Where he could possibly be? Do you want to go to Ballakeighan because you think he might be there?'

'I don't know what I think any more. Even what I believe. Only that David could never be capable of being what the police believe him to be. That Lock, I can see what he thinks about David in his eyes. What else can he think when all the evidence points that way?' She got up and began to pace the room. Janet came in with a tray of coffee and then left.

'Is there something else on your mind? You can tell me.'

She smiled. Yes, she was right to trust and like him. She had always trusted her instincts with other people and they rarely led her astray.

'There was something – perhaps I'm making too much of it – something David said the night before he disappeared . . .'

'Go on.'

'We've always had this – this uncanny knack of almost knowing each other's minds; being able to communicate without speaking. I had the feeling that night that David was keeping something back from me – what about I don't know. But when I asked him, he just said that we'd have a long talk the next day, after he'd got back. And he never did.'

'You think it was something important, to do with the fire?'

'I can't be sure. I only know that whatever it was, it was playing on his mind.' Restlessly, she began to pace the room. 'If only it hadn't been so late, if only I'd insisted he tell me then . . .'

'You weren't to know he was going to disappear.'

She smiled a little wanly.

'Yes, of course. It's easy for me to say that with the benefit of hindsight. But ever since I haven't been able to get it out of my mind. Because whatever it was I'm convinced that it's linked closely in some way with his disappearance.'

'Only time will tell.' Ryan moved towards the table. 'Shall I pour the coffee?'

'What bad hostesses you must think we are! Christabel vanishes upstairs and I leave you to look after yourself.'

'The years I spent living with my father and no woman about the house, I'm used to looking after myself.'

'If you miss him as much as I miss mine, then I understand exactly how you feel.'

Ryan fell silent and she knew it was a subject he didn't want to pursue. She poured the coffee and they sat down beside the fire.

'Are you certain that you really want to come with me to the Isle of Man? I won't hold it against you if you change your mind and back out.'

'Backing out of things isn't my way.'

She smiled. 'I'll be more than grateful for your company. I wasn't relishing the journey; and then again I have no idea what my reception's going to be like when we get there. My uncle telephoned Michael Stranahan, who takes care of things for us there, and he said the feeling against the Ismays after the fire was declared arson is running high.'

'Ignorance has a lot to answer for.'

'Women lost husbands and children lost fathers in that inferno. I know they have a right to be bitter.'

'But it wasn't your fault.'

'That's what I hope to convince them of.'

SEVEN

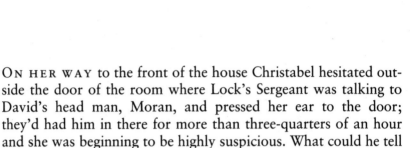

ON HER WAY to the front of the house Christabel hesitated out-side the door of the room where Lock's Sergeant was talking to David's head man, Moran, and pressed her ear to the door; they'd had him in there for more than three-quarters of an hour and she was beginning to be highly suspicious. What could he tell them that David's wife and sister could not? Most likely trying to poke their noses into family business that didn't concern them. She pressed her ear closer, but it was no use. The doors were all original Elizabethan, three inches thick and virtually impenetrable to sound. All she could hear from the other side was an indistinct kind of mumbling. Exactly, no doubt, what the original owner had intended as an antidote against eavesdroppers in the dangerous days of religious persecution and court intrigue.

She moved away, frustrated and angry, wondering who had just at the moment rung the bell at the front door. Or had she imagined that too, like she'd imagined seeing David in the garden from her window yesterday morning? It was the tablets and the vile-tasting medicine that the doctor had given her that was mud-dling her mind.

Janet appeared, hurrying towards her and bearing a crisp white card.

'Was that the bell?'

'Yes, ma'am. A gentleman to see you. If you will.'

Christabel took the card and looked down at the name and address: *Guy Vogel. The Hermitage, Epsom.* Somewhere in the recesses of her memory, she recollected the name. David had gone to a couple of bloodstock owners' receptions where Vogel had been, and some gathering at his house several months ago; alone, because she'd been recovering from her miscarriage. She remem-bered him saying that Vogel was a wealthy South African with a passion for English horses and a charming wife, but that he himself was cheap and vulgar.

She glanced up.

'Did you show him into the morning room?'

'The drawin' room, ma'am; there's a fire in there. Mornin' room's still a bit of a shambles from where the workmen have been doin' the damp patches. Shall I say you're not at home?'

'No, I'll see him.'

Before the war it would have been unthinkable to call on a perfect stranger and expect her to receive you straight away. Christabel remembered the complicated, almost sacred rituals of polite society in which she'd been schooled, the habits of half a lifetime that died hard, but that the advent of war had forced nearly everyone to jettison; the leaving of the calling card, the waiting for the recipient to respond; always receiving visitors before noon in the morning room; only in the drawing room after. Nobody seemed to bother any more. The war had swept away so much of what had always been important to her and what she believed in; her mother would have turned in her grave to see her now: receiving someone she had never met in the drawing room before noon.

She opened the double doors and saw him standing there.

'Mr Vogel?'

'Mrs Ismay, I'm delighted to meet you.' His South African accent was thick, staccato, guttural. He was – as David had already said – glaringly *nouveau riche*; his suit was expensive and the gold stickpin on the lapel of his jacket was too large and too obvious; his cravat was too bright. But not even her mother could have faulted his manners. He held out his hand ingratiatingly, stooping down towards her in a polite half-bow from his considerable height. Perhaps it was his lean build that made him seem exceptionally tall.

'Please forgive me for intruding on you at a time like this, and without warning. But the police called at my house yesterday, asking questions about a motorcar that had been found abandoned in Bush Wood. As you may know, my house is on the opposite side and they wanted to know if any of us had seen or heard anything suspicious. Unfortunately, nobody in the house was able to help, and the policeman wouldn't say what it was all about. Then I heard by chance when I went into Epsom this morning that the motorcar belongs to your husband. Something about his having gone missing. Since I've already met him on two or three occasions – and got on with him very well – I was sincerely disturbed.' He smiled, showing large square teeth. 'I came here straight away to ask if there's anything I can possibly do.'

Vulgarly dressed and *nouveau riche* he might be, but Christabel warmed at once to his sympathy.

'That's most kind of you. Please, take a seat. Would you like some sherry?'

'If it's no trouble.' He waited until she'd rung the bell for Janet and sat down before taking a seat himself. Another good mark. 'Mrs Ismay, I've no wish to pry – and I hope your husband will reappear very soon. Goodness knows what's at the bottom of all this. But who will run the estate for you in his absence? Such an enormous responsibility is a big worry for you; and, in my view, one that a lady such as yourself shouldn't be burdened with at such a time.'

Nobody else had so much as thought about that; the effect on her, the strain, the intolerable pressures. She liked him more every moment. It was all very well for Emmeline, going off to Balla-keighan without a backward glance; easy for her to say that Moran or Haynes or Charles Ismay were there on hand if there was any trouble. She was leaving Christabel right in the middle of an appalling mess that was becoming a scandal. Janet had sent two more newspaper reporters away since the news about David's abandoned car had been made public, but if they kept coming back again after Emmeline had gone, what then? She was beginning to dread the sound of the telephone bell, too. It seemed extraordinary to her that only a stranger like Guy Vogel really understood.

'You're very kind.' She found herself, for the first time in days, able to say what she really felt while he listened in sympathetic silence, nodding occasionally to agree with what she said. 'So you see, it's mainly the press that I'm worried about: what they can't find out by one means or another with their poking and prying, they just make up. I don't know which way to turn.' He noticed, from the corner of his eye, that the long, slender hands holding the glass of sherry had begun to shake already. 'As for the run-ning of the stud, we have good, reliable men. And my husband's uncle would always come here and take over, if Emmeline asked him, while she's away. But she won't. When I suggested it she said that it wasn't necessary because she doesn't expect to be away that long.'

'She's going away?'

'To Ballakeighan, where our stud was burned down. She wants to talk to the people there, see if there's anything to yield clues as to how the fire could have started.'

'A task for the police, I would have thought.' His mild admonition, artfully placed, was accompanied by a charming smile.

'Yes, I thought so too. But you don't know David's sister. Once she makes up her mind to do something, wild horses wouldn't stop her.'

'That's the trouble with young people, isn't it, Mrs Ismay ... yourself, I'm sure, excepted ...' Another beaming smile. 'They think only of the moment. Without considering the effect on others ...'

He had put into words what she herself had been nursing in silence for days, ever since the whole thing had happened. Emmeline was only thinking about herself.

'I know she's as anxious about David as I am. They're very close.' A shade of resentment there? Vogel leaned forward in his chair. 'I suspect she wants to find out something before the police do. Just for her own satisfaction.'

'Ah ...'

Vogel was watching her intently, assessing: fine-featured, golden-haired, grey eyes, the colour of wild rabbits' fur; a pale complexion that reminded him of silk. The proverbial English lady. They said back in South Africa that it was the dampness of the English climate that gave their women the beautiful skins for which they were famous; now he could see that for himself. Something about her delicacy and grace reminded him of Adeline.

He said, 'I think perhaps I've intruded on you for long enough. You must forgive me. But since I already knew your husband I felt I had to come to you and offer my help the moment I found out what had happened. Please don't hesitate to contact me at any time if you should feel in need of anything at all.'

But she didn't want him to go yet.

'You've lived in England for just a few months.'

'We came here not long after the Armistice, yes. I'd been interested in buying into English bloodstock for a number of years, something my father always wanted to do but never did. Fine horses have always been a particular passion of mine. I bought the old Abbey, renamed it and had it furnished and modernized from top to bottom. And, of course, it's in a perfect position between Epsom and London. Close to the racecourse, but set back enough on the other side of the wood to give us privacy.' He smiled. 'And I also purchased a castle in Scotland which I can use for the shooting season.'

'Do you intend to stay in England, Mr Vogel?'

'I'll have to return to South Africa once or twice a year, for business reasons. A permanently absent owner is courting trouble. That was the first lesson my father taught me. Like your husband here, I have good men in charge in my mines at Klerksdorp, but it doesn't do to leave everything in their hands.' He put down his empty glass. 'Is your sister-in-law in the house now?'

'She left early this morning, to go over some legal matters with my husband's lawyer in London. She won't be back until later tonight.'

'Please tell her that I hope she'll feel free to call on me at any time, should she need help of any kind.'

'You're more than generous.' They both stood up. Christabel rang the bell for Janet.

'Does your wife like England, Mr Vogel?'

'She loves the country and the people, but she's having the greatest difficulty in adjusting to your climate. Cape Town, even in the depths of winter, is very different.'

'So I should imagine.'

The medicine that Dr Aynsley had left for her to calm her down was beginning to take effect; Vogel's voice sounded further away from her than it had, her surroundings were becoming blurred. Janet had appeared with Vogel's coat and hat.

'You must both have dinner with us at The Hermitage; my wife would be delighted to meet you. And I hope that at some time in the near future I myself can be of service to you both.'

She heard herself make some polite answer, then they shook hands. When Janet had shown him out she went back into the drawing room and sat down, clutching at her head. She felt sick, dizzy, legless. The room and everything in it was spinning round and round, faster, in front of her eyes, yet ten minutes before she'd felt perfectly normal. Janet's voice, cutting across the confusion, came from the direction of the door.

'That's the South African millionaire everyone's bin talkin' about around town, isn't it, ma'am? I must say, he seems a charmin' sort of gentleman.'

'Yes, Janet. He is. He is.'

EIGHT

'THIS HAS BEEN a wasted journey – do you know that? I left Epsom on the first train when it was barely light and spent the last hour battling through the London traffic to get to you. Now you tell me that the best advice you can give is for me to sit back and do nothing!' Maurice Delauney opened his mouth to speak but Emmeline was quicker. It closed again, the words unsaid. 'David's still missing. Rumours have already started to fly about the stud and the fire. Our name's being dragged through the mud all over again and I won't stand by and see it happen. Whatever you think, I'm going over to the island to dig out the truth for myself. Any way I can!'

'You'd be foolish to interfere in the investigation already being carried out by the police. You can't hope to find out anything else. It's their job, for God's sake! All you'll do is go charging in and antagonize them, and that won't be good for you or for David. Wherever he is.'

'And where do you think he is, Maurice? Hiding on the island, or abroad, perhaps, like the Inspector so unsubtly hinted at. And I always thought policemen had no imaginations! He even suggested that David had been unhappy with Christabel for years, and had planned everything down to the last detail so that he could run off with another woman!'

'It isn't impossible.'

She bore on him with an expression on her face that made him shift quickly back in his chair.

'You dare even think it!'

'I said, it isn't impossible. Can't you look at things from the police point of view? They don't know anything about him. They have to consider every single feasible possibility. You know that.'

If only she'd stop pacing. Pacing, pacing, pacing endlessly, up and down the cluttered office, clenching and unclenching her fists. She was a whirlwind, a raging torrent; her anger and her impatience with his calm, rational, ordered lawyer's mind was overpowering. She was a reincarnation of Anna Brodie.

'Emmeline, don't fight me. I'm on your side, and David's, wherever he is, whatever he's done. No, please hear me out. I'm not saying that he's done anything. I can't even begin to speculate on what's really happened . . . only time will tell. But take my advice. Stay calm. Stay in England. Stay as far away as you can from Ballakeighan. You don't seem to have even thought of this, but it's my duty as the family lawyer to point it out. Rumour got to work on the island about how that fire started even before the wood had stopped smouldering; I know that from the police reports. There's bound to be enormous hostility on the part of some of the local people. Remember, four local men lost their lives in the fire. They left wives, children, bereaved parents. Widows with no man to provide a livelihood, the very roof burned away from over their heads. There's almost certain to be bitterness. Until the truth is uncovered about how the fire started, the insurance company refuses to pay out and they go on suffering.'

'You know that isn't true! As soon as we got the news David had money sent out to everyone within twenty-four hours. And he sent each family a personal letter, telling them that he was shocked and horrified and that he was coming out to the island as soon as he could make the arrangements to get away. I know every word that was in those letters because I co-signed each one. They know how much he cared.'

Delauney ran a hand through his hair. If only she hadn't come, if only she'd leave well alone; this was no woman's work. It was almost impossible to have a calm, rational, unheated discussion with a woman. They were always brimming with emotion, ready to spill over. Demanding the impossible at once. It was the war that had done it, sweeping away the old order of things and all the barriers that went with it. Emancipation, strident suffragettes marching in the city streets; chaining themselves to railings and smashing the windows of cabinet ministers and politicians to get their way. Emmeline Ismay was one of a new breed of women. Independent, strong-minded, with a will of iron beneath the deceptive, beautiful, feminine façade. Here she was now, dressed in the height of fashion with her ankle-length sealskin coat and extravagant Parisian hat, blue eyes flashing indignation from beneath the flimsy lawn veil. A devil in disguise; the proverbial Trojan horse. Nobody expected a dragon breathing fire from beneath such an image.

'Well, is that it?' she was demanding now. 'Is that all you have to say? Is this what I've wasted an entire day in London for, to hear you stating the obvious and telling me to be a good little girl and go back home?'

'Emmeline, please listen to me. . . .'

She gave him one parting look of withering scorn.

'You can go to the devil!'

She slammed the door of his office behind her with such force that the glass shook, in danger of shattering. The clerk and the typist in the little room outside gazed at her furtively, as if afraid that she might hit them. Karl Ryan snatched up his hat and jumped from his chair to walk beside her; he held open the door and she went through. In single file they went down the narrow, winding stairs.

'He calls himself the family lawyer!' she finally burst out on the pavement outside. '*Do you know what he said?*'

'I couldn't help hearing what you said to him.'

'A whole day. Wasted. Waiting for trains. Fighting our way through the traffic and crowds. And all for what? We could be half-way to Ballakeighan by now!'

'Let's find somewhere and have something to eat.'

She stopped walking and looked at him.

'Only a man would think of food at a time like this.'

He smiled. 'All that travelling, doing battle with family lawyers. Got to keep your strength up. We used to say that in the bush.' The single, tell-tale word had slipped out, before he'd realized his mistake. She picked up on it instantly.

'Does that mean that if I agree to go to a restaurant to refuel my depleted resources, you'll tell me more about yourself, your life before you came to England?'

'I never make promises I can't keep.'

So his past still hurt him enough to want to go on avoiding. She felt baulked, but she understood.

'A word is enough to a wise woman. All right. The Café Royal is only five minutes' away. Let's go there, shall we?'

'Wouldn't an ordinary eating place do?'

'We can go to an ordinary eating place back in Epsom. Since we've come all the way to London on a wild goose chase we might as well eat in style.'

'I won't argue with that. It sounds very grand. The Café Royal. Isn't that where Oscar Wilde used to dine?'

She looked at him sideways with dry humour.

'You won't find him there now.'

He had never seen so much opulence; glitter, luxury, light. The starched, white linen tablecloths so brilliant that their very whiteness hurt his eyes. Exotic flowers on each table, silver cutlery, music; it was like a ballroom in a palace, lined with mirrors and lit by gigantic, elegant chandeliers. Food seemed almost secondary in such a setting.

He glanced around him as they were ushered to a table; he noticed how men were looking at her, how the women glanced with envy as she walked by. Yes, he couldn't deny that she was beautiful, or that since he'd first met her unexpectedly the lively feelings of affinity and comradeship had grown between them in a remarkably short space of time; he hadn't expected that, hadn't been prepared for it, and he knew that he must ruthlessly stifle and set them aside before they had a chance to take hold. To get too close to her would be fateful. Emotional involvement, a sentiment he'd believed had been long dead within himself, was something that he must go on being determined to do without. Up until now he had never had any difficulty achieving that.

He stared down at the French menu without really reading it.

'Have you decided?' Her voice cut through his tumult of thoughts, forcing him to come back to the present. He smiled.

'I'm not fussy. Whatever you choose, I'll have that too.'

'Well, you certainly aren't fussy. What if I pick out something you don't like?'

'I'll suffer in silence.'

She laughed; then as quickly the laugh vanished again.

'What is it?'

'That's the first time I've laughed since David vanished. When I suddenly came face to face with the fact that I might not ever see him again, I thought I would never laugh again.'

105

'Why shouldn't you see him again?'

She swallowed.

'I don't know. None of all this makes sense to me any more. I've lain awake for hours letting everything go round and round in my mind but I'm still no wiser for it. I don't know how much progress the police have made because they won't tell us anything. He hasn't contacted my uncle in Northampton or our agent in the Isle of Man. Where in God's name is he? Where can he possibly be?'

Ryan wanted to lay his hand on hers for reassurance, but he restrained the impulse.

'There's always a perfectly logical answer to every question. It just takes time to find it.'

There was a pause, while the waiter returned to take their order. Emmeline had chosen a bottle of white wine, and he poured the pale, golden liquid into their cut-glass goblets before going away again. She rested her arms on the table and leaned towards him.

'You must be right. If I didn't believe I'd find him again I'd go mad and end up as hysterical as Christabel. All I can do is follow my instincts and go to Ballakeighan to see.'

He lowered his voice.

'Ask yourself this question: who would your brother be likely to go to for help apart from you and the rest of the immediate family?'

'Michael Stranahan. He manages a big stud near Onchan and he was the first on the scene after the fire, to take charge on David's behalf. He took all the horses that were saved back to his own place and then sent us a telegram. He was a marvel.'

'Just one thing puzzles me. Why have the stud on the island to begin with? Why not here, with the rest of your bloodstock, in England? It doesn't make sense. For one thing, because of the distance factor you can't keep an eye on what's going on. When a crisis happens – like now – you can't be on the scene quickly enough and don't even know what's happening until it's too late.'

'The stud belonged to our American great-grandfather, Jerome Charpentier. Our mother was an only child and she inherited it. The grazing is so fine that it's stayed in the family down the years; some of my father's best winners were bred there. Another big advantage – at least, before the war dragged the whole racing industry to a halt – was that the place was too far away to be plagued by touts.'

'And it was financially viable?'

'It would have been jettisoned long ago if it hadn't been.'

'What about the people who worked there?'

'David would have offered them work here or given them financial compensation. That's the thing about him, the thing the police refuse to understand. He cares about people, especially people we're responsible for, people who've given their lives working for us. I know what they think – that he staged the fire for the insurance money because it had become a white elephant he wanted to load off. But it isn't true. He said they'd accuse him. He said that to me on the night he disappeared.' A bitter note came into her voice. 'And I told him he was being ridiculous.'

'That's the way the police think. Straight and narrow. If a square piece of evidence doesn't fit the round hole, cut off the corners until it does.'

She managed a weary smile.

'You have a clever way of putting things, Karl.'

It was the first time she'd used his first name and she'd done it without thinking; she regarded him already as a friend, a connection to her father, someone she could rely on and trust; it seemed a natural thing to do. But he heard it with a jolt. Like the forbidden word he'd unthinkingly leaked only a few moments ago that might have given her a clue to his past, it had slipped out unobserved until it was too late. She was no longer Miss Ismay and he was no longer just Ryan; he knew then that they'd passed beyond the barrier from which there was no return.

The waiter brought the meal they had ordered and their conversation turned to other, less dangerous things. Christabel's state of mind, Emmeline's reluctance at leaving her, whether or not she'd be seasick on the boat.

'I'm sorry, I shouldn't have said that. It isn't a subject I should be talking about at a time like this.'

'I'm not squeamish. Anyhow, we've finished.' He reached in his pocket for his wallet, but she surprised him by laying a hand on his arm.

'No, I must pay half.'

'A lady doesn't pay when she's in my company. Emancipated or not.' He smiled, and gently moved her hand away. 'Besides, the lunch was my idea.'

'But mine to come to the Café Royal. Fair's fair.'

He caught the waiter's eye and signalled.

'We'd best take a taxi cab to be in time for the next train.'

'If you won't allow me to contribute to the lunch bill, then the least I can do is to invite you to stay at the house. Christabel asked me to, anyway.'

There was a pause while he extracted some money from his wallet and laid it on the little silver tray. The waiter thanked him profusely and moved off.

'I appreciate the gesture, but I don't think it would be a good idea.'

She raised her eyebrows.

'Why not? We'll be leaving for Ballakeighan in the next two days. It's simpler if you stay at the house.'

'If your father had still been alive, I wouldn't have hesitated. But it's different now. With David absent, for a virtual stranger to become a house guest under the same roof as two ladies wouldn't be quite the thing at all.'

'But you're not a stranger. My father and yours were friends. You knew my father when he lived in America. It isn't the same thing at all.' He'd expected her to react with anger and she had.

'I've already booked in at the hotel in Epsom. All my baggage is unpacked. And we're leaving to catch the boat in two days' time. No sense in changing things now from the way they are.'

'I bow to your superior wisdom.'

'Shall we go now?' he said.

Christabel held the lamp higher, as she inched her way carefully through the path of ancient debris all around her, the old picture frames stacked against the attic walls, the battered travelling trunks and faded old hat boxes whose silk ribbons had long since succumbed to mildew and damp. She set the lamp down and brushed dust and cobwebs from her clothes. So many abandoned relics from the past, all long since forgotten: crates of discarded toys, old curtains, piles of musty books; obsolete saddles and riding tack mounted on hooks along the wall. Enormous trunks, their locks long since broken and the keys lost, stuffed with out-dated gowns. She went over to one, and lifted the heavy lid.

There was the acrid smell of moth balls; neglect, decay. She reached inside and rummaged in the contents, turning each over, almost lovingly, in her hands. Sadness, nostalgia. A past she missed and would do anything to resurrect again. How delicate and feminine, how beautiful they were, the gowns that other generations of Ismay, Russell and Brodie women had once worn. There was a black silk dress, with elegant, hand-embroidered ruching, a matching blue velvet half-cloak, with ermine trim; a pale pink gauze ball dress, with white silk ribbon bows and flounces over a crinoline, pink and white lace ruffles sewn around the sleeves and neck; a riding costume, in dull green velvet with a fitted jacket, accordion pleating at the hem. Gloves, delicate petticoats, a variety of broken, discoloured fans; a piece of gold fringing, a strand of broken beads. She went on turning each of them over, until she came at last to the bottom of the trunk. Something glittered, in the dim, weak light, and she reached in and uncovered it. Slowly, almost reverently, she eased it out.

It was more beautiful than any of the other things she'd found in the old trunk; by the style it was also the oldest. Lovingly, she turned the material over in her hands. A ball gown of white tarlatan over layers of stiffened silk, a single line of ruched flouncing at the hem, the entire bodice, and the hand-embroidered flowers in white silk that decorated the overskirt, covered with tiny seed pearls and sequins that twinkled and glinted in the light. There were patches of yellow discoloration here and there; some of the sequins and seed pearls were missing. She tried to imagine the beautiful young woman who had once worn the gown.

There was an old, cracked cheval mirror propped up against some boxes on the opposite side of the attic wall. Christabel went over to it and held up the ball gown against herself. As she stared into the dirty and pitted glass, she caught sight of the china doll, lying on its side beside a wooden box. The blue glass eyes seemed to gaze beseechingly at her; the tiny hands stretched out in mute appeal. She laid down the gown and went over to pick it up.

It was a French Jumeaux baby doll, with huge, lifelike eyes and golden hair; real hair, fashioned into corkscrew curls that framed its round, almost human face. Christabel reached out and stroked its cheek. She touched the hair, the faded blue velvet dress, the tiny hand; she noticed that one of the fingers had been broken. She wondered who it had belonged to; why it had been left up here among the rubbish and the discarded old boxes and trunks. It seemed to her almost an act of sacrilege.

She cradled it in her arms as if it was a real, living thing. Her baby would have been like this, she knew it: delicate pink and white features, blue eyes and golden hair. The child she'd longed for and then lost; part of herself, part of the man she loved. As she gazed down into its face she felt her throat begin to tighten, tears prick cruelly behind her eyes.

'Mrs Ismay!' She heard Janet's calling with a start. 'Mrs Ismay, are you up there?' There were footsteps, then fresh light shone dimly at the far end of the long attic room. Janet appeared, puffing and out of breath, at the top of the winding stairs. 'Oh, you are up here, ma'am!'

'What is it?' Her voice was irritated, almost sharp. She held the doll against her so that Janet would not see it.

'Miss Emmeline's back from London. Just got in. It seems Mr Ryan's gone back to the 'otel at Epsom. She's askin' for you, ma'am.'

'All right. I'll be down in a minute.'

There was something strange about her, different. Janet frowned.

'You all right, ma'am?'

Christabel turned away abruptly. Why didn't she go, why didn't she leave her alone? Why was she peering at her like that?

'Of course I'm all right.' She clutched the doll tighter to her. 'I said, I'll be down.'

When Janet had gone she hurried over to the door and picked up the lamp. Then she stood listening for several more minutes until the footsteps had died away. She closed the door softly behind her, then blew out the lamp.

She stood on the landing, listening. Voices drifted up faintly from the hall. A door slammed. Then there was silence once more. Christabel went down to the next floor and opened the door of the nursery.

Everything was exactly the same as she had left it. Even without turning on the lights she knew where each single item had been placed, the position of every piece of furniture. There was a full moon, and its bright silver rays shone through the window across the floor and onto the elaborate lace-covered cradle in the middle of the room.

110

Christabel went over to it and gently moved back the covers. Then she laid the doll inside.

For several minutes she stood there looking down at it. No cradle should be without a child. It looked so real, so lifelike lying there, just like her own baby would have done. The room no longer seemed as if it was empty any more.

She smiled. She reached out and tenderly touched its cheek again. If only David could be here to share this with her. If only he would come back and see.

NINE

SHE WAS WARMING HER HANDS by the roaring fire, her cheeks and vivid eyes unusually bright. She seemed very animated, confident. Had Delauney given her good news?

'That fool? I told him to go to the devil. He said his firm had been the Ismay lawyers for thirty years; I told him that was thirty years too long.' She went over to the big oak sideboard and poured herself a glass of brandy. 'It was a waste of time. A whole day gone, all for nothing. He advised me to stay here, keep away from the island at all costs and co-operate with the police.' She took a hearty gulp of the brandy. 'I asked him whose side he thought he was on.'

Christabel was horrified.

'You mean you quarrelled with him? That he didn't give you any news about David?'

'What news would he have of David that we haven't? He wouldn't know anything that we don't already. He should have been down here, on the first train out of London, as soon as David went missing. He should have been here in this house when we were invaded by the police. Lawyers are supposed to give you protection and advice, aren't they? He hasn't given either. Except to tell me what Lock has already said: leave well alone. Well, I don't need Delauney to tell me what to do; I've made up my mind already.' She held up the brandy to Christabel, who shook her head.

'You're going then?'

'I have to. Don't you see that? Karl Ryan's coming with me so you've no need to worry about me. I'll be safe with him. When I spoke to Charles on the telephone he said that he would have been glad to accompany me if I wanted him to; but I know he's been ill and it'd be a long journey for him to make. You know how to reach him if you need to. Moran will take care of every-thing outside while I'm away; Janet and Winifred are always a tower of strength. And I'll be back again before you know it. Hopefully with some concrete news.'

'Why didn't Delauney think you should go?'

'Oh, some rubbish about the local people turning against the Ismays because of the rumours about the fire, and because now that the place had burned down they've lost their livelihoods and their homes. You know as well as I do that that just isn't true. David sent money as soon as he was told what had happened. And Michael Stranahan took on all the men. Delauney was just throwing obstacles in my path.'

'What did he say about the creditors?'

'As soon as the rumour that the fire might have been arson got about, he was deluged with letters from their lawyers threatening writs. I suppose that was predictable. They lost valuable, some irreplaceable bloodstock in the accident and they want compensa-tion. To satisfy all their claims we'd have to sell almost everything ... yes, it's as serious as that.' She leaned against the mantelpiece and sighed. 'If we don't make them acceptable financial offers, then they'd simply sue us, and we'd end up losing more because we'd be saddled with all their legal costs as well. So we have no choice. If arson is proved then the insurance company won't pay out and all the compensation has to be found from our own resources. You understand what that would mean?'

'But they can't take everything away from us! It isn't fair. This is our home. The business is David's livelihood.'

'That's why I'm going to Ballakeighan to see if I can dig up something that will exonerate David and save the business. Maybe I'm grasping at straws. But I don't intend to sit by and do nothing.' Christabel recognized the determination in her eyes. 'If we have to go down, we'll go down fighting.'

For a few moments there was silence between them. Emmeline turned and held her hands towards the leaping flames of the fire, comforting after the long, cold journey home, waiting on the platform for the Epsom train.

'What's that you've got?'

'A visiting card. I had a visitor while you were away.'

'Oh? Who?'

'Guy Vogel, from The Hermitage. You remember David met

him a few times when I was ill? The South African who bought the old Abbey and refurbished it. You would have liked him, I know you would. He was a charming man.'

'Isn't he the one with all the money from gold mining, who has a fancy to buy himself a place in the local gentry? David said he was vulgar and *nouveau riche*.'

'I doubt if David said more than a couple of sentences to him. You know how many people go to those bloodstock dinners. Anyway, he was wrong. He told me that the police called on him to ask if anyone in the house had seen the car being abandoned in Bush Wood, and when he found out about what had happened he came straight over here to see if there was anything he could do.'

'That was very neighbourly of him.'

'Our other neighbours and so called friends might take a leaf out of his book. Since all this happened not one of them has called or telephoned. One whiff of trouble and they don't want to know.'

'Yes, you're right. I'm sorry I missed him.'

'David went to a racecourse committee meeting dinner at the house and he said that it was the last word in luxury. He said they had electric lighting in every room!'

'How modern. While we poor, old, antiquated Ismays have to make do with gas, like most other people in these parts. Refurbishing that huge place must have cost him a small fortune.'

'He also said that he bought a castle in Scotland for the shooting season.'

'That's pushing the boat out, isn't it? He must be rolling in money. But then if he has gold mines in South Africa then he can buy almost anything, anything for sale, that is. I suppose he thinks he can buy himself into bloodstock, hobnobbing with all the big owners round these parts. Why else would he hand over five thousand pounds to the Epsom Racecourse Committee to repair the grandstand, then host the most lavish private dinner since the coronation and invite everyone who's anyone as guests? But if he thinks he can buy himself into the Jockey Club, he's got a shock coming. His accent alone would knock them dead.'

'I thought there was less of that sort of prejudice against outsiders since the war?'

'Don't you believe it.' She turned as Janet appeared at the door to call them to dinner. 'Some things never change; at least they're not likely to for another twenty years. Even my father wasn't acceptable as a member to the Jockey Club, because he'd been involved in those murder trials years before merely as a witness. As a young man he'd been employed by the crooked American trainer Enoch Wishard, and later on after he'd met my mother and reformed, he turned queen's evidence so the rest of the gang would be convicted. One of them had been responsible for murdering my mother's first husband, and fled to France with the others afterwards. Nobody knows where he went from there, but he made the mistake of turning up in England years later, and my father recognized him. Didn't David ever tell you about it? He was arrested and found guilty, and Daddy was the chief prosecution witness at his trial. He was hanged for what he did. But even though he would never have been brought to justice without Daddy's evidence, the Jockey Club still wouldn't elect him in. I suppose they thought his character was already stained after his misspent youth.'

Emmeline was reluctant to leave the warmth and comfort of the fire; it seemed pointless to her to traipse all the way from one room to another just to eat, when there was only the two of them: she'd rather have made do with something on a tray beside the fire. But Christabel would have been shocked at such a suggestion. Meaningless pre-war rituals meant so much to her.

Emmeline looked at her from the other end of the long table, wondering if it was just her imagination that Christabel seemed suddenly preoccupied with something else; for the whole of the meal she scarcely spoke a word.

'So, did Guy Vogel say anything else to you?'

Christabel stared at her for a moment before answering.

'He's invited us both to dinner tomorrow. And to meet his wife.'

'We'll accept, of course. I'd be fascinated to see inside his house – or should I say palace? Do you know what David called him? King Midas.'

Ryan took the key to his room from the desk clerk and went upstairs to the second floor. The hotel maid had lit the fire in the bedroom and in the small sitting room that adjoined it, and the curtains had been drawn. The bed was turned down; a small tray

115

with the bottle of whisky and water jug that he'd ordered stood on a small circular table to one side of the room. He went over to it and poured himself a drink.

She wanted to leave the day after tomorrow. That didn't leave him very much spare time to do what he had to do; he should have tried to get over to the house before yesterday, when he'd been expected. But there was no help for it. It was impossible to go in daylight, and tomorrow evening would be too late. It was tonight or nothing.

He put down the empty glass and went over to the window; luckily, they'd given him a room which overlooked the back of the hotel gardens. Beyond the garden wall he could just make out the rise and fall of Epsom Downs, a shadow of greens and blacks. He'd instructed them at the desk that he wouldn't be down to dinner and was under no circumstances to be disturbed.

He walked across to the door and locked it; he left on the light so that it could clearly be seen from outside. Then, carefully, slowly, dexterously, he eased open the sash window and peered cautiously out. Left and right. Nobody was in sight.

It was a long drop from the window on the second floor to the ground behind the hotel, but the strong, whip-like vine that grew up the side of the wall was more than sufficient for someone of his experience to make full use of. He slipped out onto the narrow window sill, silently pulling down the window until it was closed; in a few minutes he was standing on the grass below.

It was a distance of four miles from here to the other side of Bush Wood. On foot, dodging in and out of hedges and the undergrowth, he calculated it would take him no more than three-quarters of an hour. It was nothing, compared to what he'd been used to.

He edged noiselessly forward, along the hotel wall. A single glance over one shoulder to check that all was quiet and clear. Then he was gone.

TEN

THE POLICE HAD STILL NOT brought back David's car; the journey over to The Hermitage was made instead in the grand old Ismay landau, with the best carriage horses and young Harry McCaughan on the box. Emmeline never stood on ceremony with anyone who worked for them and kept up a stream of lively conversation with the boy for the whole fifty minutes that it took them to reach the house, while Christabel, sitting next to her in silent disapproval, barely spoke a word.

'A string o' gold mines 'e has, is it?' Harry said in his high, sing-song voice as the horses trotted in perfect unison along the Epsom road, 'an' wouldn't I like to have a few nuggets out o' one, an' all!'

'Maybe he'll give you one, if you ask him nicely.'

'The divil 'e will! Jaysus, but himself is a right tall fella, Miss Emmeline. I see him when he called upon the missus, while you was up in London. An' hair as red as a fox's brush!' He shook his head and laughed. 'Do you reckon wi' that big, twirlin' moustache o' his, he tickles 'is missus an' makes herself sneeze every time he kisses her?'

'Harry, be quiet at once. You're a very wicked boy.' She was smiling, but beside her she felt Christabel's chilly disapproval.

Only The Hermitage roof was visible above the tops of the trees as they drew nearer. At the massive new gates, the landau turned into the drive and both of them leaned forward to get a better view, but the building was in deep shadow. Lights streamed from several windows in the house, making pathways across the neat lawn. Emmeline noticed classical statues placed at exact locations in the garden, looking ghostly in the evening light.

'It's very impressive; David said it was.' Christabel spoke for the first time, in something of her normal voice. 'It's all been landscaped, every inch of it. It must have cost a fortune for this alone. It was an overgrown wilderness before he came and bought the Abbey.'

'It isn't the Abbey any more,' Emmeline said. They'd clattered to a halt outside the magnificent front entrance, and two liveried footmen had appeared from nowhere. 'He's re-Christened it The Hermitage; God knows why.'

'Yes, I do know that.' Her tone was almost pettish. 'He already told me.'

Young Harry McCaughan was doubling on duties. He slipped down from the box as light as a feather to open the landau door and help them out. At the same moment a tall figure in evening dress appeared in the huge frame of the open door. Though she'd never met him Emmeline knew at once who it was: the height and the flaming hair and moustache from Harry's description could never have fitted anyone else.

Guy Vogel looked at her. The light from the hall and the moonlight from above them emphasized her striking appearance; sequins glittered on her pale mauve silk gown; the rhinestone fillet that circled her dark hair reflected its colours in her eyes; they were blue, he noticed at once, but a brilliant turquoise colour, a colour he'd never seen a woman's eyes before. She wore a gold necklace, with matching earrings and bracelet around her wrist; everything about her exuded a parallel grace and self-confidence. He had underestimated her. Christabel, for all her perfect English rose looks, seemed pale and insignificant beside her.

He mustn't show surprise that she was so different to the young woman he'd been expecting. He'd wager every stone in the Abbey that Emmeline Ismay was no one's fool.

He smiled with all the charm he could muster, and advanced on them, holding out his hands.

'Ladies! I'm honoured. Please come inside ... There'll be another frost tonight, if I'm not mistaken.' He kissed her hand and then Christabel's; though he should have kissed her sister-in-law's first, or better still, only shaken hands, she could understand why Christabel was so impressed by him; manners had changed so sharply since the war.

They walked with him into the hall. She stood and looked all around her. David had been right; the refurbishment of the old interior had been undertaken on a lavish scale, no expense had been spared. It was decorated in white and gold, with heavy, elaborate French Empire furniture, enormous gilded clocks and bronze statuettes that all sat oddly side by side with the English racing paintings that covered nearly every wall. She could feel his eyes on her, questing for a reaction, and from politeness she gave him an approving nod though hardly anything except the paintings appealed to her own sense of taste. It was all over-gilded, overdone, almost vulgar in its blatant ostentation, as if its owner was trying to force the onlooker to acknowledge the limitless wealth that had purchased every piece and assembled them together.

Only one thing seemed to be missing. There was no sign of Vogel's wife.

He led them along a wide corridor that seemed to have no ending, each side hung with massive antique tapestries depicting scenes of medieval hunting. He paused, and drew attention to one of them, and she could sense his pride and pleasure even more keenly than in the gilded, over-furnished hall.

'Magnificent pieces of history. And priceless works of art.' He smiled. 'I also purchased a rare manuscript from an antiquarian bookseller in London, on this same subject. Every tapestry depicts a scene from the art of hunting different animals. This is the hunting of the boar.' She looked at it, at the faces of the huntsmen, all alike, the stilted limbs, the wrong perspectives; the only vivid, lifelike thing was the scarlet stitching representing blood. 'When the boar is tired out by the hunt, it turns and faces the hounds; the huntsman slows his horse to a trot, stands in his stirrups and tries to hit the animal with his pike, which he holds in the middle of the haft and throws in an arc like a javelin. If the blow is well aimed, the boar lets out a roar and the pack leaps on him. Then the hunter has to dismount and kill the animal with his sword. Ingenious. So was the method they had of killing wolves.' He moved on to the next scene. 'The huntsmen stuffed huge chunks of raw meat with curved needles or fish hooks in pairs, then took them to the forest and spread them out along the ground. The famished wolves would swallow the meat without chewing it and die with their insides torn apart by the needles.'

There was a pause, while Vogel waited for them to speak. But Emmeline simply turned away from the tapestries and walked on, Christabel in silence beside her.

119

'They were specially imported for me from Brussels by a specialist in Great Audley Street. Remarkable pieces, every one of them.'

The turquoise eyes looked coldly at him.

'They explain, certainly, why wolves, wild bears and boars have long been extinct in this country.'

'You disapprove of hunting, Miss Ismay?'

'I disapprove of any form of cruelty to animals; and any fight where the numbers are more than one to one.'

He should have expected her to say that, and he also realized his first mistake. He ought to have anticipated her reaction – typical woman – and simply not drawn attention to them at all.

They had reached the end of the tapestry-lined corridor and he stepped back to usher them into the drawing room.

The old, original fireplace had been ripped out and replaced with a marble monstrosity from sometime in the middle of the late-Victorian age. It was a mass of gargoyles, wild beasts' heads and writhing serpents, all heavily gilded and lacquered; there was an enormous brass fender with red plush velvet seats, which looked as if it had been taken from a West End gentlemen's club. The remainder of the room was painted in lavender and gold, with matching pieces of French furniture from a variety of periods.

Emmeline glanced around her while Christabel went and stood beside the blazing fire.

There was a sofa and matching chairs in carved gilded wood, upholstered in vermilion damask; around the walls a set of Louis XV chairs, gilded and covered in hand-woven embroidery; a console table in delicate filigree work, surmounted by the classical bust of a woman. There were several clocks, the largest and most ornate of them in pride of place on the hideous mantelpiece; the paintings in this room were smaller and were all of eighteenth-century allegorical figures.

She spread the silk overskirt of her evening dress and sat down.

'Will Mrs Vogel be joining us soon?'

He was across the room, pouring champagne into gilt-rimmed crystal glasses. He glanced up.

'Forgive me, I should have told you at once. Unfortunately, my wife is unable to join us this evening. She has a very bad headache. She was so disappointed to miss meeting you.'

'I'm so sorry. I hope she'll be better very soon.'

He handed them each a glass of champagne.

'She's in good hands, her personal maid is a qualified nurse, and a treasure. But I suspect myself that these headaches she seems plagued with are brought on by the damp and cold.' He turned to Christabel. 'As I told you before, Mrs Ismay, she finds it extremely difficult to cope with the English climate.'

'There are times when we have difficulty coping with it,' Emmeline answered with her dry sense of humour. She noticed that that amused him. 'But won't your wife find the climate in Scotland even harder to bear than ours down south? My sister-in-law mentioned to me that you'd bought a castle there for the shooting season.'

'A purely selfish indulgence on my part, I'm afraid. Firearms and weaponry are two special passions of mine. I have an extensive collection in my gun room that you ladies might be interested to see.'

'Yes, we would.'

Vogel went on sipping his champagne.

'My father was a brilliant marksman. What he didn't know about weapons wasn't worth knowing. He taught me to shoot, and how to look after my guns. He always was a firm believer in a man having a special interest in life. His was horses. Of course, I share that passion too and, fortunately, so does my wife, Adeline. No doubt she'll get used to our visits to Scotland; what a beautiful, wild place it is! All those different shades of heather, the mountains, the winding streams. And the mists. I love those wonderful, eerie Scottish mists. So much space for a man to breathe up there, and none of the heat and dust of South Africa.'

'Is your castle habitable?'

'It is now. After I spent three months and a small fortune on restoring it. It has a magnificent baronial hall – breathtaking. And a superb stone staircase leading from the hall to the upper floors. I'm told the clan used to gather there at the long table in the old days, and plot to restore the Young Pretender. True or false, it really doesn't matter to me! But I like to think it is. I've bought a huge collection of native Scottish weapons to decorate the walls, literally hundreds of the choicest and best preserved pieces. Pikes, axes, dirks, crossbows of every size and type. The collection, like my tapestries here, is a thing of beauty in itself.' Emmeline

121

couldn't miss the look, and the tone, of pride.

'Your collection here, did it take long for you to assemble?'

'The past year. I've purchased some of the finest examples of the gunsmith's craft. Sheer masterpieces. In themselves a feast for the eyes and a joy to look at.'

'And you also have a keen interest in horses?'

'As I was telling Mrs Ismay. My dream – and isn't it every racing man's? – would be to own a Classic winner. We have racing in South Africa, like most civilized countries, but there's nothing like the English turf and never will be.'

'You have no established stable as yet. Is that your plan?'

'In time. I'm a novice at these things. After meeting your brother I'd intended to come over and discuss buying a selection of your yearlings on his advice, but before I'd been able to make arrangements to see him this tragedy suddenly happened. So I've decided to wait a while. After all, I'm in no hurry. We intend to make our permanent home here, in England.' He turned to Emmeline. 'And you have absolutely no idea what could have happened, where your brother might be?'

'Neither of us has. His disappearance is a total mystery. Of course, that hasn't stopped the inevitable gossip. You can imagine what line that has already begun to take. The whispers about the cause of the fire, then David vanishing. We've chased away droves of newspaper reporters up till now, but I suppose we can't hope to do it forever. Sooner or later – certainly when I come back from Ballakeighan – I'll have to make a statement.' A bitter tone came into her voice. 'The power of the press, Mr Vogel. Their subtle insinuations have done more damage to our reputation than anything else.'

'If only there was something I could do to help you.'

'Your sympathy and understanding of the situation are more than enough. So far, you're the only neighbour who's taken the trouble to speak to us since the fire. Everyone else, people we've known for years, have taken the greatest care to keep conspicuously out of the way.'

Vogel gave her a knowing look.

'Fair weather friends, Miss Ismay. I know the breed well. And, believe me, I've had my own fair share of them.'

'I don't doubt it.'

'Adversity has a strange effect on people; people you've trusted, people you've known intimately for maybe many years – when their loyalty is tested for the first time many of them are found sadly wanting. It's a useful, if sobering lesson to learn.'

'And maybe a blessing in disguise. At least it'll cut down our Christmas card list this year.'

He laughed loudly.

'I like your sense of humour.' He refilled her glass with champagne. 'Tell me, this trip of yours to the Isle of Man, are you completely convinced that it won't be a waste of time? And isn't it a little too hazardous for a young lady to be travelling such a distance on her own?'

'I won't be alone. Just after David disappeared an old friend of my father's arrived in Epsom, and he's offered to come with me. He's been a tower of strength.'

'I wish you both a safe and fruitful trip.'

Christabel began asking Vogel questions about his paintings and Emmeline fell silent, looking momentarily into the roaring fire. She thought of David, standing there that night at the turn of the stairs as he'd smiled and blown a kiss towards her, then turned and disappeared into the darkness. The last time she'd ever spoken with him, seen him, the memory of it imprinted in her brain. She remembered the sound of his footsteps echoing on the floor, then the heavy door opening and closing shut; finally, the yawning silence.

A door was opening now and one of the overdressed, liveried footmen was standing at the entrance to the room.

'Dinner is served, sir.'

He got to his feet, standing back while she and Christabel walked out in front of him. The dining room was every bit as elaborate and ostentatious as the rooms they'd already seen, but Emmeline had long lost interest in her host's opulent surroundings. She felt empty, depressed, maddeningly helpless, a sudden impatience to be gone so that she could pack and be on her way to Ballakeighan. She'd telephoned Vogel and accepted his invitation of the day before on the spur of the moment, driven out of her mind by the brooding Christabel and the all but silent house. Now she was almost wishing they hadn't come. But it was too late for regrets.

She suddenly realized that Vogel, from the head of the table, was talking to her.

123

'Tell me something about your bloodstock on the island, Miss Ismay. Was much saved from the fire?'

'Very little. Most of the best mares were lost; and they, of course, had been sent over to us to be served by Ballacragan. None of the foals managed to survive. We're faced with a ruinous bill for compensation to the mares' owners; and the insurance company have refused to pay out because of the rumour of arson.'

'Tragic. Appalling. They have concrete evidence then?'

'According to our family lawyer, almost certainly. But I want to see it for myself.'

Vogel maintained a respectful silence for a few moments. It was much too early to pry too deeply.

'Your stallion, Ballacragan – I understand that he's a full brother to the 1913 Derby winner, Craganour. He's safe?'

'One of the few. My brother's agent in Onchan, Michael Stranahan, has him at his own stables until he can be shipped back to England. Then he'll stand here. Until we have a clearer picture of the stud's long-term future.'

'Would you rate him as good as Craganour?'

'Infinitely better. If the war hadn't broken out when it did and ruined his racing career, he would probably have been one of the finest colts of all time. His sire, Desmond, was champion sire in 1913 and his dam Veneration II was a half-sister to Pretty Polly. He had six races as a two-year-old against the highest class crop of two-year-olds that we've seen for a long while, and he beat them all in great style. He was a true stayer: he could manage anything up to two and a half miles without losing pace, with breathtaking finishing power. He was unextended in every one of his races and we never found out how good he really was. Another case of fate intervening and what might have been.'

'The 1913 Derby was a remarkable race.'

'Yes, it certainly was. The winner disqualified and a suffragette throwing herself under the King's horse in the middle of the race. Of course, it all started with the feud between our uncle, Charles Ismay, and Eustace Loder, the senior Jockey Club steward. I won't go into all the reasons for that now, but a feud it certainly was. Craganour won the Two Thousand Guineas but the judge, a protegé of Loder's, gave the race to Louvois. That should have shown my uncle what way the wind was blowing. The Derby was

124

certainly one of the roughest in history. The French jockeys said afterwards that they felt as if they'd been in a bullfight. My uncle had stood down Craganour's regular jockey because of his indifferent riding, and given the ride instead to the American Johnny Reiff. You can imagine that added fuel to the fire. The outsider Aboyeur was the horse that did all the bumping and boring as they got inside the last furlong, and he tried to savage Craganour. But when Craganour came in first Loder objected to his winning on the grounds that he'd interfered with the second horse. Untrue. The stewards' enquiry that followed was a farce. Lord Rosebery took no part in it because he had a runner in the race, and the other steward was a nonentity; to all intents and purposes Loder conducted it alone. With him in the chair, my uncle knew the dice were loaded against him. He was so sickened by the whole affair that he sold Craganour to an Argentinian breeder later that year.'

'So he lost the Derby through Loder's malice and British bloodstock was deprived of a potentially great horse. That would have made me very bitter.'

'Loder's actions were a disgraceful misuse of power. And the very antithesis of sportsmanship. Disqualifying a man's horse for something he didn't do because you hate his owner! But everyone who knew the truth said my uncle was the moral victor. Whatever Loder did that day nothing could alter the fact that Craganour came in first.'

Vogel seemed to be pondering something.

'This feud between your uncle and the Loders, is there any possible chance that they might have something to do with the fire? I'm speaking purely in confidence, of course.'

'The police have already asked my uncle about it. He told me when he telephoned. And the answer's no. Eustace Loder died of Bright's disease in 1914. He never married and all his racing stock passed to his nephew, a totally different kettle of fish. He was one of the first to agree that Craganour should never have been disqualified from that Derby. In fact, my father always thought he was ashamed of what his uncle did.'

'Does your uncle have any horses in training now?'

'He lives in Northampton, quietly. And no, he doesn't. For the last few years he'd suffered from ill health.'

'I'm sorry to hear that.'

'He contracted sleeping sickness while he was on active service in North Africa. But he always took the greatest interest in my parents' horses. Old passions die hard.'

Christabel turned to Vogel.

'Won't you tell us a little about your own family history? You were born in South Africa?'

He laughed good-naturedly.

'Not much to tell. My family are nowhere near as fascinating as yours. My father made a lucky strike in the Klerksdorp gold fields about fifty years ago. He never looked back. All I've done is carry on what he started. We've had our own share of tragedies: my eldest brother was killed in an accident down one of the mines and my first wife died when she was just a young woman. It was a long time afterwards when I could bring myself to think of marrying again.' He rose to his feet to close the avenue of conversation. His brother's accident, his first wife's death, were subjects that he didn't intend to dwell on. 'Well, ladies, we appear to have finished dinner. Shall we adjourn to the gun room?'

'No one knows exactly when gunpowder was invented. It was certainly in existence by the beginning of the fifteenth century. In 1460 James II of Scotland was blown in half by a faulty gun at the siege of Roxburgh. You see, history is another passion of mine.' Vogel had been watching Emmeline carefully all evening, not certain yet whether he'd managed to gain her total sympathy. He couldn't be sure what she was thinking about him. But he was determined that she wouldn't go away regarding Guy Vogel as just a rich, ignorant Afrikaaner. They walked on, side by side. 'Some believe it was the Chinese who first mixed the ingredients; others the Arabs while Europe was still struggling in the Dark Ages. I suppose we'll never know for sure.' He opened the double doors of the gun room and stood back for her and Christabel to walk in.

It was a man's room, the white walls relieved only from their plainness by the variety of weapons they displayed: swords, battle-axes, elaborate daggers with carved and embellished handles; crossbows, ceremonial pikes. At the far end of the room she saw two suits of armour displayed on dummies, polished and buffed to a brilliant shine. In the middle stood a line of mahogany

126

showcases, displaying the pride of his collection.

He took a bunch of keys from his pocket and unlocked one of them.

'As I said, it's always fascinated me, the origins of arms. Did you know that the Byzantines used "great fire" against the hordes of Islam who besieged Constantinople in the seventh century? Perhaps they were the first to use it?'

Emmeline smiled.

'You certainly have a very impressive collection.' She moved over to where he stood and looked down into the showcase. 'Another version I seem to remember hearing about in far off school days was that gunpowder might have been invented by Roger Bacon, a Somerset man. He was thrown into prison for his writings which contained a cryptogram. Rearranged, it proved that he knew the secret of gunpowder even if he didn't actually invent it.'

The look of surprise on Vogel's face amused her; discreetly she moved on to the next cabinet.

'These duelling pistols are early eighteenth-century, surely? And by the look of the carved initials on the side of the handles, for royalty, no less.'

'The pride of my collection. Made in 1729 for no less a personage than Frederick the Great. They were converted to percussion in about 1830, but still retain their original splendour. Beautiful things.'

'Warfare was so gentlemanly in those days, wasn't it? Elaborate uniforms and ritual, extravagant rules. No comparison to the knee-deep mud in Flanders, flooded trenches, the rotting bodies of horses and men, barbed wire and dead, uprooted trees.'

There was an artist's impression of the Black Prince on horseback on the far wall and Emmeline went over and stood in front of it.

'I wonder what he would have thought of the war to end all wars?'

'A fascinating supposition.'

'Gunpowder certainly had an enormous effect on modern warfare; medieval Europe, like the rest of the world, fought with weapons that were merely variations on a common theme . . . the sword, the lance, the axe, the bow. The English longbow was feared all over Europe after the Battle of Crecy, with good cause.'

'Handled by a professional at two hundred and fifty yards it produced a hail of arrows, a concentrated effect that remained unequalled until the American Civil War.'

'Maybe our army would have done better to have used it on the Somme.'

Vogel relocked the cases.

'It's stimulating to have a young woman who knows something about the history of such a subject. My wife, I'm afraid, considers it a bore. I often spend hours, up here alone, taking out various pieces from the collection and oiling and polishing them. Most are still in perfect working order.' He replaced the keys in his pocket. 'Well, ladies, may I suggest a brandy before you return home? And next time you come to dinner, I hope that my wife will be here to meet you.' He turned out the gun room lights.

'I can't help noticing that so much of the house has been decorated in gold. A predominant colour scheme, you might say. Is that to brighten the interior or is it in homage to your father's beginnings in Klerksdorp?'

'Perhaps a little of both. Mostly because in my life gold has always had pride of place for its pure beauty as much as for its monetary value. Think about it. Its charisma permeates our language, wouldn't you ladies agree? We talk about "a heart of gold", or "a golden opportunity". A golden wedding celebrates fifty years of marriage, we talk of someone being "as good as gold". What makes gold the noblest of all metals? Its greatest strength is its indestructibility; unlike silver it doesn't tarnish. Acid can't corrode it. Did you know that gold coins have been unearthed from buried treasure hoards after two centuries looking as bright as they did when they were new? Remarkable, isn't it?' Vogel sat down beside Emmeline. 'To primitive man, the first appeal was obviously aesthetic. Gold gleamed warmly at him from the beds of streams; he found it easy to work. It was beautiful and versatile, more workable than any other metal. It was almost as soft as putty, so malleable that it could be hammered cold by even a primitive goldsmith until it was a thin translucent wafer; did you know that a single ounce of gold can be beaten into a sheet covering nearly one hundred square feet?'

'No, I didn't know that.'

128

'My father always taught me that gold was much more than a thin vein of yellow in a lump of rock. Like my own collection of beautiful things, I prize our yield from the mines just as highly with obvious justification: without it none of the other things would exist. But it's a thing of beauty in its own right.'

'And the largest single export in your country?'

'As far back as 1910 gold made up that amount of South African exports, yes. The Royal Commission of 1914 estimated that forty-five per cent of the Union's total revenue was attributable directly or indirectly to the gold mining industry.'

'But in the mid 1800s I believe it was Russia who led the world in gold yield. Is that true?'

'Yes, true enough. When my father was a young man he mined in Russia – with considerable success, too. Couldn't stand the climate, though. Or the people. And ever since the Revolution outsiders have been wary of funding any exploratory ventures in that direction. No need to ask why. I wouldn't care to turn my back on men who thought nothing of the wholesale massacre of their own Royal Family, would you?'

'The murder of Romanovs was shocking. But the men who overturned the Government and the rule of law were fanatics; and nobody can reason with fanaticism.'

The magnificent French mantel clock that Emmeline had noticed when they'd arrived chimed the hour as she finished speaking, and she suddenly realized how late it was and how much longer they'd stayed than she'd planned. She stood up and Christabel got to her feet too.

'I'd forgotten the time. We really should be going.' She shook hands with Vogel. 'I haven't finished packing and there's still a lot to do before tomorrow. But thank you for your hospitality. We must return it sometime.'

'The pleasure is all mine.' He turned to shake hands with Christabel.

'I'm so sorry we couldn't meet your wife. Please tell her that we hope she'll feel better soon.'

He escorted them back to the brightly lit hall where the footmen were waiting with their wraps; then Vogel turned and looked once more into those clever, brilliant eyes. Clearly he'd underestimated her. Her knowledge of weaponry and her comments about the gold industry back home were, he strongly

129

suspected, the tip of an iceberg; she knew far more about both than her politeness was willing to reveal. He must tread more carefully than he'd thought.

'Good-night.'

He watched them climb into the landau. For an instant he caught a glimpse of pale mauve silk, the glint of sequins in the light; then she was gone and the landau was disappearing into the darkness, clattering away along the drive.

The footman closed the front door. Vogel turned and went upstairs.

'Well, my dear, our guests were so disappointed that you were too unwell to make an appearance. I apologized for your absence, of course.' He had closed the door behind him and he was leaning against it. She came forward, and stood in front of him.

'Guy, why are you doing this? Why wouldn't you let me come down?'

'Another time, perhaps, when you can be trusted. If you ever can.' He reached out and touched her shoulders and she shivered. 'I can't be sure of you any more, can I, Adeline my darling?' A cold smile that never reached his eyes. 'I can never be sure again that you won't betray me.'

'There was nothing between me and David Ismay! For God's sake, why can't you believe that?'

'I believe the evidence of my own eyes.'

'He was only being polite that day in the garden! Can't you see that?'

Vogel came nearer to her and she stepped back, away from him.

'Please credit me with a modicum of intelligence, my dear. I saw the way he was looking at you.' The look in his eyes terrified her. 'Since you clearly have no idea how to behave in the presence of men whom we hardly know, to protect your good name and mine you've left me with no alternative but to keep you from mixing with them ... for the foreseeable future.'

'You can't keep me locked away up here!'

'I shall keep you here for as long as I see fit. And until you learn that flirting with other men is something that I shall never allow any wife of mine to indulge in.'

'It isn't true!'

'Don't lie to me!' He took hold of her with both hands and shook her. 'Don't ever lie to me, do you understand? Otherwise you know exactly what I'll have to do.'

'Please, Guy, let go of my arm. You're hurting me!'

'You don't even know the meaning of pain!'

The silhouette of a woman in maid's uniform suddenly appeared in the open doorway of the adjoining room.

'Do you want me to settle her, Mr Vogel?'

Slowly, he let go of his wife's arms and pushed her away. She sank down onto a boudoir chair and began to cry silently.

'There's no need now. They've gone. Tomorrow the Ismay girl leaves for the island.' He glanced down at the sobbing Adeline. 'While she's gone I can start to pull a few strings, put plans into action. The ball's in my court.' He signalled the other woman over to the window embrasure and lowered his voice. 'Ensure she sees no newspapers yet. Should any neighbours call unexpectedly while I'm not here, she isn't well enough to see any of them.' The woman nodded. 'Ismay's wife, she's of no account. But the sister, she'll need careful watching. She's clever. She's got a first-class brain. But then that makes everything so much more interesting – and more satisfying when I finally win.' He glanced over his shoulder at his wife. 'For her sake I just hope that she doesn't become too clever for her own good.'

Behind them, Adeline had got up.

'Guy, I can't take much more of this . . . I hate it here. Please.' A pleading note had come into her voice. 'When are you going to take me back to Cape Town to see my father?'

'When it suits me, my dear, when it suits me. And when I decide the time is right for us to go.'

'But I haven't heard from him for so long, not even a single letter . . .'

'I told you, his health isn't good. Don't I pay a small fortune for him to live in the lap of luxury, being waited on night and day? He's got everything he could possibly need, everything that money can buy. You read the last letter his housekeeper sent us. His hands are so swollen now that he can't hold a pen to write in either of them.'

She went over to the little escritoire and opened the top of it. She brought out an envelope and held it out to him.

131

'I wrote this to him this evening, to pass the time. Guy, please have it sent for me. The mail takes so long.'

He smiled and took it.

'Yes, of course, my dear.' He leaned forward and kissed her forehead, very lightly. Across the top of her head he exchanged a glance with her maid, Livia De Haan. 'Let Livia help you get ready for bed. It's late now. And you look a little pale.'

'When can we go out? Even for just a drive? You promised that we could go to London – '

'And so we shall, all in good time. But I have business interests to sort out first. They must take precedence. You forget, despite your indiscretion, how proud of you I am and how anxious I am to show you off to the outside world. Sleep well, my dear.'

He left her there, standing in the middle of the floor gazing after him. Downstairs, in the empty drawing room, he opened the letter she had given him and read its contents.

Then he smiled, tore it into several pieces, and threw the pieces one by one into the fire.

ELEVEN

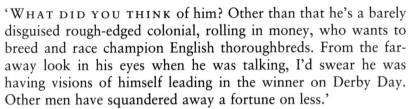

'WHAT DID YOU THINK of him? Other than that he's a barely disguised rough-edged colonial, rolling in money, who wants to breed and race champion English thoroughbreds. From the far-away look in his eyes when he was talking, I'd swear he was having visions of himself leading in the winner on Derby Day. Other men have squandered away a fortune on less.'

'I liked him,' Christabel said, 'didn't you?'

'There wasn't anything to dislike; not that I noticed. Other than his taste in furnishings and decoration. King Midas – David was right. Didn't those tapestries make you feel sick, too?'

'I didn't like them, no. But I would never have said so. You made it so obvious, Emmeline.'

'They were revolting. Exquisite needlework glorifying scenes of torture and death. It made me realize what cruel people medieval men were.'

'I think he was very proud of them. He considered them works of art.'

'Maybe an interesting insight into his mentality, wouldn't you say, the obsession with killing and weapons of hunting and war? But then I don't suppose he really looks at the pictures in terms of what they show but of how much they cost. A pretty penny, I shouldn't wonder.'

'I'm sorry we didn't meet his wife.'

Emmeline flopped down in the nearest chair. It was so late, later than she'd meant them to stay. And there was still so much to do before tomorrow. She hadn't intended to accept the invitation at all before she left, but she'd fitted it in because Christabel had looked in need of an evening out away from the house.

'Well, I'll say this for him. Vulgar and *nouveau riche* he might be, but he certainly entertains his guests in style. And the whole house was so warm!' She sighed, wishing she was already in bed. She hated the nightly journey through the big, musty-smelling, icy hall, the countless flights of stairs. 'He certainly isn't a snob; and for that I think I can forgive him almost anything.' A note of anger came into her voice now. 'Where are all our esteemed neighbours since news of the fire came? Not a telephone call of sympathy; not a single note. Not even after David disappeared. One whiff of scandal and there's not one of them to be seen.'

'People are like that; it was exactly the same after the *Titanic* sank. If you were an Ismay nobody wanted anything to do with you. Even an Ismay by marriage.'

'Well, we can live without them. Shall we go up now? Another five minutes and I'll fall asleep in this chair.'

Christabel sat down opposite her.

'We must talk, Emmeline, about David, before you leave. Do you think he could be somewhere on the island? That he went to Michael Stranahan for help?'

'I won't know that until I get there. But if for some reason that we don't know about he is, he won't be with Michael. After what the police uncovered I've no doubt they've put a watch on Michael's house. They'd know at once if any strangers went either in or out.'

'But David could have panicked when he thought about the consequences of the fire. He could have gone to Michael Stranahan before the police thought to look.'

'Have you ever known David to panic about anything?'

'Everyone has their breaking point. Maybe he reached his. He seemed so preoccupied and troubled in those few days before he left.'

'Christabel, can we talk about this tomorrow?'

'But you're leaving tomorrow. You said that after you'd gone into Epsom to the bank you were meeting Karl Ryan and going straight up to Liverpool by train. We won't have time then.'

Emmeline restrained her feelings of weariness and impatience. She lay back resignedly in the chair.

'Christabel, David is my brother. And I know he'd never go off and not tell either of us where he was going without a cast-iron cause. Beyond that we can only speculate, which is a waste of time. There's no point. All I'm sure about is that his disap-

134

pearance has something to do with the fire.'

'He's your brother, yes. But my husband, too. I know you think you understand him better than I do – '

'That isn't true!'

'Are you certain there isn't anything that's happened that you haven't told me?'

Something in Christabel's manner made Emmeline sit up.

'What are you talking about?'

'Was there anyone else? Tell me the truth, Emmeline. I have a right to know. I've lain awake night after night since he went and run every possible reason through my mind until I felt I wanted to scream. You say his disappearance must have something to do with the fire, but I wonder if that's true. I may not have your brilliant intellect, but I do know that the most common cause of disappearing husbands is that they've gone away with another woman.'

Emmeline was on her feet.

'I don't believe I'm hearing this! Vogel's champagne must have gone straight to your head! Do you really believe my brother is the kind of man who'd walk out on his wife; the wife he loves, the wife he cares about more than anyone else in the world? You do him an injustice!'

'But does he care for me more than anyone else in the world? Ever since I lost my child, I've wondered. Hated myself for even thinking it, hated myself for suspecting that he didn't care as much as he did before. I wondered if he blamed me in some way, if he thought it was my fault. When I really needed him to talk about it, he told me I should put it all behind me in the past, where it belonged. Ever since then all he seemed to care about was the success of the stud.'

'That doesn't mean his feelings for you have changed. Don't you understand what he's been up against, fighting to keep the business afloat after the post-war slump, fighting to keep all our people in their jobs? Even though our total bloodstock is down this year because David believes in quality and not quantity, he wouldn't hear of laying off any of the men. In better times, maybe he'd be willing to make drastic cuts, but he knows what would happen to them if they lost their places here. David would never reward loyalty by throwing men on to the dole queue. And you know that as well as I do.'

'You still haven't answered my question.'

'I've answered it twice over. David loves you and nothing could ever change that. What you don't understand, or want to understand, is that your marriage isn't the only thing he has to think about.'

Christabel went over to the bell rope and tugged on it hard.

'If you're ringing for Janet she won't come; I told her before we left that she and Winifred could go to bed. And don't look at me like that. Have some thought for both of them. They're up hours before you are and they don't usually go up until long after we do. It was the least I could do.' She was suddenly sorry for sounding so harsh; she smiled wanly. 'Look, I'm sorry. I'm leaving tomorrow and I don't want to quarrel with you before I go. If you need help undressing, I'll do it.'

'Thank you. But I can manage perfectly well by myself.' The war had made lady's maids an endangered, if not an almost extinct breed, with girls preferring to work in the factories that manufactured uniforms and bombs, instead of slaving for half the wages in a big house, at some spoiled society woman's constant beck and call. Christabel was still living in the past.

When she'd gone Emmeline lay back and covered her tired eyes with her hands, giving her time to go upstairs.

If only what she'd said about David hadn't started to sow the first seeds of doubt in her mind.

Christabel made her way up the darkened stairs. She paused at the landing and looked back into the hall, deep in shadow. Janet had turned down her bed and lit a fire in the grate that was still glowing; a gas lamp flickered beside the bed on the other side of the room.

She went over to the mantelpiece and lit a candle, then quietly closed the door of the bedroom behind her and made her way to the nursery.

She stood beside the cradle, gazing down into the blue glass eyes of the doll she had laid inside. She reached down and touched its cold cheek with the fingers of one hand. She smiled. Then she bent down slowly and kissed it.

In the half-darkness, the soft golden light, it looked so real to her lying there.

TWELVE

RICHARD LOCK PUT HIS HAND over his mouth to stifle another yawn, then took another swig from the big tin mug of hot, strong tea that the desk constable had just brewed for him.

'Strong and sweet, laddie,' he'd grumbled, the first time they'd brought him a piddling little cup of tepid liquid the colour of flour water. 'Something with a bit of guts in it, nice and hot. That's how I like it. Not this half-cold piss you call tea!' They could do with a kick up the backside, the lot of them. Rural Epsom was a long way from the Yard.

In front of him his desk was piled with mounds of papers. Dozens of statements, from the fishmonger's boy who'd caught a glimpse of David Ismay in his motorcar, driving to catch the train to London, down to the stud workers, his own uncle, and the two maids who worked in the house. Not a single clue in any one of them.

It was getting light now, and he and Barnes had been up all night, except for half an hour when they'd taken it in turns to put their feet up on the chair in the corner and snatch some sleep. His eyelids weighed heavy. He took another swig of tea. David Ismay had vanished into thin air nearly two weeks ago and they were still no further into finding out where he'd gone or why.

His own theories and personal suspicions were no use at all; it was hard facts that counted. So far they had none. Nobody who had been closest to him could think of anyone who'd hated him enough to do away with him. All Lock had was that a man had disappeared and his vehicle found in a wood had been in the opposite direction to the one everyone had thought he'd gone in, including his own wife and sister. He was in deep personal and financial trouble. The possible motives for his disappearing from the face of the earth seemed simple enough: charges of arson, manslaughter and fraud were more than sufficient to be going on with. One thing that had emerged from the mass of statements from anyone that knew him proved one thing to Lock if nothing else. David Ismay was a man with deep feelings of family pride. With disgrace and ruin facing him, wouldn't that kind of man choose to take the easiest way out?

But if he'd committed suicide then where was the body?

A thorough search of every square yard of Bush Wood had yielded nothing. From the time that he'd said goodnight to his sister on the evening he'd got back from London, nobody else had seen him. Lock wondered whether anyone would again.

Another woman, his other theory? It was still a possibility. Ismay could have planned for months ahead, he could have arranged to meet her near Bush Wood and left his own motorcar deep inside to delay discovery – as indeed it had – while fleeing with her to some unknown destination. True, his sister had treated the merest suggestion as an insult, and undeniably they had been more than close, but that meant nothing. Plenty of times in his career Lock had come across men whose wives and families were shocked to find out that they knew little about them after all. It wouldn't be the first time.

Only one thing spoiled his theory: if Ismay had run away with another woman to avoid detection and disgrace, what was he using for money? Enquiries had proved beyond doubt that no withdrawals had been made from his account at the local bank; no property or bloodstock had recently been sold that hadn't been carefully accounted for. So what was the answer?

It had annoyed him when his own Sergeant had pointed out the obvious answer that he, with all his years of experience, had somehow missed.

'Another bank account. He could have had another bank account. Shall I set the wheels in motion, sir?'

'It could be a hell of a long job; he could have opened one almost anywhere.'

'London, I'd say, was the most obvious place. Where else did he travel to, in the course of business?'

'Ballakeighan, Isle of Man – Liverpool, where he caught the boat.'

'Or anywhere along the route. He's no one's fool, sir.'

'You're telling me. Get on to it, no delays. I want results, and quickly.'

The tea in the tin mug had grown half-cold and he was tired and irritable. The station Sergeant poked his bearded face around the office door.

'Tell young Watson to fetch me another cup of tea!' He rubbed his hand around his face, feeling the day-long stubble of beard. After this lot, he'd have to grab himself a shave. After all, he was down from the Yard and he had an example to set. 'Well, what is it? Are you deaf?'

'No, sir. Please, sir, that young woman's waitin' to see you. Says she won't go until she does.'

Lock and Barnes exchanged glances.

'What young woman?'

'Emmeline Ismay.'

Christabel leaned against the window of the toy shop and pressed her face forwards onto the window pane. She smiled.

Inside, she could see a hand-carved rocking horse, with real horsehair tail and mane, just like the one she and her sisters had had, so long ago in the big old playroom. Dobbin, they'd christened it, and squabbled over which one had the longest ride. There were boxes of toy soldiers with a lifelike fort, and little clockwork toys that you could wind up and that moved all by themselves along the ground. She could see a lifelike monkey, that banged together the tiny cymbals in its hands when you wound the key; a musical seascape automaton, with its model ship tossing in rough seas, the background with a model train crossing a viaduct, all so lifelike. There were huge dolls' houses and furniture for the rooms inside; a clockwork battleship, teddy bears of every size and shape. A keywind musical blacksmith's forge; a toy train, a Noah's ark with pairs of every animal you could think of, exquisitely carved in wood and painted and glazed. She peered in further to the back of the shop.

At the back of the counter, displayed side by side along the rows of wooden shelves, were a variety of china dolls.

She pushed open the door of the shop and went inside.

'I'm very busy, Miss Ismay. What can I do to help you? You're leaving today, isn't that right?'

She leaned against his door.

'To answer your first question, when are you going to send back my brother's car? To answer the second, I'm leaving as soon as I'm finished here.' She let her eyes rest deliberately on the big clock hanging on the wall above his head. 'I have a train to catch, Inspector Lock. Like you, I'm running short of time.'

The insolent little bitch! And after he'd been up all night, slaving through that bloody mountain of statements and papers! For a moment he was speechless.

'Well, have your men finished with the car or not? I want it back.'

'What's the hurry, Miss Ismay? You can't go anywhere in it.'

'Oh, why not? Has someone taken all the petrol?'

'You don't drive, miss, surely?' Barnes burst out.

'Of course I drive! Why shouldn't I? My brother taught me.' Their astonishment amused her. 'There's nothing unusual about women driving motorcars any more. The Duchess of Sutherland drove a Mercedes Simplex 40/45 to a ladies' automobile meeting in London, as long ago as 1904. Besides, we were considered good enough to drive ambulances in the war, weren't we, when there weren't enough men to go round. Why should it be different now?'

'I've never met a lady what drives, anyway,' Barnes said. 'Not an ambulance or a motorcar.'

'Well, you have now.' She looked from his face to Lock's. 'Have you finished with my brother's car or not?'

'Not yet, miss, we haven't. But I reckon it'll be back for you when you get home from Ballakeighan. I wish you luck.'

'With the car or trying to find what happened to my brother?'

'Both, I'm sure. Though I've no need to remind you that when we come across ourselves in a few days' time, I'd be obliged if you'd stay out of our way. Just a friendly warning.'

'You think I might destroy some vital evidence if I found any?'

'I think you're far too intelligent to do that, Miss Ismay. That would make you an accessory after the fact.'

'After the fact of what?'

He could feel his patience stretching into a narrow strand; and yet there was something about her that he couldn't help taking to. Nobody could say that the girl didn't have spunk.

140

'That remains to be seen. Mr Ryan still going with you, then?'

'He is. And I'm more than grateful for his offer of help. A little help is worth a lot of pity. Something our genteel neighbours might think about, if they could bring themselves to peep at the real world from behind their velvet curtains.' There was anger in her voice now. 'People we've known for most of our lives haven't even had the decency to come and call.'

'Ah, that's just human nature, Miss Ismay. I can tell you a lot about that. And a funny thing it is, too. People don't like getting involved in things like this; makes them feel uncomfortable. Don't ask me why – it's just the way it is.'

She opened the door to let herself out before either of them could do it for her.

'I don't suppose it's any use me asking you if you're any closer to finding out what's happened to my brother? Even if you did know something, you wouldn't tell me.'

'I'm sorry. There's no positive news. But I wish you a calm sea journey and a pleasant trip.' He was thinking how striking the girl looked, like a fashion plate for all her talk of driving motorcars and women's rights to do as they pleased. She was wearing a charcoal-coloured gabardine suit over a pale silk blouse, black patent leather ankle boots with silver buckles and gauntlet gloves. Her cloud of dark hair and those astonishing eyes were striking beneath the wide brim of a black and white beaver hat. He suddenly realized that he was staring at her and covered his confusion by standing up. He remembered to ask after her brother's wife.

'She's with me now. I left her looking into some shop window. Harry McCaughan will drive her back.'

'She doesn't mind being all alone in the house while you're away, then?'

'She won't be alone. Most of the men who work for us live nearby, and there are two maids in the house. If she'd wanted to, my Uncle Charles would have come down to fetch her, or even stopped in the house. But she turned down his offer because he hasn't been well himself for the last few years, and I hope not to be gone very long. If she needs to speak to him we have the telephone.'

Outside, walking along the High Street, Emmeline pondered Lock's words. After the scene last night, she was more troubled

141

than she'd admitted to anyone about leaving Christabel alone. Wandering from room to room in the house, her imagination running riot, a prey to all her worst fears about why David had vanished, haunted with memories and ghosts from the recent past. Suddenly, she was overwhelmed by guilt.

There was no sign of Christabel. She had most likely gone into one of the ladies' gown shops, or the new milliners. When Emmeline reached the hotel fifteen minutes before she was due to meet Karl Ryan, she decided to make a telephone call. She opened her black kid handbag and took out Guy Vogel's card; then she lifted the receiver of the hotel telephone and gave his number to the exchange.

The line buzzed and crackled, then clicked, and a strange, heavily accented voice, not Vogel's, came through. She asked to speak to him.

His wife was bound to have recovered, and she would be about Christabel's own age. Why hadn't she thought of this before? He'd said if there was anything he could do to help, they had only to ask him. No better idea than for the Vogels to pay Christabel a few social calls.

The little shop was unexpectedly crowded; but she'd forgotten, of course, that it was only six weeks to Christmas. How silly of her to forget. She'd always loved this time of the year ever since she'd been a little girl, with the fir tree in the hall festooned with pretty decorations, the holly and the mistletoe, the piles of carefully wrapped gifts for her family and friends. She'd loved her first Christmas as David's wife when his parents had been alive, even the first Christmas of the war. But it was all different now. She thought of the old hall standing dark and silent and brooding, and she wanted to cry.

There were laughter and voices all around her as she moved slowly in between the shoppers and the attractive displays, pretending to examine the musical automaton, the clockwork monkey, the workmanship of the hand-carved rocking horse in the window, with its real leather saddle and bridle, horsehair tail and mane, brightly painted, lifelike face. She picked up an animal from the Noah's ark and turned it over in her gloved hand.

The shopkeeper was serving another customer. She put down

142

the wooden animal and edged her way towards the counter, and the row of china dolls behind. Oblivious of the noise and bustle all around her, she stared at each one, so fascinated that she forgot all sense of time, even where she was.

She began edging her way through the crowded shop towards the door now, desperate to leave. There was a couple standing in the far corner examining a dolls' perambulator, whispering and giving her strange looks. No one she recognized. Nobody she knew.

She didn't want to meet anyone who knew the family; prying, probing, insinuating, asking questions about David. Outside the shop she looked almost furtively from left to right, then hurried back to where Harry McCaughan was standing waiting beside the trap.

'Why, there you are, Mrs Ismay ma'am,' he said cheerfully. 'Miss Emmeline's waitin' for you in the White Hart Hotel.'

Without answering she scurried away again, glad that she'd worn a hat with a chiffon veil to hide her face; she imagined that everybody was looking at her, staring, gossiping behind their hands about her and David and the fire.

Gratefully, she caught sight of the hotel sign and hurried towards it, almost colliding with a couple who were coming from a nearby doorway.

She almost burst into the crowded foyer. And there, in front of her, she saw Emmeline and Karl Ryan.

THIRTEEN

EMMELINE WAS SEASICK on the boat going over to Ramsey harbour; but the moment they touched land, she was almost herself again. She had forgotten how glorious the island scenery was at this time of year, when the autumn was so much milder than on the mainland and with the leaves turning wonderful shades of jade and copper, and the rich, diverse mixture of deep wooded valleys and purple-covered peaks, so stark a contrast to the grime and dirt of Liverpool. The clean, sharp air was the perfect antidote to her anxiety and depression.

As they walked side by side towards the horse-drawn cab where the driver was busy loading their two small valises, Karl Ryan gave her a look of concern. 'Are you sure you feel all right? You're very pale.'

'I'll live, I expect.' A ghost of a smile.

He'd cracked a joke about her luggage.

'I thought women never travelled anywhere without humping at least ten trunks apiece, and every one big enough to hold a full-grown mule.'

'Oh, now you're mocking.'

'Yes, I am. But not you.' He helped her into the cab and gave the driver the directions. 'Is this Michael Stranahan expecting both of us?'

'Yes, I sent him a telegram a week ago. You'll like him. I know he'll like you. Please God he can give us news of David.'

'Don't get your hopes up too high, and then have them dashed. He might be as much in the dark as all the rest of us. I hope for your sake he isn't.'

'The police will have been to talk to him already, but he'd never give David away if he knew where he was. He's the kind of man who's always put personal loyalty above the law.'

144

'That's certain to endear him to the police.'

'They'd never find out.'

'Like we said before, they've most likely put a watch on the place.'

'Michael's friendship with my brother was well known all over the island; and his father and ours did a lot of bloodstock business together in the past. We'll have to be careful, that's all.' Another sudden thought. 'They could easily follow us, too, if they think that I really know where David is.'

'It's more than possible, yes.' He smiled. 'We'll just have to be more clever than they are.' He looked around them, from the window of the cab. 'Did you say this was the capital?'

She laughed. The sole hotel and the rows of small, scattered shops seemed pretty but hopelessly provincial compared to the towns back home. But that was the special charm of the little place.

'Wait until we leave the town behind. It's out in the wilds then.'

She hadn't exaggerated. The driver had taken the coast road from Ramsey along towards Maughold's Head, then turned inland towards Onchan, half-way between Douglas and Clayhead. Ryan stared in amazement all around them. The scenery was certainly spectacular; the view from the sweep of Maughold's Bay was one of the most breathtaking that he'd ever seen. But the island, once they'd left the perimeter of the town, seemed largely uninhabited.

'There's a cottage, to the left of the rise,' Emmeline said, almost defensively. 'I told you, there are more people living in the south of the island than there are in the north or in between.'

'I'm impressed,' he said, simply.

'So was my mother's grandfather. You can understand now why he chose this place. He bred some outstanding animals here, in his day. But a lot of people regarded him as an eccentric.'

They fell into a comfortable silence, engrossed in the magnificence of the passing scenery. Unwillingly, he thought of home, of scenery that reminded him sharply of the rolling, autumnal countryside moving before his eyes; of heat and dust, extremes of blinding heat and devastating cold. Alike and yet unalike, for there was no lurking danger hiding here.

He glanced sideways at her. She was becoming impatient now; edgy, drumming her gloved fingers in a tattoo on her lap, sitting

145

forward, willing the distance between them and Onchan to grow less.

They caught sight of Michael Stranahan's large, grey, isolated house at the same time, set against the backdrop of an enormous hill, covered with a dense forest of trees.

She turned to him, her relief and excitement barely suppressed. She was like a greyhound, tense, alert, straining to be let free from its leash.

A figure appeared on the steps leading from the house; their arrival had been seen from the windows. Michael Stranahan, he supposed. They were still too far away to see clearly.

At the gate, she jumped down from the horse-drawn cab and ran away up the drive, shouting and waving her hand.

'Yes, they've been here, Emmeline. They came the day after the fire.' The introductions had been performed, Margaret Stranahan had made a huge pot of strong, steaming coffee while they sat in earnest discussion around the fire. 'Willy Flanagan was the first one over. He rode from Ballakeighan like the devil was after him not long after the fire had started. We'd not long gone to bed. Nobody knows how it started. The lads fought tooth and nail to save the horses, but the heat was too fierce for them to get in to reach them.' Her face was white, completely colourless. She clenched her hands together until the knuckles showed white. She bit her lip. 'They were all in their beds when it first began, the police say in the hayloft. After less than half an hour the blaze could be seen for more than twenty miles. The sky was red with it.'

'What do you think, Michael?'

'He isn't here.' A moment of unbearable silence; all her hopes dashed. 'I'd tell you if I knew anything at all, you know that. The police seemed to think that I knew more than I was letting on, but I soon set their records straight. As David's friend and because his head stud man was killed in the fire, I told them I'd take over temporary responsibility for the horses that were safe and sound.' He looked away from her face. 'There aren't many, Emmeline. Thank God Ballacragan wasn't burned to death in that inferno. That would have broken David's heart.'

She got up, slowly. She went and stood closer to the fire. The flames seemed so unthreatening, so innocuous; her vivid imagination conjured up the scene of that terrible night, the screams of the dying horses as they were burned alive, the men running with buckets of water, helpless, hopeless. The stud itself was no longer important; the buildings meant nothing to her at all. Bricks and mortar could always be rebuilt. It was the lives of the men and the animals that mattered.

'You know already that the insurance company have refused to pay a penny until they're satisfied the fire was an accident. Now that the police here and back in England are virtually convinced that David paid to have it arranged – you can see how their minds work as to his motives – it looks as if the cost of the compensation for the families of David's workers who died and the owners of the mares that were stabled on the stud will have to come out of the estate's pocket. After four years of war, with virtually no profit, you can imagine that that kind of money will take everything we've got: the bloodstock, the stud at home, maybe even the house . . .'

'They haven't proved anything against David! Christ Almighty, everyone on the island knows what kind of man he was!'

She smiled, wanly. The long, tiring journey had taken more out of her than she cared to admit. But she would never give up, never give in to the notion of defeat.

'The money isn't important. All I want to do is to clear my brother's name.'

'Are they saying he's gone into hiding?'

'They think he arranged the fire for the insurance money, then realized that he wasn't going to get away with it. He vanished on the very day Lock and his minion from the Yard intended to come down to question him. In their eyes that's too much of a coincidence. Only his car was found.' She glanced at Karl. 'Karl found it, abandoned in Bush Wood.'

'But their theory doesn't make sense. If he decided to disappear, what would he use for money? If he was guilty of arson or conspiracy to it, what would he gain?'

'That they haven't told me. But they believe it because otherwise their whole case against David would collapse.'

Stranahan got to his feet, angrily. 'The whole idea is crazy! Only a lunatic would believe David could be mixed up in anything like that. The stud was his whole life and always has been, except for the years when he was away at the front getting shot at for his contribution to the war!'

'The police are deliberately keeping me in the dark – what else should I expect? But they said a box of matches had been found close to the scene of the fire, and a five-pound note with some other incriminating items, inside an isolated shepherd's hut here on the island. They traced the serial number and it corresponds with numbers of other notes withdrawn from David's bank account in Epsom. The implication being that the money taken out that day was to pay off whoever started the fire. The money was withdrawn about three months ago, when David was due to pay off all the tradesmen's bills. He likes to settle their accounts in cash. How that one five-pound note got where it was found is something I'd love to find out!'

Stranahan began to pace the room.

'It's a mystery from beginning to end. I can't even begin to understand any of it. But I do know this and I told the police when they came here; I've known David Ismay for more than ten years. And there's no man more honest, loyal, or straight-talking. Straight as a die, that's what I said to 'em. I stand by that. And I reckon I'm a bloody good judge of men.'

Emmeline sighed. She sat down again beside Karl Ryan. 'All the way here – on the boat coming over, driving up to the house – I kept hoping against hope that I was going to find the answer. That you'd tell me David was here. I should have known better.' She stared into her cup of undrunk coffee. 'But I would still have come, even if I'd known that I wasn't going to find him. I owe it to the men who worked for us. I have to talk to the families of the men that died. And the police here. I suppose I shall have to talk to them, too.'

For the first time, Karl Ryan spoke.

'Have the people here any ideas of how this fire got started?'

'Michael?'

He looked uncomfortable, almost shamefaced. 'This isn't easy for me to say, Emmeline, but you might as well hear it from me before you hear it from anyone else. Not everyone knew David as well as I did. After all, he didn't live here among the Manx people. But when the box of matches was found, and then the money in the hut, rumours started flying around. I don't know who started them. I don't even know how they found out. After all, what the local police found was supposed to be highly confidential information, but these things have a way of leaking out.'

'Are you telling me that the local people think David is guilty?'

There was an awkward silence before Stranahan replied, 'You have to understand that the families of the men who died are very bitter. There's no way that that fire could have started on its own, Emmeline. It was deliberate arson. Who and why, as yet, nobody knows.'

She got up.

'It seems I arrived on the island just in time. If Maggie can show me where my room is, I'll go and change into my riding clothes. Let me see Ballacragan, and then I'm going to ride straight over to Ballakeighan and tell them the truth there for once and for all.'

'That wouldn't be a very wise thing to do.'

'Why is that, Michael? Do you think because I'm an Ismay they'll try to lynch me? This is twentieth-century civilization, not the wild west.'

'If you insist on going, I'm coming with you. And we'll take a dozen of my own men.'

'I'm going with her,' Karl Ryan said.

'That's right, Michael. But I appreciate the offer.' She smiled, so that he wouldn't think she was being ungrateful. 'It's better if I go alone, you must see that. If I ride up with you and a posse of your workers, they'll mistrust the Ismays even more than they do already.'

All that way, the car, the train, the boat. The endless, boring hours of travelling, and then nothing. David had never been here at all.

'If you don't want me to come with you is there anything else I can do?'

She smiled, and kissed him on the cheek. He'd always been a good friend to David; and now, against his best interests, to her, too.

'Yes, if you will. Saddle us a couple of good, strong horses. There's a long way to go.'

FOURTEEN

CHRISTABEL WATCHED from the upstairs window as the postman came slowly down the drive on his bicycle, the mailbag strapped firmly in place behind his back. She could see a large, oblong shape outlined against the sacking, and her heart began to beat with excitement. It must be it, the parcel she was expecting from London. How fast and efficiently they'd dealt with her order, made less than a week ago.

Like a child, she watched from her hiding place behind the curtain as he propped his bicycle up against the wall and rang the bell. She saw the front door open and Janet's aproned figure take the parcel from him with the rest of the day's mail, exchange a few pleasantries and a comment about the weather, then the front door closed and he went off along the drive, whistling as he cycled.

She turned and dashed out of the room and down the stairs to the first landing, meeting Janet on her way up.

'Oh, Mrs Ismay, ma'am! The post's just been. Most of it's for Miss Emmeline, as usual; but there's a couple o' letters and this parcel for you.'

'Thank you, Janet.'

She ran back to her bedroom and tossed the letters unopened on the bed. Her hands tore feverishly at the brown paper wrapping that covered the parcel, then pulled away several layers of pink tissue to reveal a long, white box. She held her breath, a feeling of pure pleasure enveloping her that she hadn't experienced since she was a child.

She lifted the lid and there it was, the German bisque doll she had seen in the Derry and Toms catalogue. More beautiful. She reached inside the box and touched the hand-made clothes, marvelling at the delicacy and skill of the stitching and

150

embroidery; she touched the real human hair that had been fashioned into long, glossy, corkscrew curls; its face, so lifelike that from a distance it seemed almost like a real, live child . . .

She left the letters unopened. They were unimportant. She cradled the doll in her arms and, humming softly to it, took it to the nursery on the second floor that she now kept locked.

She opened the door and slipped inside. Nobody was allowed in here now, not even to polish the furniture or to dust. This was her special place, her private sanctuary. None of them would understand. Except David . . .

Emmeline could see the black, burned-out shells of buildings in front of them from the road. Not one, except the stable where the stallion Ballacragan had been kept, was left standing. Curious that that alone had escaped the awful wrath of that devastating fire. To other people's eyes, suspicious.

She understood how they would feel. In their place, she would feel bitter, too. She remembered her own feelings from the past, when the *Lusitania* had been torpedoed and sunk and her mother and father died; the rage, the burning need to have revenge. In her wild grief then any one of them who could have been held responsible would do. The captain who had ignored the warnings of the German U-boats; the navy, the Government, the American President who had refused to enter the war, even though most of the lives that had been lost were the lives of his own countrymen. She could sympathize with the families of David's workers now.

The whole area had been roped off, she could see a group of men standing with the island policemen that Michael Stranahan had told her were still examining the site.

She dismounted and led her borrowed horse towards them, Karl Ryan at her side. Not for the first time, Emmeline was grateful he was there.

'There's bound to be hostility,' he'd said, on the long ride over. 'You have to be prepared for that. Remember, the fire devastated their lives, in more ways than one. It has yours. But when rumours spread, some of the suspicions are sure to stick.'

'I thought they knew my brother better than that.'

They fell silent as she approached. Her eyes searched their faces, some the faces of men she knew, for a sign of amity, a

151

flicker of understanding; she saw none and her heart sank.

'George Sullivan. Henry Stevens.' She smiled. 'It's good to see you again.' Her voice sounded flat, strained, ill at ease. She could have cut the hostile atmosphere with a blunt-blade knife. 'I came as soon as I could; I can't tell you what I'm feeling when I look around and see all this.'

'Miss Ismay.'

Her brain thrashed around desperately to find the right words, but her entire mind was blank.

'What can I say to you', she said at last, 'that hasn't been said already?'

'Joseph Lynch and William Hallagan tried to get in to pull out the mares alive,' Henry Stevens said, in a cold, toneless voice. 'I tried to stop 'em. Flames was too fierce. It was an inferno in there. But neither of 'em would listen. Fought us off, they did. *Mr Ismay's horses are in there*! They was the last words they ever said . . .'

A tear welled up in one of Emmeline's eyes and ran slowly down her cheek. She dashed it away.

'I know what they did. Without any of you even telling me. I know because I know what kind of men they were.' She let her eyes rest on each of them in turn, including the policemen who hadn't yet spoken, but were looking at Karl Ryan suspiciously. 'All of you, too, know what kind of man my brother was. Knowing that, I've no doubt that any ugly rumours you might have heard that link his name with this fire, you'll treat with the contempt they deserve.'

'You were magical, do you know that? You left those flat-footed crushers struck by lightning. They never got a word in edgeways. And your brother's men, yesterday, when you'd finished every one of them was eating out of your hand.'

'Should that make me proud of myself, do you reckon?'

'Stop wearing that hair shirt and give yourself a pat on the back for a change. You deserve it.'

They were walking the horses along the top of the Ballabeg cliffs, side by side. She was hatless and the strong breezes that blew in from the open sea lifted and fanned her thick, shoulder-length hair. It seemed a hundred years ago when David had chided her for cutting it. How shocked Christabel had been! *'Emmeline, how could you? Your beautiful hair!'* They walked on, then paused beside the cliff path leading to the rocky beach.

'That's quite a view. It's a beautiful island. Not what I expected.'

'What did you expect?'

'I don't know, but something different. Not this. There's peace here. Tranquillity. No danger. No wars.'

'That's a strange thing to say.'

'Not really. Where I come from there were always wars: civil wars, private wars. As soon as one stopped then another began. That's just the way it was.' She waited for him to elaborate but he didn't.

'I'm interested. Why don't you tell me more?'

'Like I said once, there's nothing in the past that I want to remember. Most of it I'd prefer to forget.'

He was staring out beyond the headland now, to the sweep of the bay and the undergrowth that covered the steep drop from the cliffs, a haven for island birds and wildlife. She looked at his strong, sun-burned profile, the colour that not even the English climate had been able to fade. She felt a peculiar affinity with him, almost as she'd once felt with David, and yet she still knew so little about him. Somehow that no longer seemed to matter.

'You're very quiet.'

'Thinking, that's all. Just thinking.'

'A penny for your thoughts?'

He smiled at that.

'I was thinking that I'd like to climb down those cliffs, and walk over the big boulders around the bay. Do you want to come?'

She rubbed her hands together briskly. The cold wind made her eyes water.

'Have you seen that drop? It's more than two hundred feet!'

He jumped up and pulled her up beside him.

'Only two hundred? And I thought it was nearer three.'

There was always a special feeling about treading where no man, or woman, has trodden before. The pathway down the steep, rocky cliff face was longer and harder than she'd imagined, but the unexpected exertion lifted all the anger and the depression she'd been feeling, away. Concentrating on securing her footing, she had no time to think about things that she'd rather not think about: the return to England, facing the police, the rumours and speculation, the army of her brother's creditors. She had shut them all out for now. But she knew that none of them would go away. Everything she'd ever loved and believed in was being threatened: her brother's honour; the family's good name; the house she'd lived in all her life, as loved by her as it had been by everyone who'd gone before and left in it something of themselves. Was it all to be for nothing?

For a single split second her attention wandered. She cried out in alarm as her foot slipped. Another moment and she might have been spinning downwards onto the rocky floor below. But Karl Ryan's arms shot out and grabbed her so tightly that she shouted in pain and surprise. For a moment he held her so that she could steady herself; then, inch by inch, he helped her down to the safety of the wide natural shelf in the cliff face several feet below.

'Are you all right?'

'It was all my fault, I'm sorry. My attention was somewhere else.' She looked up into his face and managed to smile. 'Thanks. If it hadn't been for your quick thinking I wouldn't be all in one piece. That'll teach me to go climbing in places I shouldn't go.'

'Are you sure you're all right?' He glanced downwards, down the rough jagged path where she might have fallen. 'You might have broken your neck. Or a few bones.'

'The trouble with me is that I can never resist a challenge. It was a stupid mistake to make.'

'Do you want to go back?'

Carefully, she began to rise to her feet.

'It's safe enough if you take care. Come on.'

At the bottom she picked up stones and began to toss them into the water.

'I always loved doing this as a little girl. David and me. That's how it always was. We used to see whose stone could make the biggest ripples.'

'I'll bet you always won.' He was standing beside her now, watching as she threw the stones.

'It was about fifty-fifty, I think. David used to laugh because I'd never give up. You know the way brothers and sisters fight? We never did. I suppose that's strange, isn't it?'

'Were you always that close?'

'Yes, even after David married Christabel. At first I think she resented me because David and I always did everything together. And she wasn't really interested in the bloodstock; she didn't realize how important a part the stud played in David's life. She wanted to change him. And of course she made the mistake that a lot of women make: she thought she'd succeed.'

'They weren't happy?'

'I didn't say that. David never told me that he wasn't. It was only that last evening, when I had that strange feeling that he wanted to talk, that he needed to tell me something, that the doubts started coming into my mind. I've thought of little else since. I think if they'd had children Christabel would have been in her element; that was all she really wanted to make it all complete. She still hasn't got over her last miscarriage.' He went on watching her throwing her stones.

'What will you do when we get back? If David still doesn't reappear? Sell everything to meet his creditors?'

'I don't think I'll have a great deal of choice.' Her face was set grimly. 'I have to face all David's angry creditors on my own; Delauney says the owners of the mares and foals who died will have to be compensated as soon as possible to prevent multiple lawsuits, something we can ill afford to happen. A string of court cases with all the attendant publicity would be disastrous. The insurance company have refused to pay, so the cost would have to come directly from our own pocket. The effect on the stud finances from such an exodus of cash would be crippling. And fatal. I'd have no choice but to sell.'

'Won't they wait for their money?'

'I doubt it. Most of them are in bloodstock breeding for the money, and the animals they lost can't be replaced. If I know anything about them they won't be satisfied with the mere financial replacement of their lost stock; they'll insist on additional compensation as well. "Potential earnings" they'll label it.'

'What does that mean?'

'That if a breeder loses a champion brood mare, just offering him what he paid for her won't do. He'd argue, probably with every right, that she'd be worth much more than that – exactly how much is going to be the bone of contention. After all, if she

155

bred a foal a year for the next ten years, that would add up to a lot of money, depending on the sire and how many winners she produced. That's what couldn't be replaced.'

'I'm beginning to understand. But can't you tell them all to go to hell?'

She smiled.

'Yes, I could. But it wouldn't do me any good. The breeders would sue for negligence even if the police exonerated us from any blame about the fire. And they probably will sue, unless Delauney can persuade them not to. Do you think any of them would pass up the chance to cash in on our misfortune?'

'They sound like a bunch of bastards to me.' The word had slipped out. So long since he'd been in the company of respectable young women. 'I'm sorry, I didn't mean to say that.'

'Don't apologize, because you're right. They want Ismay blood just like they did at the public enquiry after the *Titanic* sank, and they mean to get it.'

'Is there anything else I could do to help?'

'You've done quite enough already.'

She looked at him with affection. Yes, David would have liked him, too. And Cornelius. It was strange how fate worked, how it brought complete strangers unexpectedly together. But then she could never really think of him as a stranger, even if his father had never known hers all those years ago. He'd replaced David in her life somehow; and she didn't feel that lightly. He was here, now, when she most needed him.

She wanted to change the subject. The fire, David, the stud, the creditors; they were all beginning to weigh her down.

'There's another colonial settler in Epsom, did I tell you? A man called Guy Vogel.'

'Oh?'

'One thing he has plenty of, and that's money. Not surprising since he has gold mines back in South Africa. He has a passion for English thoroughbreds, he told us. David would probably have done some business with him if he hadn't gone away.'

'Is he a friend of yours?'

'Not yet. The night before we left was the first time I'd met him. David mentioned him in passing, but I never took much notice at the time, especially after he said he was vulgar and *nouveau riche*. King Midas, David called him! Maybe that was a

156

little cruel, but he didn't mean it like that. He really is. It's incredible, the inside of his house – everything is gold, gilded. Almost like a shrine. Very flamboyant, of course; startling, overpowering. I wasn't sure whether I liked him at first ... but, like you, he's extended the hand of friendship where people we thought were friends have proved that in times of trouble they don't want to know. Maybe he has a heart of gold, to match his furnishings.'

'He'll find England a lot different to South Africa. What part does he come from?'

'He talked about Klerksdorp, and Cape Town. He seems to have adapted and integrated into the local community very well. Spreading money on impoverished waters hasn't done him any harm, either. He's donated five thousand pounds to repair the Epsom grandstand roof. I expect a few people will talk about him behind his back, but to his face they'll be all politeness and smiles. Money talks.' She stretched. 'His wife doesn't like our climate, though. A pity. She was too ill to come down and meet us.'

'Tell me more about them on the way back.'

'You tell me more about your father. I love hearing about those days.' She smiled and dusted down her clothes. 'Do you know, I've lost all sense of time. We'd better go back now.'

He took her arm.

'Are you sure you're all right? No twisted ankles?'

'I think I can just about manage to scramble back to the top.' She let him help her. She turned and gave a last, sad look all around her, wondering if she would ever see that view again. 'It's so peaceful here. Nobody on earth knows where we are. If only we didn't have to go back at all.'

She knew that something had happened by the expression on Michael Stranahan's face. She stiffened. Her heart beat faster. The perspiration felt wet and sticky in the palms of her hands. Steeling herself, she slipped down from the saddle and slowly began to lead her tired horse back along the drive.

'What is it, Michael?' she asked him before he could speak. And then she saw it at the same time as Karl Ryan. The strange horse-drawn trap at the front of the house; a uniformed policeman standing watching them from the cover of a tree beside the drive.

157

'It's Lock, the Inspector from England,' Michael Stranahan said, as he came towards them. 'He's been waiting here to see you for the last two hours.'

'You've found my brother? You have news about him?' There was an eerie silence in the room, while her eyes searched their faces in vain. No hope.

'Miss Ismay, before we left England further discoveries about your brother came to light. Our enquiries revealed that he'd opened a series of bank accounts, in London and at several provincial banks along the route he'd usually take to come to this island.'

'What?'

'In his own name, granted. But the size of the accounts, and their location, lead us to believe that he'd been planning to leave the country for some time. Significant withdrawals had been made within the last few weeks before he disappeared. So far, none of that money has been traced.'

She felt sick and giddy; spots danced before her eyes. 'I can't believe it.'

'I'm afraid the facts don't lie.' He took a step towards her. 'Did you know, Miss Ismay, of the existence of these bank accounts? Your brother's accountant certainly did not. The revelation came as a complete surprise. Have you any idea, because he hasn't and neither have we, where these enormous sums originated from?'

'Of course I don't! I don't accept any of this!'

'The evidence the local police have against your brother is overwhelming. The box of matches. The five-pound note. A tin containing gunpowder, all found in that shepherd's hut.'

'He didn't put them there! He was at home in Epsom.'

'But he paid the men who did. The day before the fire, witnesses saw three strange men arriving on the Liverpool ferryboat. It was obvious they were all travelling together. We have clear physical descriptions. Yet none of them sought bed and board for that night at any of the hostelries or hotels anywhere on the island. Where did they go? What were they doing? At six o'clock on the morning after the fire they took the ferryboat back again. Petrol and lamp oil were stolen from a local grocery shop only hours before the stud went up in flames ... and one empty oil container has been found buried in the rubble after the fire. I'm sorry, Miss Ismay; the coincidences are too great. Your brother was directly responsible for that fire and the loss of four men's lives. There's so much evidence against him a blind man could see it. A general alert has been put out to place him under arrest . . . as soon as he's found.'

'No!'

'Just a minute,' Karl Ryan said. 'Something here doesn't make any sense to me.'

Lock smiled his detached, professional smile.

'Forgive me, Mr Ryan. But I must point out that this matter has nothing whatsoever to do with you.'

'It has everything to do with me. I found David Ismay's car and his father and mine were friends of many years' standing; that's one of the reasons I'm here now. And after the past few weeks I've come to one or two conclusions of my own. You haven't got any clues to what's really happened, have you? So you need a convenient scapegoat to explain away the fire and David Ismay is the only one you can come up with.

'But tell me this. If David had all that loot stashed away in secret bank accounts – hardly secret if they were opened in his own name – what the hell did he need the stud insurance money for? Tell us that.'

Emmeline had stopped shaking; suddenly, she felt very calm.

'The insurance, Mr Ryan, was far larger than all of the individual bank accounts combined. It was a risk – for him – well worth taking. Men have committed cold-blooded murder for far less. His strategy seems crystal clear now. The accounts were set up along his escape route so that he wouldn't arouse suspicion by withdrawing a large amount of money from his own Epsom bank before he vanished. We might never even have discovered them, but for an idea from my Sergeant.' A glance at Barnes. 'We followed up a single theory, and uncovered far more than we could ever have hoped for. Our next step is to find and arrest those three men.'

'They're automatically guilty because they're strangers? It could just as easily have been someone on the island.'

'The Manx people are a close community, Mr Ryan. Hasn't Miss Ismay here told you that? Where you come from, it might be usual for one man to slit his neighbour's throat without a second thought. But they're more civilized here.'

'If you weren't a policeman I'd take you apart for saying that.'

There was a heavy silence. A piece of charred wood fell noisily onto the hearth from the fire; in his basket across the room Stranahan's dog stretched and yawned in his sleep.

'Miss Ismay,' the voice was softer, more gentle now, 'you may not believe this, but I'm truly sorry to be the bearer of ill tidings. Just another unpleasant part of the job. Someone has to do it. But for the moment, we shan't need to question you any further. I'm satisfied that you, at least, know nothing of these events. But I must leave you with a word of warning. If your brother should attempt to contact you and you were to help him in any way at all, you would be an accessory after the fact.' He paused, to let the enormity of his words sink in. 'I don't need to remind you of what the consequences of that would be.'

She waited until he'd reached the door before she answered.

'Whatever they are, I would never betray my brother. But then I think you know that already.'

He looked back at her. There was despair in her face as well as defiance. Yes, he felt sorry for her. Right from the beginning he'd had no option but to admire her loyalty and her guts; pity that no-good brother of hers had left her high and dry to shoulder all his responsibilities. He didn't deserve her. But even presented face to face with almost incontrovertible evidence of his guilt, she still chose to believe that he was innocent. That was the tragic part.

He said, 'Goodbye, Miss Ismay. I wish you a pleasant journey home.'

It didn't surprise him that she did not answer.

'Michael, I need to be alone. I have to be, just for a little while. Before we go back.' She felt herself falling, her strength draining away. 'I'll saddle up Ballacragan and ride up to the top of Fairy-kell Peak. I can think up there.'

'Ballacragan? You can't use him like a saddle horse.'

'Why not? Stallions need a good strong gallop as much as any other horse. That's what they were made for. Besides, what difference does it make? It'll most likely be my last chance to ride him. When the creditors meet he'll have to be sold like everything else we have to pay off all the debts.'

160

Stranahan knew her too well to try to argue.

'Won't Karl go with you?'

She looked at him and smiled, sadly.

'There are some things that I can only work out alone.'

She spent the remaining days on the island, restlessly roaming alone, trying hopelessly, desperately, to find some reason for the fire. And failed.

The small boy stayed where he was, peering out at her from behind the clump of trees, while she sat on the grassy knoll with her hair blowing out behind her in the strong wind. She was holding a piece of twig in her hands; breaking pieces off and flinging them into the air. A few feet away, the black stallion, reins knotted and hanging loose across his neck, cropped at the thick, lush grass with relish.

It was only when the boy's tiny shadow fell across the ground that Emmeline turned, startled to find that she wasn't alone.

He stared at her with wide, round eyes.

'Well, who are you?'

Nervously, he stuck his hands in his trouser pockets. He mumbled his name and kept stepping backwards.

'I'm Emmeline Ismay.'

His eyes suddenly brightened.

'Th-th-th-they s-set your stables o-on f-f-f-fire, didn't th-th-they?'

'Yes, they set them on fire.' She turned her head and looked down to the steep incline in front of her, where the peak rolled away to the valley below. Savagely beautiful.

'It w-w-was the G-G-G-Germans.'

'Wicked men. Evil men.'

'Th-they gone n-now, haven't th-th-they?'

She smiled. Poor little Manx boy, with his nervous twitch and painfully laboured speech. She thrust a hand in her pocket and found a coin for him. He stared at it as if he was hypnotized.

'You're a long way from home, aren't you? Does your mother know where you are?'

He went on staring at the coin, then back up into Emmeline's face.

'I must be going now, too.'

161

FIFTEEN

IT WAS NIGHT before they reached home. The journey had seemed endless. As they drove along the winding approach towards the house, Emmeline could see the lights from the downstairs windows twinkling through the wall of trees.

Everyone had heard the sound of Karl Ryan's motorcar. She caught sight of the men clustered in a group together in the courtyard; Janet and Winifred stood side by side on the steps outside the front door.

'Please, come in with me. Please stay with us for dinner. It's been a long way for both of us.'

He smiled.

'I know that. But I think you need to be alone the first evening back. You have to explain what's happened to Christabel.' He got out and unstrapped her single valise of luggage. 'If you need me, you know where I'll be.' He kissed her lightly on the cheek. Then he was gone.

She stood there, oblivious of them watching from behind her, as the car reversed and went back along the drive. As it took the corner, he turned and waved, and she somehow moved her wooden limbs enough to wave back. The sound of the engine grew fainter, then faded into silence.

She turned and walked back towards the house.

'You didn't do it!'

'How could I? It was far too great a risk. Someone could have been watching, they might have seen me. Stranahan was with us nearly everywhere we went; I had a suspicion that the police might have her followed, just in case she knew where Ismay was and led them to him. I couldn't take that big a chance.'

162

Vogel lay back in the huge leather buttoned chair; he lit a cigar and began to draw deeply on it. 'You had enough time with her; couldn't you have made some other opportunity?'

'I already told you, it was impossible. If it hadn't been then I would have done it. But if anything had happened to her the one time we were on our own, it would have looked suspicious.'

'All right, I know I can take your word for it. Always better to leave a job rather than bungle it. You know what you're doing. And the price to pay if you make a mistake.' A sly smile. 'It's just that if you'd been able to get her out of the way it would have made the path to Christabel Ismay smoother.' He got up languidly and went over to the fire. He flicked the ash from his cigar into the hearth. 'Do you know, I'd swear that woman's wandering in her mind. I went over there, like I promised Ismay's sister, and got her talking. She let drop quite a few very interesting things. Like who inherits the business if Ismay doesn't turn up. She seemed perfectly normal when I first arrived. She talked, offered me sherry. Then it was like a curtain had come down and she was different, some other person. If I had just her to deal with, the whole thing would be a piece of cake. But it's the other one that bothers me, more's the pity. Still, more ways than one to skin a cat. It wouldn't surprise me in the least if all this sent Christabel Ismay off her head.'

'Is that any wonder, after everything she's been through? And with the news that the police have put out a warrant for his arrest, she'll go through more.'

'You don't feel sorry for her? Not you, of all people! All her life she's been cossetted and pampered; she's never even had to think for herself. No backbone.'

'That isn't her fault.'

'Pity, from you?'

Karl Ryan was standing at the window. He stared out, downwards across the lawns that lay in darkness except for the thin, golden shafts of light that came from the downstairs rooms of the house. There was no moon, but he could see the ghostly white outlines of the classical statues, glowing like phosphate in the dark.

'No, not pity. There's no pity left inside me any more. I just don't like waging war on women, that's all.'

'Oh, I wouldn't call it that; aren't all women a means to some end? Besides, remember that the female of the species is often deadlier than the male. Christabel won't be left destitute by this. Some distant branch of the family are bound to come along and take her in, *noblesse oblige*, when the scandal's died down. And it will. She'll spend the rest of her life wondering what happened to her husband if no one finds him, and being grateful for the roof over her head. But the other one . . . now what happens to her is something I find a fascinating subject.' Ryan made no movement, no response. 'When Ismay's creditors have finished picking all the meat off the business's bones, there won't be much left over for her: not even a horse to put a saddle on. But a girl with looks like that, even with the name Ismay, can still take her pick. If only I wasn't married already!'

Ryan didn't laugh at the joke.

'How long do you want me to keep up this charade, Vogel?'

The other man's sharp, pale eyes gave him a long and penetrating stare.

'What's all this, Karl? Not getting cold feet, are we? Because if you were, well, that wouldn't be very good for your father's health, now would it? But then I don't need to remind you.'

Ryan was familiar enough with danger at close quarters to recognize the scent of it now. He forced himself to smile.

'You've misunderstood me. Like I said, I just don't like waging war on women.' He looked straight into Vogel's eyes without blinking. 'And it isn't my style, playing chaperone and guardian angel. I told you that before, remember?'

Safe ground again now; Vogel smiled and walked across the room to pour himself brandy. 'Of course, but who else could keep their ear to the ground with the Ismay girl and pass for genuine like you? Well, you're half genuine; can you see Oortman doing it, or Kraal?' He let out a loud, coarse guffaw. 'She'd see through them in two minutes. No, you stay exactly where you are until I say it's time to bow out.'

Pieter Kraal turned up the wick of the oil lamp and then set it down carefully on the floor while he found the right key. It took his big, calloused, clumsy fingers several minutes to locate the right one because they all looked alike to him and he could never remember whether the key to the undercroft was the fourth or the sixth one on the right. He cursed when the first key he tried was the wrong one. But after several more minutes the door was open and he was walking heavily down the steep, winding stone steps, the oil lamp held high above his shoulder.

When he reached the bottom he began walking along the wide stone passageway that ran parallel to the old cellar, at the end of which was a heavy, iron-studded door. When he reached it he pounded it with his enormous fist and called out a few words in Afrikaans. It creaked open.

'Vogel wants you, upstairs,' he said in the same language to the man who opened it. 'He's waiting in the gun room. Now.'

His companion grunted an answer and went away.

Kraal put down the oil lamp and rubbed his hands together. Christ, it was enough to freeze a man's arse off down here! He cursed again. He hated England, the cold and the damp that got into the very marrow of your bones and made every one of them ache as if you were an old, arthritic man. He wondered how long they'd have to stop here, while the boss man upstairs played out his crazy little charade, acting the role of an English country gentleman and settling old scores. He spat on the flagstone floor. Only a madman would want to live in a mausoleum like this, stuffed full of meaningless ornaments and fancy pictures, in a country where it never stopped raining and a man was lucky to get a sight of the sun once a month.

But Vogel had always paid his men well. Sooner or later when his twisted mind was sated and he'd tired of playing his little game, he'd sell up and go back to Cape Town, to the big, sprawling colonial house that his father had built fifty years ago with the gold from his Klerksdorp mines.

A low, agonized groan suddenly disturbed Kraal's thoughts. For a few minutes he stood there and listened; then he picked up the lamp and shuffled down the passageway until he came to another door. There was a small, grilled window in it, and he pushed back its wooden cover roughly and peered through.

The tiny, windowless room had been the cell where erring novices were sent for penitance by the Mother Abbess. There had once been a miniature altar at the far end, undecorated except for an altar cloth of gold and a single crucifix; but it was completely empty of furniture now. From the stone block wall, someone had fixed a pair of medieval leg irons of the closed shackle type, and the man who lay semi-conscious on the icy floor had long since become almost oblivious of their tortuous pain.

Kraal's eyes gradually became accustomed to the darkness.

The shackles had been placed upon his legs and then hammered shut. Each one weighed more than fourteen pounds, making it impossible for him to escape ... even if he was able. But his racked, beaten body, covered with bruises and open wounds thickly encrusted with dried blood, had long since been incapable of any movement; all he could do now was breathe.

Kraal snapped the grille shut again. It was no concern of his what Vogel did, or why. He'd have his reasons. But Kraal felt faintly uneasy because this wasn't the wilds of South Africa where a man might do what he would to his enemies or those he reckoned had injured him, with virtual impunity. In the bush a man could make his own laws.

This was England; and the man who lay in a broken mess of cracked bones and torn, bloody flesh was well known in these parts, and the police all over the country were running round in circles looking for him. Having the policemen from the village knocking on the door was getting a little too close for comfort.

He heard the sound of his companion coming back again. The wick in the lamp was beginning to give off smoke, and he adjusted it, swearing beneath his breath when it went down too far and almost went out.

The other man spoke in Afrikaans.

'Vogel says it's time that he was moved.' He jabbed a finger in the direction of the grilled door. 'He still won't talk ... everything we've done to him, and he still won't talk. He's a tough bastard, I'll give him that.'

'He won't last much longer. He's been like that for three days.'

'He'll talk. We're taking him to the castle; that's our orders. He won't last out there. No man could.'

They walked back along the passageway together, one behind the other because of its narrowness.

'What is it that he won't say, that Vogel wants to know?'

The other man shrugged.

'There's only one thing that'd make him upstairs mad enough to break a man's body apart. Have you forgotten what happened to Kathleen van der Louew and her lover fifteen years ago?'

'That's only hearsay, we never worked for him then.'

166

They were at the foot of the winding stone steps now; light gleamed from the bottom of the door from above.

'No, but we both know men who did.'

SIXTEEN

THERE WAS NO SIGN of Christabel. She put down her valise and looked around the empty hall.

'Oh, Miss Emmeline, I'm so thankful you've come back!'

'Where's Mrs Ismay, Janet?'

'That's it, miss. She's had the pair of us worried sick! Locked herself in that nursery, she has. She's asked for all her meals there. Neither of us is allowed to go inside, not even to clean and dust. Mrs Ismay's orders. Winifred or me have to take her her meals on a tray and leave it outside the door.' Janet was working herself up into a state of agitation. 'It's Mr Ismay goin' missin' what's done it, miss. It's the grief that's turned her brain . . .'

Emmeline marched in the direction of the stairs.

'Don't be ridiculous, Janet. Let me go up and see.'

She ran towards the staircase and then up it, leaping the steps in twos and threes. Christabel's bedroom was empty; a small fire flickered in the grate. The curtains were drawn across the windows, the bed turned down. Emmeline ran on, up to the second floor until she reached the door of the old nursery. For a moment she listened. Then she tapped lightly on the door and turned the handle to go inside. But it was locked.

'Christabel? Christabel! It's me, Emmeline. I'm back.'

There was a single moment of silence; then she heard the sound of the key being turned in the lock on the other side. When the door came open and she looked in, she received one of the biggest shocks of her life.

There were dolls everywhere. Large ones, small ones; dolls with exquisitely made Victorian costumes and dolls with modern clothes. Dolls with fair hair, dolls with dark hair. Dolls dressed as babies, dolls dressed as children. They were propped up along the mantelshelf and on the window ledge; one sat on the nursing chair, another on the rocking horse. On the couch across the room there were dozens more.

Slowly, her astonished eyes came and rested on her sister-in-law's face.

'They're beautiful, aren't they? I wish David could see them.' She was holding one in her arms. 'This is my special one, my special baby doll. Can you see how fine the stitching is on this Christening gown? It's all hand-embroidered, Emmeline. And feel her hair. It's so soft . . .'

'Christabel, where did you get all these? Where have they come from?'

'I bought them.' Emmeline watched in wordless astonishment as Christabel kissed the doll on its cheek, then bent down and laid it gently in the empty cradle. Away on the island for more than three weeks and she never even asked a single word. No questions about the fire, about David. As if none of it mattered any more. She went on staring around her in numb astonishment.

'What's happened to you? Why have you done all this?'

Christabel came over to her and put her arms around Emmeline's neck. Her eyes were bright. Her face was full of barely suppressed excitement, like a child's.

'It's for the baby. They're all for the baby.' Happily, she smiled. 'I only found out after you'd left for Ballakeighan. Emmeline, I'm going to have David's child . . .'

'Christabel, that's wonderful! Why didn't you send me a telegram to say? And why have you shut yourself up here without a fire?' She held the icy hands in hers. 'Come down, where the fire is, I've so much to tell you.'

Christabel suddenly seemed to revert to something of her former self.

'You didn't find David, did you?'

'No.'

'Michael Stranahan?'

'David hasn't been on the island. If he had Michael would have been the first to know. It was just a shot in the dark, anyhow.'

'What about the police?'

Emmeline sighed. She leaned wearily against the door. Then she explained to Christabel about the bank accounts.

'Nobody knows where the money could have come from. I've been through every account book and every ledger line by line

169

and I can't find a single clue.'

Christabel's grey eyes took on a strange, vacant look.

'Did he win it by gambling?'

'David? Gambling?'

'Where else could it have come from?'

'Christabel, do you understand what all this means? You do know what I'm saying, don't you? The police have proved that the fire was started deliberately, and they think David arranged for it to be done. As soon as they release their findings to the press, the whole story will be splashed across every newspaper in the country. The creditors are demanding that their losses be met; the insurance company won't pay out because it was arson.' She paused, so that everything she said could sink in. 'There's no way we can stay here, Christabel. We have no choice but to sell everything and go.'

'*No!*'

'If we don't, the creditors will only declare us bankrupt and take everything we have in any case. Let's do it with some vestiges of dignity. That's about all we have left now.'

'This is David's house! My child's house!' Her voice grew to a shout. 'My child will inherit this house one day, whatever anybody tries to do. And no one else will ever live in it!'

'We have to face reality whether we like it or not. I'll have to telephone Uncle Charles and contact Delauney in the morning. He can call a meeting of all the creditors and we'll do a deal.' Christabel was scowling at her. 'And let's face it, this house is far too big for just the two of us, you must see that. Ever since the war we've gone on fighting, struggling to make the bloodstock business pay against gigantic odds. If David was still here and the fire had never happened then we could have pushed on, and won. But all that's changed now. It's no use fighting against impossible odds.'

'I *won't* go! If they try to make me leave I'll lock myself in here and barricade the door.'

'There's no point in trying to talk to you when you're like this. I'll go back downstairs.'

She was half-way along the landing when Christabel rushed out of the nursery and shouted after her from the top of the stairs.

'You could borrow the money to go on!'

She stopped.

'No bank would lend it to us. And what could we use as collateral, except the house? Look at the state it's in. People don't want to live in houses like this any more. It belongs in the past.' The words were like bile in her mouth. 'Look around you, open your eyes. It's 1919, not the end of the last century. All around us there's been a huge spate of building; the whole place is changing.' She ran a hand through her hair in frustration. 'I know how you feel. I feel that way too. I was brought up in this house and I've lived all my life in it; I love it like I love my family. Like the horses it's a part of me that I'll never forget. And I don't want to. But it's no use, Christabel. We have to sell or be forced out. I'd never let it come to that.'

She went away down the remaining stairs, went into the drawing room where there was a fire and sat down in a chair. Christabel came in so quietly behind her that she jumped when she suddenly heard her voice from the doorway.

'Guy Vogel came to see me while you were away.'

'Yes, I asked him if he'd cared to call, with his wife. Since we'd already met him and dined with him, I thought Mrs Vogel would make pleasant company for you while I wasn't here.'

'I didn't meet her, she's still not well.'

'I'm sorry to hear that.'

'He's buying some bloodstock from a London-based company, to start a racing stable. He asked my advice about bloodlines – not that I was able to be of much help. I told him to wait until you came back, and ask you instead.'

In spite of everything, Emmeline managed a weary smile.

'So he wants to buy himself a Derby winner! He thinks that the more he pays the better he'll get. Does he know anything about horses at all? And I don't mean the ones he uses to carry the ore up from his mines. What was the name of the company? If they think he's a novice with money to burn they'll fleece him for everything they can get!'

'I don't remember the name, just that he was buying from them.'

'He'd better take care until he knows just who he's dealing with. Why doesn't he use a local bloodstock agent?'

'I don't know that. Why don't you ask him yourself? I knew you were coming back today so I invited him and his wife for dinner tomorrow night. You don't mind, do you?'

171

'No, of course not. Why should I?'

Christabel came further into the room and walked towards the fire. The leaping flames cast shadows on her pale face.

'He invited us first; so I thought it was only polite to return the invitation. But I didn't really like to. Compared to The Hermitage, it seems too cold and shabby here.'

'Vogel has more money than we do.'

'Yes, I know that. But I still feel so awkward. I can't help it.' She began fiddling with her hands. 'I expect his wife has the most beautiful clothes —'

'You and I are not exactly beggarly in that department. David always made sure of that.'

'I know that, too. But a millionaire's wife . . . she probably has the most wonderful collection of jewellery.'

'I've no doubt she has; but that doesn't necessarily make her happy. Think about it. She hates the climate and always feels ill. After living all her life in Cape Town this cold must seem like purgatory, and she's probably homesick as well. Can you really envy a woman like that? She was there at the functions that David went to, but that was way back in the summer when the weather was warm. From what I've heard, she hasn't even been seen in Epsom since then. Not much of a life, wouldn't you say?' She got up and went over to the door.

'Where are you going now?'

'To telephone Uncle Charles before the exchange closes down for the night. Straight after the Vogels have left tomorrow, I have to get ready to go and see him.'

'But why? Can't you say what you have to say on the telephone?'

'No, I can't. I must talk to him face to face.'

SEVENTEEN

SINCE EARLY MORNING, snow had been falling steadily all day long; now, as night approached, Emmeline could no longer see where the drive that led up to the house began or where it ended; everywhere was a blanket of white.

She had only been to the Ismay house at Hazelbeech Hall three times in her life: after the sinking of the *Titanic*, after the 1913 Derby, and when her parents had died. This time was her fourth and she was here because of yet another disaster: the disappearance of her brother, David. The story had broken in the press on the morning that she and Karl Ryan had left Epsom in his six-cylinder Delauney Belleville to motor up to Northamptonshire, and when they'd stopped to buy newspapers on the way she was glad that they'd decided to travel by car rather than by train: alongside the pictures of David there were photographs of her, too. When they'd broken their journey at a remote little inn thirty miles from Charles Bowyer Ismay's house, she'd pulled down the veil on her hat and let Karl Ryan do all the talking, while she sipped hot punch in a corner and kept her head well down in case she was recognized.

Though it was bitterly cold and the snow began to fall faster and thicker when they resumed their journey, she was grateful for it; she could turn up the huge shawl collar of her fur coat and be swamped in total anonymity.

The house was a blessed haven of peace and quiet; the servants unobtrusive; Charles Bowyer Ismay's wife was away visiting her sister. Instantly he had made them both welcome, though he rarely received visitors and entertained even less.

The first thing Emmeline noticed when they arrived was the pile of newspapers: at the bottom the stories of the weeks before; at the top that very morning's sensational revelations about

David. Steeling herself for the worst, she'd flopped into the nearest chair and flicked through them one by one.

The *Herald* merely stated that the police wished to question David about the suspicious circumstances surrounding the fire; *The Times* and the *Tribune* both made heavy weather of the fact that he'd vanished at a crucial time. The others had published various family photographs, accompanied by several paragraphs of wild speculation, and a guarded rehash of old family history. Emmeline wilted. Everything up until this moment had been a private affair, known only to a mere handful of people; now it had burst starkly onto every breakfast table in England. She wanted to crawl away and hide.

Nobody who read the stories and the speculation would ever understand, none of them could possibly know the truth; they would read what was printed and believe everything, not questioning a single word. It was there in their newspapers so it must be true. None of the faceless millions knew David, none of them would know that he could never be guilty.

Even when Karl Ryan and Charles Ismay had sat down, she went on pacing restlessly around the room. She refused the glass of brandy he held out to her.

'I can't swallow, eat or drink a thing. I feel sick. Helpless. Angry because there's nothing I can do. I had to get away, besides wanting to talk to you face to face. I wanted Christabel to come with us but she wouldn't hear of it; she refuses to so much as leave the house. Ever since I told her we had no choice but to sell, she's been threatening to barracade herself in her room if anyone tries to force her out.'

'David's disappearance has taken a terrible toll with her. I wish she'd come to us when this first started, before Florence went visiting. She could even have gone with her. It would have done her a power of good.'

A moment's hesitation.

'She's going to have a child again.'

That had surprised him.

'But I thought the doctor advised to wait for at least another year?'

'Yes, he did. But Christabel wouldn't listen. She's clinging to this like a drowning man clings to a raft. It's the only link she has with David.'

'If we'd known about this a week ago, she could have come here with you, before Florence went visiting.'

'Christabel refuses to leave the house and she won't listen to reason.'

'But with the insurance company refusing to pay out what other choice do you have left but to go? God knows I'd help you out of this if I could –'

Emmeline managed to smile.

'I didn't come here for that. I needed a bolt hole, a place to run to and hide. I want what's left of our family around me; seeing you and being here is such a comfort somehow.'

'You both always have a home here with us; you know that goes without saying.' He turned to Karl Ryan. 'So your father worked for the Merritt Bloodstock Company when Cornelius was there? My, that takes me back a few years now. It must have been quite a shock to have travelled all this way and thousands of miles to find that – well, not to find what you expected to.' He glanced up at Emmeline, who was standing gazing from the window into the park. 'I miss Cornelius, and Rebeccah, too. The war ruined so many innocent people's lives. Tell me about your father.'

'He's been dead a few years now, like the rest of my family. Not that I ever stayed in one place too long.' He gave a rough, sketchy account of the past few years. 'When you're on your own, one place is pretty much like another. You have no roots, nothing to hold you any more. You drift, like a piece of wood in a river; you never know exactly where it is that you'll end up. But I always wanted to see England.' A silence. 'And even though nothing has worked out quite as I'd envisaged it, I'm glad I came in time to be of some help to Emmeline.'

Charles Ismay nodded. He was still unsure of the kind of relationship that existed between Cornelius's daughter and the tall, dark, young Rhodesian, but the easy way they talked together and the lack of formality between them made it obvious to him that it had become a close one. He liked Karl Ryan. And it was good to talk about Cornelius's youth with the son of a man who'd been close to him in those days.

'I remember he had a ring, a sort of signet ring – two horses' heads in silver, twined together. Funny, as a boy I used to look at that ring and wish that I had one just like it.'

175

'He never took it off; I remember it well. He wouldn't even take it off to clean it. It was his father's, I think.'

'My father hadn't seen him for years, when he came over to America on bloodstock business, and he looked him up. That was the first time I ever saw him. And the scar he had on his cheek; that fascinated me. I longed to ask him how he got it, but my mother told me not to be so bad mannered. I did ask him, when she wasn't there. And he told me the story. I suppose I felt a sort of hero worship for him then. If only I'd known that I wasn't going to see him again.'

Emmeline had come back from her place at the window. It was getting dark now. She'd started to worry again about Christabel, even though Janet was there. She wanted to tell Charles Ismay about the dolls, but it somehow didn't seem to be the right time.

'When we go back I'll have to face Delauney and listen all over again to his doom-laden prophecies about David's creditors. I told him to call a meeting of all of them and put our cards on the table. It's the only way. Prolonging the agony isn't going to help anyone. Me, Christabel, the men in the yard. I feel as if I'm responsible, as if I've let them all down. They'll all get good references and as much compensation for the loss of their jobs as we can afford, but it won't be nearly enough.'

'Emmeline, it isn't your fault. And you can't take the weight of the whole world on your own shoulders. No one can. And the men will be the first people to understand. They all know you've got no choice.'

'Yes, I realize that. But it still doesn't stop me feeling guilty.' At last, she sat down. Her limbs and body ached, the long journey had taken more out of her than she knew. 'By the way, when you were on service in Africa, did you ever come across a man by the name of Guy Vogel?'

'Africa's a very big place!'

'The name means nothing to you?'

'Is it important?'

'A South African millionaire called Vogel has settled just outside of Epsom. Millionaires aren't as common as ordinary men, even in Africa.'

'Where does he come from?'

'Cape Town. He has gold mines at a place called Klerksdorp. David met him a few times when he and his wife first came to

176

England. He's a blatant *nouveau riche*, trying to buy himself into the local gentry and the Jockey Club. Flamboyant, vulgar, a bit rough around the edges, with terrible taste in furnishings. You should see the inside of his house – if you can call it a house. It's the old Abbey on the other side of Bush Wood, and he's paid a fortune to have it refurbished and modernized. Electric lighting in every room. That impressed even Christabel. Since we accepted his invitation to dinner she hasn't stopped talking about it.'

'You don't like him.'

'I didn't say that. Nobody would say he was top of the social graces, but he has a kind of rugged charm. At least he's sincere. Ever since our troubles started he's the only neighbour in miles to have anything to do with us.'

'That's the one good thing about troubles that I've learned. When you get them you find out who your friends really are.'

'I already have.'

'And the stud, we need to talk about that. You said on the telephone that Ballacragan and some of the mares were being shipped back.'

'Yes.'

'He must be your most valuable piece of bloodstock. No point in standing him at Epsom, if you're going to be forced to sell. I know what he meant to David, and that if David was here now he'd want to do all he could to hang on to him. If you can get him valued, then I'm willing to buy – no, hear me out. I don't keep a large stable these days, but when all's said and done he's a full brother to my Craganour. I'd like to think we can keep him in the family if we can.'

'You don't have to do this –'

'But I want to, Emmeline. I want to do it. And who knows what phoenix will rise again from the ashes. Because everything looks black now it doesn't mean it'll always be that way. You have to keep believing in yourself, that in the end everything will be all right and you'll win through.'

She looked at him. Behind the lines of illness that were deeply etched in his face, he was still a handsome man. At the moment he reminded her so much of her father that she wanted to break down and cry like a little girl and she wanted him to comfort her.

'If you're sure. If you're really sure, then you can have him. I'd rather he went to you more than anyone else in the world. Selling him to some stranger, to a company who just regard him as another of their assets – I don't think I could bear that. If I can salvage just one thing from all this wreckage then I think I could muster up the strength to go back and face them all.'

Emmeline lay in the great satin bed when the rest of the house was sleeping, unable to fall into sleep herself. Her throat felt taut and dry, and there was a sharp stinging feeling behind her eyes because the tears that she needed to shed wouldn't come.

She thought about the disbanding of a hundred years' toil and achievements, the loss of the house she'd grown up in and loved. Only memories of what had once been would be left. She'd fought to the last, and her father had always told her that there was no point in going on with any fight you weren't sure of winning.

Snow on the branch of a tree glinted in the moonlight beyond the window. Strangely, she felt a curious kind of peace wash over her, now that what she had to do was fair and clear. There was no going back.

She thought of Christabel, then David, then Karl Ryan, before she finally closed her eyes and slept.

EIGHTEEN

THE STEEL BARREL of the gun glinted coldly in the harsh sunlight as Vogel held it up and lay it against his shoulder, pointing it with deft precision at the stag's head positioned on the wall several feet from the door. When the door opened, Oortman jumped and stepped back suddenly, as he found himself confronted by the sight of a double-barrelled army rifle pointing straight at his head.

He let out an exclamation of surprise and Guy Vogel burst into laughter.

'It isn't loaded, *domkopf*!' He lowered the barrel, then let his hand run across the fine silver work along the hand-carved butt. 'They knew how to make guns in those days – works of art, every one a creation of individuality.' He went on fingering it, lovingly. 'Beautiful. And deadly. What more could a man ask of a weapon than that?'

'Mr Vogel,' Oortman said, his small, suspicious eyes still on the gun, 'De Witt's here.'

Vogel glanced up.

'Then send him up to me.'

A box of cleaning materials lay open on the bare scrubbed table in the centre of the room. Vogel picked up a square of fine cloth and began to polish the steel barrel. He paused every now and then to breathe on it, then rebuff it to a deeper shine. When the door opened for a second time he went on with what he was doing. 'You've taken your time in getting here. How long since you got back?'

Karl Ryan closed the gun room door and leaned against it. 'The snowfall was heavy up there. The journey back took an extra three days.' He walked over to the table and sat down on the edge of it. 'Well, you got what you wanted in one way . . . she's selling. But not the stallion.'

Vogel instantly stopped what he was doing.

'What are you talking about?'

'She's selling it to her uncle, Charles Ismay. How the rest is going to be divided up is anyone's guess. She could sell it piecemeal at an auction, or she could sell the lot to a private buyer. Before we left she spoke to Ismay's lawyer on the telephone, and asked him to call a meeting of her brother's creditors. When their individual claims have been sorted out and agreed on, she'll make a decision about what she intends to do.'

Vogel's small, deep-set eyes were unnaturally bright; the freckles stood out against his skin.

'I wanted that bloody stallion with all the rest of it! Couldn't you change her mind?'

'It was her uncle who offered to buy.'

'Damned bloody Ismays, all tarred with the same brush. When I think of that bastard Cornelius . . .' His hands tightened around the gun. 'And while you were away, I made special journeys over to the house to see Ismay's wife, so that I could plant the seeds about the company. I had to watch every word. Even a woman as hare-brained as she is would get to wondering if I mentioned them too many times. But I think the thought's sunk in.'

'Does it really matter so much about the horse?'

An angry scarlet flush had spread from Vogel's neck to his face.

'It was his, and I wanted it. Just like I'll have everything else. I swore I'd break the Ismays and I'm already more than half-way to doing it! A pity about Cornelius; a pity my father never knew. Maybe he's looking down now and he can see it all. I'd like to think he is, somehow. Not that I ever believed there was any God up there sitting on a throne and dispensing justice. In this life you have to do it yourself.' Slowly, he turned his attention back to cleaning the gun. 'Do you know when the Ismay girl's next going to talk to that London lawyer?'

'No, but soon. I'll get word to you.'

'Good. When he shows her the offers for the business from the three main contenders, she'll be spoiled for choice, won't she?' He started to laugh, very softly. 'Like I said before, there's more than one way to skin a cat.'

'What about your wife? She still knows nothing; you haven't even let her see the local papers. You can't keep her out of the way indefinitely otherwise people will start to talk.'

'I'll deal with Adeline in the way I think fit. She's to be kept in the dark for as long as I say so. Besides, you're forgetting: like you she knows why she has to keep her mouth shut.'

For the second time, Ryan fell silent, stifling his resentment and anger; long before this he'd become prey to an uncomfortable conflict of loyalties, and he baulked against what Vogel was forcing him to do. While Vogel went on talking his mind went back over the twenty-five years of his life and he realized that there was nothing in any of them that he was proud of or wanted to remember, except for the past few weeks since he'd been in England, ironically the last place on earth that he'd wanted to come.

He recalled arguing with Vogel, remonstrating that somebody else would do the job so much better, that after all the years spent as a mercenary in the African bush or a rich colonial's private army, playing chaperone to a young well brought-up English girl was just not his style. But Vogel had overridden all his objections. And because of Vogel's vice-like hold over him he had no choice but to do what he was told.

Vogel had the best reasons for everything. None of his other men were suitable, he'd said: they were all too rough, too raw, too crude, completely lacking in all the social graces; the girl – and the police – would have seen through them in an instant. In that, at least, he'd had to concede reluctantly that Vogel had been right. Sending an oaf like Kraal, or Oortman to find David Ismay's car instead of himself would have courted certain disaster from the start. Vogel had told him that he was the only one capable of carrying off the elaborate deception, and he'd proved now that he knew what he was talking about.

The one thing Karl Ryan hadn't bargained for was that almost from the beginning he'd felt a strong attraction towards the girl.

She was striking, beautiful to look at; but he'd been involved with beautiful women before back in South Africa and plenty of other places without even being tempted to feel anything for them except lust. He'd left them without a backward thought, impervious to their tears, not caring whether he hurt them or not. But from the start the relationship that had grown up between him and Emmeline Ismay was completely different, not something that could easily be cast aside. When she'd said, almost unthinkingly, that there was something about him that reminded her of

181

her brother, he'd realized how much he'd felt flattered, knowing how close the bond between them had been. From that time onwards, he'd found it almost impossible to go on pretending, playing the role that Vogel had forced him to perform. As he'd watched her fight tooth and nail to keep the business and clear her missing brother's name against all odds, he'd felt such a depth of self-disgust and revulsion for what he was doing that he'd decided to tell Vogel that he was opting out for good.

'After she signs with one of the bloodstock companies, you don't need me any more,' he said simply. 'I've done everything you wanted, everything you've paid me to do. The police are nowhere near finding out the truth about Ismay. They've fallen for all your carefully laid trail of clues and they're convinced he's guilty. She's being forced to sell. So why do you need me around any more when she goes?'

'We'll see.'

'Vogel, I've had enough. I told you in the beginning all this wasn't my style. I want to go back to Cape Town.'

'You're beginning to sound like Adeline, my dear Karl.' Vogel held out the gun in his hands and turned it over with satisfaction. The barrel glinted brilliantly in the light. 'Keep close to her for the time being. Let me know everything she does. I want to know right away as soon as she's decided which of the companies to sell to – though she can hardly turn down the offer from Consolidated Bloodstock Holdings. And what she intends to do about the house.'

'She told her uncle she intended to put the house and contents up for public auction. She'll get more money that way.'

'Then let me know the date.'

Suddenly the room seemed claustrophobic, stifling. Ryan went over to the door and opened it wide. He longed to get away, to be rid of the crushing feelings of betrayal and guilt, but he knew that there was no way he could leave the country now without alienating Vogel and arousing Emmeline Ismay's suspicion. And besides he had no choice. He had known that before he started. Afterwards, when it was all over, he would have a lie ready about a sick friend back home, and then they would say goodbye.

Lying on his bed in his hotel room, he'd gone over and over the story in his mind. He had no doubt that he'd make it sound as convincing as all the other lies he'd told her. But a part of him that was still untouched by all the ruthless acts he'd ever done longed to tell her the truth. But he never could.

'I'll be in touch," he said, without turning round.

Vogel simply smiled.

'I won't see him, I told you I don't want to see anyone. There's nothing wrong with me; nothing wrong with this child. Send him away.'

Emmeline laid her hands gently on Christabel's shoulders, but she shook them off, angrily, with surprising strength.

'Doctor Kinane's been coming to this house since David and I were children. He's nursed you through two miscarriages and more besides. Don't you understand that because of what's happened in the past it's important for you to have the right care now?'

'You had no right to send for him! I don't need him. I don't need you. Or anyone. And I won't let him touch me. Every time he's come here I've lost my child –'

'Don't be ridiculous!'

'Go away and leave me alone!'

Resignedly, Emmeline turned away and went back downstairs, her fingers made marks in the dust that lay thick along the banisters, the wood panelling in the hall that had once been so buffed and polished that she could have seen her own reflection in it looked lifeless and dull. The house seemed even more sad and brooding than usual, at this time of year when it should already have been gaily festooned with boughs of holly and ivy and mistletoe, all ready for Christmas.

Even the drawing room fire had gone out.

'I'm sorry,' she said flatly, as Kinane turned round. 'But she won't see you. I should have guessed she'd do something like this.'

'Have the tablets I prescribed for her not helped?'

'Yes, in the beginning. But I think she's gone beyond that. Every day she's expected some news of David, convinced that he'd suddenly come back. When that didn't happen she gradually started to sink further and further into a sense of unreality, almost as if she's trying to force herself to believe none of what's happened is really true.' She sighed, deeply. 'If anything happens to this child I really think she'd go out of her mind.'

Kinane smiled.

'Let's hope we can avoid that happening.'

'You're going up to her?'

'I think I can persuade her to see me.'

He was already half-way along the hall when she remembered something and called after him.

'You'd better prepare yourself for a shock.' A pause. She cast around for the right words to try to explain about the dolls. 'She'd bought them while I was away. Not just a few. There are dozens of them, everywhere. She said they were for the child but I don't believe her. She bought them for herself.'

'I see.' He came back a little way. 'But I wouldn't worry too much; it isn't uncommon in childless women. They have to have a substitute for a child they've lost, for a baby they've never had. Some women surround themselves with pets, animals that they treat as if they were human. This is Christabel's way, a form of self-comfort. I should leave her be. After all, they're harmless enough. And soon, God willing, she won't need them at all.'

'I've been so busy, preoccupied with worrying about the house and the stud, that I haven't spent very much time with her. Maybe this is partly my fault –'

He shook his head.

'Don't ever think that. And don't be too hard on yourself, Emmeline. After everything that's happened I think you've coped magnificently. A lot of women in your place would have fallen apart.' He smiled, reassuringly. 'I'd best go up to Christabel now. I have another call to make near Bush Wood on my way back.'

'Bush Wood? You must mean the Vogel's place. Mrs Vogel is still ill?'

His face showed only surprise.

'The Vogels who live at The Hermitage? No, Mrs Vogel isn't one of my patients.'

'My mistake.' She wandered back into the drawing room and sat down to wait for him. What he'd just said puzzled her, somehow.

He was much longer than she'd thought. She threw an old cloak around her shoulders and walked outside into the gathering dusk.

The snow that had already fallen crunched beneath her booted

184

feet, the tiny footprints of garden birds dotted the untouched carpet of white that lay spread along the terrace. How sad and neglected the grounds looked now; sadder, that when the glorious profusion of colour came into being, someone else, some stranger, would be standing where she stood now. She walked on, further, past the snow-laden rhododendron bushes, the sleeping rose arches, half-buried clumps of lavender. In the eerie half-light, her imagination conjured up images of all the Brodies, Russells and Ismays that had walked here along the same path as she did now. Then herself, walking hand in hand with her mother when she was a little girl.

She turned, slowly, and looked back towards the house.

It would probably be the last time she stood here like this, the last time her feet touched this spot. She would never see the old house again in springtime, when the buds burst from their long winter sleep and the ice on the pond in the sunken garden melted. She would never watch the foals cantering in the paddocks; never sit under her favourite tree in the park with a book on her lap on a hot summer's day. Other people would live here, people who knew nothing of its history or what it had meant to her. Perhaps they would change things, uproot bushes, tear down the old tree house that her father had built for her and David when they were children. Maybe they would alter the house inside, too, in such a way that she would never again be able to recognize it, the rooms and corners and the little things that she loved.

She pulled her cloak tighter around herself and put her head down against the wind. Then, slowly, each footstep like a physical pain, she began to walk away again in the direction of the house.

She pushed open the front door and shook the snow from her boots. Her cheeks stung with the warmth after the bitter cold of the air outside. Kinane was already coming towards her from the direction of the hall.

'Emmeline . . .'

The expression on his face, the strained note in his voice sent alarm coursing through her.

'What is it, what's wrong?'

She saw his deep intake of breath. But she'd already told him about the dolls . . .

'I saw her, she let me examine her.' A pause. 'It's all in her mind, a figment of her imagination. Christabel isn't having a child at all . . .'

'I went looking for Livia; I found this in her room.' Adeline Vogel held out the newspaper to him, and he stared at the headlines on the front page. 'Why didn't you tell me? Why did you try to keep me from finding out the truth? That's why the police were here that day, isn't it? Because they'd found his motorcar abandoned in Bush Wood.'

He was furious with Livia. How could she have been so careless?

'You had no right to go searching for things in Livia's room!'

'I didn't. It was lying on the table next to her bed and I picked it up. I haven't seen a newspaper for weeks!'

Vogel turned away abruptly.

'Guy, you haven't answered my question!'

He harnessed his annoyance and anger that she should have found out before he was ready.

'What do you want me to say? Yes, that was why the police called here, to ask if any of us had seen or heard something, and no one had. That was what I told them.'

'But you didn't tell me.'

'Why should I have told you, my dear? What does David Ismay mean to you?' She saw that look of malice light up his eyes and she knew she had made a mistake. He could never contain his ungovernable jealousy for long. He took her by the wrist and squeezed it so tightly that she cried out. 'He means nothing to you. Isn't that what you told me?' He increased the pressure. 'That afternoon when I caught you flirting with him and you swore it was all my imagination. Are you saying now that that wasn't true?'

'Please, Guy, let go of my wrist. You're breaking it!'

'Answer me.'

'I told you the truth!' Tears of fear and pain sprang into her eyes. 'We were just talking together . . . that was all. Guy, I swear it!'

He pulled her round to face him, so savagely that he tore her dress.

'But what were you thinking, Adeline? Hmm? Tell me what you were thinking. Were you wondering what it would be like to make love with him, to have his hands touching your naked skin, to feel him inside you?' He threw her to the floor and grasped her around the throat until her face turned blue. The room swam in front of her eyes, her arms flayed helplessly in the air. 'You wanted him, didn't you? And he wanted you. I saw it, I saw for myself the way you were looking at him.' His scarlet face was so close to hers that she could feel the spittle shooting from his mouth. 'You didn't know that I was watching you both for a long while before I came out. I saw you laughing, smiling up into his face. You would have loved to have reached out and stroked his hair. You wanted him to kiss you!'

She was beyond speech, protest, movement. She could feel consciousness slipping, blotting out the terror and the pain. Then suddenly he let her go and she fell in a heap at his feet choking and spluttering, fighting to get her breath. Vogel took the newspaper and flung it down beside her.

'It's true. He arranged the fire at the stud, for the insurance money. When he knew it wouldn't work, that he wouldn't get away with it, he turned tail and ran. Rumour has it that he's left the country. With another woman.'

She stared up fearfully into his cruel face.

'I . . . I don't believe it . . .'

'Then you're the only one who doesn't. Even his sister does now. Even his own wife. I hear she's heartbroken.' He went on staring down at her. The look in his eyes was pitiless. 'Now that you know, you might as well see all the newspapers. I'll tell Livia to bring them to you. Then you can read for yourself what a bastard David Ismay really is.'

He didn't help her to get up. He stood by the door and watched her struggle to her feet. She touched the torn material of her dress, then the painful, bruised skin around her throat. A tear welled up in one eye and trickled down her cheek.

He walked out of the room and left her there.

187

NINETEEN

'HE'S LYING! He doesn't know what he's talking about!'

'He's a doctor and he examined you, Christabel. Didn't he explain to you that you'd made a mistake?'

Christabel folded her arms stubbornly and stared morosely out of the window, even though it was too dark now to see anything outside.

'Did you hear what I said?'

'I'm going to have David's child.'

Emmeline went over and took her by the shoulders. She wanted to shake her; she felt pity and impatience both at once. She mustn't upset her. She mustn't lose her temper. None of this was Christabel's fault.

'You have to accept the truth. If David was here he'd say exactly the same.'

Christabel threw off her hands.

'You always resented me for marrying him, didn't you? You've always hated me!' She was shaking now. 'You were glad when I lost those babies, because if I hadn't it would have been a special bond between us, something that you couldn't share. You wanted to keep your hold over him, you wanted to stop him belonging to me. I was always the outsider, the interloper, the intruder into your own little world. You were jealous when he wanted to marry me, weren't you? Because you couldn't bear the thought of sharing your precious brother with someone else!'

'Don't be absurd.'

'I came between you and you couldn't stand it. So you tried to take him away from me.'

'*Christabel!*'

'It was always you – you and David, shutting me out. You always came before I did. Even before Cornelius and Rebeccah died four years ago, I was always the odd one out. Admit it. You'd sit there, all of you, talking about the stud, about some race, about this horse or that, knowing I couldn't join in because I didn't have your knowledge. Horses, horses, horses! That's all I ever heard. Didn't any of you ever stop to think that I might want to talk about something else, something different for a change? Didn't it ever occur to you that sometimes I needed to have my husband to myself?'

'Why didn't you say that to David?'

'David never listened to me!'

'That isn't true. And if you felt that way then you should have thought twice before marrying him. You knew long before the depth of his involvement and commitment to the stud.'

'Your mother and father never wanted him to marry me; don't think I never knew that! Neither did you. Until I came along you had him all to yourself. I used to watch you, the pair of you, walking arm in arm out there by the paddocks, laughing and cracking jokes, while I was left here on my own!' Behind her, the grotesque rows of dolls stared at Emmeline with their sightless glass eyes. Christabel had picked one of them up and was cradling it in her arms.

Emmeline said, 'I think we better end this conversation before I lose my temper.'

'You know where he is, don't you? Why he went away? You want to get rid of me! It's all a plot to send me away from this house. You want me to go and live with Charles and Florence Ismay at Hazelbeech Hall. But I won't go.' Her eyes were bulging from their sockets, unnaturally bright, like the glass eyes of the dolls. 'I won't leave this house without David!'

Emmeline grasped her by the wrist and pulled the doll out of her arms.

'You're ill, Christabel! You need help. We can't stay here and you know it. You won't be going to Northampton alone. You forget that I'll be coming with you.'

'*What have you done with my husband?*'

'For pity's sake . . .!'

Christabel was hysterical. She pummelled at Emmeline with her fists, crying and screaming. '*I wish you were dead! I wish you'd been drowned with Cornelius and Rebeccah!*'

Emmeline slapped her across the face.

Instantly she stopped crying. The awful crazed look went from her eyes. She stumbled back against a piece of furniture, pushing her hair away from her face. She was deathly pale.

'Emmeline, I didn't mean that . . . I didn't. Forgive me, please. Emmeline, I'm sorry . . .'

Emmeline went over to her and put her arms around her. Christabel started to sob. Before she could help herself, Emmeline was crying too. For David, for Christabel, herself; for the loss of everything she'd lived with all her life, the end of her parents' dream.

Until Janet came and knocked on the door to fetch her, she'd forgotten that Karl Ryan had promised to call on them at eight o'clock.

'You've been crying.'

She leaned against the drawing room door.

'It's nothing. I'm all right.'

'You're not all right.' He came towards her, she felt his hands on each side of her shoulders. The touch and the nearness of him strengthened and revived her.

'Shall I pour you a drink?'

'No, thank you; I won't have one. But get one for yourself.' She didn't want him to move, she wanted to keep on feeling his hands against her shoulders.

'Do you want to talk about it?'

'It's Christabel. The doctor came today.' She heard herself repeating the events of the afternoon. It made her feel better to share them, somehow. 'A phantom pregnancy, the dolls – David's disappearance is starting to unhinge her. I should have seen it coming. One moment she seems quite normal and I think she's accepted what's happening to us; another moment she suddenly turns into someone else. I don't know what to do.'

'When you leave this place maybe it'll all come right. Away from here, all the memories she has of the past, it'll give her the space she needs to heal. Wait and see.' He released her gently, and guided her into the nearest chair. He knelt down beside her and pressed her hand. It was a gesture that David and her father had often used and she felt extraordinarily moved by it. She wanted to cry and she wanted him to put his arms around her.

'I haven't seen you since yesterday. Have you decided about the house?'

The moment passed. He got up and went over to the table where the decanter and glasses stood. Despite what she'd said, he poured her some brandy and pressed the glass into her hands.

'I meet with Maurice Delauney's partner at the bank tomorrow, to work out the details about the sale of the stud. When I spoke to him on the telephone, he said we have three main bloodstock companies interested. It's just a question of working out the creditors' claims and compensation, then making sure I get the best possible price. As far as this house goes, I think we'd get more by selling it with all the contents in a public auction. I told the local auctioneers to come while I'm at the bank, and make an inventory and a valuation. Then I can arrange a sale preview and then the auction itself.'

He sipped his own brandy.

'You've certainly settled things very quickly. What then?'

'I'll leave the lawyers in London to sort out the loose ends. Christabel and I are then free to leave ... for my uncle's. If we didn't have him God knows where we'd go.' She looked away into the fire. 'I can't bear to think about it.'

'I admire the way you've handled everything. It took a lot of guts.'

She managed to smile at him.

'If only I had a gold mine like Guy Vogel. How different it would all be then. I suppose I envy him. It must be like having a money tree in your back garden. Every time you run short you can go outside and pick some from the branches.'

For a moment he hesitated.

'Have you ever thought of going to him for help? You said yourself, he'd shown more sympathy than any of your neighbours. After the fire and your brother's disappearance, didn't you say he was the first one on the scene, offering to help? You know he wants to buy into English bloodstock. Why not sell to him or ask him to bail you out? Maybe you could even make him an equal partner.'

She looked at him incredulously.

'Ask Vogel for help? Go into partnership with him? Are you serious? I'd never do business with a man like that. Or sell any part of my father's business to him. What does he know about

191

breeding English thoroughbreds? All he really cares about are ostentation and making money. He flaunts what he is. Do you really think I could work with a man like that?'

'So you don't like him after all?'

'It isn't a question of that. I care about this stud, I care about what happens to it after we leave. Vogel's here now, wedded to the idea of turning himself into an English country gentleman, hobnobbing with the local aristocrats and landed gentry; but who knows when he'll get tired of his new game? Next year or the year after – if he stays that long – he could sell up and go back to South Africa and then what would happen? I'd be back where I started, probably even worse off. And if I sold out to him completely, what about our men? They'd be out of work, thrown onto the dole queue with the other jobless thousands, and end up God knows where. I couldn't do that to them. They've worked for this family all their lives and they deserve something better. Selling now for the best possible price I can get to an established bloodstock company is the only answer.'

'You know what you're doing.'

There was a lengthy silence between them.

'And you? Where do you go from here?'

'Everything will be settled by Christmas, won't it? With you and Christabel. When you close up the house and go north, so will I. No point in coming to a country if you don't see everything.' He smiled. 'After that I reckon I'll maybe spend a while in the States, before I go back to Africa.'

Suddenly she felt cold. She left the chair and sat down in front of the fire, spreading out her hands towards its warmth.

'We always go to the service before Christmas every year. I promised to sing the solo in the choir. Not that I shall feel like singing, after seeing this house and everything my family worked for go under the hammer. But that's life, I suppose. Nothing can make time stand still, however much we want it to; nothing can ever stay the same.'

The firelight cast shadows on her hair, across her face. The flames reflected in her eyes. He wanted to reach out and touch her, he wanted to kiss her and gather her in his arms; but he knew that if he did he would betray himself, and that there would be no going back. He wasn't worthy of her. He had no rights. And if he told her the truth, she would hate him.

'When you go to sing in the choir a few days before Christmas, would you mind if I came too?'

'I didn't know you were religious.'

'I'm not. But when I leave I'd like to take some memories away with me: an English church at Christmastime, snow, icicles on the churchyard gate, people wrapped in furs. Not something we get in Africa. That's the way I'd like to remember it. And you.' He forced himself to speak the next words. 'Even though we probably won't meet again, it'll always be a sort of link, somehow. Wherever you go; whatever happens to me.'

She turned around and moved closer to the fire, so that he wouldn't see she was crying.

TWENTY

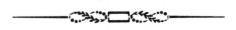

ADELINE VOGEL went over to the door and grasped the huge iron-ringed handle in both hands. Holding her breath, she turned it slowly, inch by inch. Then she stopped to listen. No sound. Peering out from behind it she looked along the corridor outside, its walls lined with the oil paintings her husband seemed to be obsessed with, and saw with relief that there was no one in sight. No sign, either, of Livia De Haan, who she'd sent down to the kitchens for a glass of milk to get her out of the way.

She ran along the carpeted passageway, then down a flight of steps, trying to remember if she was making in the right direction. It still seemed crazy to her that after all this time she could still get lost in her own house; so many corridors, so many flights of stairs, so many rooms and doors that all looked exactly alike. She stood there for a moment, turning this way and that. Then she opened another door and cried out in alarm as she suddenly came face to face with Livia.

'Mrs Vogel.'

Colour drained from her face.

'I . . . I was just going down to see if there was any mail . . .'

The other woman's smile didn't reach to her eyes.

'Yes, there was mail, madam. But it was all for Mr Vogel. I've put it on his desk. There was nothing for you today.'

'But my father – I wrote to him weeks ago. He should have answered by now!'

'You know that he isn't strong, madam. That his sight is very poor now. Mr Vogel read you the letter he received from Mr Bausche's housekeeper, don't you remember? She said he was well in himself but couldn't hold a pen in either hand.'

'But I –'

Livia De Haan took her firmly by the forearm and propelled

her back in the direction from which she'd come.

'You really shouldn't be out here, you know. Mr Vogel said that you were to lie down in your room until this afternoon. He'll blame me if he comes back and finds you're not there. We don't want that to happen, do we, madam?'

'Livia, he said we were going to a presentation, a dinner, in the public rooms at the racecourse grandstand.' She put her hand to her head and tried to think clearly. 'He did say that, didn't he? Or did I imagine it?'

'He did say it, madam, but it isn't for some time yet. He's to be guest of honour, for the contributions he's been making to the racecourse fund. Now, why don't you come back to your room and rest? Then you'll feel fresh when you go down to dinner later.'

They reached the door of her rooms and Livia stood back to let her go inside. The glass of milk stood on a silver tray in the middle of a small table. Adeline went over to it and picked it up.

'It's so cold, Livia. So bitterly cold. Could you please send somebody up to put more wood on the fire? I'm afraid it might go out.'

'Yes, I'll do it right away.' She hesitated in the frame of the door. 'I wouldn't go wandering about the house, if I were you. You know that Mr Vogel doesn't like you to do that.' She smiled, coldly. 'I'll be back later, to help you dress.'

Adeline heard the sound of a key turning in the lock on the other side.

'She's getting cunning; I told you so. She sent me downstairs for a glass of milk and she didn't even want it. And she's been asking me questions about David Ismay and his sister. You'll have to be careful.'

Vogel cut the end from a large cigar and lit it with a taper from the fire.

'I'll have to do something about her father. She's no longer satisfied with the letters from his housekeeper. Housekeeper! If only she knew.' He laughed, softly. 'I must find somebody who can write a fair imitation of the old man's hand, and send a few lines. That'll keep her quiet.'

Livia De Haan sat down unbidden in the nearest chair.

195

'Do you think it's wise of you to take her with you to the grandstand dinner? In public, with all those people, you can't be beside her every minute. It's a big risk.'

'It's a bigger one if I keep her shut up here. Our dear neighbours will begin to talk. The beautiful Mrs Vogel, Rapunzel in her tower. No, I won't have that. There must be no gossip, not a whisper. I've run through the whole gamut of plausible excuses – her health, the climate, there's nothing left. I have to take her. She has to be seen if not heard. I don't think I've got much to worry about, not while I'm holding the trump card.'

'Will the Ismay girl be there?'

'I doubt it. She'll be too busy packing her bags. Think of it. At a single stroke, I've wiped the slate clean. Destroyed the Ismays and turned them out of Epsom. If only my father could be here now.' He drew deeply on the cigar. 'Let me tell you something about revenge, Livia. It isn't only sweet; as the Italians say, it's a dish best savoured cold.'

'You really hate them, don't you?'

'You of all people don't need to ask why.'

Yes, Livia De Haan understood. She knew what the agonies of jealousy meant, the pain of long-nurtured resentment, the thirst for revenge. She remembered her girlhood in Cape Town, living in the shadow of a younger, prettier sister who had been her parents' pride and joy. She remembered the way people would pet and fuss over her, how she herself had been pushed aside; she remembered, bitterly, the way young men at dances had singled out her sister and left Livia standing alone on the edge of the ballroom. Until the day she had thrown a cup of acid in her face and evened up the score.

She never forgot the three years that she'd spent in a girls' reformatory. And she'd learned that a girl with brains could very often do better than a girl who had nothing more than a pretty face, for beauty faded. Yes, she understood Guy Vogel's bitterness. David Ismay had been handsome, too. But did it really matter whether he'd done what he'd done because of what had happened to his father, or because of the way Ismay had looked at his wife.

She got up.

'You won't take her to the castle yet?'

Vogel shook his head.

196

'After the grandstand dinner. When we've left, you'll be in charge. The others have been told already that while I'm away they take their orders from you.'

'Is there anything else?'

'She isn't to wear any gown that reveals her bare shoulders, or too much of her bare arms. See to it.'

When Livia had gone he went over to the window and stared out into the night. He could see stars, faint and twinkling, silver against the backdrop of blue-black sky. Sweat had broken out in beads across his forehead; sweat was damp and sticky in the palms of his hands. Desire for her raged in him, desire for that soft, smooth, white flesh that shrank whenever he touched it, the look of fear and loathing in her eyes that she could never hide.

He clenched his fists and crashed them down with rage. It was happening all over again. The impotency that had cursed him when he'd been married to Kathleen van der Louew, his first wife.

TWENTY-ONE

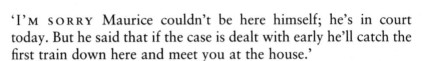

'I'M SORRY Maurice couldn't be here himself; he's in court today. But he said that if the case is dealt with early he'll catch the first train down here and meet you at the house.'

'That was very generous of him,' answered Emmeline, drily. She looked across the desk at David's bank manager. She took a deep breath. 'Well, gentlemen, shall we get down to business? The sooner this is over and done with the better it'll be. I've already broken the news to the men.'

Delauney's partner pushed three sets of papers towards her across the desk.

'Basically, these represent the highest three offers for the stud, so we whittled the initial list of would-be purchasers down to a short list: Consolidated Bloodstock Holdings, the Amalgamated Bloodstock Company, and the largest, Anglo-French. Consolidated, as you can see by these figures, have made by far the largest offer, and we recommend that you accept.' He opened his briefcase and took out more papers. 'As you instructed Maurice, he contacted each of your brother's creditors and asked them to submit a figure that they considered adequate financial compensation for their stock that perished in the fire, plus additional losses that would represent what they would have expected offspring from that stock to make on the present market. These are their final figures. We've both been over them very carefully, and I think by and large you'll agree that they're fair. But if you're not happy about any of them do say now.'

Emmeline took the papers from him and read through them. 'Half of them, I dare say, could be reduced by a third or more. But no matter; I've done with haggling. Let me sign the sale papers, pay them all off and have done with it.'

Delauney's partner picked up the bill of sale and gave it to her, but his elbow caught the pile of papers on the edge of the desk and they toppled over and spilled across the floor.

'I'm so sorry, how clumsy of me!'

She knelt down to help him retrieve them when a name on one of them flew up and instantly caught her eye.

'What's this?' She picked it up incredulously and held it out towards him. 'Guy Vogel, one of the Directors? You never told me he had anything to do with Consolidated Bloodstock Holdings. How long has he been associated with the company?'

'I've no idea.'

'I believe he's also a majority shareholder,' David's bank manager said. 'Of course, he does have an account with us, but I'm afraid I'm not at liberty to say more than that. But I do know that he has quite extensive plans to enlarge the company so that it rivals Amalgamated and Anglo-French.'

Emmeline was dumbfounded.

'And not a word of this to me. Not a whisper. He made out that he was a complete novice in the bloodstock game, pretending that he needed my advice on buying horses to be put into training. And all the time he was scheming to buy the stud.' Anger flared. 'I should have realized, when I compared the price Consolidated were offering and the prices offered by the other two bloodstock companies. He instructed the company secretary to offer more than our stud was worth so that I'd be sure to sell to him and not one of the others.'

'Emmeline –'

'And I almost fell for it. I was completely taken in. If you hadn't knocked down those papers and I hadn't seen his name I would never have found out until it was too late. That's what he wanted.'

'It'd be madness to turn down Consolidated's offer just because you don't like the man! Think about it. If you don't accept then most of the money the sale of the house makes will have to go towards paying off David's creditors. Accept Vogel's offer and his purchase price for the stud will cover all their claims in full.'

'No. I won't sell to him. I want the stud to be run as David ran it, I want our men's future jobs secure. With a man like Vogel, who cares about nothing but profit and glory, the entire place would be split up and scattered. I couldn't do that to them. And the bloodstock. We have more than fifteen barren mares, and

199

another dozen who are too old to breed from any more. Our policy has always been to turn them out to grass, so that after a lifetime's racing and stud service they can end their days in peace. Do you think a totally profit-orientated man like Guy Vogel would carry on a policy like that? Before the ink on this paper is dry he'd have sent them all to the knacker's yard for dogs' meat!'

'Emmeline, I think you ought seriously to reconsider this.'

'I've already made up my mind.' She tore the bill of sale in two and threw it down. 'I sell to Anglo-French. My father did a lot of business with them in the past and I can accept their offer with a free mind.' She picked up a pen and dipped it in the ink well, then signed her name at the foot of the bill of sale with a flourish. She pushed it back to Delauney's partner across the desk. 'When the money's received into our account, arrange to have all the creditors paid off; what's over I want distributed to all our men.'

So it was done, an era was over. She glanced down at her signature on the bill of sale and felt a lump in her throat.

There was no point in staying, no point in saying anything more. She picked up her gloves and handbag, then thanked them and walked out.

It was the first time she'd seen Delauney since their argument in London. So close to Christmas, the undecorated house seemed even more cold and cheerless. She'd greeted him formally, almost coldly, when Janet had shown him in to David's old study where she sat working. She let him stand there for several minutes before she offered him a chair.

There was no reciprocating rancour either in his expression or voice. Almost at once she felt guilty. She was behaving very badly. It wasn't his fault that David had vanished, that she'd lost one stud and had a few hours ago been forced to sign away the other one. She hadn't agreed with any of the advice he'd given her, but he was a lawyer; in his place no doubt she'd have done exactly the same. She'd made him her whipping boy and now it was time to make amends. There was no point in doing otherwise. Her father had always taught her that nobody should ever be too proud to say they were sorry.

She motioned him into a chair and looked at him across the piles of papers and ledgers.

'I've accepted the offer from Anglo-French Bloodstock.' She gave him a brief account of what had happened. 'Your partner thinks I'm crazy to turn down Consolidated, but he did me a bigger favour than he'll ever know. If he hadn't been so clumsy I would never have known that Guy Vogel was behind them and I'd have sold to him without knowing. Until it was too late.'

'I thought you liked him. You said he'd been one of the few local people to care. You've dined with him, he's been quite a frequent caller here, isn't that true?' He took out his cigarette case. 'So he's vulgar and *nouveau riche*. He's a clever business-man with social pretensions. That doesn't make him an ogre with two heads.'

'I should have known better. The fire and David's disappearance stopped me from seeing things clearly. Beware of King Midas bearing gifts.' He asked her permission to smoke and she nodded. He took out his cigarette lighter and flicked it. 'He invited us over to The Hermitage for two reasons – to show off his gold-encrusted mausoleum of a house and to find out what I planned to do. A wolf in sheep's clothing. I always knew there was just something about him I didn't quite like, something I couldn't quite put my finger on.'

'All right, so the man's devious. That's how he gets on in the world and all successful businessmen are the same. You can't hold that against him.'

Emmeline smiled.

'You think by accepting a lower offer from Anglo-French I'm cutting off my nose to spite my face. But you know how I feel about this place. I can't help the way I am. I tried to think about what my father would have done if he'd been here; what David would have advised me to do. I think I know the answer. If I didn't care, if I didn't have a conscience about the horses and the men who've worked for us all these years, if I could just sell out to the highest bidder and then walk away, it would be different. But you know me and you know that I could never do that.'

'Yes, I know. And I admire you for it. But lawyers don't advise their clients out of sentimentality.'

A moment of silence. She looked around the room. 'I never knew there'd be so much to sort out. All these old papers and dusty books. Stud records and obsolete accounts dating from

201

before the war. And there's still a shelf full of ledgers earlier than that in the old gatehouse.'

'Looks like you've got your work cut out.'

'I want to leave everything neat and tidy for the Anglo-French accountants when they take over. David used the old gatehouse as a temporary office when he first came back from the front and the house was still being used as a Red Cross military hospital. There's more dust in there now than study records.'

Delauney smiled and leaned back in his chair.

'That's the worst part of moving, isn't it? I know. I helped my father with his files and God knows what else when we moved from Trinity Buildings to Lincoln's Inn. We had thousands of packing boxes. When you open up all the old cupboards and drawers that have been locked for years you don't realize how much stuff is packed away in them. I told him what we needed was a gigantic bonfire.'

'Shall I ring for Janet to bring you a drink?'

'That would be pleasant; then I must go. How is Christabel, by the way? The house seems unusually quiet.'

'She hasn't been well. But then you knew that already.'

'Yes, and I'm very sorry for it. Please give her my best regards. And your uncle? You're going to live with him at Hazelbeech Hall?'

She laughed, shortly, and a little bitterly.

'We don't have anywhere else to go.'

He looked embarrassed.

'He's a good man, Charles Ismay. I always liked him. Does he still keep any horses in training?'

'A couple of steeplechasers, I believe. But after what happened to him in 1913 I think he's pretty disillusioned with the flat.'

'But you said on the telephone that he's buying Ballacragan from you. Does that mean he intends to use him for breeding?'

'I doubt it. We all know what the stallion would fetch on the open market, but the reason he wanted him was quite different. We're a sentimental lot, we Ismays ... surely you've already found that out for yourself? Keeping the horse in the family and what he represents means that we don't quite lose everything.'

She could see that he understood. They chatted for a few minutes more while he drank the brandy Janet had brought him, then he looked at his watch and stood up, ready to go.

'I'd better be on my way then. No knowing if we'll get more snow and I'll get stuck in a drift on my way back to the station. Give my best regards to your uncle. Have as happy a Christmas as you can under the circumstances, and a safe journey north. And always remember you can contact me at any time if you need any advice.'

'Yes, I'll remember. Till we meet again, then.' She hated goodbyes, they were too final and too depressing. Even saying goodbye to Maurice Delauney.

He had been with her for more than an hour and they had hardly mentioned David at all. It was almost as if he'd somehow ceased to exist. She watched him walk from the porch to the waiting horse cab; he got in and waved and it moved off along the drive. For a moment she could hear the rumble of the wheels and the sound of the horse's hoofs, then there was silence.

She turned away and went back inside the house.

Although with the finality of the sale she felt that a weight had been lifted, she felt unaccountably miserable and depressed. She went along the corridor to the hall, her footsteps echoing on the tiled floor. The doors to every room now stood open, and Janet and Winifred had been busy covering everything with white sheets while she'd been away in Epsom. She looked at the shrouded furniture, the walls bereft of their pictures. She walked into the old library that had been her mother's favourite room and stood staring at the rows of empty shelves, the crates of books stacked up against the damp-stained walls.

There was a tight feeling in her throat, a burning sensation at the backs of her eyes. She could remember where every single item had once been, the clocks, the little china cherubs on the mantel-piece, the Staffordshire dogs that had stood at each end. The sporting prints, the writing desk, the chairs on each side of the fire.

There were no velvet curtains at the big windows now; like everything else they'd been taken down and packed away. The grate stood cold and empty, swept clean of ashes.

In the distance she heard the front door bell faintly ring, Janet's footsteps in the hall. So Karl had come early tonight. She went out to meet him, ready to tell him what had happened in Epsom this afternoon. But when she reached the hall it wasn't Karl Ryan who was waiting for her there.

'*You!*'

'Good evening, Miss Ismay.' Guy Vogel stood at the foot of the staircase dressed in evening clothes, hat and cane in each hand. 'I received a call from my bank a few hours ago.' His voice was like ice, echoing around the empty hall. 'It was very foolish of you to accept Anglo-French's offer, and turn down mine. I think I can safely say that you'll live to regret it.'

'Don't threaten me.'

'Threaten you? Why should you think such a thing? I merely state the obvious. Clearly, you have no business sense. Otherwise you would never have allowed sentimentality and personal prejudice to influence your decision. A good thing you have sold the stud, before your unrealistic ideals forced it into bankruptcy.' He smiled, coldly. 'But then, what else can one expect from a woman?'

Slowly, she walked towards him across the floor. They stood a few feet away from each other now.

'If you'd been honest with me then I could have respected you for it. But you set out from the beginning deliberately to lie and mislead. You only pretended concern and sympathy for your own ends, isn't that true? No doubt a man like you would think anyone a fool for doing something out of principle and not profit. But there are some things in this world, Mr Vogel, that are above price. I don't like the way you do business. And I think it's time for you to leave.'

He didn't move.

'You despise me, don't you? From that first time you came to my house. You only came out of curiosity, to see what I had. I saw through the veneer. All the things I prized, none of them made any real impression on you at all. I could see what you were really thinking under all your politeness and charm. Your contempt showed in your eyes.'

'Does it really matter to a man like you what I think? Do you really care if I say you're nothing but a coarse, arrogant, self-important social climber, a miner with the dirt still encrusted under your nails, who's grown rich on the sweat and toil of other men?' The leer on his face disappeared. 'You don't belong here. You can't buy what it took my family four generations to build. You don't have the class. Go and be the guest of honour at the Epsom grandstand committee's dinner – you paid enough for your invitation. But just remember that putting on a top hat and an evening suit won't turn you into a gentleman.'

For a moment she thought he was going to strike her. A dark red flush spread from his face to his neck; the freckles stood out vividly against his skin. But suddenly the sound of someone at the front door and Janet's voice stopped him from what he was about to do. Emmeline looked beyond him and saw the figure of Karl Ryan.

'Shall I throw him out?'

'Mr Vogel was just about to leave.'

He gave her one parting glance of anger and malice; then he replaced his hat and stalked out. His heavy footsteps rang loudly on the bare floor, then the front door slammed.

'Are you all right?'

She smiled, relieved to see him.

'Yes, I think so. But I'm glad you came when you did. I think he was tempted to hit me after what happened in Epsom today.'

'He wouldn't have dared.'

'I think a man as ruthless as Vogel would be willing to dare anything. To get what he wanted.'

'Do you want to talk about it?'

'On the way to the service.' She moved towards the stairs, hesitating for the first time since she'd known him to say what she was thinking, unlike her, at a loss for words.

She knew it was time now for the parting of the ways. He'd come unexpectedly into her life, almost at the same time as her brother had vanished from it; in great measure he'd helped to fill the void that David had left. He'd been a helper, a mentor, a friend. As long as she lived she'd always be grateful to him for that, thankful that he'd been there when there was no one else to turn to. Saying goodbye to Karl Ryan was going to be the most painful goodbye of all.

The lights from the tall stained-glass windows cast coloured shadows across the carpet of snow that covered the churchyard. Porchlight tumbled from the open church doors, the faint strains of organ music filled the stark, crisp night air.

As they made their way through the lych gate and along the path towards the doors, Emmeline was aware of the way people were looking at her – unobtrusively, covertly, not certain whether or not it was safe to catch her eye. She understood, suddenly, that even though she had spent her life living among most of the other people gathered in the church, she'd become a stranger, an embarrassment, a name in their newspapers connected with a scandal. Perhaps it had been a mistake to come at all.

She remembered only snatches of the service; a single prayer, a fragment of a Christmas hymn. She mouthed the words through wooden lips, her eyes fixed on the stained glass windows behind the altar, the candles burning by the chancel arch, the row of choirboys standing in line behind the stalls. Then she remembered that she'd promised to sing the solo of *Ave Maria*; she roused herself and squeezed past Karl Ryan and Christabel and began to walk self-consciously along the aisle.

From his place near the back of the little church Ryan watched her as she stood there, her soft, smooth skin illuminated by the candlelight, her dark hair falling on the white fur collar of her velvet cape; then her exquisite voice rose up into the silence and swelled, dwarfing the faint accompanying strains from the church organ. Effortlessly, it rose higher and then held the top note for a fraction too long, because her eyes were full of tears and, by the light of the candles behind her he could see one well up, spill over, and trickle down one side of her face.

In that moment he knew that he loved her as he had never loved anyone in his life, and that he could never see her again.

TWENTY-TWO

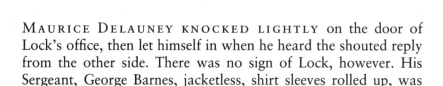

MAURICE DELAUNEY KNOCKED LIGHTLY on the door of Lock's office, then let himself in when he heard the shouted reply from the other side. There was no sign of Lock, however. His Sergeant, George Barnes, jacketless, shirt sleeves rolled up, was alone, sorting through a mountain of dusty old papers and books.

'We spoke before, in London, if you remember. I'm the Ismays' lawyer.'

'Yes, I know. Never forget a face.' He smiled, but he looked tired, Delauney couldn't but help notice. His skin had a greyish pallor; there were circles beneath his eyes. He gestured to a rickety chair. 'I s'ppose you've come down to tie loose ends up, what with the sale of the Ismay place and all that. A bit like me, really. A policeman's work is never done.'

'My train to London doesn't leave for another half-hour. I thought I'd call in on the off chance that you might have made some progress in finding my client.'

Barnes perched himself on the edge of the desk.

'He's vanished into thin air. That's all we know. In fact we're no further on now than we were a month ago. Frustrating, isn't it? But don't worry. If anything turns up you'll be the first to know.'

'You've made no progress at all then?'

'Like I just said. Not a dicky bird. Some cases are like that. We've followed up every lead we had, every single clue, every sighting – and ended up where we started. David Ismay walked out into the fog one morning and then ceased to exist. I'm stumped, I don't mind telling you. But my gov'nor, he reckons he got out of the country right at the beginning, that he's abroad somewhere.'

'And you don't?'

207

'Maybe he'll surface somewhere or other, sometime; maybe nobody'll ever see or hear of him again. Almost like black magic, isn't it? But to someone who's been in police work as long as I have, it isn't always that strange.' He made himself more comfortable. 'You get someone's husband or wife who goes missing – no explanation, no feasible reason why. Their family says they acted normal right up to the time they disappeared; they had no worries, no reasons to want to leave. The family swears blind they've been kidnapped, murdered, Christ knows what else. Because they think they know 'em through and through. But it doesn't always follow, you see. More often than not they turn up right as rain somewhere else, sometimes living under another name, sometimes even with another husband or wife. Well, you're a lawyer so you know about these things. None so queer as folk, ay? David Ismay, now he had plenty of reason to want to disappear, but . . .'

'Go on.'

'. . . There's just something . . . I don't know what, niggling, right at the back of my mind. Call it instinct, a hunch, just a funny feeling, but as hard as I've tried to make it, it won't go away.'

'You don't think he's guilty of arranging that fire?'

'All the evidence says it can't be anyone else. Nobody else had a motive. And yet when you read through all the statements from people who knew him, worked with him, his family and friends, you say to yourself a man like Ismay wouldn't do something as terrible as that. I interviewed all of 'em: maids in the house, stable boys, tradesmen, neighbours. None of 'em had a bad word to say about him. It just didn't make sense. So there was this big conflict in my mind and it left me with two simple conclusions: Ismay was either a Jekyll and Hyde or the evidence we've dug up so far was planted there by somebody else.'

'So what are you saying?'

'It brings us back to enemies and motives. Nobody hated him that much. At least, nobody we know of. But that doesn't mean they don't exist.'

'But it's a remote possibility.'

'That's why I'm going through all this – just in case. All we want, all we need is just a single thread. One tiny piece of evidence. If we get that, then all the other pieces begin to fit.'

Delauney checked his wristwatch.

'That late already . . . well, I'd best be on my way unless I want to miss that train. Good luck. And a happy Christmas.'

Barnes laughed wearily.

'This is the third Christmas I've worked in four years.'

When the lawyer had gone a uniformed sergeant came into the little office. He glanced down at the half-drunk mug of cold tea. A grey film had settled on the top of it.

'Just going off duty now. Night shift's coming on. By the way, does the Inspector want a watch kept on the Ismay girl?'

Barnes shook his head and stretched.

'No point, not now. They're going north, to the uncle. In the beginning when he wasn't sure, he thought it was best to have her watched, just in case she knew something she wasn't telling us and led us to her brother. But I think we can safely say she's in the clear now.'

'All right, Sarge. Good-night then.'

'Have one for me at the pub.'

She sat beside the bed for a long while after Christabel had fallen asleep, unable to rest, unable to sleep herself. She looked round dully at the boxes of dolls that Janet had already packed, the trunks of clothes, the bulging valises, the pile of hat boxes scattered around the room. Then she turned and glanced down at Christabel's sleeping face.

She looked like a small, pale, vulnerable little girl again, lying there with her long golden lashes against white cheeks, a strand of fair hair falling across the pillow. Their last night in old Brew House.

Emmeline got up and found the cloak she'd worn for the service in the church and draped it around her shoulders. Quietly, she went out of the room and walked along the bare floorboards of the landing. She stood looking down into the silent, empty hall.

Where the velvet curtains had been taken down and packed away, the moonlight cast long shadows across the floor. The whole house seemed curiously alive with ghostly images and voices from the past that she remembered, the past that was so painful to let go. Like that last night with David, she thought of her mother as she best remembered her, gliding gracefully down these same stairs in one of her exquisite gowns, the sequinned train rippling across the carpet, sparkling like foam; she could hear her brother's boyish laughter, her father's voice calling to his dogs. In the empty sheet-shrouded room that had once housed a gleaming grand piano, she remembered her mother's cousin Lottie singing, the crowded drawing room and guests' laughter. But only the forlorn sound of her solitary footsteps echoed in the stillness all around her now.

Slowly, a tear spilling down one cheek, she walked downstairs.

There was something of indescribable sadness about the rooms of the empty house, a house that has once been happy, somewhere cherished and loved. Other people would come and live here, other people who knew and cared nothing about its past. They would bring strange furniture and strange pictures, and different faces would look out of the windows on to the gardens and flowers that she'd loved. Other hands would touch the bannisters that her hands had touched. Other feet would walk where hers walked now.

She opened the front door and went out into the snow.

She had no conception of time; every clock had been taken down and packed away. When everything had been sold those same clocks whose gentle ticking and melodious chimes she'd loved, would sit on other people's mantelshelves, in strange rooms, striking the hours for people she would never know.

She walked on, her booted feet crunching in the crisp snow, as she made her way to the old gatehouse at the end of the drive. The chilly air was bracing, it stung her cheeks, it soothed her tired eyes. When she reached the door she fumbled in her pocket for the key, and let herself inside.

It was so long since she'd been here. Everything was covered in thick cobwebs and dust. There was only an old table and a pair of broken chairs in one of the tiny rooms, relics of their occupation during the war when the main house had been used as a military hospital. She walked in and out of the empty rooms, not even understanding why she had felt the need to come here after so long.

There were no curtains at the windows. The light from the full moon shone into the shell of what had once been her home, making the light from the candles she'd brought with her almost superfluous. But she stooped and lit one of them just the same. Her tall shadow fell across the ceiling and the wall as she went up the narrow staircase to the semi-circular room above, the room David had once used as an office. She gazed sadly around her. She was glad she'd come to see the old place for the last time.

She could sense his presence here. His handprints lay in the thick dust on the old battered desk, along the shelves from where he'd taken the old stud books; she noticed his footprints in the dust that coated the bare boards of the floor. Then, as she held the candle higher, something in the empty grate caught her eye.

There were a few blackened, charred sticks, half-burned pieces of coal and wood. Since they'd left no one had bothered to clean out the grate. There among the debris of the last fire was a crumpled ball of paper, speckled with soot from the unswept chimney.

Emmeline stooped down and picked it up.

She spread out the paper in her hands. And as she read the hastily scribbled note with astonished incredulity, she knew that she'd stumbled at last on the first clue to where David had gone.

TWENTY-THREE

HER HANDS WERE SHAKING as she pushed the crumpled sheet of paper into her pocket; as fast as she could, she scrambled back down the little narrow staircase and ran through the lodge, not waiting to lock the front door. She slipped and stumbled in the snow as she ran back along the drive towards the house, where she raced through the rooms and up the stairs.

Christabel was still fast asleep. In her state of mind, no point in waking her. She flung open the door of the adjoining room where Janet started up in bed.

'Lord love us, Miss Emmeline, whatever is it? You scared the life out o' me!'

'Janet, don't say anything. Just listen.' She knelt down by the bed and gripped her hand. 'I went to the old gatehouse, and I found something. A note that my brother had been sent just before he disappeared. I'll explain later. I have to leave now, there isn't much time. I'm taking his car.'

'Miss –'

'I'll be back here as soon as I can. But if I'm late I don't want you and Mrs Ismay to wait for me, do you understand? When the men come to take away our luggage, just go with her to the train. You have the tickets. Remember to change for Northampton station at Waterloo.'

Janet struggled up among the bedclothes, rubbing the sleep out of her eyes.

'But miss, if you've found somethin', shouldn't you take it to the police?'

'I can't do that, they've got a warrant out for his arrest. I have to find him first, before they do.' She squeezed Janet's hand even tighter. 'Janet, you must promise me that you won't tell anyone, swear it!'

'Of course, Miss Emmeline. You know I wouldn't –'

'Even if I don't get back in time to catch the train, and Christabel asks where I am, you mustn't tell her anything.'

'But miss, where is it you're going?'

Emmeline got up.

'I can't tell you. It's not that I don't trust you, Janet; but if anything went wrong I don't want you to be involved. It's better that way.' She rushed to the door. A quick smile of reassurance. 'I'll be all right. Just make certain you and Mrs Ismay don't miss that train.'

'I'll be careful, miss!'

But Emmeline was already running back towards the stairs.

She had the keys to David's car in her handcase. She took them out, praying that when she cranked it the engine would start. It was a long time since she'd driven; she was more used to riding on horseback, but all the bloodstock and the hunters had been taken to John Martin's stables, and it was too late to call him up.

At the top of the drive she turned right and went on for several miles, until she reached the junction of the Dorking and Epsom road. Only three miles into Epsom, another mile to the racecourse and to the grandstand building where the dinner with Guy Vogel as guest of honour was being held.

She glanced at her pocket watch: ten minutes to midnight, ten minutes before the evening ended. If only she wasn't too late.

Lights were still streaming from the big windows. She could hear the sound of music, chatter, laughter. There were private carriages as well as chauffeur-driven motorcars lined up behind the building on one side. Changing down gears, she steered the car into an empty space and switched off the engine, ignoring the astonished stares from the male chauffeurs when they realized she was a woman.

She straightened her hair, brushed the creases from her long sweeping cape, and hurried into the vestibule on the ground floor.

'Have Mr and Mrs Vogel left the building yet?' she asked the nearest doorman.

'Why, no, madam. They're running a bit late. Mr Vogel's guest of honour and nobody's likely to leave until he's finished making his speech.'

She smiled.

'I need to speak with Mrs Vogel urgently. May I go up?'

213

'By all means.'

It was months since she'd been inside the grandstand building; she was impressed by the expensive redecoration and refurbishment that had been carried out, no doubt paid for by Guy Vogel's ambiguous largesse. She paused at the entrance to the ballroom, taking care that Vogel, from his place at the centre of the long table, did not catch sight of her.

She moved back against the wall, while her eyes searched the faces of the assembled guests.

There were many faces that she knew; a few she didn't recognize. The long tables were covered with snow-white linen cloths, heavily decorated with massive silver candelabra and elaborate tiered bowls of hothouse fruit. Crystal glittered in the strong light of the chandeliers, almost every face was turned towards Vogel as he went on speaking, his staccato, thickly accented voice difficult to understand from the distance that she stood. Then her eyes moved along the faces at the centre table and stopped on one who could only have been Guy Vogel's wife.

She was unusually pale. The cheekbones coloured by a touch of rouge accentuated her whiteness rather than disguised it. Her hair was dark, caught up in jewelled combs away from her pretty, heart-shaped face. She wore a gold necklace set with diamonds, a matching bracelet on her narrow wrist. She appeared not to be listening to what her husband was saying; even from where she stood Emmeline could see her eyes darting nervously back and forth, her hands fidgeting with the cutlery on the table. Suddenly, unexpectedly, she glanced up and caught her eye.

They had never met, yet somehow Emmeline felt she knew. She stiffened in her seat. She looked down agitatedly into her lap, then glanced up again, then away. As Vogel finished speaking and the assembly broke into applause, Emmeline moved quickly through the open doors and mingled with everyone else. The chairman of the grandstand committee gave his short closing speech, and as guests then began to rise, she edged her way towards Adeline Vogel's place.

'Mrs Vogel?'

The shoulder beneath her hand shuddered. She jumped, as if someone had struck her.

'I'm sorry . . . Have we met somewhere?'

'We almost met, on the night your husband invited myself and my sister-in-law to dinner at The Hermitage. But you were too ill to come down. I'm Emmeline Ismay.'

Around them the sound of chatter and laughter grew louder. Adeline Vogel glanced furtively in the direction of her husband, but his back was towards them as he talked animatedly to someone else.

'How do you do. I'm sorry I was unwell ...' Another glance towards her husband. Nervously, she picked at the ring on her hand. 'Did you want to speak to my husband before we leave?'

Emmeline stared into the fear-filled green eyes.

'No, Mrs Vogel. I came here to speak to you.'

Adeline Vogel had no time to answer. Striding towards them, pushing his way almost rudely through the crowd came Vogel himself. His long, tall shadow fell across the table and she cowered beneath it like a dog that has been whipped by its master.

'Well, what a pleasant surprise.' His eyes glittered with barely-concealed malice. He took his wife firmly by the arm. 'Miss Ismay, I see you've already made yourself known to my wife.'

'We had invitations for this evening, but we could scarcely come after all that's happened. And we're leaving for North-ampton first thing tomorrow morning. My uncle has an estate there.'

'I'm sure we both wish you a pleasant journey. And happy Christmas. Perhaps the New Year will bring you a change of fortune.'

She could have struck him. She could see by the expression in his eyes that he wasn't in the least fooled, and she cursed her bad luck. Another few minutes and she could have said what she'd come here to say.

'We, too, are leaving for the north. My castle in Scotland. I've hired a large local staff, arranged a special shooting party for Boxing Day – our first Christmas away from South Africa. A novelty for both of us.'

Emmeline realized that she'd been recognized. Several people were glancing her way. She felt sick with frustration and disap-pointment, but she forced herself to smile.

'I'm glad to have got here in time to have met you, Mrs Vogel. And I'm sorry we didn't meet before. But no matter. I was here in time to say goodbye.'

She moved away into the crush of guests, then let herself be swallowed up in the crowd.

So they were going to Scotland. As she made her way back hurriedly to David's car she pondered the thought that if Adeline Vogel was as delicate as her husband made her out to be, Scotland in December was the worst place he could have chosen to take her.

One thing was certain in her mind. For some reason that she had to find out, Adeline was terrified of her husband and he'd gone out of his way to make sure she mixed with the outside world as little as possible.

But she had no doubt that the answer to that and her brother's disappearance lay in the crumpled note that she held in her hand.

'What did you say to her? *Answer me!*'

'Nothing! Guy, I swear it!'

He hit her again and she went reeling.

'Don't lie to me.' He towered over her, his hand raised to hit her once more. 'No woman lies to me, do you hear? My first wife tried it and I broke her neck.' He took her by the wrist and yanked her to her feet, then he shook her violently until her teeth chattered. '*What did she say to you?*'

'Guy, I'm telling you the truth. She only told me who she was. There was no time for her to say anything else.' Sobs began to rack her body; her legs refused to bear her up. Across her face where he'd struck her a long, livid red welt had come up. It throbbed with pain. 'That's when you saw her and came across . . .'

His long, tall shadow fell menacingly across the floor.

'You discussed me with him, didn't you? You had to. There's no other reason why his sister would come all that way just to try and speak to you –'

'No, Guy, no!'

'What did you tell Ismay? *What did you say about me?*'

'I never spoke about you; I swear it, on my father's life. Please, let me go, Guy. I'm so tired, I want to go to bed and go to sleep –'

He grasped her savagely by both wrists and swung her to her feet. He fastened his big hands around her neck and began to squeeze. The freckles stood out on his skin like spots, sweat was pouring from his brows.

'Sleep. You wanted to sleep with Ismay, didn't you, my dear?'
His voice grew louder until it seemed to fill the whole room.
'Answer me before I throttle you!'

'No!'

His dinner jacket was crumpled, his cravat had come untied.
He dashed away the perspiration on his face with the back of his
hand. He let her go suddenly, unexpectedly, and she stood there
in front of him crying and holding her bruised neck. Then he
slapped her, hard, across each side of her face.

'*Livia!*'

The connecting door to Adeline's bedroom opened, letting in a
soft fall of light. Livia De Haan stood in the frame of the archway
impassively, as if the sobbing, dishevelled woman cowering in
front of him was invisible.

'Do you want me to give her a dose?' She was holding a small
brown glass bottle in one hand, a cloth in the other. 'She's
hysterical.'

'Not until I've finished with her.' He took Adeline roughly by
the hand and dragged her into the bedroom. Then he flung her
down on the bed. 'Undress her.'

'What happened tonight? Did something go wrong?'

'Near the end, Ismay's sister turned up. No, not as a guest.
They're leaving Epsom first thing tomorrow morning. But my
back was turned and when I looked round she was talking to
Adeline.'

'She wouldn't have said anything. She wouldn't dare.'

'That's all everyone was talking about tonight. The fire and
Ismay's disappearance. By the time we get back from Scotland in
the New Year let's hope it's all blown over.'

'No news stays on the front pages forever. Of course it will
have.'

'Are the trunks packed?'

'Losch did them this afternoon.'

'Tell him to load them on the car. Get rid of everything in the
cellars. Have the whole place scrubbed clean. I want no traces
left. Check it yourself when they've done.'

She went without another word, closing the door so softly that
Vogel didn't even hear it.

Adeline dragged herself off the bed; she stood against the lintel,
her dark hair dishevelled, tendrils of it sticking to her deathly pale

face. The silk evening dress she'd worn for the committee dinner was creased and ripped in several places. Her green eyes were red and swollen.

'You know something about his disappearance, don't you?' Her voice sounded hoarse, cracked with emotion. 'Guy, where is he? Where has he gone?'

For the first time Vogel smiled. There was a leather-bound book lying on the table and he picked it up, stroking the fine binding and tooled gold lettering of the title with his fingers.

'*Dumas*. I always loved Dumas. Every novel he ever wrote I collected and had specially bound for me in the finest leather. These gold letters . . . do you see?' He held it out to her. 'Blocked with real gold leaf.'

'Guy –'

'I've read them all a dozen times over. *The Black Tulip*, *The Three Musketeers*. *The Count of Monte Cristo* . . . and my favourite, *The Man in the Iron Mask*. That plot always fascinated me, where one man had his own brother thrown into a secret prison so he'd never be a threat to the throne, encasing him in an iron mask so nobody would ever see his face . . .'

Terrible realization suddenly dawned on her. Trembling, she came towards him.

'No, no. *You wouldn't dare!*'

His cruel lips turned up at the corners in a ghost of a smile.

'If you'd read Dumas, my dear, instead of those foolish women's novels, you'd come to understand what lengths a man is prepared to go to to protect his own interests.' Before she could answer he crossed the space between them and grabbed her by the hair. He twisted it in his hands until she screamed.

'Shout all you want to, my dear.' Another twist, more agonizing pain. 'Nobody will ever hear you.' A cruel laugh. 'That, you see, is the beauty of this house . . . like the castle. You could torture a man to death and nobody would ever hear a thing.'

Sick with disappointment, Emmeline drove back in the direction of the house. It lay there among its background of waving trees and undulating lawns, a jewel in a hollow. The last time she would come down the drive like this, feeling that she'd come home. Soon it would belong to others.

If only Karl Ryan hadn't left, if only her uncle was here. The exchange had long since closed down for the night. She couldn't contact him until the morning and then it would be too late.

There had never been any secrets that she knew of between herself and David, and yet he had never showed her the contents of the note. Now she knew, at last, what it had been that he wanted to talk to her about that night: Adeline Vogel and himself.

She slowed down and changed gears as she turned into the sweep of the drive past the old gatehouse, the line of trees, coming to a halt in front of the house. Her booted feet echoed through the empty rooms as she made her way back upstairs through the corridors and hall. Christabel was still sleeping, but Janet had heard the sound of the approaching car and was waiting for her on the landing.

'Miss!' She'd thrown a blanket around herself and pulled on her shoes. The bedroom door stood half open; Emmeline could see that while she'd been gone Janet had rekindled the fire. 'Oh, miss, I've bin that worried about you. You all right?'

'Janet, I want you to listen to me very carefully. You must do exactly as I say.'

'What's happened?'

'I can't go with you and Christabel today. No, please don't argue. Hear me out. As soon as the telephone exchange opens in the morning, I shall put through a call to my uncle. I'll explain that you and Christabel will be coming on without me. There's something I have to do, Janet, something I have to find out. I can only do it on my own.'

'Is it about your brother?'

'Yes.'

'But what are you goin' to do, Miss Emmeline? You're not goin' back to that place on the island to look for him?'

'No, not there. Somewhere else. You see, there's somebody who I think can help me find where he is, but they're too afraid to speak the truth. I have to see them when they're alone so that they'll tell me.' She looked earnestly into Janet's worried face. 'If it was safe to tell the police what I think then I would. But I can't risk that. They wouldn't listen; they'd arrest him before he had a chance to prove his innocence. He had nothing to do with starting that fire, nothing to do with the death of those four men. There's no other way, Janet. This is something I have to do and I have to do it alone.'

'Isn't there anything I can do to help you?'

She smiled. Janet looked at her with eyes that reminded her of her father's docile, faithful old lurcher dog. She remembered how she and David had cried their eyes out when it went deaf, then blind, then caught distemper and had to be shot. Strange, that she should think of that now.

'Don't tell Mrs Ismay anything I've said. And look after her for me.'

TWENTY-FOUR

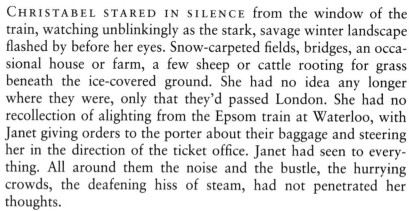

CHRISTABEL STARED IN SILENCE from the window of the train, watching unblinkingly as the stark, savage winter landscape flashed by before her eyes. Snow-carpeted fields, bridges, an occasional house or farm, a few sheep or cattle rooting for grass beneath the ice-covered ground. She had no idea any longer where they were, only that they'd passed London. She had no recollection of alighting from the Epsom train at Waterloo, with Janet giving orders to the porter about their baggage and steering her in the direction of the ticket office. Janet had seen to everything. All around them the noise and the bustle, the hurrying crowds, the deafening hiss of steam, had not penetrated her thoughts.

She lay back in their first class compartment, swathed in rugs and furs, thinking back to the time that seemed so long ago when she'd first met David Ismay.

The time, the place, the house where they'd met had long since gone from her mind; all she could see, with startling clearness, was the tall, dark, handsome man who'd gazed down smiling into her face.

She could hear his voice. The touch of his hand on hers was still warm. They walked together, in a direction she'd long forgotten, side by side. She could not remember what he'd said, only that his words had pleased her. He had made her laugh. He had made her smile. She remembered the delicious nearness of his body, the peculiar scent of his hair. She remembered his hands, long and tapering; things of beauty without being effeminate, masculine and powerful without being coarse.

She could see the vases of flowers that decked out the big, fashionable church. She could hear a choir singing. There were faces that she knew among the congregation, faces that smiled at

221

her as she walked by on her father's arm. There was a long, scarlet carpet in front of them that seemed to stretch for miles, and she remembered reaching the end of it where David was.

She'd turned round then, and handed the beautiful bouquet of roses to a figure that stood behind her, a young girl who looked startling like him with dark hair and bright, turquoise-blue eyes. She remembered thinking how unusual they were, and how David had told her that he'd inherited his brown eyes from his Canadian grandmother, Lily Meissenbach. And laughed.

She turned woodenly from the window. She came back to the present. High above her head on the luggage rack she could see their smaller travelling cases, each one with labels that bore her name. Opposite her sat Janet, her knitting in her lap, the needles click-clicking relentlessly, stitch on stitch.

Christabel frowned. She stared all around her without understanding. She no longer knew where she was; she no longer understood why she was here. The train was moving, but where was it taking her?

'David?' she said, suddenly, into the silence. Janet looked up quickly. 'Where is David? Janet, where has my husband gone? Has he gone to fetch the baby?'

'There, Mrs Ismay, ma'am. Not far to go now. Nearly at Northampton station, we are. Just a little way longer to go.'

Christabel stared at her as if she had never seen her before.

'Northampton station? Why are we going to Northampton station? We don't live there. Ask David why we're going to Northampton station.'

Janet threw down her knitting and changed seats.

'It's all right, ma'am. We're going to Hazelbeech Hall, where Mr and Mrs Charles Ismay live. Mr Ismay'll be there when we arrive to meet us in his motorcar. He'll be so pleased to see you again –'

'Charles? Why will he be there to meet us? Where is David? Tell Emmeline to go and find David . . .'

'Miss Emmeline isn't here, ma'am. She had to stop behind in Epsom to see to some business or other. She'll come on later. She spoke to Mr Ismay this morning on the telephone, early . . .'

Janet looked helplessly from the window, watching the monotonous landscape go by. All the way from Epsom, then from Waterloo and not a word; now this. She prayed fervently

222

that Northampton wasn't too far off now. If only she wasn't here with her alone, having to cope, having to humour her. She struggled up, her footing uncertain in the rocking carriage. This was a fast stretch now.

'Ma'am, I shan't be above a minute. I'll just nip out along the corridor and find the guard. He'll tell us how far we've got to go.' She slid back the compartment door and hurried out.

She edged her way along the narrow corridor, past the occupied compartments of other carriages, feeling panic, nervousness, envy. Envy for the passengers who sat there, unaware of her predicament; some asleep, some bent over a newspaper or a book, unknowing, unworried. If only Winifred had been with her, if only she hadn't been left alone. In her state of mind, Mrs Ismay might be capable of anything. Why, look at that roomful of china dolls!

The train seemed to be slowing down now; gratefully, she glimpsed the unmistakable uniform of a guard a little way ahead. She wasn't used to travelling on trains. She hoped she could find her way back to their compartment and not get lost. The guard glanced up from checking tickets, and caught sight of her. She called to him and waved her hand.

The words came tumbling out one over the other, in a rush.

'How long till we get into Northampton station? Only it's my lady, you see, mister. She's not well, not herself. Just lost her husband, she has.'

'Oh, dear me. Not ill, is she? There's no doctor on the train, not unless it's among the passengers.'

'No, nothing like that. More a bit wandering in her mind. The sooner we get to Northampton, the better it'll be. We're bein' met there.'

He pulled out his fob watch and opened the lid.

'Another fifteen minutes, that's all. Just another fifteen minutes.' The sick feeling in her stomach felt a little better. Her heart had stopped racing now. Please, God, let the train be early. Please let it.'

'Thanks very much,' she said.

'Need a hand, do you, with the baggage? I can get a porter to see to that.'

She smiled gratefully.

'That'd be very kind, mister. If you would. I don't know the number of our carriage, though. Do you think it'd be too much trouble to show me the way back?'

Fading daylight moved across Emmeline's closed eyelids, the train jerked and began to slow down. She could feel the power of the brakes beneath the carriage, the screech of the wheels on the metal tracks, then a deafening blast of steam.

She opened her eyes suddenly, she sat up.

Though she'd dressed in her warmest clothes she realized she was shivering. She turned up the deep collar of her coat and drew on her gloves. Her fur muff lay beside her on the seat and she picked it up, together with the single valise and her leather drawstring bag. As the train pulled slowly into the station, she stood up.

Only four other passengers alighted besides herself. Hurrying, heads down, battling against the flurries of snow and icy wind. It was much colder than she'd expected; even in her long fur coat and fleece-lined boots, Emmeline shivered. She surrendered her ticket, then walked out from the station into the street outside.

As she walked along, trying to get her bearings, she was suddenly aware that people were turning to stare at her. She hesitated outside the window of a tiny dress shop. Though her English clothes were understated and not flamboyant, they were the height of fashion; she looked strikingly different to everyone else. What she needed was total anonymity. She was too obviously a stranger, too glaringly conspicuous.

She took a deep breath and went into the little shop. Because of what she had to do it was essential that she must not be remembered.

A few moments later she came out again, a dull tartan cape draped around her shoulders, hiding most of the fur coat beneath, its huge matching hood concealing the top part of her face.

Her footsteps were firmer, more confident this time. She began to walk in the direction of the small inn where the shopkeeper had told her she could take a room.

'Sit down here, Janet, and tell me everything that happened.'

'It was like this, sir. The night before we were leaving, Miss

Emmeline shakes me awake and tells me that there's something she has to do. I was half-asleep, I was, I don't mind tellin' you. Thought for a minute I was havin' some kind of funny dream.'

'Didn't she tell you anything at all?'

'She said it was best not to, because she didn't want me to be involved if anythin' went wrong. But I know it was somethin' to do with her brother. I heard her go downstairs, then out the front door. Then I heard a cranking noise and the sound of Mr David's motorcar being started up. She went off down the drive.' She felt uncomfortable sitting here, in the big, grand drawing room with all the upholstery brocade and satin. She wasn't used to it, it didn't feel right somehow. It gave you a queer sort of feeling, being out of your usual place, even though there was nothing grand or stuck up about Mr and Mrs Charles Ismay. Like Miss Emmeline had always done, they made her feel she was part of the family.

'Think, Janet. Take your time.'

'She said before she went – I remember this because it put me all in a flurry – that if she wasn't back the next mornin' when the men came to take the luggage to the station, we was to leave without her. Well, sir, that got me really in a stew, I can tell you. I couldn't go back to sleep. I was goin' to get dressed but I decided not; I just sat up waitin' for her to come back. I made up Mrs Ismay's fire to keep the room warm.'

'But she came back?'

'I was that relieved when I heard the sound of Mr David's motorcar. I looked out of the window and saw her comin' back into the house. But she was drawn-looking, not herself at all. She said somethin' had gone amiss and she hadn't bin able to do what she wanted, and we still had to leave without her the next day. I was to take care of Mrs Ismay. She said she was puttin' a call through to you early next mornin', soon as the exchange opened. An' I heard her speakin' to you, while the men was bringing down the luggage.'

Charles Ismay glanced to where his wife Florence sat.

'The line was so bad I could scarcely make out what she was saying. She told me she was following on later, that there was something she had to do. Then I told her what I'd found out about that South African fellow she didn't care for, the one who tried to hoodwink her about buying the stud. She didn't com-

225

ment, didn't say anything. Several times I had to shout and ask her if she was still there. Not that there was all that much to tell, except a bit of malicious gossip . . . there always is, about a man who's made as much money as he has. Before I could ask her any more questions, she'd rung off.'

Florence Ismay said, 'Janet, is there anything else at all that you can remember?'

'Well, there was just one more thing, ma'am. I asked Miss Emmeline why she didn't go straight to the police, if she'd found out somethin' they ought to know. But she said that if she did that they'd be sure to arrest him, and she had to clear his name first. She wouldn't tell me nothin' else.'

Florence smiled.

'You've done marvellously, Janet! Coping with all the luggage and Mrs Ismay on your own; getting the tickets, changing trains. Go on now and get yourself something hot to drink and a good square meal. Our housekeeper, Mrs Swifte, will take care of you.'

'Thank you, ma'am.' She got up and bobbed a curtsey. 'If I do remember anythin' else I'll be sure to tell you.'

The moment they were alone Florence's smile faded and she began pacing and wringing her hands.

'Charles, I don't like this! I don't like any of this at all. What can have come over Emmeline, behaving in this way? I'm so worried. Look at the weather. Where is she? Where can she possibly have gone? And what can she have found out about David that the police couldn't?' A pause. 'Do you really think she can have any idea where David might be?'

'I don't know, how could I? But we have to trust her judgement. If she didn't want to tell anyone it was for a very good reason. She knows what she's doing. And she isn't Rebeccah and Cornelius's daughter for nothing!'

'Can it be something to do with this man, this Guy Vogel? Why did she ask you to find out about him?'

'She didn't exactly, the idea was mine. After what she said I decided to send a cable to Robert Lewis – you remember Robbie, who I hunted big game with while I was in Africa? As it happened, Vogel is a big man out there, he owns half of the Klerksdorp fields. I think his father was a bit of a rogue – no roots, living in one country and then moving on to another; probably living half on his wits and half on shady business deals, always one step ahead of the law. That's what Robbie thought, anyhow. But he also heard rumours about the circumstances of his first wife's death – nothing provable, just local talk. You know how people like carping at their betters. Vogel has the reputation of being a hard taskmaster, and he isn't popular. But what man in his position is? If he wasn't tough with his men they'd probably run amok. They're a rough lot, the kind of scum who work in the mines.'

'What else did Robbie's cable say?'

Ismay shrugged.

'You can read it for yourself. There was gossip when his first wife died. Her father was Claud van der Louew, another big name in the gold mining industry. She was his only daughter and when he died all his mining interests passed into Vogel's hands.'

'Is that all?'

'She fell down the stairs when she was pregnant, and broke her neck. There was a rumour that it might not have been an accident. The talk was that Kathleen van der Louew had a lover, and Vogel found out.'

'Didn't the authorities think it was a suspicious death?'

'No. And afterwards Vogel stayed a widower for nearly fifteen years. That seems to suggest to me that he must have loved her deeply, and found it hard to come to terms with her death.'

'Or lost his faith in women.'

He went over to the window and stared out at the falling snow. He couldn't rid himself of his feelings of uneasiness and disquiet; they lingered on like an unwanted guest. He was becoming increasingly disturbed about Emmeline, despite everything he'd said to reassure his wife that she was safe.

'Charles, you can't just sit here and do nothing. We have a responsibility towards her. And now that David's not here there isn't anyone else to take care of her.'

'She isn't a child.'

'No, but she could be in some kind of danger. I just feel it. The exchange hasn't closed down for the night yet. There's still time for you to telephone the police.'

He ran a hand through his hair, prey to a conflict of feelings.

He knew his wife was right but if he did what she wanted him to it would be premature, a betrayal of Emmeline. She'd begged Janet not to say anything to Christabel, who was, after all,

David's wife; she'd told her it was important that nobody should know where she'd gone to, that she needed a chance to clear his name.

He made one of his instant decisions.

'Florence, she isn't a fool, far from it. She's already proved that. She went all the way to Ballakeighan to try and find out the truth about the fire, to try and find evidence to clear David's name. She may have failed in that but we have to keep faith with her now and give her the chance. She'll contact us when she's good and ready. After what she told Janet, how can we be justified in interfering? We'll give her one week. If we don't hear from her by then – then, yes, I'll call Lock in London.'

'What about Christabel?'

He turned back from the window. He let the curtain fall back into place, shutting out the cold, snowscaped night.

'Poor Christabel. Even before David vanished, she was disturbed in her mind. Anyone would have guessed it, after all those miscarriages. That's why she tried to convince herself that she was going to have another child. And why she's surrounded herself with all those incredible dolls.'

'Charles, I think she needs help, more than we're capable of giving her. I think you should call up your doctor and arrange for her to see a specialist.'

'If Emmeline can find David, I don't think Christabel will need anything else at all.'

The little tap room was crowded and local trade brisk when Emmeline came down the narrow, spiral staircase from her room above, and made her way to the landlord over at the bar. He was a big, jovial Scotsman, with hands like sides of ham and thinning, fair hair that stood out on his scalp like a hog's bristles. His eyes twinkled as they looked at her.

'Good evenin', Miss Brodie. Supper's served in the next room at half-past seven. Fresh fish from the loch or good succulent roast Scotch beef.'

'Can I have both?' She smiled, wanting to strike a balance between being amicable but not over-familiar. 'The food was dismal on the train. I fell asleep and missed the second sitting for dinner, and there was nothing left. They gave me a plate of sandwiches instead.' She pulled a face. 'The bread was as dry as chaff.'

There was so much she wanted to ask him, but she had to extract the information without arousing his suspicions. Strangers, especially English strangers, attracted attention in these parts.

She'd invented a Scottish ancestor and used her great-grandmother's maiden name when she'd arrived and taken the room.

'Ye can ha' just what your heart desires, bonny lass.' He tapped the bottle in front of him on the counter of the bar. Ay, she was a bonny one all right! He'd already noticed how the men kept turning to get a look at her. 'Ha' a wee dram on the house to warm yoursel' through. It's a bitter night, an' that's a fact. An' bad weather for travellers.' She smiled back guardedly, sensing that he was fishing for more information. 'Wi' a name like Brodie, even though I ken ye aren't Scots, I'll wager your family came from around these parts?'

'A long time ago, before my time.' She gratefully accepted the drink. He was right, she needed warming through. 'I'm on my way to meet my brother in Edinburgh. He's spending Christmas with friends.'

'Edinburgh? That's a fair distance to travel, an' on your own. Snow's thicker that way. 'Tis the wrong time o' year for long journeys, I'd say. Ye'll ken that as ye go through.'

She went on drinking the brandy in small sips.

'I noticed a fair-sized castle lying to the left of the forest as the train came through.' Deliberately, she kept her voice casual. 'I suppose that belongs to some old Scottish baronial family, who farm the land here as well?'

'Castle Drago, ye'll be meanin'? Ay, no, bonny lass; Clan Drago hav'na lived there for years. 'Twas the upkeep, before the war started, that forced them to sell. Duncan Drago had to let it go. Pity. Foreigners ha' got it now. Some gold miner from Cape Town bought it for the shootin'.'

'They live there all the year round?'

'No, just come up for the shootin'. Arrived, only a couple of days ago, with servants and his wife.' He refilled her glass and then his own. 'Don't see much of 'em, not down here. They keep themselves to themselves.'

'What about supplies for the castle? Don't they send down for what they need?'

'Ay, one o' their men comes down, wi' a big order, meat, flour, spirits, fresh milk an' eggs. Ol' Taggart takes it up there on his cart.'

'Do they entertain much?'

He put his head on one side. She wondered if she was asking too many questions.

'They only hobnob wi' the local laird, Ian McCormick from Rothestayne, an' his lady. Reckon they're up here again for the shootin'. That's what McCormick's ghillie says. Makin' a party of it tonight, by the cartload o' stuff goin' up in Taggart's cart. Why, he'll need to make two journeys of it, an' that's a fact.'

She thanked him for the glass of brandy. She knew now how she could do what she'd come here to do. She gave him her most charming smile.

'Is there a livery stable around here, where I could hire myself a good horse?'

The hog's-bristle eyebrows drew together and he half-laughed, half-frowned.

'Don't tell me ye can ride, bonny lass ... a slip of a thing like you.'

'A little.'

TWENTY-FIVE

FLORENCE ISMAY KNOCKED several times on the door of the room, but there was no reply. She knocked again – louder this time – and called out; but still no answer came from within. Taking a deep breath, she opened the door and looked inside.

Christabel was sitting in a chair beside the window, staring expressionlessly over the snow-covered, landscaped park. She had turned off the gaslights, only one of the curtains had been drawn. Looking quickly around her, Florence could see that Janet had unpacked and put away her clothes. The trunks and boxes that contained her collection of china dolls had also been emptied, and she'd arranged them in rows and groups around the room, with several clustered together against the head of the bed.

She did not look up when Florence came into the room. She made no movement, not even to turn her head. She went on staring ahead of her, until the silence became unbearable.

'Christabel, are you coming down to dinner?'

At first, there was no response; then, when Florence repeated the question again, the large, sad grey eyes turned and fixed on her face.

'Where is Emmeline? Has she gone to buy tickets for the train? Janet . . . I must get Janet to pack my things . . .'

'Christabel, shall we go downstairs together?' She went over to the nearest gas lamp and turned it up, bathing the room in soft, pink light. 'Charles is waiting to talk to you.' She held out her hand and smiled.

'It's so thick, the snow. I wish it would go away. So cold. Everywhere's so cold . . . David will have trouble starting the engine of his motorcar . . .'

'Christabel –'

231

Christabel got up suddenly and began to stare all around her. She frowned.

'Where am I? What am I doing here? This isn't home –'

'This is Hazelbeech Hall, Christabel. Northamptonshire. It's Charles's house. You know where you are, why you're here. Emmeline explained it to you. This is your home now. You've come here to live with us.'

'I must find David . . . I must go home, Florence . . . I have to go home. Can't you see, I can't stay here? David will be waiting for me at home . . . He'll be wondering where I am . . .'

She turned the horse's head in the direction of the deep woods that covered the sloping bank, and set him into a canter. With deft artistry, she steered him lightly, expertly in and out of the trees, her sharp eyes on the ground ahead, alert for hidden ditches or potholes in the icy, uneven ground. When she glimpsed the daylight through the woods from the opposite side, she pulled him up and dismounted, and led him to the edge of the forest on foot. She tied him securely to the trunk of a tree in the clearing, and, on her hands and knees, crept carefully to the top of the rise.

She took the telescope from inside her cape and focused it on the castle below.

She could imagine how wildly beautiful it would look in summer, the severe grey stone softened by the riot of flowers and brilliant-coloured shrubbery in bloom inside the gardens and grounds, the crenellated turrets made less forbidding by a blue, cloudless summer sky. Now in the stark depths of a Scottish winter it made a cold, forlorn landmark to the backdrop of the dark, brooding woods and snow-covered hills.

She looked down and saw the lowered drawbridge, men moving to and fro inside the courtyard, dogs loose and barking nearby. Yes, of course, Vogel would have dogs.

She shifted her position, pointing the telescope in the direction of the rows of narrow windows, the ground floor doors that she could just make out on the other side. A plan had already formed in her mind; all that she had to do was to carry it out. But could she? Hidden inside one of the barrels on Taggart's cart it should be easy enough to get inside the castle. But once inside she had to find Adeline Vogel, and then get out.

232

If the McCormicks had been invited to dinner, it should be easy for her to escape when they took their leave; but was the landlord's information reliable enough for her to take that chance?

It was too late to back out, too late to go back. She was already convinced that Adeline Vogel knew something vital about her brother's disappearance and she was determined to find out what it was.

She folded up the telescope and put it away. Then she went back to where her horse was tethered in the clearing, and led him by the bridle deeper into the woods. Nobody would find him here.

At dusk, she would make her way down to Taggart's yard and hide herself somewhere in his cart. Then she would get into Vogel's castle and do what she had come to do.

TWENTY-SIX

MICHAEL STRANAHAN WHISTLED to his dogs and began to make his way back along the path that skirted the little row of flintstone cottages. The wind was bitter, and he turned up the collar of his fleece-lined working coat. The snow had held off so far; but by the feel of the air there'd be a hard frost tonight, he'd warrant.

He walked on along the path briskly, calling to the dogs as they lagged behind, sniffing and ferreting in the undergrowth. He caught sight of Annie Bevan's boy, Thomas, playing with a whip and top, up ahead.

'H-h-hello, M-Mr St-Stranahan!'

'Hello, young fellow.' He ruffled the boy's thick mop of black curls. It was a shame, he'd always thought, that the boy suffered from a painful stutter and his widowed mother never had much time for him. Not surprising, when she'd lost her man in the war and had a sickly father and three more children to look after. The boy's impediment made him shy and he had no friends. 'How are you today? And how is your mother?'

The boy grinned.

'She's w-w-well enough, th-thank you, Mr Stranahan, sir. S-so am I. See what S-Santa Claus give me for Ch-Christmas!'

'Why, that's a fine whip and top, isn't it? The best I've ever seen.' He fought down a smile, while the boy took it up and fell into step beside him. 'And what else have you been getting up to? On your best behaviour, I hope?'

'Oh, y-yes, Mr Stranahan.' His stuttering did not seem so painful now. If only someone could find time to spend time talking to him, it'd be half-way cured. It was a pity, it was a shame. And he was a bright lad, too.

'I've g-got a secret, I h-have!' A conspiratorial tone now.

234

'Have you now!'

'If I t-tell you, do you th-think you c-c-could give me s-sixpence?'

Stranahan stopped walking and put his hands on his hips. The little tyke!

'Sixpence?'

'If I had sixpence, I could b-buy myself a real g-g-good c-c-catapult, I could. N-not like those ones you make yourself. A real g-good one. And some sweets. I c-could buy some liquorice sticks and sherbert, too!'

Stranahan smiled. Annie Bevan wasn't only a war widow; two of her brothers had worked for him before they'd joined up and got blown to bits on the first day of the Somme; her husband had fought at Ypres and never came back.

'Would your mother like it if you got yourself a catapult? Now, catapults can be pretty dangerous things. Remember the story of David and Goliath?'

'Well, I know th-that, but I could sh-shoot Germans, couldn't I?' He squinted up at Stranahan with his round, dirty, freckled face. 'Germans k-killed my d-d-d-daddy, they did.'

For a moment Stranahan was silent. They walked on until they reached the end of the row.

'Threepence, for the liquorice and sherbert.' He smiled, and dug into his pocket for a coin. 'If you promise me not to eat it before you have your tea.'

The boy's eyes lit up.

'Oh, th-thank you, Mr Stranahan, sir. Th-thank you v-very much. Do you want to know my s-s-secret now?'

'Oh, I don't think you should tell me, do you? After all, if you did then it wouldn't be a secret any more.'

The boy stopped walking, hovering at his cottage gate. He looked over his shoulder.

'There are Germans on this island, there are. I s-s-seen them.'

'Germans? Of course there aren't any Germans. The war's over now, Thomas. There are no Germans here.'

'The K-Kaiser sent 'em, I bet. He's angry, isn't he, b-because they lost the war? We b-beat 'em! That's why they c-came here and lit that f-f-fire – burned all them b-buildings right down to the g-ground . . .'

Stranahan stiffened. His heart began to beat very fast.

235

'Buildings, Thomas? Do you mean Mr Ismay's buildings down at Ballakeighan?'

'Yes, those ones! It w-was the Germans what did it. I saw 'em, I d-did. They made a hide-out in the w-w-woods, just like a fox's l-lair.'

Michael Stranahan knelt down and took him firmly by the shoulders. He looked hard into his face.

'Thomas, you mustn't tell me lies.'

'God's honour!'

'I want you to tell me everything you know, everything you saw.' A pause. 'Didn't you know that the police on the island have been looking for the wicked men who started that fire?'

The boy looked down at his feet.

'But I'm f-f-frightened of Germans, Mr Stranahan. They eat babies, don't they? If you t-tell, they'd come back for you and st-stick a bayonet in you and roast you alive!'

'Nonsense.' He stood up. He took him firmly by the hand. 'Thomas, this could be very important. I want you to come with me and show me where you think you saw them.'

'But —'

'I'll explain to your mother later, when we come back.' A sudden thought struck him. 'Why did you think they were Germans? You've never seen Germans before.'

The bright, round little eyes gazed up at him. He smiled, dipped into his trouser pocket and brought out the stub of a burned out cigarette.

'Th-they left this behind. I found it. See,' he pointed, holding it out in the palm of his grubby hand. 'It's got a funny-s-sounding name on it, foreign. And I heard them talk. I w-was in my hiding place, my special h-hiding place waiting for the b-b-badgers, my s-secret hiding place, in the f-fallen trees ... But I couldn't tell anybody, could I, or else they'd roast me and eat me alive! They d-do that, Germans do. I heard p-people say.'

Stranahan looked down with disbelief at the faded, barely decipherable lettering on the stub of the cigarette. Not German, but Afrikaans, the language he remembered from his service in the Boer War.

He said, almost in a whisper, 'You heard them speak?'

'When they went by, an' I was h-hiding ... f-funny voices, they had. Funny-sounding voices. An' they didn't t-talk in English, not like us. That's how I kn-knew. They were Germans, weren't they, Mr St-Stranahan? Are they going to invade the i-island?'

Stranahan took the piece of stub from the boy's outstretched hand and held it in his own. So small, seemingly insignificant. But worth a man's life, an entire lifetime's reputation. He suddenly realized that he was trembling, shaking with a feeling that he could neither describe nor understand.

He knew now beyond any doubt that David Ismay had been innocent, that he'd never had anything to do with the fire at all.

He began to run back to the place where he'd left his motorcar as fast as his legs would carry him. The boy staring at him in astonishment, his two dogs running on behind.

Slipping the bag of raw meat into her deep pocket, Emmeline left unnoticed the little inn's crowded tap room. The bought cape of dull tartan slung around her shoulders, the big hood pulled down to shield her eyes. The wind was cruel, strong, icy. Head down, her face obscured, nobody she passed gave her a second glance. At the entrance to Taggart's yard she paused, hesitating, looking carefully all around her. Beyond the yard gates she glimpsed the loaded cart, the sacks and barrels covered with a weather-proof tarpaulin to protect them from the weather. There was no sign of Taggart himself; the men had gone away to eat their dinner. She allowed herself to smile. Casting another quick glance around her, she edged her way towards the cart using the cover of the wall, then climbed carefully inside underneath the tarpaulin. She had abandoned her first idea. The barrels were too heavy to lift down alone and be replaced with an empty one. And it would take too long; someone might walk into the yard and see. It was much better this way.

She crawled in between the boxes on the furthest end of the cart and squeezed herself behind them. All she had to do was wait.

It took far longer than she had expected for the cart to wend its way through the rough, uneven track that passed for a road. The horses stumbled, the wheels rattled and stuck. Every now and then she could hear the grumbling and curses of the driver, freezing on top of the box. Several times she heard him shout abuse to the horses, then the irritable cracking of his whip; but the cart went no faster than before.

She dare not move the tarpaulin and look out. Only when the ground seemed to be more even, and the tired horses' pace quickened, did she realize that they were on the drive that led up to the castle itself.

There was a sick sensation in the pit of her stomach. Her heart had begun to beat faster, anticipating what still lay ahead. As the cart at long last clattered over the drawbridge and across the moat into the courtyard, she held herself ready, waiting and tense, for the moment when she would have to leap out.

From her cramped hiding place she could hear voices. There were heavy footsteps; from a tiny chink at the edge of the tarpaulin, she could see two pairs of men's legs. The voices were more muffled, moving steadily away. Lifting the side of the tarpaulin nearest to the castle wall, she quickly jumped down from the cart and crouched beside the wheel.

It was too far to run to the door where the supplies were being taken; too risky. Taggart's man and the manservant who had come out from the castle were standing in her path, close together, heads bent over a list of the supplies. She took her chance.

Casting a rapid glance upwards towards the windows to make sure there was nobody looking down to see, Emmeline ran to a half-open door that had once been a carriage house or a large stable. Lucky that other comings and goings had already disturbed the snow, so disguising her footprints. Vogel's motorcar gleamed in the darkness.

She moved to the cover of the wall. From the chink in the half-open door she watched as two more men came from the castle and carried the boxes and barrels inside. After what seemed an interminable time, the cart stood empty and Taggart's man took his payment and went on his way. The huge door opposite where she was hiding banged shut, and there was silence once more.

She sank down onto the floor, and drew her knees up to her chin. She let her eyes rove over the long, gleaming metal of the car, tucking her hands deep inside her cape to ward off the bitter cold.

All she had to do now was wait.

TWENTY-SEVEN

'MISSING, and she's made no contact of any kind for more than a week?'

'She may be somewhere where there's no access to a telephone. There may be some other reason why we haven't heard from her.' Charles Ismay glanced across at his wife, then back to Lock and Barnes. 'I've already told you my reasons for not calling you in until now. My niece is a bright girl and I know perfectly capable of taking care of herself. It isn't so unusual these days for a young woman to travel alone. But I promised my wife that if we didn't have word from her when a week had gone by, we should do something.'

'Mr Ismay, you might as well know that in the beginning we put a watch on her, just in case she led us to her brother. It's usual in these cases. Then we decided that we were satisfied she didn't know where he was, and called off the tail. But one interesting piece of information did come through from one of our men in the Epsom area. She was seen talking to the Vogels on the night of the grandstand committee dinner, the night before Mrs Ismay and her maid left to catch the train here. I understand the Vogels are spending the New Year in Scotland. Is it possible that your niece might have gone there? She was on terms of friendship with Mr Vogel, isn't that true? We understood that he'd visited Brew House several times and she and Mrs Ismay had been guests at his house.'

'Are you saying you think David's in hiding somewhere in the wilds of Scotland and Emmeline is travelling up to find him?'

'It could be possible.'

Charles Ismay hesitated. Although he'd kept his promise to his wife to contact the police when the week was up and there was still no word from Emmeline, he now had serious misgivings

239

about what he'd done. Clearly, they thought that Emmeline knew where David was and that they'd been mistaken in not continuing to keep a watch on her. At the unspoken question in his wife's eyes he imperceptibly shook his head, so subtly that nobody else noticed it. Family loyalty came first. Until it was absolutely necessary he had no intention of telling them what Janet had told him.

'David Ismay vanished into thin air,' Lock went on. 'Despite our blanket watch on all the ports, nobody of his description was ever sighted trying to leave the country, at least not by legal methods. But Scotland could be another thing altogether. I'd say it was the perfect hiding place. Bonnie Prince Charlie certainly kept himself hidden from the redcoats there! Much of it is uninhabited and dense, thickly wooded terrain, impossible to reach except on horseback or on foot. I suggest that your niece may have known that her brother was making for the lowlands right from the beginning – so there was no need for them to have any contact – and is on her way there now. That the Vogels have a castle there and will be there for some time gives her a good cover story. If we caught up with her she has merely to say that she's travelling north to visit them.'

'And if Mr Vogel doesn't confirm her story?'

'We haven't been able to speak to him yet. Unless this weather shows signs of clearing it could take some time before we do. And, of course, your niece had no idea that you'd get worried and contact us. Are you certain there's nothing else that you think we ought to know?'

He had no choice now but to bluff it out.

'Only what I've already told you. That Emmeline telephoned us on the morning they were ready to leave, and said she had some loose business ends to tie up. She said she'd follow on in the next few days.'

'Excuse me, sir.' Barnes was looking down at something lying on the table. He picked it up. 'May I ask you who this is?'

'Why, yes. It's an old photograph that that young Rhodesian Karl Ryan gave to Emmeline. Christabel had it in her bag when she arrived here. It was taken years ago when Cornelius was a young man, working for the Merritt Bloodstock Company in the United States. That's where Karl's father and Cornelius first met . . . he looks so young there!'

Barnes went on studying the picture.

'And the other two men?'

Charles Ismay came over and glanced across his shoulder. 'This is Rufus Waldo. He came to England with Cornelius in the 1880s and married Emmeline's mother, Rebeccah Russell. Before your time, but a famous case. He was deeply involved with the notorious betting ring run for crooked American owners by Enoch Wishard. Cornelius was young and foolish in those days; he got involved but in a lesser way. The marriage to Rebeccah wasn't happy and he fell in love with her himself. In the end he turned queen's evidence and most of the gang were caught. But that's all water under the bridge now, and so long ago. The other man? I couldn't say who he was. Just somebody else who worked for the Merritt Bloodstock Company, I suppose.'

Barnes looked up.

'Would you mind if we kept this photograph for a short while, sir? I'll see that it's returned to you. Just something I'd like to check up.'

'Please do.'

'What did you want it for? An old faded picture of Emmeline Ismay's father –'

'Can you hand me that pencil, sir? It's just a hunch . . .'

'What are you doing, Barnes, for Christ's sake?'

Barnes took the pencil from him and began to shade in and thicken the eyebrows and the hair of the fourth man; then very slowly and very carefully he pencilled in a long, twirling moustache. They both stood there, side by side, staring down at the altered picture. Lock picked it up and held it up to the light almost incredulously.

'Vogel!'

Adeline Vogel went over to her elaborate, lace-draped dressing table and sat down silently in front of the mirror. Like everything else in the large, circular room it was expensive and opulent, the colour gold dominating every piece of fabric and furniture. The drapes were of gold brocade, heavily fringed with gold tassel work; the boudoir chairs and the scrolled legs of the little reading table were all finely worked in gilt. Eighteenth-century pastoral works adorned the walls; the curtained four-poster bed, a magnificent work of art in itself, dominated the entire room. It had been especially imported from Versailles and was reputed to have once belonged to Queen Marie Antoinette herself.

But none of the trappings of wealth and power meant anything to Adeline; unable to find happiness or peace within herself, she had never felt so low in spirits or more depressed.

There had been no answer to any of the endless letters she'd sent her father in Cape Town; a single reply, from his housekeeper, telling her that he was unable to write. Although the letter spoke of his general wellbeing and assured her that he thought of her constantly, she felt curiously dissatisfied and ill at ease. If only she could see him for herself, if only Vogel would let her go back. How much she hated it here, even more than The Hermitage, with the sight of the forlorn, monotonous landscape from every window in the castle. How she hated those sloping mountains and endless hills, the miles upon miles of green nothingness now thickly covered in snow, how much she loathed the high ceilinged, echoing rooms and vaulted passages, too big and wide to be homely or comforting. Like a bird in a gilded cage, she'd spent every day since their arrival pacing up and down, biting on her fingernails, longing to be free.

But there was no escape. Ever since her marriage, the marriage she'd never wanted, to a man she'd feared and loathed, she'd known she was little more than just another of her husband's carefully guarded possessions.

Livia De Haan had come into the room from the antechamber that adjoined it, and Adeline stiffened. For the briefest of moments, their eyes met fleetingly in the mirror before Adeline looked away. Then she slowly picked up one of her hair brushes and began to draw the bristles through her dark, silky hair. She kept her eyes on her own face. Beyond the mirror, moving silently about the room, she was aware of the figure of Livia De Haan. Every now and then, from the corner of her eye, she could see the other woman pause, and look up from what she was doing, to watch her.

The silence went on, grew worse. She laid down the brush, and began to make a pretence of opening the little pots and boxes on the dressing table, containing powder and rouge. After several more minutes, Livia De Haan came over and stood behind her; and, still without speaking, opened the velvet-lined casket in her hands. In silence, Adeline turned her head and glanced down at it, her eyes looking without pleasure on the contents that winked and glittered in the light.

Livia De Haan lifted the gold filigree necklace from its scarlet bed, and lay it against Adeline's neck. It was cold against her skin and she shivered; but still she said nothing. Next came the matching bracelet, the earrings, the hair combs with their decoration of lions' heads in wrought gold, with tiny diamonds for the eyes. As she lifted and twisted Adeline's hair into place, then held it up each side with the golden combs, she pulled it by the roots painfully. And still she had said nothing, not even a single perfunctory word of greeting.

Adeline hated the touch of those long, dry, cold hands. The sly look in her dark eyes, the colourless cheeks, the secretive, unpleasant expression that hard face always wore. There was no warmth there, no humanity, no compassion. Suddenly Adeline could bear the closeness of her and the oppressive silence no longer. Starting up from her stool, she almost pushed Livia De Haan away.

'Why are you looking at me like that? Why don't you say something?' She was near to tears. 'You enjoy watching me suffer, don't you?'

Livia De Haan's face never even changed expression.

'Suffer, madam? What have you ever had to suffer? Mr Vogel has given you everything; everything that any normal woman would desire. Possessions that any other woman would give her eyes for. Perhaps you don't realize how fortunate you are.'

Adeline's throat felt so tight and painful that it was an effort to swallow, to speak.

'Fortunate? To live like this, to be nothing more than just another of Guy Vogel's possessions?' The indiscreet, angry words tumbled out, one by one. Even as she spoke she knew what this outburst would mean, but somehow she could not stop herself. 'Is there any woman in the world who, if she knew the truth, would change places with me?'

Tears stood in her eyes. But she would not let them fall. She would never give Livia De Haan that satisfaction.

'Why do you stay here, working for him? Tell me why. Is it

243

because he pays you so well? Or is it because you enjoy being a gaoler to me?'

For the first time, there was movement on Livia De Haan's face. Her thin, bloodless lips turned up slightly at each corner.

'Why, madam, I really don't know what you're talking about. Mr Vogel, it's true, has always been a more than generous employer. But to suggest that you aren't free to go about the castle as you wish is completely untrue. I think you know that.'

'I can go anywhere I want to in the castle; but not outside. I can never go outside unless someone else is with me.'

'No lady would dream of going out in public unescorted, madam. No true lady. Standards in England have, I've already observed, fallen badly since the war. Perhaps that is to be expected. But a lady in your position – that is quite a different matter. Surely you see that? Mr Vogel would never dream of permitting it.'

'And we both know why that is, do we not?' As soon as the words had left her lips, she knew she had made a serious mistake. She could not call them back. They had been said. Livia De Haan's thin mouth changed back to a single, narrow line. The hooded eyes glittered beneath their heavy lids.

'I wonder if Mr Vogel ever told you, madam, that I used to be personal maid to Kathleen van der Louew, his first wife? Did you know that?' There was no answer. Adeline stood there, staring at her, like a dumb thing. She could not speak. She could not move. 'Did you also know, I wonder, exactly how she died?'

She willed her frozen voice to say something. Suddenly, despite the blazing fire in the huge fireplace in the room, her whole body was icy cold. Fingers touched her spine.

'What are you talking about?'

Livia De Haan had gone over to the door of the little ante-chamber. She paused, her hand remaining on the latch.

'She fell down the stairs, and broke her neck. She might have saved herself that, had she taken more care. I should think about that, madam. I should think about that very carefully indeed.'

Adeline moved towards her.

'What are you saying? That Kathleen van der Louew's death wasn't an accident? Tell me!'

'I can tell you nothing, madam. Except to give you a piece of very valuable advice. Advice that your predecessor chose to ignore . . . to her own cost. Never displease Mr Vogel. And never betray him. If you do, let the consequences be on your own head.'

She had gone before Adeline could reach her. On the other side of the door, she could hear the key turning in the lock. She grasped the latch in both hands and shook it. She battered on the door with her fists. She called out, she screamed. But there was only silence.

She turned away. Restlessly, she began to pace up and down. They couldn't keep her here. There were guests, important guests, coming to the castle. What excuse could he make if she didn't go down? He dare not risk setting tongues wagging; he had told their last guests that she was ill, and it had been a lie. Why was he doing this to her? What did he hope to achieve? She would never love him, she had never wanted to be his wife. But her father . . . she'd had to do it for her father . . .

She closed her eyes, hot bitter tears of despair began falling through her fingers.

Suddenly, in the adjoining room she heard the sound of Livia De Haan cry out, then a piece of furniture overturn.

Instantly, she stopped crying and ran towards the door.

'*How did you get in here?*'

'Never mind how I got in. Where's Vogel's wife?'

For a few brief moments they faced each other across the space of the little antechamber, then Livia De Haan made a wild lunge for the bell. Emmeline was too quick for her. She rushed towards her, pushed her with such force that she toppled backwards with a shout of pain, then crashed into a chair. Emmeline picked it up and belted her across the head. She flung open the connecting door.

Adeline Vogel stood there in the middle of the room with her hand in her mouth, face wax-white, staring at the sight in front of her. Her terrified eyes focused slowly, frozenly on the still form of Livia De Haan, lying among the wreckage of broken furniture.

'*Livia!*'

'She's out cold. Quickly. Find some belts and scarves and help me to tie her up. Then we'll drag her under the bed.'

Adeline did as she was told but while Emmeline tied her ankles and wrists, she stood by uselessly, still in a state of shock. 'Don't just stand there. Give me a hand to pull her over to the bed.'

Emmeline grasped hold of the arms; Adeline took the feet. They dragged the unconscious body of Livia De Haan across the floor and pushed it beneath the huge four-poster bed where the heavy voluminous drapes hid it completely from sight.

Emmeline stood up. Then she opened her drawstring bag and took out the letter.

'Well, where is he? Where is my brother?'

Adeline's face showed only bewilderment. Woodenly, she reached out and took the single crumpled sheet of paper and read what was written on it. She looked up fearfully into Emmeline's angry blue eyes.

'I didn't write this. I know it's been signed in my name, but it isn't my handwriting. It's Livia's.'

'I don't believe you.'

'I swear it!' Suddenly galvanized into action, she hurried over to her escritoire and hunted frantically through the drawers. 'I'll prove it to you! Here, see, this is my handwriting. Compare it to this note and you'll see that it's completely different!' Emmeline looked through the assortment of letters, notes, entries in an old battered diary. She realized that Adeline Vogel was speaking the truth.

'But you know where he is, don't you? You know something about the disappearance of my brother. If you didn't you wouldn't have behaved the way you did at Epsom grandstand that night. You were scared out of your wits.'

A tear welled up in the corner of Adeline's eye.

'Please, you must go. You must leave here before anyone sees you. If he found you here I can't say what he'd do. It isn't safe for you to stay –'

'I came here to find my brother and I don't intend to leave without him.'

'You don't understand. I can't expect you to . . . but Guy, my husband, he's insanely jealous. He isn't like other men. Yes . . . you're right, I'm afraid of him. But if you knew him like I do, if you knew what terrible things he's capable of, you'd understand why.'

A pause.

'Were you having an affair with my brother David?'

'No! I scarcely knew him. We'd met only three times. I was

lonely, I was homesick, I was unhappy . . . he was so charming, so fascinating; I'd never met a more attractive man. Yes, I was drawn to him, like a moth's drawn to a flame. He was everything Guy was not. But Guy can't bear other men to look at me, to pay me attention. I'm just like all his other possessions – nobody else is allowed to touch them. When he saw us together in the garden that day he exploded with rage. Later, when all the guests had gone he accused me of . . . terrible things. His jealousy makes him completely irrational, it makes him violent.' She was trying not to cry, trying to control her shaking voice. She sank down onto one of the boudoir chairs and covered her face with her hands. 'He became obsessed with the idea that your brother wanted to seduce me.'

Emmeline stood over her while she sobbed.

'Why do you stay with him? Why in heaven's name did you ever marry a man like that in the first place? Did you just marry him for his money, because you wanted to be a rich man's wife?'

'You still don't understand!' Tears coursed down her face. 'I had no choice. He forced me to marry him. My father was a partner in Guy's company in Cape Town; Guy wanted me. But I loathed him, the sight and touch of him made my skin crawl. Guy did something . . . to the company records, that made it look as if my father had been stealing money from the company funds. It wasn't true!' She dashed away fresh tears. 'But he said that if I didn't marry him he'd expose my father and he'd go to prison. *It would have destroyed him!* He isn't a young man; he isn't strong, I didn't have any choice –'

'Your father is dead.'

Adeline stopped crying. She rose to her feet, her eyes transfixed on Emmeline's face.

'No, no, he's alive . . . I've had letters . . .'

'My uncle Charles Ismay was in Africa several years ago. I asked him if he could find out anything about your husband, and he cabled a friend in Cape Town. The morning I left Epsom I spoke to him on the telephone and he read out the reply.' She hesitated before speaking the final words. 'Your father died of a coronary thrombosis three years ago. A few months after your marriage to Guy Vogel.'

'It's impossible!'

'There is a death certificate.'

247

'*No!*'

Suddenly, there was a sound in the antechamber; they both froze. Then Emmeline heard the deep, gruff, heavily-accented voice of a man. She darted behind the door as it opened.

'What is it, Losch?' Adeline Vogel's voice was surprisingly cool, calm. 'I didn't hear you knock.'

'I'm sorry, Mrs Vogel, but I'm looking for Livia . . .'

Adeline went and sat down at her dressing table, picked up the silver hairbrush and began to pull the bristles steadily through her hair.

'Then when you find her, please send her up to me. I need her help to dress for dinner.'

'Yes, Mrs Vogel.' He turned away, the door slammed shut.

'Quickly, before he comes back! You have to get out of here!'

'Not without David.' She laid her hand on Adeline's trembling shoulder. 'I know you must be shocked and devastated by the truth about your father . . . but you must help me. I know David's here. I must find where.'

The green eyes looked up at her. A tear ran down one side of her face. Visions of her father, sick, ill, suffering. Dead, and he'd even kept that from her. She felt so overwhelmed with hate and grief at the same time that she did not know which emotion was the stronger.

'My husband is a great admirer of the novels of Dumas. He boasted to me that his favourite was *The Man in the Iron Mask*. And that that was the way a clever man could dispose of a rival who threatened him. It was when he told me that, that I knew what he'd done to your brother.'

'*Dear God!*' All the colour drained from Emmeline's face. David had been led into a trap by a madman; and, like Dumas's Prince Philippe, imprisoned in a dungeon.

Her back against the wall, she paused outside her husband's dressing room door, ears straining for the slightest movement or sound. Nothing. Her heart beating faster, she slipped inside and went to the little carved cabinet that stood beside his bed, and opened it. Her shaking fingers groped inside until they felt the bunch of keys. Selecting one, she opened the desk in one corner of the room and pressed the little button that slid back to reveal a false panel in the row of pigeon holes. There were two keys there. She grasped them and stuffed them into the front of her bodice, then carefully closed and relocked the desk.

Outside, Emmeline kept watch.

'These are the right keys, I'm sure of it. I watched him once, when he was giving them to Losch. They're not the keys to the wine cellar. He keeps those in the kitchen.'

Emmeline took them.

'Go back to your room. Try to keep your head, behave as if nothing's happened. Show me the way first.' She took her hand. 'We can make sure he's punished for all the things he's done. But I have to get David free first.'

Noiselessly, they walked on tiptoe and single file to the end of the long passageway, then down a flight of steep, narrow stone steps. Another corridor loomed ahead of them, and Adeline pointed to the door at the very end of it.

'You can reach the dungeons from there, but there is another door, another staircase, that opens out near the top of the steps that lead down into the banqueting hall. It's too risky to use now, with his men walking in and out, but later, when it gets dark, the hall will be clear.'

'I'll find the way.' She had already broken into the gun room upstairs. Cradling the pistol that she'd taken, Emmeline left Adeline Vogel and ran as fast as she could towards the door.

The second of the large, cumbersome keys fitted the antiquated lock. She inched the heavy door open, wincing as it creaked loudly, then with a last glance behind her slipped inside.

There was an overpowering, sickening smell of dampness, filth, decay; she moved in almost total darkness, feeling her way down into the bowels of the earth, down the sloping stone staircase, the wet and grimy walls. Gradually, as her eyes became accustomed to the gloom, she gazed around her with gathering dismay.

Everywhere, the walls had been hung with restored instruments of medieval torture.

There were scolds' bridles, thumbscrews, maces, leg-irons, balls and chains of various sizes. Wrist and ankle shackles, a gibbet, an array of spiked iron collars; manacles, iron masks, a Scavenger's daughter. And there, in the very centre of the gloomy, stinking chamber, a rack.

Incredulously, she walked up to it and then around it.

It was an iron frame, about six feet long, with three rollers of wood within the metal structure. The middle of these, with iron teeth at each end, was governed by two stops of iron, the parts of the machine which suspended the powers of the rest when the unhappy sufferer had been sufficiently strained by the cords. She examined the wooden rollers more closely.

There were dark stains upon the wood. Peering closer still, Emmeline could make out that the stains were dried blood, and that there were more around the body of the rack itself, strewn across the flagstone floor. As she looked still closer, difficult in the almost nonexistent light, the bloodstains seemed to make a trail from the rack to the far end of the chamber beneath a tiny grilled window, where she could just see the top of what had at one time been the castle cesspit.

Following the bloodstains, a sick, raw feeling in the pit of her stomach, she moved tensely across the floor. When she reached the edge of the cesspit, she looked down through the holes of the rusty iron mesh that covered it.

And, by the meagre stream of moonlight that fell into it from the high window, she saw what remained of her brother David.

TWENTY-EIGHT

'You've found Emmeline and David!'

'No, sir, I'm afraid we haven't. But we certainly found something else.' Lock produced the photograph they'd taken from him less than twenty-four hours before. 'I'm sorry to come here so late, but this is urgent.'

'I don't understand.'

'The fourth man. My sergeant thought that face reminded him of somebody in Epsom, someone he'd recently seen, and he was right.' He took another picture from Barnes. 'This is a copy we had made of the photograph we borrowed – a little different, you'll notice, because Barnes added a few pencilled in details.'

'I still don't recognize him.'

'We've been up all night chasing records, and there's no possible mistake. This man in the picture with Ryan's father, Waldo and Cornelius Ismay is Frederik van Gheest. He worked for the Merritt Bloodstock Company, then came over to England with the Enoch Wishard syndicate, and spent two years of active participation in their criminal activities. When Cornelius turned queen's evidence against the gang and most of them fled to France, van Gheest followed Waldo to Scotland and murdered him for the syndicate to stop him talking. Then he disappeared. Years later he turned up again in England and Cornelius recognized him. He was hanged for Waldo's murder at Pentonville prison.'

'I was living in New York then.'

'Yes, sir, we realize that. Otherwise it's highly likely that you would have attended van Gheest's trial at which Cornelius was chief prosecution witness.'

Suddenly Charles Ismay understood.

'The other photo!'

'With a different hairstyle and no moustache, Barnes wasn't sure. But now we are. This is the spitting image of Guy Vogel – van Gheest's son.'

'His son?'

'Van Gheest's wife's maiden name was Vogel. And I don't think any of us can be in any doubt why after all these years his son has come back here.' A pause. 'Cornelius may have died in 1915, he's out of reach. But his son and daughter are not.'

'*Jesus Christ!*'

'We've cabled the Scottish police; we're leaving for Vogel's castle now.'

'I'm coming with you!'

'David Ismay could already be dead, your niece in serious personal danger. You see, not only was she last seen talking to the Vogels that night in Epsom; the following morning, we've established, she purchased a ticket to Scotland and left on the early train. Nothing has been seen or heard of her since. You were the last person to speak to her. The clerk at the railway station was the last person to see her alive.'

From underneath the four-poster bed, Adeline heard the muffled sounds of Livia De Haan coming to.

It was almost time for her to go down to dinner, almost time to steel herself for another charade, hostess to her husband's unsuspecting guests. She was trembling. Grief, rage and fear all jostled inside her, making her nerves frayed and raw. She sat on the edge of her dressing stool feverishly biting her nails. Louder now, the sounds of struggling from beneath the bed.

She sprang up, rushed into the next room and knelt down by the little medicine cabinet, but it was locked. She fetched a poker from the fireplace and smashed it open in a frenzy. Then she took out the hated brown glass bottle that contained the chloroform Livia used to make her pass out.

She rushed back into the bedchamber and threw back the heavy brocade hangings on the bed, then she dripped out the colourless, strangely smelling liquid onto a handkerchief and clapped it firmly over Livia's nose and mouth. For a moment her eyes rolled wildly and she shook her body from side to side. Adeline pressed harder and harder until she went limp, her eyes closed and her head drooped to one side.

A loud rapping on the door made her almost jump out of her skin.

She flung back the bed hangings, stuffed the handkerchief in the nearest drawer and quickly sat down with her brush in her hand. Losch had come back again.

'Have you found Livia yet? I shall be late dressing for dinner if she doesn't come soon.'

'No, Mrs Vogel. We can't find her anywhere. Mr Vogel, he sent me up to tell you that he's just had a message from the Laird. There's been another snowfall there and he can't come.'

Alarm ran through her.

'What about the roads to the village? Are they impassable as well?'

'They're clear up to now, as far as we can tell. We might be cut off if there's more snow tonight. But no need to concern yourself about that. We have enough supplies to last for three months.'

When he'd gone she put down the brush and covered her face with her hands. The brief moment of defiance and bravery had passed. She reverted to herself again, the puppet he'd made of her: a prisoner, afraid, unsure. For a moment she forgot about David Ismay and Emmeline and remembered that her beloved father was dead. The finality of it overwhelmed her.

She would never see him, speak to him, again; she would never hear his voice. And for the last three years she had been writing letters to a dead man.

She laid down her head among the boxes of jewellery that covered her dressing table, and wept.

Emmeline had lost all concept of time. She couldn't remember how long she'd stayed there, pressed flat against the slimy wall, trying to stop the trembling in her limbs. It was like the old, childish nightmare, when she floated along the deserted decks of the doomed *Titanic*, calling for her brother, searching for him in vain.

David was dead.

She opened her eyes and blinked the water from them. Somehow she managed to pull herself together. She was all alone and she was trapped. Vogel was a madman, his personal servants were no more than hired thugs who would do anything at his bidding. She could count on no more help from the pathetic figure of Adeline Vogel. Her only hope of staying alive was to escape from the castle without being seen and go at once to the village police.

Taking a deep breath, she made her way step by step up the narrow, winding little staircase that led to the landing above the banqueting hall. When she reached the top she laid her ear against the heavy door, listening for any sounds. When she heard nothing, she opened it carefully inch by inch, and cautiously, her fingers shaking, peered through.

Lights were burning along the walls; the glow flickered and highlighted the polished metal of the suits of armour and shields, the old weapons that hung there for decoration. There was no sign of anyone for as far as she could see. Quickly she slipped out and closed the door softly behind her. Because there was nowhere else from this spot to the door below that could possibly hide her if somebody suddenly came along, she knew that to get away she had to reach the hall below unseen, without making the slightest noise. Steeling herself, she began to run. Her heart was pounding. As she reached half-way between the landing and the bottom of the staircase, Guy Vogel suddenly appeared in the middle of the hall.

For a moment there was only astonishment written across his face. Then it vanished, leaving only an arrogant, malicious leer. Emmeline froze in her steps.

'Well, Miss Ismay, what an unexpected surprise.' He called out loudly in Afrikaans, and two men came running. 'Pointless in me asking why you're here. I can see by the look on your face that you've managed to find out the truth.'

There was a terrible dry, tight feeling in her throat.

'*You murdered my brother!*'

'Not murdered, Miss Ismay. Executed. That isn't the same thing.' He came forward so that he now stood at the very foot of the stone stairs. 'That's what happens to people who commit crimes, isn't it? We execute them. I couldn't kill your father for testifying against mine and sending him to the gallows, because he's already dead. But your brother was an acceptable substitute.'

She stared at him without understanding.

'What are you talking about?'

'My father worked for the Wishard racing syndicate when they operated here nearly forty years ago ... very successfully and profitably, until Cornelius Ismay betrayed them and turned queen's evidence against them. Didn't you know that? Most of them managed to get away, including my father. He went to South Africa and made a fortune. But he made the mistake of coming back to settle old scores. Your turncoat, law-abiding father recognized him and he found himself on trial for the murder of another member of the old syndicate, your mother's first husband, Rufus Waldo. They hanged my father at Pentonville prison. And the Ismays just went on climbing upwards.'

'They hanged him because he was guilty!'

'What my father did was nothing compared to yours! He betrayed his own friends to the law and got commended for it!'

'That isn't true. When he was young and foolish he got involved with the syndicate; but what they were doing to horses for huge sums of money soon sickened him. That was why he did what he had to do to stop them.'

But Vogel was no longer looking at her. His eyes had moved beyond her to something behind at the top of the staircase.

'Grab her, De Witt!'

She spun round, and came face to face with Karl Ryan.

'What are you doing here, Karl? You said you were leaving the country!' Her mind refused to reason. 'Why did he call you De Witt?'

'Because that's his real name.' Vogel had begun to laugh, very softly. 'Do you remember the photograph he gave you, the picture of his father and Cornelius, taken when they worked for the Merritt Bloodstock Company in America all those years ago? My father was in that picture, too. Yes, I see that surprises you. With less hair, thinner eyebrows, without my moustache, not many people would ever spot the likeness. But it's true. You see, Miss clever Ismay, my father wasn't the only member of the syndicate that Cornelius betrayed. He betrayed Karl's father, too.'

They looked at each other. Then as Karl De Witt and Vogel both moved towards her at the same time, she pulled out the gun she'd stolen from the collection upstairs. She flattened herself against the wall.

255

'Don't come any closer, either of you. I'm not afraid to use this.'

Vogel smiled.

'I don't doubt it. If it worked. You stole it from the gun room, didn't you? Yes, I thought so. But unfortunately you won't be able to use it. The weapons here have been specially adapted for display only. A bad choice for such a bright girl. You can load it with ordinary ammunition, but it's impossible to fire.'

Emmeline pulled the trigger. There was only a feeble, impotent clicking sound. In the split second that followed Vogel's shout of command, Losch and Oortman dashed up the staircase towards her. But neither of them reached her. Karl De Witt hit Losch with a stunning blow in the face that sent him spinning backwards into his companion, and both of them toppled down the stairs.

'Emmeline, run!'

Vogel's face turned red. His eyes were round and wild, the livid freckles stood out on his skin. With a shout of rage and a string of invective in Afrikaans, he pulled a long, pointed pike from its holding on the wall. But before he could lunge at Karl De Witt there was a sudden movement up above them on the galleried landing.

Adeline Vogel stood there, a medieval crossbow in her hands.

He stared up at her as if she was a ghost.

'My father's dead and you never told me. You hid it from me, because you knew that while I thought he was still alive you'd keep your hold over me. You hounded him to his death. And you let me go on writing letters to a man who's been dead for more than three years.' Her mouth turned up at the corners in a cold, bitter smile. 'For what you did to him and what you've done to me, I intend to repay you, Guy.' She tightened the weapon in her hands; so many times she'd watched him as he'd practised loading and firing it, she could have done it blindfolded.

Without another word, before any of them could move or speak, she released the bolt and sent it flying downwards.

Vogel fell dead where he stood.

TWENTY-NINE

EMMELINE SAT IN THE CHAIR in the police sergeant's office, a large blanket thrown around her shoulders, a chipped metal mug of tea with brandy in it cradled in both hands. There was a fire burning brightly in the little grate, a smell of paper and leather. From the next room where the door was ajar she could hear her uncle's voice talking to the policemen. The sound of it soothed her, comforted her. At last she was safe. At last she could go home.

There was a sound of footsteps behind her. The door closing shut, someone drawing up a chair. She turned and looked into Charles Ismay's face and her eyes filled up with tears.

Without saying anything at first, he pulled her head gently towards him and held her while she sobbed.

'How did you know where to find me? How did they guess what happened?'

'Until Lock's Sergeant followed his hunch about the photograph, they had nothing but question marks and loose ends. Frederik van Gheest did know your father and Karl De Witt's, and Guy Vogel was certainly his son. When Cornelius was a young man drifting around with no real purpose in his life, it was easy enough for him to get into bad company; Rufus Waldo's, for instance, your mother's first husband. But after Cornelius met Rebeccah and became more and more disillusioned and sickened by what the syndicate were doing, he turned against them. You know that story. Van Gheest killed Waldo to stop him talking, and then fled abroad. He went to Klerksdorp and made a fortune in gold mining. But he never forgot Cornelius or how much he'd loved the life in England. He made the mistake of coming back. When he was recognized and arrested, your father testified against him. Easy to see now why Vogel hated the Ismays so

257

much. He held Cornelius responsible for his father's death.'

'He didn't know about the *Lusitania* until he came to England . . . that's when he decided to kill David instead.'

'He would never have got away with it, though he very nearly did. It wasn't only the clue in the photograph, but the boy I told you about at Onchan, who'd seen Vogel's men at the time of the fire. Michael Stranahan's telegram came just in time. Lock got a warrant to search The Hermitage and they found evidence that someone had been held in the cellars. It didn't take more than the threat to their own skins to make the servants there talk. What they weren't able to tell the police, Livia De Haan did.'

Emmeline had stopped crying. Slowly, she took out a handkerchief and wiped her eyes.

'I can't believe . . . I can't believe that I'll never see David again . . . and Christabel! How can we ever break this to Christabel?'

'It won't be easy. I know that. But we're a family and we have to stay together and try. And you know what all this means, don't you? The business, the stud. I've made telephone calls to Anglo-French Bloodstock and Delauney in London, and he says they're willing to sell it back to you.' He smiled. 'The insurance company is going to pay you full compensation for all the losses in the fire.'

She choked back fresh tears. She could scarcely speak.

'What is it, Emmeline? Isn't that what you wanted? It means you can go back to Epsom. You can carry on the business in the Ismay name.'

'Karl De Witt. He betrayed me.'

'Yes, I've already spoken to him. I know what happened –'

'All the time I trusted him, he was Vogel's man. He took his orders. He took his blood money.' Her voice was bitter. 'He spied on me. Everything I said, everything I did he reported back to Vogel. And all the time, fool that I was, I thought he was my friend.'

'I'm not defending what he did. But I do know that he had nothing to do with David's death.'

'I never want to see him again.'

'You won't have to, after today. When the police have finished talking to him he'll most likely be leaving the country. For good this time.'

'*Talking to him?*' She got to her feet, outraged. 'You mean they haven't arrested him?'

258

'There could be charges, yes. But I think they'll waive those, for the evidence he can give against Vogel's men. The men who really murdered David.'

'And am I supposed to be grateful?'

There was a movement behind them by the door, and they both looked up.

'Emmeline?' Across the space of the little cluttered room she and Karl De Witt faced each other. She realized, grudgingly, that if it hadn't been for his sudden change of heart back at the castle, she would undoubtedly have lost her life. But it made no difference to her feelings of outrage now. She'd given him her trust and friendship and he'd cold-bloodedly used them for his own ends; he'd pretended to care for her while all the time he'd been hand in glove with her family's enemies.

'I have nothing to say to you.' She grabbed her uncle's sleeve quickly. 'No, don't go. I don't want to be alone with him.'

'I'm sorry you feel that way. I suppose I can't blame you. But I couldn't leave and go back to South Africa without seeing you. And I wanted to tell you the truth.'

She laughed, mockingly.

'The truth? From you? What else can you tell me except that all this time you've been Guy Vogel's man? Who are you? Can you tell me that now? Karl Ryan or Karl De Witt? Or have you got some other name that I don't know about?'

'My real name is De Witt. My mother's maiden name was Ryan.'

'Really? And how many other things about your colourful nomadic life are true? Not that you ever told me much. Too dangerous. You might have slipped up and given yourself away. That time in London, at the Café Royal – *the bush*, you said, before you realized you'd told me something you didn't want me to know, a clue from your past that you could never talk about. I'm right, aren't I? What were you before you came to England, before you worked for Vogel? A mercenary, isn't that true?'

'It isn't as simple as that.'

'Oh? I would have thought it was very simple. Mercenaries are soldiers of fortune; they have no principles, no loyalties, no respect for either life or death. They maim and kill without mercy, they work for any man or Government who can pay their price. Like whores, they sell themselves to the highest bidder.'

259

His face was grey and taut under the onslaught of her insults. But he could hardly blame her for what she thought because he'd had no chance to tell her the truth.

'I don't want to listen to any more of this. I don't want to hear what you've come to say.' She moved closer to her uncle. 'If you've come here to tell me more lies, or to expect me to thank you for saving me from Vogel's men, you can forget it. I wouldn't believe anything else you told me. And the only reason you saved me was because you knew if you were caught it would look better for the record.' She was determined not to break down and cry in front of him. 'Now will you please leave me alone and go away!'

THIRTY

FLORENCE ISMAY replaced the telephone receiver and sank down onto the couch. She smiled with relief. She was close to tears. She covered her face with her hands in sheer relief while her maid hovered about in the background, anxiously.

'Ma'am, is everything all right? Have they found Miss Emmeline?'

'Yes, they've found her. She'll be coming home soon.' She felt as if an enormous weight had been lifted. She was safe, they'd reached her in time. He would tell her everything when they got back from Scotland.

'It's a little early in the day, I know, but I think I could use a good stiff drink of brandy.' Almost as if he'd divined her thoughts, her butler appeared.

'Mrs Ismay, I'm sorry to disturb you, but it's Mrs David. She's not in her room. And we can't find her anywhere in the house.'

'She must be here.'

'She isn't, madam; we've even searched the attics. And one of the gardeners says he thinks he saw her more than half an hour ago running towards the folly in the park.'

'*What?*'

'He's sure he wasn't mistaken.'

'Dear God, gather all the men. Search the grounds, every inch. She must be there!'

'I already took the liberty of doing that, Mrs Ismay. But she's still nowhere to be found.'

She crouched low in the snow-covered, overhanging branches of the fallen tree, listening, watching; but no one approached. She had watched them like this from the cover of the other woods, the woods that skirted the estate of Hazelbeech Hall, running to and fro from the house, looking for her, calling out her name, their panic evident even from the distance from where she was hiding, because they could not find her.

Janet would have discovered that she was missing. She was fond of Janet, she had always been fond of Janet. Good Janet, loyal Janet, Janet who had always understood; Janet had been a part of the long-distant past that she remembered, the past that was gone and would never come back. But even Janet would not understand why she had to do this thing, why she must leave her uncle's house. She did not belong there. It was not her home. Home was the sad, silent, empty building that she could see through the trees as the ground sloped from this spot where she hid to the grounds and gardens of Brew House below.

Night was beginning to fall; the air was crisp, freezing. But Christabel did not feel the cold any longer. She looked down through the bare limbs of winter trees, the twisted clumps of dead wild plants and bracken, and saw the house as it would have been had they never left.

Lights would be streaming from all the great windows, casting a soft, warm, golden glow across the snowy landscape, the fallen leaves and snow-strewn grass. There would be a roaring fire in the big drawing room, and David would sit beside it with his dogs at his feet, every now and then glancing up from his book or newspaper to smile at her, or reach out and touch her hand. Emmeline would be standing by the window, looking out; Christabel could see the fall of her thick dark hair upon the velvet of her dress, the glow of the firelight upon her creamy cheek. Someone would come in and throw more wood and coal upon the fire.

Slowly, stiffly, for she had crouched here in hiding for many hours, Christabel stumbled from the wood and made her way downwards towards the house. Florence Ismay's purse, and the crumpled remnants of her railway ticket fell from her hand into the snow, but she did not pause to retrieve them. It did not matter any more, she did not need money, she did not need anything but to be home, where she belonged. She should never have left, never let Emmeline send her to Hazelbeech Hall. David would not know where to find her. David would not know where to look.

She went on walking, slipping a little, stumbling in the ice-covered drifts, but she kept her eyes fixed rigidly upon the house ahead.

She reached the front door and took her old key from her pocket. Her gloved fingers pushed it deep into the lock, and with a creak the great door swung open. There was little light. Only moonlight from the great bare uncurtained windows where the downstairs doors had been left ajar found its way into the gloomy, brooding, silent hall. But it did not matter; she could find her way blindfold. Down, down she went to the kitchens. Someone would have left candles and matches there.

The big stove was cold and quiet. No heartening, comforting warmth came from its dead, burned out ashes. No meal was cooking on its hob. She touched it, and the coldness of it burned her hand.

When she had found the candle and lit it, she carefully retraced her steps back towards the stairs.

There was no roaring fire in the drawing room; there was none in the morning room, the study, the library, the great dusty, empty hall. Dead leaves were scattered here and there across the floor. Her footsteps echoed with a strange, hollow sound.

There were marks along the walls where once pictures had hung. The great painting of Anna Brodie above the first landing on the stairs. She could see them, she remembered every one. She remembered that a carved oak settle had stood just there, opposite the plaster mantle, and all along the edge of the hall there had been matching chairs. A longcase clock had struck the hour; in the semi-darkness she fancied that she could see the rich gleam of its mahogany casing, the light reflecting upon the gilded face. She remembered its chime, deep and melodious, and how it had echoed about the hall.

She glanced upwards towards the grand staircase. Holding the candle aloft, she began to mount the stairs.

The long, bare landing loomed ahead of her, the deserted bed-rooms to left and right. She walked on, steadily, surely, past every one. She knew what they would look like inside, the great canopied beds hung with satin and brocade, the elegant dressing table where she had once sat, while David had brushed her long, thick, golden hair. She could see his laughing face reflected in the mirror, and her own. She could see the rose garden below her window and smell its sweet, cloying scent when she flung the

263

windows wide. She had walked with him there, out on the terrace, along the box hedges, arm in arm. She could see the clumps of lavender, the gaily coloured borders, the lingering, overpowering scent of stocks. Deep beneath the lily pads of the sunken garden, she could see the fishes swim.

The door to the nursery was already standing open. Heart racing, hands shaking with excitement, Christabel went inside. A pile of discarded curtains had been abandoned in one corner of the room. Some wooden boxes, all empty, with little wisps of straw they had used to pack china. She set down the candle on the window ledge. She stood there for several moments looking all around her. Then she knew what it was that she had to do.

There was a For Sale notice on the fence that bordered the grounds at the top of the drive. Strangers would buy the house. Strange furniture would stand in the rooms and strange pictures on the wall. Some other person would sit beside the drawing room fire where David had sat; some other woman would walk in the gardens where she had walked, some other woman would pick her flowers.

She remembered that there had been a jar of lamp oil left in the scullery beyond the kitchen. Without the candle, she made her way slowly back downstairs to retrieve it. Her steps did not hesitate, did not falter. She knew every corner, every turning, the height of every stair. When she had brought it back to the nursery she knelt down upon the floor beside the pile of curtains, and sprinkled it across them, around them, then in a trail from the room.

She could not let strangers come here. She could not let strange voices echo in the hall and in the rooms that she and David had walked in and loved. No one else would live in this house that belonged to them. No one else would make this their home, because it would always be David's, always be hers.

Calmly, her hands steady, a faint smile on her face, Christabel lit the match.

Lock was watching her across the room as she made ready to leave. She fastened the buttons on her coat and pulled on her gloves, then she turned and smiled at him.

She'd lost weight since he'd seen her last in Epsom and her face was pale, but neither of those things surprised him after all she'd been through. Normally, he wasn't given to sentimental feelings; twenty years in the police force chasing hardened criminals had put paid to most of that. But credit given where it was due; he couldn't help admiring her courage and gumption. She was certainly made of the right stuff, the Ismay girl. He supposed that now her brother's name was clear, she'd go back down south and start up the family business again; most likely she'd go and breed a great Derby winner with that big black stallion of hers. And he wished her well.

He'd almost forgotten something. As she went to shake his hand he took out the photograph Karl De Witt had given her when they'd first met, and gave it to her. But she shook her head.

'No, I don't want it. You keep it instead. Tear it up, keep it in your files. I have plenty of other pictures of my father. I don't need this one. Besides which, I don't want anything of his.'

'Karl De Witt? But I thought he was quite a special friend of yours. He told you the truth about his connection with Vogel?'

She frowned.

'He started to make a half-hearted attempt at saying sorry, if that's what you mean.'

'You mean you didn't give him the chance to explain?'

'What else could he have told me other than that he worked for Guy Vogel as a paid spy? After what he did I think he's lucky not to find himself thrown in gaol!'

'But he had to do it. Here, read his statement. That was his father in the picture with the others, yes, but his father was only fifteen or sixteen years old when he was roped into working for the betting coups syndicate; he was never any more than an ordinary errand boy. He had no idea what Wishard and the other big guns were up to, until one day he came in to work and found the whole place deserted and everyone gone. He went back to America for a while, then got taken onto a ship bound for South Africa. It was several years afterwards when he was living in Cape Town that he met Frederik van Gheest again, and his son Guy. He knew by then that van Gheest had more than dirtied his hands working for the syndicate, and he didn't want anything to do with him. He ended up in Rhodesia and married the daughter from a neighbouring plantation. He did very well. Karl De Witt was born there in 1893. Then he had to go away on business and while he was gone, the entire family – all except Karl and his nurse – were massacred by Nbebele tribesmen. They came down from the hills and burned the whole plantation to the ground.

'For a while De Witt lived with his father just outside Cape Town, then, when the war started, he fought against the Germans in South West Africa . . . and I expect a lot of other things before that that he'd rather forget; it's a tough corner of the world. After van Gheest had gone back to England and got himself hanged for his numerous crimes, Guy van Gheest decided on his trail of revenge. Van Gheest had already taken his wife's maiden name Vogel when they married – easy now to see why. Guy Vogel was certainly his father's son, as you've already found out. You know what he did to Adeline's father to force her into marriage with him. He threatened, cowed, manipulated anyone he wanted to use. He looked around him and found exactly what he wanted to get revenge on the Ismays. Karl De Witt was perfect. His father had known yours and he could produce the photograph to prove it. He could clearly remember the small, personal details that would convince you he was genuine. Nothing could have suited Vogel's purpose better – except for one thing: De Witt refused to do it.'

'I don't understand.'

'Vogel told him that if he didn't play his part, he'd betray his father to the authorities as a member of the syndicate. It didn't matter that De Witt's father had had nothing to do with their criminal activities. Vogel knew enough about his background from his father to have made more than a convincing case. Karl De Witt had no choice. If he didn't do Vogel's bidding, his father could have spent the rest of his life rotting in some gaol. At worst, he could even have found himself hanging at the end of a rope. What would you have done in his place?'

There was a terrible tight pain swelling in her throat.

'Why didn't he tell me any of this? I would have understood! Why didn't he just tell me the truth?'

'In the beginning he didn't dare to. His father's life was at stake. Isn't blood supposed to be thicker than water? At the end, well, you just said yourself, you didn't give him the chance.'

Panic coursed through her.

'Where is he?'

'He said he was going to catch the next south-bound train.'

Her eyes flew to the big clock on the police station wall. She called out frantically to her uncle.

'I must borrow somebody's car. Or a horse. I don't care which but I must have it now.'

She stumbled up the little flight of steps, slipping and sliding in the calf-deep snow. In the distance she could hear the approaching sound of the train, the heavy lumbering of the engine and the hiss of steam. She ran past the ticket window and out onto the platform, then she paused for breath.

It was almost deserted, except for the tall, solitary figure at the opposite end, leaning on his single trunk of luggage.

As the train came into the station and the sound of his name in her throat was drowned in the deafening noise, he turned and saw her.

For a moment she thought he was going to board the train, but his hand fell away from the carriage door. Behind them the whistle blew and the guard on the platform waved his flag. For a moment she was totally blinded by a huge cloud of thick, white, billowing steam. Then the train lurched forward and began to move off, and the acrid-smelling cloud from the engine blew away.

He was still standing there, at the other end of the little platform. Then each of them began to run towards the other.

EPILOGUE

The taxi slowed down and then drew to a halt as it reached the summit of the hill. The driver stopped the engine, then got out and opened the door for his passenger to step outside. She thanked him in a low, well-spoken voice; while he stood there beside the car she walked away from him, pausing on the edge of the slope that dipped down towards the old blackened ruins of the house beyond the trees.

She would not go closer to them than she was now; she did not want to see the broken chunks of stone, the glassless windows, the roof that opened to the sky. That would hurt too much. She would not walk along the pitted, weed-strewn drive, she did not want to see the tangled wilderness that had once been the gardens. She would not walk among the ruins of the house she'd loved and lived in so many years ago, the house that poor demented Christabel had put to the torch and died in, in her unhappiness and grief.

She'd had to see it again, after so many years in South Africa, the years of rebuilding with Karl everything that she'd lost here. She'd had to look at it for the last time.

She went on gazing down, seeing it not as it was now, a crumbling, deserted pile of stones and blackened timbers, but as it had once been in the days of its glory. She saw the great panelled hall festooned with holly and mistletoe and ivy boughs; the fir tree bright with tiny candles and little wooden figures; the pile of gaily wrapped parcels hanging in its branches and strewn around it on the ground. She could hear the sound of her brother's laughter; she could see her father's smile, her mother's evening gown, its sequins twinkling and glittering in the light, sweeping across the scarlet carpet as she walked slowly down the great staircase to join them in the crowded hall.

271

Strange that after all these years a lump had risen in her throat. Tears stung unexpectedly behind her eyes.

'Mrs De Witt?' said the man behind her, intruding into her half-dream. 'If you wish, I can take you down a little further. Closer to the entrance to the drive.'

Emmeline smiled.

'No. No, thank you. This is close enough. I've seen what I wanted to see.' Turning away, she began to walk back towards him. Her dark hair, the veil of her hat, fluttered together in the breeze. She let him help her back inside the car.

She did not feel sadness any more. Her memories were happy ones, outweighing the painful and the bad. These she would treasure in her mind, like jewels locked inside a casket; they would belong to no one else.

As the ruins of the old house disappeared behind her, she closed her eyes, smiling, and thought of Karl.